Constant Fear

Constant Fear

Strength Comes From Within

K.A. Hudson

Arrowsmith Publishing

This novel is entirely a work of fiction. The names, characters and incidents portrayed are the work of the author's imagination. Any resemblances to actual persons, living or dead, events or localities are entirely coincidental.

ISBN: 978-0-6452708-0-8 (Paperback)
ISBN: 978-0-6452708-1-5 (Ebook)

Printed & Channel Distribution: Lightning Source | Ingram (USA/UK/EUROPE/AUS)
Cover Designed—Laila Savolainen, Pickawoowoo Publishing Group
Editing—Eddie Albrecht, Pickawoowoo Publishing Group
Publishing Consultants/Interior Design—Pickawoowoo Publishing Group
Arrowsmith Publishing: www.arrowsmithpublishing.com.au
About the author: https://kerriehudsonauthor.wixsite.com/website-1
For enquiries, write to: rights and permissions via publisher.

Dedicated to my husband.
Thank you for your faith, support and unconditional love.

1

Chapter One

Today mother gave me an ultimatum. Marry Eugene Gallagher or enter a convent and take vows.

Mother, a resolute woman, ran her family and her multitude of local committees with the same degree of rigid control. The matriarch of all she surveyed. Her word was law. I had just upset that world and disagreed with her plans for me.

She waved a rigid forefinger in my face and said, 'Constance Lee O'Hara, I've had just about enough of you. There's nothing wrong with Eugene, he's a delightful man. Rich and with a profitable business, we'd want for nothing.' White globs of spittle formed in the corner of her lips as she emphasised her words. 'Why can't you be more like Sarah? She never created a fuss when I set her up with Frank. In fact, you should be happy Eugene is willing to take you on.'

'Well, I'm not happy, not for myself or Sarah. Frank is a self-centred, egotistical git who will never love her the way she deserves. As for Eugene, he spits when he talks, combs his sad excuse for hair over his bald patch, and he's old, Mother. Good grief, his wife only died six months ago – probably from boredom.'

'Constance, that's a dreadful thing to say. Eugene is not boring...why he has the most wonderful stamp collection.'

'Well, you marry him then,' I snapped. A stupid thing to say, I know, but I was determined not to buckle under the pressure this time. My whole future was at stake. 'Good god, Mother, its 1970 not the eighteen hundreds, girls don't marry some old bloke just because their parent has designs on his bank account. I won't do it.' I pulled my shoulders back and stared at her in defiance.

She took a step forward, pushed her face close to mine and glared. The pupils in her eyes were so large they appeared black instead of their normal gooseberry green. 'While you live under my roof, young lady, you *will* obey me. I set the rules around here.'

I took an involuntary step back from her intensity and sucked in my breath. It was now or never. 'Fine,' I said, 'straight after Sarah's wedding, I'm taking option three.'

Her eyelids closed and opened in a long slow blink of surprise. 'Option three? There's no option three.'

'Yes, there is...and it doesn't involve taking vows at some mouldy old convent or getting married to some even mouldier old man. I'm packing up and moving to the mainland.' I held my breath and waited for the full extent of her wrath to be unleashed.

Mother's mouth dropped open. She turned purple in the face, the ultimate weapon for getting her own way. The flap of loose skin that hung below her chin quivered and her round piggy eyes bulged. It only needed steam to blow out her ears to complete the picture. Chubby fingers rose to her breastbone.

'Tom...' she gasped, waving her other hand around, reaching blindly for a chair.

Dad, who'd been trying to merge into the leather of his armchair and avoid the argument, rose and guided her to a seat. Mother moaned, rolled her eyes as if about to faint.

'Tom...' she wheezed, 'my heart...it won't take the stress. Speak to your daughter – I don't have the strength.'

My father is the light of my life, and I would do anything he asked. He was also mother's greatest weapon against me. Tears stung my eyes, but I refused to let them fall.

'Daddy, please...don't make me...,' I whispered.

Mother groaned, drawing in a shaky breath. My head dropped as I saw my future snatched away.

'Prue, *stop* this at once.' My head shot up, surprised at my father's tone. In all my twenty-one years, I'd never heard him raise his voice or defy my mother. 'Let Constance enjoy her life. If you don't, I will never forgive you.'

My heart swelled, so full of love for my father who risked even more misery for himself by standing up against her bullying me into a life I did not want.

***

Finally, I was out of there. I'd given up arguing with Mother about the dress, hat and gloves she'd insisted I wear.

I didn't get to say goodbye to Sarah. She and Frank were on their honeymoon and mother told me to stay away. Some honeymoon. Frank took her camping and fishing at Seal Beach two kilometres from home. He'd insisted they rough it in a tent and not waste money on a motel, the cheapskate. That's certainly not the honeymoon I know Sarah had dreamt about. When I said so in mother's hearing, she told me to mind my own business.

'Sarah's married and Frank makes all the decisions concerning her,' she said, taking up her usual domineering stance, hands on hips, breasts thrust forward.

I cocked my left eyebrow and said, 'Yeah, but it wouldn't have hurt him to give her a pleasant holiday to start their life together.'

'It's your silly ideas on life that are your downfall,' she snapped.

Yeah, poke away mother, it only makes me more determined to get away.

I heard from one of my friends that Frank invited a couple of his mates to join him and Sarah. The men spent the entire time fishing and drinking while she sat and froze on the beach. What a horse's arse.

* * *

'Goodbye, Mother,' I said, giving her a dutiful peck on the cheek. She leant forward as though to hug me and whispered, 'You've made your bed, young lady, now lie in it. Never darken my doorstep again.'

So much for motherly love.

Dad drove me to the airport. It was quiet in the car. Mother's last words still stung me. Staring out the passenger window, I watched the apple orchards flicker by and wondered if the fruit on the mainland would taste as fresh as here. Soft rain gathered in large skittering trails along the glass. My vision blurred and I realised not all the moisture was on the window. I rubbed the unshed tears from my eyes. With a heavy heart, I turned my head and studied my father's strong fingers as they gripped the steering wheel.

'Daddy?'

'Yes, my precious girl?'

'You will look after Sarah, won't you? I don't think Frank's a very nice man.'

He reached over and patted my knee. 'I'll do my best, Constance.'

At the Hobart Airport departure door, I clung to my father as he wrapped his muscular arms around me in a big bear hug. 'Constance, I love you...very much. Be careful...it's a dangerous world out there.' He kissed both my cheeks and took a small step back. 'Now go, enjoy your life.'

'Daddy, why don't you come with me, we can run away together.'

He straightened his shoulders and placed a gentle hand on my cheek. 'Tempting...but no. I need to stay to look after your sister. Now, do you have everything?' He began patting his pockets. 'Money, do you have enough money?'

'You've already given me plenty,' I said, covering his searching hand with mine.

He looked at me and smiled. His emerald-green eyes crinkled at the corners. I reached up and stroked his smooth cheek, memorising the look and feel. He gave me a whimsical smile, so I nailed him with a big raspberry kiss.

'Daddy, you're such a fusspot. I'm going to be fine. I'll write to you and Sarah every week, I promise.'

My eyes stung with unshed tears. I flapped my hand towards the car. 'Go, before the traffic across the Tasman Bridge gets bad.'

The memory I took away with me was of my father jumping rain puddles like a little kid as he trotted back to the Cortina. A last wave and he was gone.

I dumped my hat and gloves in the rubbish bin.

* * *

As I climbed off the plane, Melbourne's summer knocked me for six. Wavy lines of heat rose from the tarmac. A hot breeze carrying the strong smell of aviation fuel stung my cheeks. The sun's rays had a bite that burned on contact and sucked the moisture from my skin. I slung my backpack over my shoulder and hustled over to the relative cool of the terminal. Uncle Richard and Aunty Gladys had promised to pick me up. They weren't really my aunt and uncle, but old friends of mother's. She was still trying to maintain her control and had organised for me to billet with them and their daughter Betty. Living with them would do for now.

I pushed my way through the large clutch of people waiting to greet their loved ones, studying the faces milling around me. I spotted Uncle Richard, tall and smiling. I lifted my hand to wave and hurried over. He hadn't changed much over the years since I'd last seen him. His back was still ramrod straight, a few more wrinkles maybe and less hair, but on the whole he looked fit and well. Aunty Gladys was a bit of a shock though, no longer skinny, she now resembled a large, round ball and didn't walk so much as rolled from left to right to get around. Scooping me up, she pulled me into a big motherly hug that wrapped her breasts around my face, nearly suffocating me.

With a clang and a rattle, the ragged conveyor belt started its endless circling. Baggage spewed from a hole in the wall. I pointed to my small white case and Uncle Richard plucked it up as if it weighed nothing. We ploughed through the press of people still waiting for their luggage and shot out the first door that led to the car park. The soles of my shoes squelched and stuck to the sun softened bitumen as we hurried over to the car.

Aunty Gladys wriggled her bum backward and squeezed into the front seat of the red Toyota Corona. Her large bosom filled the cab of the sedan. With tightly permed grey hair she looked like an overproofed muffin that had exploded at the top.

Uncle Richard loaded my suitcase and denim backpack into the boot, slid neatly behind the wheel and smiled grimly at me in the rear-vision mirror. He applied his long slender fingers in a death grip to the steering wheel and carefully steered the vehicle out into the traffic. It was a forty-minute drive to Elsternwick where they lived, and I don't think he blinked for the entire journey.

Aunty Gladys, chubby face wreathed in a cheerful smile, leant her head back on the car seat, seeming to speak to the ceiling.

In a high-pitched squeaky voice, she said, 'It's lovely to see you, Constance. How's your mum? Is she keeping everything in order back home?'

'Oh, you know mother,' I replied, not wanting to say too much on that subject.

'Yes, love, I do,' was Aunt Gladys's enigmatic reply. 'We're so pleased you've come to stay. Now the other children have left home it is so quiet...you'll be good company for Betty. You remember our Betty?'

I nodded, and she continued to prattle on. 'Betty was sorry she couldn't come to meet your plane, but she had to work. She works on the perfume and cosmetics counter at the Myer Emporium in the city. They're having some sort of sale at the moment, something to do with clearing stock left over from Christmas. Betty wasn't happy about not getting the time off but one has to earn a living. I understand she's organised a sales assistant position for you – but I'll leave that for her to tell you about.'

'Oh, that's excellent, aunty. I wasn't looking forward to traipsing around the city, job hunting in this heat.' I watched the wavy heat haze hover over the bitumen road through the windscreen. 'Is it always hot like this?'

'Well, love, it is summer.' Aunty Gladys gave a chuckle. At odds with her speaking voice, her laugh was soft and musical. 'Victoria has much warmer weather than you're used to in Tasmania – but overall it's been a reasonably pleasant summer this year. I suppose others would call it hot, but I don't notice the heat anymore. I hope you won't find it too unbearable.'

Lifting my shoulder in a quick shrug, I said, 'Well, like anything, Aunty Gladys, I'm sure I'll get used to it. So, how're the grandkids?'

Aunty Gladys smiled at the mention of her favourite subject. For the rest of the trip, she chattered on, filling me in on all her family news. Uncle Richard stoically drove on with a hunted look on his long angular face, fingers welded to the steering wheel.

2

Chapter Two

'This'll be your room, Constance. You'll be sharing with Betty,' Aunty Gladys said.

She gave the beige painted wooden door in front of her a hard shove – I glanced in. A cyclonic mess of clothes and shoes lay before me. The doors of the old brown wooden wardrobe hung open, discarded outfits draped in careless abandon across the top, others pooled on the floor underneath. My nose crinkled in disgust as I eyed the walnut dressing table separating the twin beds. At least I think it was walnut, hard to tell because of the used cosmetics, discarded tissues, and chunky jewellery strewn over its surface.

Aunty Gladys casually kicked a pair of black platform heels to one side and took a step into the room. I wondered if we'd need a rope to find our way out.

'Betty's been having a bit of a clean out,' she said, pointing at the clothing piled up on one bed.

'That'll be your bed, just throw those things over on the chair. Betty can put them away later.'

I gathered up the pile and caught a whiff of stale sweat. The clothes were dirty...they needed to visit the laundry tub not be put away. I added them to a pile already living on the chair.

'Betty's cleared you a drawer for your things. I'll leave you to your unpacking, love. You'll find sheets and towels in the linen press just outside in the hall. Help yourself to anything you need and sing out if you can't find something.'

With a placid smile on her plump lips, she turned and roll walked her way from the room.

I decided against using the drawer. Its base was sticky with spilled red nail varnish and covered in cigarette ash. There was no hanging space.

Standing with hands on hips, I looked around and wondered how anyone could live like this? I rolled up my sleeves, threw everything on my side of the room into a heap and shoved it over to Betty's side. I gave a satisfied grin – she can deal with that lot when she gets home.

With room to move, I set about unpacking. Or maybe not! Finding nowhere to put my stuff, I changed to plan B and slid my neatly packed suitcase under the bed. Dusting my hands together, I smirked – well that's my unpacking taken care of...now for my bed.

I sat and bounced on the mattress. It passed the comfort test. I shuffled my way back through Betty's flotsam and opened the linen press in trepidation. The household linen, laundered, folded in crisp neat piles, and stored with sachets of potpourri, emitted a wonderful bouquet of sweet-smelling flowers and freshly cut grass. So, Betty's slovenly ways were not an inherited trait. I grabbed a set of white sheets and made up my bed, smoothing a happy, sunny-yellow bedspread over the top. I slid my PJs and journal under my pillow.

Satisfied I'd organised my things as best I could, I wandered down the short hallway into a combination dining-lounge. I found Aunty Gladys sitting erect in a brown leather recliner, chin on chest, taking forty winks. Her mouth was making little putt-putt noises as she breathed out. Not wanting to disturb her slumber, I tiptoed across the dingy beige carpet to a doorway on the other side of the room. This led me into a bright and cheery kitchen. A single bowl sink sat under the window with pristine pale-yellow laminated benches on either side. The refrigerator set against the wall on my right, had a green glass vase on top, full of freshly cut roses. It was a cheerful room, with sunlight filtering through lace curtains.

I slipped through the doorway on my left, past a washing machine and cement trough, and out into Uncle Richard's realm – the garden. I found him hoe in hand, sweat pouring down his face, turning over soil and compost in the rose bed. The man's mad; it's far too hot for this sort of activity. His arm brushed against a blossoming red rose bush, and the air filled with its wonderful fragrance. I took a long deep breath, filling my nose with the delightful scent. Hearing me, he turned and looked over. He smiled as he removed the faded-blue cloth hat from his thin thatch of grey hair and used it to wipe the river of sweat from his brow.

'Hello lass, Gladys see you right, you all settled in?'

His deep voice had a beautiful Irish lilt that played like music in my ears. I wondered how a man from Derry County in Ireland ended up serving in the Australian Army, marrying a girl from Tasmania, and living in Melbourne. I must ask one day.

'Yes, thanks, Uncle Richard. Aunt's having a catnap at the moment, so I came out to look at your gorgeous garden.'

Uncle Richard beamed. Leaning his tall, angular frame on the hoe, he looked around.

'Aye, it's not bad for this time of year. It takes a lot of water, to keep it looking this way. Let me show you around.'

Slipping my hand into the crook of his arm, we strolled over to the shade of the Jacaranda tree and spent a lovely hour chatting.

* * *

Dinner time came and went, still no Betty. I smiled across the room at Uncle Richard. He lay back in the brown leather recliner, replete from his evening meal. One of his plaid slippers hung precariously from a toe. A pair of half-moon reading glasses perched on the tip of his nose offered no reading assistance. His book lay open across his chest, where it had fallen as sleep had overtaken his pursuit of the written word. Now and then, he gave a mighty snore and smacked his lips together before blowing out a puff of air.

I cleared the last of the dirty dishes from the dining table and carried them out to the kitchen sink. Picking up the tea towel, I wiped as Aunty Gladys washed.

She smiled. 'Thanks love, it's nice to have the help.'

I returned her smile with one of my own. 'Not a problem, Aunty. Thanks for the lovely dinner. It's been ages since I've had roast chook.' Selecting a pot to dry, I went on, 'I was wondering, how long you guys have been living here?'

'Well love, we've been here since Brian was ten, he's thirty-five now. Must be twenty-five years, but it's all changing now. There are new houses going up everywhere...and big. Brian was telling me, he works in the planning department of our council, some city bigwig is planning on building a mansion over near the beach – Joshua Estate, he wants to call it.'

I fitted the lid to the pot I'd just dried and started on the next one. 'You don't approve?'

'Selfish...it'll limit access to the beach.'

I shrugged, not understanding the implications, and changed the subject.

'Do you miss Tassie?'

Aunty Gladys's arm, a blur as she scrubbed the roasting pan, said, 'Yes and no, love. I miss some of my friends – I don't miss them knowing and interfering in my business. You know what they're like.'

'Yeah, sure do. You can't even scratch yourself without word going around.' I glanced around the pretty kitchen, 'Where do you want these pots to go?'

Aunty Gladys lifted a wet finger, pointing to the cupboard next to the stove, and asked, 'How's Sarah doing?'

Putting the pots away in the cupboard, I hung my wet tea towel over the oven handle and was careful how I answered her. Who knows what might get back to mother's ears.

'She's fine...just got married. A lovely church wedding and a divine dress. She married Frank Watkins...do you remember the Watkins family? Good friends of mother's.'

'Oh yes, love, I remember them. Beryl Watkins, or Sims as she was then, and I went to school together. The three of us, Beryl, your mother, and I were as thick as thieves in those days. We still write occasionally, Christmas and birthdays mostly. Beryl married Donald Watkins just after I left and had Frank the following year. Gosh, he must be twenty-three years old now. Don was a bit of a rake in his day, nothing in a skirt was safe from his wandering hands I can tell you, but Beryl soon sorted him out. Are your folks happy about the marriage?'

Frank's certainly a chip off the old block I thought as I leant against the bench and folded my arms across my waist.

'Mother was ecstatic, I'm sure she arranged the marriage. She certainly pushed Frank at Sarah – went on and on about his attributes.'

'You don't like him, love?' asked Aunty Gladys. She pulled the plug and rinsed the suds down the drain.

'Oh, he's alright, I suppose. It's just...I heard some worrying rumours.' I paused, but the urge to speak got the better of me. 'He's bossy, tells Sarah what they're doing, where they're going. I never once heard him ask her what she wanted. He'd never let me tag along when they went out either – said it was his time with Sarah. It felt more like he was cutting her off from us. Mother reckons I'm jealous and have to accept her life's changed, there's no place in it for me. I shouldn't lose her just because she's gotten married, should I?' I could hear a touch of exasperation in my voice and said, 'Sorry.'

'Hmm, yes...well love, give it time. New life and all that,' said Aunty Gladys. She picked up the kettle and held it up to me, 'How about a nice cuppa?'

We'd just settled at the dining room table when the back door slammed.

'Hello love, good day?' sang out Aunty Gladys, to the click of heels of tiles.

'Brilliant, Mums, brilliant,' was Betty's sarcastic reply as she entered the room.

Aunty Gladys gave her a gentle smile, took a sip of tea, and said, 'There's some dinner keeping hot in the oven and a fresh pot of tea on the bench.'

Betty pulled a face and said, 'No dinner, Mums, I couldn't face it. A cuppa would be great.' She made no move towards the kitchen, so Aunty Gladys got up. A moment later, I heard the rattle of a cup and saucer. Betty looked me up and down and said, 'You're here then.'

Hmm...I ran my gaze over her short bobbed black hair, held in place by a thick layer of hairspray and eyes heavily layered with black mascara and eyeliner. Her mouth, painted with thick bright red lipstick, hurt my eyes. Affecting a sultry walk, Betty crossed the room and sank into the chair beside me, kicking off two-inch stiletto heels. Her brown eyes seemed glazed and unfocussed. A distinctive odour of cigarettes and liquor tickled my nose. Aunty Gladys returned and plonked a cup of black tea in front of her.

Glancing in her father's direction, Betty took a sip and drawled. 'I see Pops is the life and soul of the party again.'

Aunty Gladys, settling back in her chair, cup in hand, paused and looked over at her husband's reclined figure.

'Now love, your Dad's had a very busy day. Driving in all that traffic to collect Constance, well you know how he is when the roads are busy. It was all very stressful for him. He spent the afternoon in the garden digging and hoeing out the rose bed. The Best Garden competition's next week and he wants the garden to look its best.'

The corner of Betty's brightly painted mouth lifted on one side in a slight sneer. She must have seen some emotion cross my face because suddenly her whole demeanour changed.

'Pops doesn't need to spend all that time in the garden Mums, he's a shoo-in to win Best Garden. His garden is divine, I haven't seen better anywhere, it's even lovelier than Queen Victoria Gardens and they've got a team of gardeners working on theirs,' she drawled. Lighting a cigarette she drew in a deep lung full of smoke before blowing it out towards the ceiling. Aunty Gladys leant over to the buffet, against the wall, and grabbed an ashtray. With a deft flick of her wrist, she slid it with enough force across the table to stop neatly in front of Betty.

'Yes, it's lovely, but it takes a lot of hard work to keep it that way. Anything worth achieving in life takes work. Things aren't just given to you on a platter, you know.'

Oh, you crafty old devil, you're not so blind to Betty's faults as you pretend.

'So Constance,' said Betty, choosing to ignore her mother's dig, turned her gaze towards me. She blew a lung full of smoke at me and asked, 'How was the trip? Dreary, I suppose.' She waffled on, in a rough sultry voice, not giving me a chance to reply. 'Oh well, never mind, you're here now. We're going to have such fun together. Did Mums tell you about the job I wangled for you?'

I nodded.

'Yeah good, well you start work Monday. The supervisor's a stickler about what you wear...you'll need a black skirt and white blouse, like mine. Now I've had a hell – sorry Mums – a really busy day, I'm turning in.'

She stubbed her cigarette half out and left it to smoulder in the ashtray. Slipping her feet back into the black shoes, rose on those impossibly high heels and sauntered out of the room, taking the self-absorbed atmosphere with her.

* * *

Late into the night, I lay in bed staring through the gloom at the shadows dancing on the ceiling from the streetlights outside. Sleep eluded me. I could hear a soft snore coming from the bed beside me. It might have been a mistake coming here.

After finishing my tea and clearing up, I'd said goodnight to Aunty Gladys and sought my bed. Propped up on three pillows, Betty lay smoking a cigarette. As I shoved my way into the room, sweeping her newly discarded shoes aside with my foot, she'd given me a blank stare and said, 'Tidy little thing aren't you.'

Depositing the butt into an empty drink can, she threw it on the mess already living on the dressing table, sank under the covers, rolled to her side, and began to snore.

Sighing I rolled over to face the paint-chipped wall and waited for sleep to overtake me.

3

Chapter Three

I woke early, and in the dappled morning light shining through the window I lay and read while the rest of the household slumbered. Betty may have planned to stay in bed for the entire day, but I was restless. It came from not being allowed to stay in bed after seven, not even on special occasions. Mother would have a fit if she knew I was still in bed. Restless and uncomfortable, I got up, pulled on my green floral dressing gown and slid my feet into slippers. My quiet movements must have awakened Betty because with a hacking cough she sat up, looked at me for a moment in incomprehension. Her face was a mess. Mascara and eyeliner formed black circles around her watery red eyes, while a slash of scarlet lipstick ran along her cheek. She resembled a lopsided woman in a Picasso painting. Running a hand through her hair – still lacquered in a layer of spray – left it pointing at the ceiling like a burnt-out forest. Awareness slowly sank in and she groaned. Flopping back on her pillow, Betty threw her forearm over her face and muttered, 'Oh God, kill me now.'

I snickered under my breath, finished knotting my gown and said, 'Good morning, Betty.'

Judging by the glare I received I don't think she appreciated my cheerfulness.

I waded through her mess and headed to the kitchen to put the kettle on.

Betty staggered from the bedroom, coughing and hacking. She stumbled down the hallway and slammed the bathroom door. The water ran for a long time. The girl that finally emerged bore no resemblance to the creature I'd previously encountered. Freshly shampooed hair bobbed in soft curls around a clean, sweet angelic face. I studied her and noticed a slight yellow tinge to her skin, an unhealthy sign. Not enough moisturiser or something else?

She flashed a sparkling, even-toothed smile.

'Morning Constance, any tea in the pot?'

Stunned at the complete change of personality, I poured her a cup of tea and offered the pale pink milk jug. Betty shook her head and amazed me with an apology.

'I'm sorry about yesterday and my grouchy mood. I had a shit of a day at work. My bitch of a supervisor was riding my tail all day. Look, I want to make it up to you, how about we go shopping in the city. Stores are open till noon. We can get the things you need for work and have a slap-up meal somewhere. Would you like that, Constance?'

Prepared to give her the benefit of the doubt and revise my opinion based on our first encounter, I said, 'That sounds like a great idea, Betty. It'll be fun to check out the latest fashions.'

She snuggled deeper into her ruby dressing gown and picked up her cup. 'It's going to be terrific having you around. There's so many great places we can go, movies, clubs, the beach. We can even double date.'

'I don't know about that.' I'd never been on a proper date but didn't want to admit my lack of experience in that area, so with a small laugh I said, 'I don't know anyone to date.'

'That's alright, I know a couple of great blokes. Kane and Jerry are terrific guys...I'll introduce you. You'll love them.' A small smile lit her eyes and touched her lips. 'Kane's my fella. He's got this terrific job and we get to go to some fabulous places. Nightclubs, racetracks, cafes, those types of places and...he can get us tickets to anything we want. We only have to ask.'

'That sounds exciting, Betty, but are you sure he won't mind me tagging along when you go out together?'

'No, he loves having me by his side when they're working, but sometimes the boys get tangled up in business matters and that can be a real drag. It'll be great having you along for company...and you can partner up with Jerry. He'll like that.'

Betty gulped down the last of her tea and jumped to her bare feet, 'Come on then, let's go tart ourselves up and head into the city. I hear the shops calling.'

Shopping with Betty was not for the faint-hearted. We trooped around all the high-end clothing and shoe stores, road-tested and discarded a vast array of garments, and giggled over some of the latest weird fashions. I picked up a couple of modest skirts and tops for work. Too modest for Betty's taste, but as I was the one who had to wear them, I opted for comfort and professionalism. Betty racked up an enormous sum on her store accounts. I wondered how she could afford all the things she bought.

My feet felt three sizes too big for my leather shoes, so I dropped a hint for us to find a café and indulge ourselves with a cup of tea and something to eat. Betty worked to her own agenda and ignored my suggestion. Instead, she let out a loud, harsh whistle that hailed a passing taxi.

'I want to show you something,' she said, as we piled into the back seat of the black and white cab. A strong stale smell of old perspiration and nicotine hung in the air, so I cracked the window and slipped my throbbing feet out of my leather shoes.

Betty rapidly issued directions to the elderly Greek driver, 'Beaconsfield Parade, St Kilda', before settling back in her seat and sighing.

It turned out she'd found us some digs. A boarding house, in a prime location, only twenty minutes from the heart of the city. The three-storey building, with a red-brick facade faced the beach. The main road stood between its front steps and the golden sand of the beach. How good was that? I didn't remember ever discussing sharing digs with Betty or even moving out of aunt and uncle's house but, according to Betty, it was always the plan. I must have slept through that bit.

Gloating at my surprise, Betty said, 'It's all organised. A twin-share's available from the first of next month. That gives you a couple of weeks to get Mums and Pops on board.'

'Me! Why me? Why do I have to do the dirty work? They're your parents, and it's your idea,' I said, crinkling my nose in disbelief at the effrontery of her.

'Yeah, it'll be dead easy coming from you,' she said, tucking a lock of hair behind her ear and fiddling with the big hoop earring dangling from her lobe. 'You just need to tell them that staying at our place was only ever a temporary thing until this room became available. It would be lovely, '*cause we've become such good friends*', if I could come and live with you. I could act as your chaperone, you know, help you find your feet.'

I shook my head. As I glanced up I noticed the taxi driver watching us in his rear-vision mirror, amusement written all over his face.

'That won't work, Betty. Your folks will never believe that.'

Betty lit a cigarette, narrowed her eyes, and glared at me through the smoke haze. Without looking, she tossed the dead match out the window.

'Yeah, they will...my folks are a walk over – very naïve – it'll be dead easy.'

I lifted my eyebrows at her reasoning and gave a mental shake of my head – is this girl for real.

'Look, this is all you need to say,' and with a placid smile on her painted red lips, Betty instructed me on what to say. I felt like an actress following a script as she made me rehearse during the taxi ride home.

* * *

It wasn't until that evening I finally got to eat – sort of. We never got the promised lunch or even a cup of tea, and I was starving. It was late afternoon by the time we arrived home. A delicious aroma from the stew, simmering on the stove, pervaded the entire house. My stomach cramped in pain and anticipation. Lugging our packages to the bedroom, I folded and packed my new clothing away in my suitcase and put the paper carry bags into the bin. Betty threw hers into the wardrobe, not bothering to unpack.

I left her lounging on her bed and went into the kitchen, opened the cutlery drawer and started setting the table. Aunty Gladys gave me a smile that warmed my heart.

'Thank you, Constance.' She raised her voice and called out loudly, 'Wash up you lot...dinner's being dished up in five minutes.'

Yes, I gave a mental fist pump, finally some food. I dashed into the pretty blue and white bathroom to scrub the day off my hands.

'Come and get it, you lot.' The call resounded around the house.

I joined a smiling Uncle Richard as he emerged from his chair, and together we trooped into the bright and cheery kitchen. I grabbed a bowl from the stack on the bench and lined up behind him at the stove. Aunty Gladys, wielding a large stainless steel ladle, served out big meaty scoops of delicious looking stew. She filled my bowl to the brim and plonked a freshly baked, crusty bread roll on top.

'There you go, love...there's plenty more in the pot, if you want seconds.'

My stomach gave a loud growl.

Betty tipped most of her food back into the pot.

'No roll, Mums, I'm not hungry.'

Not hungry! Did this girl ever eat, I wondered? No dinner last night, a cup of tea for breakfast, no lunch and not even a sniff of afternoon tea. Wow, how does she do it? I certainly can't. I need my meals.

I waited in polite anticipation, my hands clenched in my lap until everyone had taken a seat at the table. I lifted my spoon loaded with stew. The smell hadn't deceived me. The tender beef covered in wonderful rich gravy tasted sensational. The inside of my cheeks tingled and my tongue danced in delight as I chewed. I almost groaned outloud it was so good. Then Betty ruined everything by speaking.

'Oh, by the way Mums, Constance has something important to discuss with you and Pops.'

The food formed a hard rock in my stomach. I lost my ability to swallow. Ambushed, I repeated my speech, just as Betty had me rehearse.

'It's a nice room, Aunty Gladys, and they're strict about us being in early at night. The doors have locks and no one, other than residents are allowed upstairs.' I finished my lame story and tried to maintain eye contact.

Aunty Gladys paused her chewing and stared at me wordlessly for at least a minute, before swallowing.

'Well, I suppose it will be okay for Betty to go, as you'll be living with her. But,' pointing her stubby index finger at me to emphasise her words, 'if for any reason it doesn't work out, you come straight back to us, love.'

Pasting a small smile on my lips, I nodded in agreement and felt like a real heel. I stared down at my food, loaded my spoon and waited for the cold lump in my stomach to ease. It didn't. I carefully laid the spoon in the bowl and excused myself from the table, my appetite gone.

4

Chapter Four

I was brimming with excitement as Betty and I caught the 7.30 bus into the city for my first day at work. Dressed in a knee-length black skirt, modest white silk blouse and flat, black slip-on shoes, I was prepared for a day on my feet.

The old olive-green and white bus, with its impossibly hard vinyl seats, took well over an hour to rumble along its route. We rushed in the staff entrance five minutes before opening time. It took us ages to walk from the bus stop to the door because Betty, clad in a very short skirt and very high stiletto heels, found walking at any speed difficult.

The floor manager, glasses perched on the tip on her nose with a beaded chain looped from them around her neck, stood tapping her watch face and glaring as we hurried in.

'Your station please, Miss Ryan. The doors are about to open.'

Betty sashayed her way over to the perfume counter, picked up a sample bottle, and spritzed herself with scent. She then posed herself decorously behind her workstation with a pasted smile on her face. The manager continued to glare at her for a moment. Then it was my turn. She wrinkled her nose and ran steel-grey eyes from the top of my head to the tip of my toes in a detailed examination .

'Good, at least you're well-dressed, Miss O'Hara. My name is Mrs Morris. You'll report directly to me. I do not tolerate tardiness, rudeness or dishonesty in my staff. So, you will show up on time and complete your work before leaving each day. You will not leave early unless I have given you approval, which I shall not. You will be meticulous in your duties. You will always be polite to our customers and your co-workers. If a customer is rude to you, you will not be rude back. Instead, you will smile politely. If a customer is slow, unsure or difficult, you will smile and be helpful. There will be no fraternising with other employees or men during work hours. You will remain professional at all times. Do you understand, Miss O'Hara?' she asked. Her tone brooked no argument.

'Yes, Mrs Morris.'

'Good. Follow me and we'll get you started.'

She turned on her heel and marched towards an array of glass and steel shelves that sparkled in the bright store lights. The department store doors opened and a flood of customers entered.

'You'll be working in the shoes and accessory department.'

I spent the morning under the instruction of Mrs Morris. I learnt about my duties and customer service approach. By noon, when I was permitted a half-hour lunch break, my brain was crammed so full of what to do and what not to do, I was too scared to even lift a finger without permission. Mid-afternoon, Mrs Morris allowed me to serve my first customer. A young blonde-haired woman with pursed lips. She wandered the shelving, picking up shoes in a desultory manner. Mrs Morris lifted her meticulously arched eyebrow at me in permission, so I took a brisk step forward.

'Good afternoon my name is Constance, may I help you with anything?'

'Oh hi, I'm Susan. I am looking for a comfortable work shoe.'

'What sort of work do you do, Susan?'

'Office work, long hours. I'm looking for something with a low heel. My feet get so sore and my legs ache if I wear anything with a heel for too long. You'd know what that's like, working as a shop assistant and on your feet all day.'

Smiling at her in understanding, I said, 'Why don't you sit down, Susan, I've got the perfect shoe for you.'

Going over to a glass display case, I selected the Gucci square-toed flats with a bamboo horse-bit detail at the toe.

'Wow, they're gorgeous. Do you have them in a size six?'

'I'll just slip out the back and check.' I hurried into the stock-room. High on one of the upper shelves, I spotted the box I needed. I clambered up the ladder and put my hand out to pull what I needed from the stack. A hand slid up the back of my leg towards my thigh. I dropped the box and tilted sideways on the step. Two hands grabbed me by the waist and a gravelly male voice said, 'Careful there, young lady we don't want you hurting yourself now.'

I looked around at the clean shaven, middle-aged man, with an unpleasant smile on his thick lips. He was creepy, and I didn't like the way his hands were touching me. Betty rushed in. The heel of her two-inch stiletto shoe caught the middle of the man's foot and he yelped in pain and let go of me.

'Oh...I'm so sorry, Mr Owens. I'm such a klutz,' Betty feigned.

'You should be more careful. What are you doing back here, you're not in shoes?'

'I came to tell you that Mr Grace was just here. I think he's looking for you.'

He gave a quick nod and hobbled away. Betty looked at me and said, 'Sorry, should have warned you about old Handsy Owens. He tries it on with all the girls.'

I bent to retrieve the box of shoes from the floor and gave a small shudder. 'He was horrible.'

Mrs Morris appeared in the doorway and said, 'What's going on in here? Betty, stop gossiping and get back to work. Miss O'Hara your customer is waiting.'

'Sorry Mrs Morris, I was having trouble with the ladder and Betty was just giving me a hand. I have the shoes now.' I said, holding the box up. Betty gave me a wink and slipped from the room.

Looking slightly mollified, Mrs Morris nodded and said, 'Alright then, but hurry before you lose the sale.'

I followed her back out onto the sales floor and gave my customer the shoes to try on.

'Hmm...they feel nice, like slipping on a soft glove,' said Susan, standing to admire her small feet in the mirror. She twirled her right foot on its toe and watched the reflection in the mirror.

'I have a beautiful bag that will go nicely with those,' I said and handed her a pearl grey Gucci suede and leather clamshell clutch.

Susan's face lit up in delight, and as she ran her hand over the soft leather, her blue eyes sparkled. 'Oh, it's gorgeous. I must have them both. Thank you so much, you've made my day.'

While I rang up the sale, Susan nattered on about the woes of shopping. I smiled at her as I placed the change in her hand.

'Thank you for shopping at Myer Emporium. Have a lovely day,' I said, remembering the instructions Mrs Morris had given me on the best way to close a sale.

In a cheery voice, Susan announced she would be back soon for me to accessorise her engagement outfit. A small glow of satisfaction warmed my heart and pushed away the creepy feeling Handsy Owens had left. My first customer wandered away with a radiant smile on her pretty face. Mrs Morris, standing like a forbidding statue in the background, gave a single nod of her head. High praise indeed!

The day passed in a whirl. I counted my blessings by having a modicum of success and no difficult customers. Whenever I went into the storeroom, I took a careful look around first to make sure Handsy Owens wasn't in the vicinity. There was no way I was going to get cornered by him again.

The store doors closed at exactly five o'clock. I restocked the shelves, ensuring they were all ready for the next day. Once that task was complete, I took a quiet stance at my counter, hands clasped in front of me while Mrs Morris inspected my work. I could see Betty in the background, jigging from foot to foot, impatient to be off. I ignored her antics until Mrs Morris gave me permission to leave.

'How'd you go today?' Betty asked as we trotted down the city street towards the bus stop. 'Mrs M's a stuck-up old cow, isn't she? I think if she sucked her skinny cheeks in any tighter she'd turn into a prune.'

I laughed at the image of the thin, grey-haired Mrs Morris with a prune face.

I answered Betty's question with a quick description of my day. 'She was very strict. Watched me like a hawk, but once I got over my nerves, I enjoyed myself. Mrs Morris seemed happy with my work.'

Betty grabbed my hand. 'Come on, we've just got time for a quick snifter before the bus,' she said.

Tugging me along in her wake, she pulled me towards the door of a pub. With a loud laugh, we half fell into the open foyer that divided two sets of swing doors. The reek of stale beer and cigarette ash burnt my nose and made me sneeze. To the right, someone had propped open the doors to the smoke-filled public bar. Half a dozen men leant against the highly polished bar staring into their beer glasses looking for the answer to life. Our entrance caused them to look up in dismay at the intrusion of two women into their sanctum.

Betty tossed her head in contempt and pulled me towards the closed frosted glass door marked 'ladies lounge'. Leaning on the door with her shoulder, she pushed it open to reveal an empty room. The black and white checked flooring and six green laminated tables were about as attractive and welcoming as the male patrons. Betty pointed to a hatch in the wall. It opened onto the end of the bar in the other room.

'Get the drinks will you. I'll grab us a table. Make mine a scotch and ice.'

The stop at the bar for a drink on the way home from work became a regular pattern of our workday. Betty would always grab a table while I paid for the drinks. One glass of wine was nice, but I learnt quickly to tell her I was short of cash, otherwise Betty, who never opened her purse to pay, would keep drinking.

* * *

After two weeks of working under Mrs Morris's eagle eye and avoiding creepy Handsy Owens, my nerves were beginning to fray. Then one morning I heard a rumpus near the ladies' toilet. Mrs Morris rushed out to investigate. When she returned, she had two bright red splotches of anger on her cheeks.

'Miss O'Hara, you're ready to work unsupervised now. I'm leaving you in charge of the floor.'

'Thank you, Mrs Morris,' I replied, careful not to show my relief.

She left in a hurry, heading for the elevator. As soon as the doors dinged shut, Betty raced over.

'Did you hear? Handsy Owens got caught perving in the ladies' toilet.'

'Wow.'

'Wow's right...I think old prune face is about to get a promotion.'

'Promotion?' I asked, confused by the leap from Handsy being caught perving to Mrs Morris getting a promotion.

'Yeah, he was manager of the entire department – she's next in line.'

A customer came in at that moment, so I did what I'd been trained to do, leaving Betty to return to her counter.

It had been a busy and successful sales day. Checking my till and sales dockets balanced correctly, Mrs Morris ventured to say that it was nice to see the department flourish under my competent hand.

5

Chapter Five

Betty was being a drama queen about packing up her room. I think it was because she had to do something about her mess. I quickly cleared out of the house, announcing loudly I had urgent letters to post. Once outside I leant with my chin on my crossed arms on the front garden gate. I closed my eyes as I enjoyed the morning sunshine on my face. A smile tugged at the corner of my mouth as I listened to the wailing that was drifting out of the open bedroom window.

'Crap, now I've broken a fingernail. Can't someone else do the packing or even give me a hand.'

Aunty Gladys put a stop to Betty's complaints by saying, 'Well love, if you don't want to pack that's fine, don't pack and stay here, it makes no difference to us.'

'Is someone pulling the cat's tail?'

A deep masculine voice penetrated my quiet enjoyment of the sunshine. My eyes popped open in surprise. Before me stood a handsome young man who gave the impression, he'd just stepped off a surfboard. Scruffy and tousled butterscotch hair framed a boyish angular face and laughter lines surrounded bright hazel eyes.

'Sorry, I didn't mean to startle you, I just thought with all the gnashing and wailing going on, someone was giving the cat a hard time.'

Before I could stop it, a bark of laughter escaped my smiling lips. Clamping a hand over my mouth, worried Betty might hear me and demand my help, I muffled the noise to a snort. I took a moment to drink in his short, muscular frame before answering his cheeky question.

'No, no cat. My friend is packing her suitcase.' I held out my hand, 'Hi I'm Constance, do you live around here?'

He adjusted the backpack hanging off his shoulder and put his hand in mine. His grip was warm and strong as we shook hands.

'Hi, I'm David Wellard, stoked to meet you.' Pointing to his bag, David revealed his gappy white teeth, which added a real cheekiness to his smile. 'I'm on my way to check out some digs right now, but I'm not sure it'll suit me, a bit far from the surf for my liking. How about you, little pixie, do you live here in this magnificent garden?'

I felt the corners of my mouth lift in amusement. I didn't see any reason not to answer his query.

'Not for much longer. My friend Betty and I are moving out today. We've gotten ourselves a room, in the boarding house on Beaconsfield Parade. Do you know it?'

'No. Beaconsfield Parade...that's in St Kilda, right?'

'Yeah'

'Is it in a good spot?'

'It's right on the beach. The surf club's nearby and within walking distance are cafés and restaurants. Anyway, that's what all the commotion's about. Betty's mum is making her clean up her mess before we leave.'

'Constance, are you around? Can you come give me a hand?' Betty's whine floated out the window.

Scrambling out the gate to join David on the footpath I said, 'Sorry David got to dash before she finds me and I end up doing her packing.'

David laughed at my evasive manoeuvres.

'It's been awesome meeting you, Constance. Maybe I'll look you up at your boarding house, and if this place doesn't work out, I might even try my luck there for a room.'

I lifted my hand and waved to him over my shoulder before hurrying around the corner and out of sight of the house. There I slowed to a casual stroll and took my time to post my letters to dad and sarah. I wondered if they were getting my letters – I hadn't heard from either of them since leaving home. It made my heart ache being cut off from them.

Spotting a phone box at the end of the street I decided to call home. I dug some loose change from the pocket of my denim shorts and checked the time on my watch. 'Yes,' I exclaimed, 'Mother should be at the church guild meeting.'

I fed some coins into the slot and listened to the ringing at the other end of the line. It went on for ages. Disappointed I was about to hang up when a stern voice said, 'O'Hara Residence.'

My heart sank, 'Hello Mother, its Constance. How are you?'

'What do you want?'

'Nothing I just rang to say hello to you and Daddy.'

'Well don't do it again, and you can stop writing as well. I have burnt your letters. You are not welcome in this family.' The phone clicked in my ear as she hung up. I stared at the receiver in my hand. I now had the answer to my question. A heavy weight took up residence in my chest. With a slow dragging step I returned to the house determined to make a success of the new life before me.

Betty was sitting on a bulging black suitcase, trying unsuccessfully to secure the latch. I don't think she'd actually folded anything, as escaping items of clothing looked like they'd been scooped up and shovelled in. The room looked larger now with the floor clear – all

Betty's shoes now lived in a large cardboard box standing in the corner.

The empty wardrobe, except for a lonely wire coat hanger dangling on its rail, echoed with the sound of her voice.

'Give us a hand will you, Constance. I can't get this bloody thing closed.'

Kneeling in front of the suitcase, I added my weight to hers and between us we snipped the latch. I must remember to stand back from the explosion when she releases it.

* * *

Our gear sat on the footpath in front of our new digs. Uncle Richard wrapped his powerful arms around me in a bone-crunching hug. Unshed tears stung my eyes.

'Take care, young Constance. Don't get pushed into doing anything you don't want to. Remember lass, it is alright to say *No*, especially to missy over there.' His comforting voice hummed through me like an Irish lullaby. I was going to miss him.

Much to Betty's chagrin, Uncle Richard held her close and kissed her soundly on both cheeks. She wriggled and complained until he let her go, but he had the final say. Leaning out the driver's window, he shouted out an Irish endearment as he drove away.

'Love you, Mavoureen.'

I don't know what Betty had in her bags besides clothes, rocks maybe, but they weighed a ton. Pushing, shoving and dragging her first two cases, we finally manoeuvred them to bottom of the staircase. There, sitting on the third step, tying the laces of a very scruffy pair of gym boots, was David. Looking up from his task, he leapt to his feet and flashed a cheeky grin.

'Hi there, do you girls want a hand with your stuff?'

Betty immediately dropped her hold on a case, fluffed her hair, and gave a sultry smile.

'Hello handsome. I'd certainly appreciate the help of a nice muscular man,' she said. With a purr in her voice and an exaggerated swing of her hips, she brushed her body against David to squeeze past him on the stairs. 'Walk this way gorgeous and I'll show you the way.'

He chuckled in amusement at her antics. 'If I walk that way, I'll do myself some damage.'

Betty threw an amused look over her shoulder, winked and continued swaying her hips as she went up the stairs and out of sight. David's cheeks took on a pink tinge. He grabbed the handle of Betty's dropped case and lifted it with a loud grunt.

'Good god. What the hell has she got in here, the kitchen sink?' he exclaimed as he began struggling up the steps, holding the case with two hands.

'Hello David, this is quite a surprise. What are you doing here?' I asked.

The emphasis on my words caused David to pause. He looked at me with a crooked smile on his lips and said, 'Well, that other place didn't work out for me. They were asking far too much rent and I'm positive the bed was full of critters. Anyway, I remembered you talking about this excellent place being right across the road from the beach. Sounded just what I was looking for. So I scooted along to try my luck.' Putting on an exaggerated whisper he continued, 'The scary but efficient Mrs Simmonds has decided that as I'm not a mass murderer, my presence in her establishment will be tolerated – her words not mine, therefore I have been honoured with a small attic room and a long list of rules. Thanks for the tip, Constance, this place is awesome. I'll be able to catch the waves whenever the surfs up. Cool hey.'

David looked down at me with a grin. Enthusiasm poured out of him in waves. I cocked my head and returned his smile with one of my own, happy he'd found a new home. Sucking air deeply into his lungs, David continued his struggle with the bag. 'Bloody hell, it feels like she's got the whole damn house in here! Is this all of your stuff?'

Laughing at his naïve question I said, 'Goodness no David, that's only the first of Betty's three cases. I've got the second one here. There's another case, a large box and my small bag still out on the footpath.'

Puffing and panting, I heaved the heavy bag up another step. David spoke over his shoulder. 'No, don't struggle with that, Constance. I'll bring it up for you, and your other stuff as well. My muscles need the workout. And...I promise, I won't break Mrs Simmonds's rules, by going into your room. I'll leave the bags outside your door, okay. We can't go getting kicked out on our first day now can we.'

Talking to the back of his purple tee-shirt, as he staggered up the stairs, I said, 'Thanks David, I really appreciate your help.'

While I dragged Betty's heavy bag into our room, David raced back downstairs to retrieve the rest of our gear. As promised, he left everything sitting outside our door. The last I saw of him that afternoon, he was jogging down the stairs, surfboard tucked under his arm and a self-satisfied smile on his face.

Our room, while nothing special, was furnished with the necessities for basic living and was scrupulously clean. Over the twin, iron-framed beds that lined a light grey wall, a long thin window was open to the cooling afternoon sea breeze. The lightweight plain green curtain billowed with a current of air and would be useless against the brightness of the morning sun. That didn't worry me,

I'm an early riser, but I think madam might have trouble sleeping until her usual noon rising time.

Dark-green chenille bedspreads covered freshly laundered crisp white sheets and smelled faintly of lemon. For me, unpacking and settling in was easy. I unlocked my suitcase and slid it under the bed. I'd found this was the best way to keep Betty out of my stuff. She was too lazy to fossick under the bed.

I set my silver-backed hairbrush, tube of lipstick and the framed photo of Sarah and Dad on the dressing table that divided our two beds.

'You can have the wardrobe, if you like Betty. I just need the two drawers on this side of the dressing table for my smalls.'

I settled back on my bed and watched in amusement as Betty did her version of unpacking. She pushed her cases against the far wall and popped the latches. Her clothes exploded onto the floor like she'd trained them to live there. Grabbing a few light filmy night things, she threw them into a drawer, but didn't bother to close it. She threw the box of shoes into the wardrobe, shut the door and turned the key to stop it popping open again. Then with a dramatic flop, she threw herself back on her bed and lay with her arm across her flushed face. Betty kicked her feet and blindly tossed the thongs on her feet across the room.

'Oh god, who would've thought moving could be so tiring. I'm exhausted.'

Betty lasted five minutes in a sprawl on her bed before leaping up.

'Where the bloody hell are they?' She searched for the discarded footwear. 'Why don't I give the boys a ring? We could go catch a movie tonight or have something to eat and then go on to a night-club.'

'The movies would be fun, Betty. I saw in the newspaper last week that they're showing *Love Story,* starring Ali MacGraw and

Ryan O'Neal this week at the cinema. I wouldn't mind seeing that. Ryan O'Neal is such a dreamboat, don't you think?'

'Yeah, he's not bad, I prefer Warren Beatty myself. That dazzling smile.'

'So, what do you think, shall we go see *Love Story*?'

'I don't think so. Kane and Jerry wouldn't be interested in that, type of movie,' Betty said, sarcasm dripping from her words.

No, I don't suppose they would, being men, I thought in disappointment.

'Well, what about that adventure flick *Airport*, it's got a heap of Hollywood stars in it? That might be alright for the blokes, full of action and drama.'

'Sounds alright, I suppose. I'll suggest it to Kane. I'll be back soon – I'll just nip down to the phone box on the corner and give him a ring. We can go out for drinks at the pub first, so you can meet the guys, seeing as they are not allowed in our room.'

The slapping of Betty's thongs, as they smacked against the soles of her feet, echoed up from the staircase as she descended the stairs. It had become increasingly obvious to me that with Betty, everything revolved around her having a drink.

It took her an hour and a half to make the phone call. I put the time to good use, taking a sticky beak around the house, making sure I knew where to find everything, especially the loo. Satisfied I knew where everything was and it was clean, I went back to our room.

I decided it was safe to put my knickers and bras into the drawers, but nothing else. I had caught Betty snooping through my things a few times and helping herself to money. She said she was just 'borrowing' – I'm still waiting to be paid back. My plain cotton knickers were safe from her grasping fingers, not being the fancy and sexy silky numbers she preferred, but I didn't trust her not to poke her nose into my journal.

Kneeling down to retrieve my suitcase, I glanced under the bed. The floor near the bed head didn't look right, one of the wooden floorboards stuck up a little. Leaning in further, I brushed a few dust bunnies out of the way and had a poke at the board. It flipped up, revealing a small recess beneath. Hmm...it seems roomy enough, might be a great place to hide my money. I carefully checked to satisfy myself there were no spiders or creepy crawlies in the hole, before backing out from under the bed. I dug my floral cosmetic bag out from my backpack and emptied most of the cash from my purse into it. I crawled back under the bed and stashed the bag of money into the hole. Looking at the space again, I added my journal. The stuff I write is personal and the only person I'd share it with is my sister. Fitting the board back into place, I crawled back out from under the bed just as Betty slapped her way back up the stairs.

6

Chapter Six

Betty, flushed and unsteady, smelt of booze when she returned from the phone box.

'Kane's real happy we're all moved in. He wants to take us out tonight to celebrate. The guys will meet us at the Beaky, that's the local pub, at seven. It's just around the corner from here. I checked the place out and guess what? They're showcasing a band tonight. '*Zoot*' or 'Hoot', something like that. So get your glad rags on girl, we're going out on the town.'

A band. Wow, sounds like fun. 'You know I've never seen a live band.' In excitement, I started dancing around the room like a loon. 'What do I need to wear?'

My silliness amused Betty. 'As little as possible,' she said, throwing back her head in laughter.

Confession time. 'No seriously, Betty,' I replied calming down. 'My mother's nothing like yours. My social life comprised of church teas and charity benefits, and then only to work. She'd never allow me to meet friends at the pub...as for going to see a live band, the world would have to end first. This is all very new to me. I need some guidance on this stuff.'

'Are you serious?' exclaimed Betty, leaning forward, eyes wide. 'Good god, your mother was that strict?'

'You've no idea.'

'Well wear something lightweight, it's February, you won't get cold. The summer nights here are as hot as the day sometimes. Besides, if it gets cool, we'll have a couple of handsome blokes to keep us warm.' Betty wrapped her arms around herself and gave a small shimmy of delight. 'Wear that emerald, short-sleeved jumpsuit, the one with bell bottoms, it'll be perfect. With your pale skin and auburn hair, you'll look divine.'

'Okay, sounds good. What are you going to wear?' I asked, eyeing off the pile of clothing sprouting from her cases.

Betty rummaged around for a moment and then held up a red outfit. 'I picked this up yesterday, it's like yours. Flared jumpsuits are so trendy just now. We can look like sisters...twins. Well, not quite twins as you're short with auburn hair and I'm rather tall and dark, thanks to my father.'

I stopped listening as a shaft of pain hit me in the chest. Oh, god Sarah, I miss you. It should be us sharing this room and getting ready to go out. What fun we'd have, with no Mother or Frank around to spoil it. Not wanting to ruin the moment with a crying jag, I pushed my depressing thoughts and feelings down deep and locked them away. Shaking the wrinkles from my outfit, I joined in with Betty's enthusiastic date preparations.

At seven o'clock, all dolled up in our glad rags, complete with opened-toed platform shoes, we carefully tripped the three hundred metres to the pub. A couple of blokes walked past us as we approached the door, looked back, and wolf whistled.

The lanky redhead cast an appreciative eye over us and drawled, 'Sexy. How about joining us for a drink?'

Betty smirked at him, took a puff of her cigarette and fluffed her hair. I giggled at my first compliment.

She cocked her hip and said, 'Sorry mate, this presents wrapped for someone else.' He looked at Betty in disappointment and gave a shrug.

'That's a shame. Next time, maybe.'

He opened the pub door for us with a gallant bow. A wave of hot air, noise and cigarette smoke hit me in the face, forcing me to take a momentary step backwards. Whoa! People crammed together in tight groups had barely enough room to raise a glass. The drinks were being ferried from the bar, held high overhead. The noise from raised voices, yelling to be heard over the other patrons, was deafening, and the band hadn't even started yet. A dense cloud of grey smoke hung over the scene, fed by the prolific cigarette consumption in the room. Even as I looked, it thickened.

Betty stands at five foot nine inches before heels. This gave her an advantage over my tiny five feet of height. She rose on to her tiptoes and looked over the crush. Identifying her target, she pointed and charged into the crowd. I tucked myself into her wake and followed close as I could. I came to an abrupt halt by bumping into her back and realised we had arrived at her intended destination.

I looked around her hip and saw two men slouched at a small four-seater pine table with their feet up on the spare chairs. Our dates, I presumed – the infamous Kane and Jerry. They had dressed alike. Hip hugging black leather jackets hung open over white polo shirts and black dress trousers.

Betty leant into the tall, lean, handsome guy, whose blond, wavy shoulder length hair was the same colour as his moustache. She plastered her red lips all over his. Must be Kane. Taking my eyes from the smooching pair, I glanced with interest at his companion, Jerry, and saw someone who was unsuccessfully trying to imitate his friend. He wore his hair and moustache in the same style as Kane, but his stringy, mousy-brown hair was limp and straight. He'd not been blessed with good looks. His face gave the impression that someone had smeared it on as an afterthought. In the past, Jerry's nose had been broken and not reset properly. It sat bent and flattened on his pock-marked cheek. A cigarette hung from the corner of lopsided plump lips.

Betty removed her mouth from Kane's. 'Hey handsome, this is Constance,' and flicked her fingers in my direction. Kane stood, towering over us all at six feet four and politely held out his hand. Placing my small hand in his to shake, I yelled over the noise, 'Hi Kane, pleased to meet you.' I turned my attention to Jerry.

With his left foot, Jerry kicked the chair in my general direction and leered.

'Have a seat Princess,' he said in a deep gravelly voice and lifted a cupped hand to his face adding, 'Drink?'

I nodded in bemusement and sat on the ungraciously offered chair. To say I felt a little creeped out by Jerry was an understatement. He gave off the same vibes as Handsy Owens. Jerry rose to his feet, lifted his brow at Kane, who nodded, and charged towards the bar. He didn't ask what I wanted. Jerry had the solid build of a boxer, everyone who saw him coming got out of his way. Those who didn't he shoved aside. No one protested at his rude behaviour.

Kane and Betty plastered themselves all over each other. Embarrassed by their antics, I turned to watch Jerry at the bar instead. He was having a heated discussion with a bloke I guessed was the pub's manager. He was dressed like the bar staff – white dress shirt, blue tie and dark trousers, only his were better quality. The manager stuck his finger on Jerry's chest, to emphasise whatever point he was making. Jerry gripped the finger, twisted it hard and then delivered a swift punch to his stomach. Acting as if nothing unusual had occurred, Jerry casually picked our drinks up and made his way back to the table. The manager, hunched over and gasping for air, staggered away into a back room. The crowd ignored everything.

Jerry plonked the drinks on the table in front of us. I looked over to check out Kane's reaction to the incident, but he just gave Jerry a chin lift.

'You give that little upstart Mr Joshua's message?' Kane asked.

Jerry laughed. 'Yeah, sure did,' he said. 'Here you go Princess, drink up.' He sat a glass of scotch in front of me.

I smiled and mouthed, 'Thank you Jerry,' but I didn't touch the drink.

Jerry's eyes squinted, and a vein stood out in his neck. 'What's the matter, not good enough for you?' The snarl in his voice took me by surprise.

'Ease up Jerry,' said Betty. 'Constance doesn't drink hard liquor, she's a white wine girl.' With a laugh she picked up my glass and tossed the contents down her own throat.

Jerry grunted, his jaw unclenched, and he turned to Kane.

'I've given that upstart ten minutes to come up with the dough. As an added lesson, I'll take him out for a drive and teach him what it means to welsh on payments.'

Kane rocked his hand back and forth.

'We'll see, mate. Let's give him some time to sweat over his actions first. If he doesn't come up with the money, we'll teach him a lesson he won't soon forget. He needs to understand this is his last chance – any more late payments and he's going fishing.'

Exactly ten minutes later, just as the band Zoot were tuning up their instruments to start the evening's entertainment, the manager came over to our table carrying a tray of drinks for us. His hand was shaking and his voice trembled as he handed Kane an envelope.

'I'm sorry Mr Hansen, I had my dates wrong.'

Kane glared at him and said, 'Don't be late again. There's no room in this business for misunderstandings. Mr Joshua won't be so tolerant with you, next time. You may even suffer a permanent retirement.'

The manager paled under his tan and gave a vigorous nod.

'Yes, I understand. It won't happen again.' He slunk away like a whipped dog.

The band struck the first chords of their opening number. Voices rose to be heard over the music.

'Come on, we're outta here.' Kane sculled down his beer. 'This place is the pits, let's go get some dinner.'

Before I could voice my disappointment about missing the music, Jerry grabbed my wrist and pulled me along in his wake. He barged towards the front door and out onto the street, with me in tow. The change in temperature almost made me cold, it had been stifling hot inside. My lungs welcomed the fresh air. I wrenched my wrist free of Jerry's harsh grasp and massaged the red mark his grip had left, to get the blood circulating.

'The car's parked around the corner,' said Kane, taking Betty's hand and leading the way. 'How's about we go to Geraldo's, that Italian place over on Lygon Street and then onto Mr Joshua's. Would you girls like that?'

'Oh goodie,' said Betty, bouncing up and down in delight. 'I *love* Mr Joshua's. You will too, Constance. There's poker, blackjack, roulette and my favourite, craps. All the big names will be there. Last time I saw two of the stars from that stage show *HAIR* and that politician and his wife. Do you remember Kane?'

Kane, an indulgent smile of amusement on his face, nodded as Betty chattered on, 'Oh, oh...and that famous horse trainer, oh what's his name? Ahh! Doesn't matter, Kane, you're the best.' She squealed and threw her arms around his neck.

Crab walking, they kissed all the way down the street. Jerry halted at the front passenger door of a light blue Holden Kingswood, placing a hand on the roof to lean on the car.

He said in amusement, 'Well I hope Kane has deep pockets if you're going to Mr Joshua's, Betty. I swear you lost enough to buy the place last time.' Then glancing at me with his brown eyes crinkled at the edges. 'Do you like to play cards and have a flutter, Princess?'

'I don't know, Jerry. I've never gambled. I have played gin rummy and whist but never for money.' My caution in trying not to appear too small-townish, backfired.

Jerry's eyebrows nearly disappeared under his hairline. 'God, where did Betty dig you up from?'

Betty spoke up for me. 'Leave her alone, Jerry. Constance has lived a very sheltered life in a small town. Not everyone's been around the traps like you and had the experiences you've had.'

Across the roof of the car, a look I couldn't interpret passed between Kane and Jerry.

'Well, mate, a bit of breaking in for you to do. You can introduce Constance to all the joys Mr Joshua's offers...and more.'

The corner of Jerry's mouth lifted. Another look passed between the two men.

Jerry glanced in my direction and said, 'Sorry Constance, I'm not used to nice girls. I live in a world full of life-hardened people who'd sell their souls for another beer. You stick with me, Princess, I'll show you a real good time – teach you how to beat the table.'

'Thanks, Jerry.' I gave him a shy smile, not really understanding what he was referring too, or maybe I did and just didn't want to appear unworldly.

* * *

Geraldo's restaurant served the most delicious pasta. Jerry, whose personality had undergone a complete change, actually asked me what I would like to eat. I'd never eaten Italian before so I asked him to choose. My request seemed to give him enormous pleasure. With a smug smile on his face he made a big show of studying the menu before ordering Spaghetti Carbonara.

Trying not to appear too obvious, I peered around the dining room in delight. The walls displayed hand-painted murals, each framed by an exposed brick arch, depicting different views of a vineyard in full bloom. The ceiling decoration was a hand painted grapevine in full fruit, bearing luscious ripe red grapes. It was like dining outside in a garden.

The men started discussing dogs and race meetings.

'I didn't know dogs raced. What sort of dogs are you talking about?' I asked when there was a pause in their conversation.

Jerry grunted, lit another cigarette, and said, 'Greyhounds, Princess. They race at Sandown Park. We mostly send the dogs to the country tracks in Geelong and Bendigo. Kane and I have stakes in a couple of mutts that do alright.'

'Stakes?' I asked, puzzled by the term.

'Yeah, stakes, you know...shares. We part own some dogs with a few of the blokes we work with, including Mr Joshua. How about we go to Sandown one night and watch them race?'

'That sounds like fun, Jerry.'

Taking a sip of the glass of wine in front of me, I said, 'Jerry, can I ask a question? Who is this Mr Joshua that you and Kane keep talking about?'

Stabbing his cigarette in the ashtray, leaving the butt to smoulder, Jerry's lips tightened in displeasure, but answered.

'Mr Joshua is our boss, Princess. An entrepreneur of some renown in Melbourne. Got his fingers in a lot of pies. He owns an exclusive club called The Orion. He also has shares in racehorses, dogs, gaming houses, clubs, pubs and escort agencies.'

As he spoke, Jerry lifted his hand to the waiter, twirled his finger around to order more drinks.

'And what do you guys do for him?'

'Kane and I monitor things, and provide protection.' Jerry started laughing at some inner joke.

'Protection?'

'We remind people when payments are due. We also find ways that people can be of help to him and keep an eye out for new business opportunities.'

My curiosity aroused, I wondered how much Jerry was going to tell me before he clammed up.

'Wow, that's a lot of responsibility. What sort of business opportunities do you keep an eye out for?'

The waiter arrived with glasses of beer for the men and scotch for Betty. He set another glass of white wine next to my first. Jerry indicated I should drink up. Taking a gulp I dropped my gaze under Jerry's intent stare.

'Confidential deals, Princess. Now, no more questions about Mr Joshua, he's a very private bloke and won't like us talking about him.'

'Oh, I'm sorry, Jerry. I don't want to get you and Kane into any trouble.'

At that moment, the food arrived and diverted his attention. Jerry started telling jokes. Who would have thought it...he could be quite a funny man, although most of his humour did have a hard edge. While we ate, he told us a story, about two old men who had each lost a leg in the war. One had lost his left leg, the other his right. They would buy one pair of shoes between them and share. The tale got quite a laugh and the atmosphere around the table lightened.

The meal was delicious, and I ate my fill. Betty pushed the pasta around her plate but knocked back plenty of scotches. I struggled to keep up with the drinks Jerry was buying me. The glasses before me lined up. The head began to swirl. When I rose after our meal I staggered. Jerry put a supporting arm around my waist.

'Whoa...here Princess lean on me.'

'Thanks Jerry. I think I had a little too much to drink,' I said, as I stumbled towards the car.

He smiled and helped me into the backseat and climbed in next to me. I leant my head against his shoulder. The car began to move and Jerry pulled me close. He covered my lips with his. I went to pull away but he held the back of my head in place and deepened the kiss. I lifted my hand to push him away but it wouldn't obey me. Jerry applied some pressure and I slid down to lay flat on my back across the seat. He covered me with his body and continued to kiss me. The car halted and I vaguely heard doors closing. I tried to tell Jerry to stop but my mouth wasn't obeying me. His hand slid my front zipper down and he pushed my jumpsuit off my shoulders. Then it was sliding down my body and onto the floor. I murmured a protest and made a grab, trying to pull it back up. He clamped my wrists together with one hand and held them above my head. With the other hand he reefed my knickers down. I cried out in protest. Jerry's mouth clamped over mine and muffled the noise. One handed he undid his trousers. His knees slid between my legs and he pushed them apart. He thrust himself inside me. Burning pain tore through me. I cried out but Jerry didn't stop. He thrust again and again. Tears ran down my cheeks. I pulled my wrists free and pushed hard against his shoulders. Jerry ignored my attempts to dislodge him. He gave one more thrust and then with a shout of delight collapsed on top of me.

I managed to slur, 'Get off me.'

He sat up and fiddled with his pants. I grappled around and found my knickers, and after a couple of attempts managed to pull them on. I started to cry harder and nausea overwhelmed me.

'I'm going to be sick,' I said, grappling for the door handle.

I fell out. Jerry followed, picked me up off the ground and pointing me to a nearby bush. I staggered over and lost my dinner and the rest of the alcohol in my stomach. When I finish Jerry handed me a handkerchief so I could wipe my face.

He pulled me against his chest and asked, 'Finished?'

I nodded and tried to push him away. He ignored me and shoved his hand inside the back of my underpants.

'Stop Jerry...I don't want to.'

He ground his groin against me and said, 'Sure you do.'

'No I don't.'

I gave a hard shove. He took a step back, grunted and ran his eyes over me standing exposed in my underwear. He gave a smirk and lit a cigarette.

'Can't blame a guy for trying...it was so good the first time.'

I glared, brushed past him and returned to the car to dress. I looked around for Betty. In the distance I could see her, naked, back against a tree, legs around Kane's waist. Judging by the noise they were making she was enjoying herself.

We piled back into the Kingswood, the men now sat in the front. Betty a contented smile on her lips sat next to me, smoking. I kept quiet. The tears now dry but the nausea still swirled around in my stomach. This was not how I planned my first time...and especially not with a man like Jerry. I was bitterly disappointed in myself for letting down my guard and allowing this to happen. Never again, I promised myself. With a heavy heart I stared unseeing out the window as Kane drove us to the far end of Lygon Street. There he turned into a small lane behind a dark building and parked. Standing in the lot next to us was a smart looking black Mercedes Benz limousine. Very flash. I'd no idea where we were, but followed along in a fog of misery. The freedom to do as I pleased had been quite heady but there were always consequences. I now had to learn to live with mine.

Kane descended half a dozen concrete steps and pressed the doorbell next to a solid looking black metal door. A small flap in the door opened, a face made a brief appearance, and then the flap closed with a clang. The door popped open and a soft light fell on our upturned faces. We trooped into a small foyer, home to a chair and table that guarded a well-lit staircase leading downwards.

'Evening Aidan, busy night?' asked Kane.

The doorman, Aidan, stood at least six foot six inches with chest and arm muscles so massive they looked as if his tee-shirt had been spray painted on.

'Just the usual crowd, but the night is young,' he said. Aidan's voice was unusually high pitched for a man his size. 'Mr Joshua was asking for you, Kane. He wants you to go find him as soon as you get here.'

'Right, thanks mate.'

Kane pointed in our direction.

'Betty, you know. The red head's Constance.'

Aiden nodded his bald head at us, stepped back to allow the men access to the downstairs staircase. Expecting us to follow, they jogged down the carpeted steps without a word.

I gave Aiden a timid smile. 'Hello.'

He smiled back at me with a look of surprise. 'Good evening, Miss.'

'Is it okay to go on in, Mr Joshua won't mind?' I asked, pointing after my friends.

'No Miss, he won't mind at all. Enjoy yourself.'

'Thanks, Aiden.'

Careful of my platform heels, I made my way down the steps without disgracing myself by falling flat on my face. Stepping out from the last stair tread, my shoes sank deeply into plush black and pink diamond patterned carpet. I spotted a toilet so I headed straight there. I looked at myself in the mirror and was surprised to see I looked no different. After suffering such a dramatic event I had expected it to show. I took a wad of wet paper towels and went into a cubicle to clean myself up. I felt a sob rising in my chest, hammering hard for release. I clamped down on the urge to cry. It would do no good. Blowing my nose on some toilet paper I flushed it all away. I took a deep breath, and when I was satisfied I was under control I went out into the club area.

Glancing around, I saw a variety of crowded gaming tables in a large open room. The well-dressed patrons were blithely throwing betting chips down and cheering lustily when they won. Overhead, a thick layer of blue-grey cigarette smoke blanketed the ceiling. Beyond the noisy gaming area, I noticed a second room, furnished with three large round tables covered in green felt. Card players sat in quiet groups, analysing their cards and chances.

A highly polished bar glowed under the bright lights. It ran the entire length of the left side of the room. Three well-dressed barmen, black suits and white shirts, scurried in a co-ordinated dance to fill drink orders. Loaded drink trays were being ferried around the gaming tables by waitresses in very high heels, bow ties and not much else. The shoes must be murder on the feet, I thought. The alcohol acted as fuel to the excitement being generated in the room, the noise level grew. Studying the faces, I noticed a range of emotions being played out, from happiness to drunken despair. Hmm...the gambling bug seems to be alive and well in Melbourne.

Betty appeared at my elbow, grabbed my hand and said, 'Come on, Constance, let's go. I don't want to miss anything.'

She towed me through the crowd, pointing out a few famous faces. She spotted Kane and Jerry across the room and dragged me towards them. Stepping into the quiet card room, I gave a sigh of relief, glad to be out of the noisy throng. Wondering where we were going, I glanced around and saw Kane head towards yet another room. This one was off to the left, hidden from the main gaming room.

Furnished with pale pink modular settees set around small black tables, the room was home to a second bar. Groups of men were being entertained by scantily clad girls. The lights and music were set at a low level, just right for intimacy. Kane made a beeline for the only table that differed from the rest. At this table sat two men, no girls, no drinks.

As he approached, Kane spoke to the man who had his back to us.

'Good evening, Mr Joshua. Aidan said you wanted to speak with me.'

Mr Joshua's head turned towards Kane, and his face lit up in delight. I looked with interest at the man I'd heard so much about. He was very handsome, about 35 years old, with chestnut brown hair that was neatly parted to the right and cut very short at the back. His clothes were superb, dark blue silk shirt, tucked neatly into tailored black trousers and soft leather dress shoes polished to a high gloss. He looked like money.

'Ah Kane, my boy, there you are. I want you to meet Detective Mullins...Roger to his friends. You and Roger are going to be great friends. Roger, this is Kane Hansen and his associate Jerry Martin. They'll be your go to people. Kane will fill you in on details. If you want to contact me, do it through him.'

The dark-haired man sitting across the table looked faintly embarrassed as we all stared at him. He nodded his head towards our group, but held out a hand to shake Kane's. Mr Joshua glanced my way and raised his eyebrow. Kane introduced me.

'Mr Joshua, I'd like you to meet Constance O'Hara. Constance is Betty's roommate and friend. This is her first visit to the gaming club. Constance, I'd like you to meet Mr Joshua.'

Mr Joshua rose to his feet and held out a beautifully manicured hand, his little finger decorated with an opal dress ring. I placed my hand in his and smiled up into his unusual grey eyes.

'Mr Joshua, it's lovely to meet you,' I said while enjoying the tingle that ran up my spine from his warm touch. Mr Joshua gave me a dazzling smile, his beautiful straight teeth gleamed white. He looked down at my hand, turned it from side to side studying the bruise that had formed around my wrist.

A slight frown touched his lips. He flicked Jerry a stern look but didn't comment.

'The pleasure is all mine, young lady. Please, you must join me.' In a gallant gesture he handed me into the chair he'd just vacated. He turned and said to Jerry. 'Get Miss O'Hara a drink, in fact get everybody a drink, while I have a word with Kane.'

I noticed Jerry's jaw clench, and the vein in his throat throbbed. With a small tight smile, he said, 'Certainly Sir.' He stomped over to the bar.

Hmm, I thought, no love lost between these two.

Kane pulled up another chair for Mr Joshua and placed it next to mine.

'Thank you, my boy.' He patted Kane on the shoulder as he sat back down. 'Now Roger here is new to our circle of friends, Kane. I'd like you to show him around, teach him how things work around here. Make sure Roger has a good time. Leave your young ladies here with me, I'll make sure they come to no harm.'

'Certainly Sir, it will be my pleasure,' said Kane. He smiled in a friendly fashion at the detective.

'Oh, and Kane.'

'Yes, Sir?' asked Kane, raising his eyebrow in inquiry.

'Take Jerry with you please, his scowl offends me.'

'Certainly,' said Kane. His tone betrayed no emotion at the comment. 'Roger, why don't you come with me and I'll show you around. There are a couple of people you might like to meet…' and still talking they wandered off together, collecting Jerry along the way.

Betty's lips were set in a childish pout. She slumped into the pink chair that Roger had just vacated. A barman appeared at her elbow carrying a tray of drinks. A large glass of scotch was deftly placed in front of her. The smile returned to her face. A glass of white wine appeared in front of me. My stomach roiled at the sight. Mr Joshua got the best of the deal, a creamy white coffee.

'Now Constance, tell me why has Miss Ryan not introduced us before now?'

I saw Betty's eyes narrow, so I smiled at her. 'I've only just moved to Melbourne. This is our first night out together.'

Mr Joshua smiled in delight at Betty 'And you came straight to my club. I'm honoured.'

Flattered Betty returned his smile. 'I love your club, Mr Joshua. You get the best people here and it's always such fun.'

I leant forward and put a tentative hand on the newspaper lying on the table. It was opened to an article announcing the relocation of the Pinacotheca Art Gallery from Fitzroy Street in St Kilda to a new building in Richmond. Mr Joshua noticed my interest.

'Are you interested in modern art, Constance?'

'I don't have a great deal of knowledge on the subject, but I've heard of the Pinacotheca...its commitment to avant-garde and providing a platform for a new generation of artists to display their work. My preference is with the old masters. I didn't realise the gallery was so close to where I live. I must go have a look before they move.'

'I, too, prefer the old masters.'

My host proved to be quite knowledgeable and we started a lively discussion about the arts and modern theatre. While I had an intimate knowledge of the arts, I was not up to date on modern theatre. Mr Joshua soon enlightened me on the latest plays currently being performed in London's West End and New York's Broadway – and all the titillating backstage gossip that surrounded those productions.

Bored by our chat, Betty slugged back her drink. 'If you'll excuse me, Mr Joshua, I think I'll go check out the gaming room.'

'Of course, my dear, here's something to get you started.' He slid a small pile of chips across the table to her.

She smiled in delight, clapped her hands like a little girl and hurried from the room.

'Constance, you haven't touched your drink? Is it not to your liking? I can get you something else.'

'I'm afraid I don't drink a lot of alcohol and I had wine with dinner. That was more than enough for me.' My stomach knotted, remembering what had happened. My throat tightened. To avoid the crying jag hovering just under the surface I focussed on something that always gave me comfort. 'If you don't mind, I'd really enjoy a cup of tea.'

Mr Joshua's smile lit the room, his bright white teeth dazzling in the dim lighting. He raised a hand and the barman dashed over.

'Tommy, a pot of tea for the lady, please.'

Tommy returned carrying a silver tray with my hot beverage. He handed a note to my host. Mr Joshua read it, frowned and slid it into his top pocket.

I took a soothing sip of tea.

'I'm sorry Constance, I have to say goodnight. I've got business I must attend to. Thank you for a most delightful evening...we must do it again soon. Shall I return you to your companions?'

I glanced at my watch. Shocked by the time, I shook my head.

'No, my boarding house locks its doors soon and I don't want to be stuck outside for the night. If you don't mind, may I use a telephone to call a cab.'

'You don't want Jerry to drive you?' Mr Joshua asked.

I broke off eye contact and dropped my gaze to my hands laying in my lap. 'No, please...I'd prefer a cab.'

Mr Joshua placed his soft, warm hand over mine and gave a gentle squeeze. 'Of course my dear, just ask Aidan to call a taxi for you. Tell him I said to put it on my account.' He then lifted my hand to his lips and kissed the tips of my fingers.

I appreciated his courteous gesture and said, 'Thank you for a lovely evening and for the taxi, you're very kind.'

Rising to my feet, I said a final farewell and left, keeping a wary eye out for Jerry. In the noisy gaming room, I found Betty having a high old time at the roulette table.

'Come on, Betty it's time to leave,' I said in her ear.

She swung around to look at me in astonishment, pouted her red lips and said, 'God no, I'm not going anywhere, I'm on a roll.'

Not bothering to argue with her I said, 'Okay, well I'm off home. Aidan is calling me a taxi. I'll see you back at our digs. Don't forget, the front door gets locked at midnight.'

'Not a problem,' said Betty, her face took on a smug, self-satisfied look. 'When I got back from phoning Kane this arvo, I snaffled that bossy old manager's spare key and hid it under the big rock outside the back door. I can get in any old time I want.'

'Well, enjoy yourself then, but be careful, money doesn't grow on trees and it's very easy to lose.' I fluttered my finger at her, in a last wave. 'See you later.'

On my way out I ran into Kane, who was emerging from a back room. Just before the door closed, I caught a glimpse of Detective Roger Mullins in the passionate embrace of a girl. He was slipping his hand up her skirt. I thanked Kane for dinner, mentioned Betty was playing roulette and that I was off home. He nodded, but seemed distracted. He headed off towards where I had just said goodbye to Mr Joshua, a camera held in his left hand. Jerry was nowhere to been seen.

Aidan telephoned a taxi and stood outside with me until it arrived. When I protested, he insisted. 'It's not safe for a young lady to be standing out in the city streets alone.'

'Thank you Aidan, I'm not used to this life. Have you worked here at the gaming club long?'

Aidan took up a wide-legged stance beside me. 'I don't always work here,' he said folding his hand in front of his waist. 'I've been Mr Joshua's bodyguard for six years. I stand guard at the door or over him everywhere he goes.'

'Oh.' I could feel my eyebrows creeping up in surprise. 'Is he in danger from someone?'

'A man of his standing is always in danger from jealous people. My job is to ensure he comes to no harm,' Aidan said. 'Are you good friends with Jerry and Kane?'

'No, I only met them for the first time tonight. Betty and I room together. She asked me to come along tonight. Do you know them well?'

'Well enough,' said Aidan. There was a lot of evasion in his reply. 'Here's your cab. You take care. It was very nice to meet you.'

I climbed into the vehicle grateful to be headed home. For a girl from a small town, out on the tiles for the first time, a lot had happened. I had been ill prepared to navigate it safely.

7

Chapter Seven

I awoke early next morning to a luxurious stretch and dappled sunlight. Sunday, and I could please myself what I did. My new bed was cosy, so I snuggled down under the covers thinking a lie-in would be nice. Then I remembered Jerry. Nausea swam around inside me along with the remnants of last night's wine. I glanced over to the bundled-up girl in the other bed – she snored with gusto and looked set for the entire day. Betty had tiptoed in about four in the morning, being very careful not to make any noise. I think that was so Mrs Simmonds didn't cotton on to her having a key rather than out of consideration for the other tenants.

The lapping of waves rolling up onto the beach calmed my jangled thoughts and produced an image of a soothing walk on the warm sand. Frolicking in the water might wash away the dirty way I felt. I snuck out of bed and pulled the covers into place. In a flash, I pulled on my denim shorts with the frayed cuffs and a white peasant shirt. A quick run of my hairbrush untangled the sleep knots from my long hair. I bundled it up into a high ponytail, collected sunglasses and shoes, and slipped from the room. Sitting at the top of the staircase, I pulled on my white canvas tennis shoes, stuck the glasses onto the top of my head and hurried down the steps.

The dining room was empty, but an urn was heating water on a table just inside the door. Laid out on a pristine white tablecloth was a neat row of tiny white coffee cups and saucers. Standing guard was a money-box labelled *beverages fifty cents* each. What a rip! The cups would only hold a mouthful. I think I'll be buying an electric kettle, teapot and a large mug this week and hiding it in my room. Vetoing my anticipated cup of tea, I headed out the front door instead.

It was a glorious morning, warm with a soft cooling breeze that lifted a wisp of hair on my brow. Drawing in a deep breath, I tasted the salty air and held my face up to the sun. I smiled as a small sense of peace and freedom began to fill me. I slipped my glasses into place and headed across the road to the sandstone sea wall. As I danced my way down the beach steps, I marvelled at how white the sand was against the azure blue ocean. I landed in the soft sand, pulled off my shoes, tied the laces together, and hung them around my neck. In delight, I dug my toes into the warm sand and laughed, not caring if people thought me mad. I looked up and down the shoreline and could see it ran in a straight line for kilometres in both directions before the coast curved. Bright flags and people wearing colourful red and yellow patrol caps and shirts grabbed my attention. I trotted up the beach to the South Melbourne Life Saving Club. As the waves softly washed over my bare feet, I watched fascinated as the Nippers carried out their drills and training exercises. When the budding lifesavers finished and were released from their duties, the beach erupted into chaos. Kids hit the water to body-surf and have fun. Parents settled back on deck chairs, newspaper in hand, to enjoy a morning of peace.

I continued to splash and play along the water's edge until I reached Lagoon Pier. I was right, the walk had done me good. I settled with one leg dangling over the edge of the wharf and my back against a pier. I refused to think. Instead, I watched the anglers trying their luck and kept my thoughts blank. Noisy sea birds circled around and screeched as they looked for a chance to steal an unguarded catch. Daydreaming and enjoying the sun, I was just drifting into a light doze when a shadow fell across my face.

'Hello Constance, you looked like a basking mermaid sent to lure sailors into your thrall.'

Opening one eye, I looked up and smiled. 'Hello David, not surfing this morning?'

'Nah,' he said, with a pout of his lips. 'It's too calm at the moment, no swell. Tides not in again until about five this arvo. If I'm lucky, I might catch a few waves after work tonight.'

'Work? Wow, it didn't take you long to find a job. Doing what?'

David settled down opposite me and hung his leg over the side of the wharf, swinging it in time with mine.

'I've scored some bar work at the Beaky pub...start noon today. You know the one I mean, just down the road from our digs?'

'Yeah, I was there last night.'

'Hey crazy, so was I. It was a mad crush, but so worth it. The band was great...I think those dudes are going make it big. What did you think of them?'

'We didn't stay for the music. The blokes we were with didn't like the place, so we went for dinner at some Italian place over on Lygon Street. After that, we went on to a gaming club. That was fun.' I left out the details of the stop between venues, ashamed of myself.

'A gaming club? Wow, you gotta be careful, Mermaid. I hear a lot of dodgy characters hang around in those places. They're illegal, you know.'

Not appreciating his tone, I snapped, 'Well, I don't think this is one of those places. There were a lot of respectable people there. I even met a policeman...a detective. I can't see the police hanging around somewhere that's illegal, can you?'

David held his hands up in surrender. 'Yeah sorry, you're right...my mistake. I've heard a few stories, that's all. Did you enjoy yourself and win big?'

I smiled to show I forgave his well-intentioned interference and said, 'I don't gamble David. I can't see the attraction, but I had an enjoyable cup of tea and spent the evening discussing the arts and theatre with a very nice man...named Mr Joshua. I think he must own the place. He certainly seemed in charge.'

David's leg faltered for a moment, he managed to rematch the swing of my leg again. He gazed out over the water, his face blank and a faraway look in his eye. 'Where is this place, Mermaid?'

I laughed at his ridiculous name for me. 'I've no idea David,' I replied. 'Betty's boyfriend drove us there, and I came home in a taxi. I don't know Melbourne's geography and didn't pay attention to the street names. Why?'

'No reason, it just sounds like a cool place to hang out in. I might check it out one night but no biggie, couldn't afford to gamble, anyway.' He glanced down at his watch and exclaimed, 'Oh shit...sorry Constance, excuse my French. It's nearly noon, I'm supposed to be at work. I'd better scoot, before the boss dude sacks me. Not a good look, getting the sack, before I've even started. You enjoy the rest of your day and be kind to those sailors.' With a light-hearted laugh he leapt to his feet and took off at a brisk jog, heading towards the pub.

I missed the distraction of his company and felt restless. My stomach gave a loud growl. I took that as a hint and started imagining a big feed of fish and chips, as I sauntered back towards the seawall steps. The sand was littered with bright umbrellas and beach towels, noisy, cheerful people, enjoying a day in the sun. As I topped the steps up to the road, I saw a man and woman leaning against a car kissing passionately. Much to the passing pedestrians disgust the man was running his hands intimately all over her body. As I turned away from the sight, two arms engulfed me and a voice whispered into my ear, 'Hello Princess.'

Before I could stop him, Jerry plastered his horrible lips on mine. I pushed hard against his chest and shoved him away, trying not to show my disgust.

'Oh, hi Jerry, I didn't see you there. You shouldn't grab me like that, you really frightened me. What are you doing here?'

Jerry pointed to the lip locked couple. I realised it was Betty and Kane.

He said in amusement, 'We've come to take our girls out for lunch. Would you like that, Princess?' Just at that moment my stomach growled again and Jerry laughed. 'I'll take that as a yes. What do you feel like?'

Remembering last night's disappointment with the band, I said before the others could scuttle my plans, 'Fish and chips...battered and hot...smothered in salt and vinegar.'

'Right you are then. Hey, Kane,' yelled Jerry, 'Put that wench down, we're going for fish and chips.'

Kane flapped his hand, but his mouth didn't leave Betty's.

Jerry gave me a crooked smile and asked, 'You wanna eat in the park or on the beach?'

Wow, I was being consulted now. What a turn up.

'A picnic in the park would be nice. There's a crowd on the beach, and the breeze is getting up. I don't want sand in my food.'

Taking my hand, Jerry tugged me towards the car, saying with just a touch of sarcasm, 'Come on Kane, drive us down to the park on the Esplanade. We are going for a picnic.'

Trying to extract my hand from his, I thought, there's no need for sarcasm, Jerry. Hell, you don't have to come...I was quite happily enjoying my day before you arrived.

* * *

Lying back on the shaded grass, under a Norfolk Pine, I floated along in the twilight close to sleep. My stomach no longer growled because it was stuffed – best fish and chips ever. I listened to Betty joke with Jerry about how she was going to spend last night's winnings from the roulette table. The air was tinged with cigarette smoke as all three puffed their lives away on the coffin nails.

'I think I might have to reinvest some of those winnings, at the crap table,' said Betty, her laugh soft and hoarse. 'Kane darling, where are we going tonight?'

Oh, no...not tonight. We've got work in the morning. I'm not starting the day in battle, trying to drag Betty's sorry arse out of bed to get there on time. I opened my eyes to protest, my words remained unspoken when Kane scuttled her plans.

'Not tonight, my sweet. Jerry and I are going out of town for a couple of days. In fact, we should be on the road now...work stuff. *But*,' he said, holding the tip of his finger against her pouting lips, 'we'll be back on Friday. How about, we go somewhere nice for dinner and then onto Mr Joshua's? You can reinvest your winnings and then buy me a new sports car.'

Betty pouted. Kane set about wooing a smile to her lips. She giggled at his antics and peace once more descended. I closed my eyes again and wished they would leave. I was just drifting off when a hot wave of nicotine blasted my face. My eyes flew open just as Jerry leant in to kiss me. His hand touched my breast. I sat bolt upright, jumped to my feet, the hair on the back of my neck standing up. I felt dirty from his touch. His jaw locked and his face turned red in anger.

Before he could say anything, I said, 'Thanks everyone, for a splendid afternoon, but I really need to get back. I've some letters to write and my folks are expecting a phone call from me.'

Betty looked at me in surprise, then at Jerry's stormy face. She reached forward and stroked his cheek.

'Jerry sweetheart, you'll look after my handsome man for me, while you're away, won't you? Don't go getting into any trouble with the girls either, you know how they are around you. It's all that animal magnetism you exude, drives them crazy. We're looking forward to you taking us out to dinner on Friday, aren't we, Constance?'

Putting me on the spot, I gave a half-hearted nod of agreement. Betty smiled and continued to pour on the syrup. Jerry relaxed and began leering at her.

'Italian or Chinese sounds heavenly, Kane darling. Now you boys had better take us home, so you can get on the road and do what you have to do, *but*,' she added with a smile at her man, 'not before you give me a kiss.'

I ignored Jerry's expectant look and occupied myself, dusting the grass off my clothing. When Betty was ready, we all climbed back into the car for the short drive back to the boarding house. But Kane didn't drive us directly there. He found a quiet spot among the undeveloped bush blocks and stopped the car. Betty climbed out and together they went for a walk. Jerry left his seat in the front and climbed into the back with me. I made a grab for the door handle but before I could wrench the door open Jerry had his arms around me and was pulling me down onto the seat. I pushed with all my might, fighting to ward him off, but Jerry was all muscle and very strong. He flicked my arms away from his face, grabbed my wrists and lay on top of me. He smeared his mouth over mine, pushing with his tongue to gain access to my mouth. I wriggled and squirmed, pulled my face to the side to no avail. Jerry was like a limpid, attached and determined. He reached down and before I could stop him he had my shorts down and his fly open. I slammed my legs closed but he wedged his knees between them and forced them apart. I yanked my hands free of his grip and scraped my nails down his face.

He pulled back and snarled, 'Bitch.'

I opened my mouth to scream. Jerry clamped his hand over my mouth and put his face close to mine, glaring. Tears streamed down my face. He ignored them and slammed himself into me. He gave a couple of quick pumps and cried out in exaltation. As quick as it was, it was still too much.

I pushed him off and shouted, 'I hate you Jerry, don't you ever do that again...'

Jerry touched his fingers to the scratch marks on his face. He stared at the blood on his fingers for a moment before saying, 'Princess, I'll do that anytime I like...you're mine.'

8

Chapter Eight

'No, you'll have to go without me from now on,' I said, planting my feet and staring up the great height to Betty's face. She had just informed me that Kane was picking us up after work and we were all going out to dinner.

Betty glared back at me and said, 'It's all arranged, besides Jerry wants you there.'

'I don't care...'

'You will. If you don't come, Jerry will just come into work and make you.'

I stared at her in disbelief. After my last experience, when we had been out with her friends, I never wanted to see them again. Evidently my wants and needs didn't come into it. From that moment on I was forced into a life I didn't want. Betty set the pattern of our lives. She'd arrange nights out and I was expected to tag along. My arguments and excuses were overridden. If I said no I incurred the wrath of her vicious temper as well as Jerry's. It wasn't beyond him to make trouble for me at work and I needed my job to save for my escape fund. I was too ashamed to tell Betty, Jerry was forcing me to have sex. Sometimes I got the impression she knew and was amused by it. I was trapped in an abusive cycle and didn't know how to free myself. I spent most of my time trying to avoid Jerry's grasping hands, slobbery mouth and being left alone in his company. I wasn't always successful.

To protect myself after the first time I went to the family planning clinic. I had to lie and pretend I was married to get the contraceptive pill, but in the whole scheme of things, that little fib was better than getting pregnant with Jerry's child.

I needed help but there was nowhere to turn.

Everywhere we went, the men had some sort of business to take care of. I got the feeling none of it was legal. Friday evenings we often finished our night out at the gaming club. Mr Joshua always invited me to spend my time in his company drinking tea and talking. Much to my relief, he didn't include Jerry in our enjoyable tête-à-têtes, in fact his presence seemed to displease him. This inflamed Jerry's temper, but I didn't care. For me, it was the only bright spot in my life.

Often Mr Joshua had someone for Kane to meet and entertain. Some of their faces seemed familiar, like they'd been in the newspaper or on television. I didn't think it was in my best interest to ask questions.

On Saturday's Betty and the men would drive to Ballarat to attend the races. I had a valid excuse for avoiding these outings. Much to Betty's disgust, Mrs Morris now trusted me with the full running of the entire floor. I'd source and select specialty items to be showcased each week, and Saturday mornings I'd travel into the city and spend the morning planning and designing the displays for the upcoming week.

Mid-July arrived and winter seemed confused. It put on a glorious display of sunny, warm weather. To my surprise, when I returned home from work one Saturday, I found Betty sitting on her bed wrestling to fit an elaborate hat to her perfectly groomed dark hair. She looked chic, dressed in an eye-catching red and black pantsuit. She glared at me through lashes layered in thick black mascara.

'It's about bloody time you got home – where the hell have you been?'

'I've been at work, Betty, like I am every Saturday. Why?' I wandered over, dropped my handbag onto the bed, fell back on my covers and kicked my shoes off with a sigh.

'You need to hurry if you're to be ready in time. The boys will be here in half an hour to pick us up.' Spritzing perfume in the air, she walked through it. I gagged at the cloying smell and pulled a handkerchief from my sleeve to cover my nose.

'Pick us up? What are you talking about Betty, where are we going?' I asked, my voice muffled by the hankie.

'Flemington of course. I'm sure I told you. It's the last day of the winter racing carnival, the Flemington Cup is being run. Half of Melbourne will be there.'

'No,' I said. Warily I shook my head, wondering how I was going to get out of this without a fight. 'You didn't tell me. I don't think I'll go...I'm tired. Besides, I have nothing flash to wear.'

Betty started pulling my drawers open and throwing stuff at me.

'I'm sure you can rummage up something. I don't know how you do it but you always look elegant, even in shorts and tee-shirt. Now hurry up...Mr Joshua is expecting you. I'm sure you don't want to disappoint him.'

Twisting my lips up in a half smile at the sarcastic comment, I wondered if she'd deliberately not told me about today to show me up. Yanking my suitcase out from under the bed, I lifted out a pale green floral dress with matching long-sleeved jacket. It's an outfit that always looks good. The jersey clung and flattered my figure. Like the proverbial LBD (little black dress), this outfit was easy to dress up and was suitable for all occasions. I slipped into nylons and a pair of low-heeled shoes. Now for my hair. I brushed it until it shone, then braided it to the right to just below my ear. I left the bulk of it loose and slid three mother-of-pearl combs along my crown. A touch of mascara, plum coloured lipstick, and I was ready.

Betty shook her head in amazement 'How do you do that? I've spent the entire morning getting ready and you do it in twenty minutes. It's just not fair.'

I smiled and to keep her in a good mood, said, 'But you look fabulous, Betty, so it's worth all the effort you've put in.'

She glowed at the compliment. Gathering our handbags, keys and each other, we headed down the stairs. Betty chattered on in excitement about the day ahead. David, surfboard tucked under his arm, was coming in the front door. His honey brown chest was hairless and glowed from suntan oil. He clocked Betty and let out a slow wolf whistle. With a smirk, she casually trailed her fingers over his chest and fluttered her eyelids as she sashayed past. I followed her out and turned to shut the door. David was watching Betty swan her way down the street towards Kane's car. He had an unflattering goofy look on his face.

Narrowing my eyes, I chucked him under the chin with my knuckle, 'Close your mouth, David, before you trip over your tongue.'

And shut the door in his face.

* * *

Moving from the car into the racecourse, I kept Betty and Kane as a buffer between Jerry and myself. When they had arrived to pick us up, he'd done his best to get his hands on me...again. I scuttled away and into the back seat of the car, before he could touch me. Now among the race crowd, I had my avoidance radar attuned to top gear so he couldn't sneak up on me.

Over the racket of the betting ring I heard Kane say, 'Could you do a minor job for me today, my sweet?'

Betty gazed adoringly up into his face, nodding her head.

'Of course, handsome. What is it you need me to do?'

Kane kissed the tip of her nose.

'There's a lady I would like you to meet. Her name is Mary.'

Betty frowned. Kane flashed a dazzling toothy smile and pulled her close.

'Her husband is the jockey, Mark Nolan, silly. I want you to make friends with her. Get to know her. Buy her a couple of drinks and get her talking about their life. You know, stuff I need, where they hang out, hobbies, any bad habits he has, that sort of thing. You can tell me what she says tonight at dinner.'

Snuggling in close, Betty purred, 'Sure, handsome, I can do that...if it's important to you.'

Giving another display of his bright white teeth, Kane said, 'Yes, it is. Now, my sweet, here is some play money for you. Have fun betting on the gee-gees,' and he slipped a large roll of cash into her handbag.

At that moment, Aidan, dressed beautifully in tailored black trousers, white shirt, burgundy tie and jacket, materialised before us. Ignoring Jerry totally, he handed Kane a thick crisp white envelope.

'Mr Joshua's wants you to take care of this. Ensure you distribute the funds before the first race. He doesn't want to be bothered with business today.'

Kane slipped the envelope deep inside his jacket's breast pocket. Aidan turned towards me, smiling.

'Mr Joshua's compliments, Miss O'Hara. He asks if you would join him in the members' area.'

Jerry stuck out his chest. 'Sod off, Aidan, the Princess is here with me.' Aiden ignored him. So did I.

'Thank you, Aidan, it will be my pleasure,' I said, as I slipped my hand into the crook of his muscular arm. We started along the footpath leading to the members' enclosure. I could hear Jerry cursing loudly behind me. Glancing over my shoulder, I saw him moving in our direction. My fingers involuntarily tightened on Aiden's arm. Kane reached out and placed a restraining hand on Jerry's shoulder.

'Leave it, mate. It's not worth the aggravation.'

'It's alright, Miss,' Aiden said, laying a gentle warm hand over mine. 'Mr Martin knows his place – or if he doesn't, he soon will.'

'Thank you, Aidan.' I said in relief and loosened my grip.

The large colourful racing crowd hardly hampered our progress. Aiden's bulk was like being attached to a tank moving through a field of hay. The crowd just parted before him. Enjoying the sense of protection he exuded, I turned my attention to other matters.

'How's that wife of yours treating you, Aidan? Is she looking after you properly?' Aidan's face glowed and he stammered. 'Oh yes, Miss. Robyn's excellent...she's having a baby!'

'That's wonderful, Aidan. You're going to be a father. You must be so excited,' I said, patting his arm. I wondered how Robyn could find shirts with sleeves big enough to house those enormous arms. 'Is this your first child?'

'Yeah,' he breathed out happily. 'Robyn and I were beginning to give up hope. Bub's due in August.'

I smiled at his excitement. I glanced up. Mr Joshua, looking extremely handsome in a skilfully tailored black suit and tie, was watching our progress towards his table. Sitting with him was a well-dressed, middle-aged couple who seemed to be overshadowed by his presence. As we approached, he rose to his elegantly shod feet. Aiden handed me over. Mr Joshua took my hand, and lifting it to his mouth, kissed my palm. A warm tingle ran the entire length of my body and my breath caught in my throat. Locking his steel-grey eyes with mine, he murmured, 'Constance, my dear, you look absolutely stunning.'

I could feel a blush burn my cheeks.

'Thank you, Mr Joshua. It's a great pleasure to see you again. Thank you so much for inviting me.'

'Please, my dear, you must call me Paul,' he breathed intimately in my ear as he placed his cheek next to mine. His delicious spicy cologne tickled my nose. I felt the urge to bury my face into his neck and breath in deeply. Stepping back, he smiled and tucked my arm through his. After drawing me close to his side, Paul said, 'Come, I have some people I would like you to meet. Donald, Trudy, I would like you to meet Miss O'Hara. Constance, my dear, this is Donald and Trudy Olsen, owners of Golden Bay.'

I shook hands with them both.

'How do you do? It's a pleasure to meet you.'

Taking the offered seat next to Donald Olsen, I went on, 'You must be very excited having your horse run today, Mr Olsen. Will it win, do you think, or are you running it for experience?'

Donald puffed out his chest and laughed heartily at my naive question. In a loud booming voice he bragged, 'My dear girl, Golden Bay is the favourite for today's cup. Golden Bay is also a contender for the Melbourne Cup this year. So, *no,* I'm not running him for experience!'

Mr Joshua gave a bored yawn and handed me a racing guide open to today's racing.

'Yes, yes, Donald, we all know the horse is having a marvellous season,' said Paul, flicking his wrist with a dismissive gesture. 'Constance, my dear, why don't you review the horses while Donald and I discuss my impending share in Golden Bay.'

Donald's loud laughter had me flinching at the assault on my eardrums. Leaning forward to look around me he pointed an aggressive finger at Paul, and said, 'Now what in the world makes you think that I'd even consider parting with a share of one of the best racehorses in the country?'

I glanced up at Paul and saw a benign smile touch his lips. His eyes had turned a cold steel colour.

'Donald, you seem to forget that I have spent a considerable amount of time and gone to a great deal of effort on your behalf. Over the years your interests have been well protected and without my help, you would not be in the position you are in today. What has been so generously given, can easily be taken away.' The smile dropped from Donald's face and his face turned a blotchy purple colour as Paul went on. 'But I know you are an appreciative, sensible man who values our friendship above all else. All I'm asking is for you to give my offer your most serious consideration.'

A line of sweat formed on Donald's brow, and his florid face lost its colour. Quickly I dropped my head and stared blindly at the form guide in my hand, pretending to study it. What the hell! Had Mr Joshua, no Paul, I must remember to call him Paul. Had Paul just threatened to ruin Donald Olsen if he didn't agree to the sale?

Paul murmured in my ear. 'Constance, my dear, now you have had a chance to study the guide, what horse is going to win race three?'

I took a blind stab at the list of names and said, 'Number Nine, Paul.'

He lifted the guide from my hand and read the name. He laughed and turned to Aidan, who was sitting like a granite boulder behind us. 'Aidan, dear boy, please go put ten on Hitman in race three at odds of 30 to 1.'

The race started, I clasped my hands together nervously in my lap. My knee bounced up and down to its own rhythm. Not being able to take the stress, I closed my eyes and listened. The roaring of the crowd was deafening. Then came the announcement over the PA. Hitman had crossed the finish line in first place.

'Oh, thank goodness he won. I was so worried you would lose your ten dollars.' Paul smiled at me in genuine amusement. Placing a knuckle under my chin, he lifted my face and placed a soft, chaste kiss on my lips.

'Excuse me for a moment, Constance, I need to organise a bank transfer of my winnings on Hitman. Trudy, would you be kind enough to keep Miss O'Hara company while I'm gone? Donald, walk with me, my friend. We can talk on the way.'

Together, with Aidan tagging along in their wake, the men headed off to the members' lounge. I watched them leave, my lips still tingling from the kiss. Turning my attention to Trudy, who sat staring off into space, her hands clenched tightly in her lap. I said, 'Trudy, can I ask you a silly question?'

I watched as her eyes refocused. She settled her gaze on my face.

'Certainly, Miss O'Hara.'

Feeling uncomfortable having this frumpy middle-aged woman speaking to me so formally, I said, 'Oh please Trudy, call me Constance.'

Trudy shook her head and said, 'No, my dear I can't do that. Mr Joshua has introduced you to us as Miss O'Hara. Until he says otherwise, I must use that title. It is a respect thing with him. Surely you know that no one may call him by his first name either, unless he is intimately attached to them.' I felt my eyes widen in surprise. Wow, and he's just asked me to call him Paul.

'Now what is your question?' she asked, ignoring my evident surprise.

'Why wouldn't the bookies just pay out the three hundred in winnings to Mr Joshua? Why does he need to organise a bank transfer?'

Trudy gave me an incredulous look and said, 'You really are an innocent, aren't you, Miss O'Hara? Men like Mr Joshua don't bet in small denominations. When he asked Aidan to put ten on the horse he meant ten thousand dollars.'

I felt the blood leaving my face. Holy shit. I had nearly lost ten thousand on a blind pick. Then the reality of the situation kicked in even further. 'Holy crap,' I exclaimed, 'that means Paul has just won three hundred thousand dollars.'

She gave me a brittle smile. 'Yes, some people get to have it all.'

Strawberries, champagne and crystal cut glasses arrived, carried on a silver tray by a smartly dressed waiter, closely followed by Donald Olsen. He looked deflated, no longer the puffed up peacock I had met earlier.

'Trudy, it's time for us to go down to the saddling enclosure to see Golden Bay.' Trudy leapt to her feet, whispering sharply in his ear, 'What happened? Is he taking a share?'

Donald made a shushing motion with his hand and said fiercely, 'Leave it, Trudy. I told him I would have to think about it, but you know there is nothing to think about...' He stomped off, leaving her to scuttle behind. I watched and felt a little sorry for Trudy.

Paul returned, a pleased look on his face, and offered me the form guide. 'Would you like to choose a horse in race five, the Flemington Cup 1849, my dear. I will have Aidan place a bet for you.'

I smiled up at him and said, 'Oh, no thank you, Paul. I'm not a gambler. I can't take the stress of having money on a horse. You don't mind, do you?'

He threw back his head and laughed. 'Not at all, my dear. Champagne?'

Handing me a glass of bubbly with a strawberry floating in the golden liquid he clicked his glass to mine and drew me close to his side.

'Scratching. There has been a late scratching. Horse three, race five has been scratched.' Came the announcement over the public address system. Punters scrambled to read their guides. 'Horse three, Golden Bay has been scratched from the Flemington Cup 1849 due to an injury in the saddling enclosure.'

'Oh Paul, what a shame. Your friend's horse won't be running. I hope it's nothing serious,' I said, as I craned my neck to see down to the saddling enclosure.

A small smile tugged the corner of Paul's mouth 'I'm sure it's nothing too serious. Now, my dear Constance, tell me have you had a chance to read the book I recommended for you?' and so the conversation was neatly diverted.

Donald and Trudy Olsen didn't return. They left the racecourse immediately after Golden Bay was scratched. The last race was under way when Paul invited me to join him for dinner and a show at the Orion Club. We were gathering our things to leave when Aidan, returning from the depths of the racing crowd, handed an envelope to Paul. Scowling as he read its contents, he apologised.

'I'm sorry, my dear, but it seems that I have some business to attend to and I'm afraid it cannot wait. Can I have a rain check on our evening?'

I placed a tentative hand on his forearm.

'Of course, Paul. I can't say I'm not disappointed, but I understand that you're a busy man. Another time perhaps.'

Paul lifted my fingers to his lips for a long and intimate kiss that curled my toes.

'No *perhaps* about it, my dear. We'll have that dinner very soon.' Then turning he said, 'Aidan, my boy, see Miss O'Hara safely into a taxi, then call your lovely wife. Let her know you will be late. We have some business to take care of.'

9

Chapter Nine

The pleasant weather had disappeared again. Despite the cold, I decided to go ahead with my usual Sunday walk on the beach. As a reward afterwards I'd treat myself to a pot of tea and the newspaper at my favourite haunt, Café Italy. I left the warmth of the boarding house, and to my amazement a small crowd had gathered across the street. A blue-faced police constable was blocking the steps down to the beach. I joined the crowd and saw David staring, unblinking, at the police activity down at the water's edge.

'Hello, David. I was going to take a walk, but the police aren't letting anyone on the beach. What's going on?'

David, the skin around his lips and eyes pinched and white from cold, didn't take his gaze from the goings-on. 'Hello, Mermaid. I don't think you'll be beach walking today. The body of a man washed up in the surf this morning.'

My hand covered my mouth and I felt sick.

'That's awful, David.'

'Yeah, wasn't what I expected to find in the surf this morning.'

I gasped. 'Oh god, don't tell me you found him? How horrible for you. What happened, did he drown while swimming?'

David pinched the bridge of his nose and closed his eyes. He suddenly seemed a lot older. 'No, I don't think a bullet in the brain counts as drowning.'

I felt the blood leave my face and my stomach churned.

'Come and share a pot of tea with me, David? It'll warm you up and might dull the shock a bit.'

With a small smile, he reached over and gave my hand a quick squeeze. 'Thanks, Constance, that's thoughtful, but I can't. I have to go to the police station in a minute and make a statement.'

Even with the buffeting wind and spray of wet cold water flying off the pounding surf, the surrounding crowd grew. It took on a carnival type atmosphere as people laughed and speculated over the police activity. I felt disenchanted by their ghoulish behaviour so I said goodbye to David, hunkered deeper into my jacket and hurried along the street to Café Italy.

My first sip of hot tea took the chill from my bones. In comfort, I perused the newspaper headlines and photos taken at yesterday's races. On page two, it surprised me to see a photo of Paul and Donald Olsen – not taken at the races. Underneath the grainy black-and-white photograph was the caption, *The new owner of Golden Bay, Mr Paul Joshua,* and below that a brief article. I read with interest.

In the surprise of the racing season, Mr Donald Olsen announced late last night that he had relinquished ownership of his racehorse Golden Bay to his good friend Mr Paul Joshua. Mr Olsen said that because of his continuing poor health he was no longer in a position to own and run the prized stallion. Golden Bay suffered a slight injury in the saddling enclosure at yesterday's race meeting, as a result the horse was scratched from the Flemington Cup 1849. Golden Bay's jockey Mark Nolan, disappointed to miss an opportunity to ride in the prestigious race, said he was looking forward to riding for the new owner. Officials claim they suspect a protruding nail in the railing of the saddling yard caused the horse's injury, a minor cut on the flank. Mr Joshua was not available for comment.

I sat back in surprise and wondered if this was last night's important business. A disturbance at the door broke my train of thought. I looked up – Jerry, Kane and Betty were making their way to my table. My heart sank. Damn. I was hoping to avoid them today, especially Jerry.

'Hello, Princess. Fancy seeing you here. Boyfriend not around?' he said with a smirk on his ugly face. He leant in for a kiss. I lifted the newspaper, pretending to fold it, and used it to block him. He threw himself into a chair in disgust and turned to yell at Sophia, the café owner's wife. 'Four cappuccinos.'

Sophia glared at the back of his head and went to make the coffees. Betty pointed to the newspaper and started chattering in excitement.

'I hear you made Mr Joshua a very happy man yesterday, Constance,' she said. Jerry's face darkened in fury and he stood up.

'Where the fuck's that coffee?' he said and stormed over to the counter.

He started an argument with Mario. I stood up, tucked my folded paper under my arm. Leaving my hot tea, I said, 'I'm going for a walk. You guys enjoy your coffee.' I stepped out onto the footpath just as big fat drops of freezing cold rain started hurling from the sky. Great.

* * *

I listened to the news report on the bus radio the next morning. The lead story was the body on the beach.

A body, washed up on the beach near the South Melbourne Life Saving Club, has been identified as Mr John Willcox, manager of the Beaconsfield Hotel. Mr Willcox, last seen at closing time Saturday night, was in the habit of going out on his boat, late at night to fish.

Police believe he fell overboard and drowned. Investigating officer Detective Roger Mullins says the death is not suspicious.

My stomach coiled into a tight knot as I recalled my conversation with David yesterday. He said nothing about the man being his boss. He had also claimed the man had been shot. The detective in charge of the case, Roger Mullins, claimed the man drowned. So who was right? It seemed too coincidental that the same Detective Mullins, who Kane had been entertaining in a back room at the gaming club, was investigating the death of someone Jerry had been threatening. I didn't know what to think or believe.

* * *

Late July, an incident occurred that had far-reaching implications for my life. I was sitting high in a mostly deserted grandstand, the cold Melbourne wind was whipping around my ankles. Slunk low in my seat, I stared as another greyhound race ended. The small crowd that had been brave enough to gather in the stands hurried off, shedding losing tickets like confetti.

Betty, huddled in the new mink coat Kane had presented to her at the beginning of the evening, rose to her feet saying, 'Wait here, Constance, and save our seats. I gotta go pee.'

She headed off in the direction of the bar – again. Great, she'll be drunk and mouthy in no time. Another night of her and Kane arguing is not something to look forward to. I was giving serious consideration to incurring her wrath and sulks for the next week by ditching them all and taking a taxi home.

I huddled further into my jacket and shoved my hands as deep as I could into my pockets, trying to warm them. I scanned the bookies' ring and caught sight of Jerry, the inevitable fag in his mouth. I noticed him pocketing a roll of cash. He must have had a win – that might help improve his attitude, but probably not. In surprise,

I watched him muscle to the front of the line at the next bookie and be handed another wad of cash. After counting the notes, he slipped some into his jacket pocket and the rest went into a small pouch he was carrying. He took a notebook and pen from the back pocket of his trousers and wrote something down. Moving on to the next bookmaker, he repeated the process. What the hell?

'What the fuck you looking at?' Kane asked.

'Nothing, Kane, I'm just cold. Can we go soon?' I asked as my chattering teeth gave a loud clatter.

'Whinge, whine...we're not leaving, I still gotta talk to someone.' He turned a circle, looking around the stand. 'Where's Betty got to, not the fucking bar I hope?'

'Ladies,' I replied, being careful not to look in the direction she had actually gone. Thankfully, Betty chose that moment to saunter back. Giving Kane a sultry smile, she traced her fingers over his cheek, and almost purred.

'Hey, handsome, can we sit the next one out in the bar? It's a tad cool out here.'

He stared at her, his face blank, then suddenly he smiled. His bright white teeth gleamed in the spotlights.

'Yeah, alright, gorgeous...sounds like a grand idea. I need to catch up with some mug first, then we can enjoy a snifter before heading off.'

Slinging his leather-clad arm over her shoulders, he had a nibble at the side of her neck, which started her giggling. They climbed down the grandstand steps.

My bum frozen and legs numb, I stood and stomped my cold feet on the ground, trying to get the blood flowing. Stiff legged and hunched deep into my jacket, I clambered along behind them. Jerry, standing at the bottom of the steps, attempted to put his hands on me. I scurried sideways to avoid him. He flicked his cigarette butt in my direction and lit up a new fag. Bastard, I thought, as I dodged to avoid the lighted butt.

Kane raised an eyebrow at Jerry and asked, 'Everything okay, mate?'

They walked ahead together, chatting. Jerry handed Kane the bag. Their conversation drifted over in my direction and I heard Jerry saying, 'All accounted for, mate. No welshers.' He sounded very disappointed.

'You give them the new collection date?' asked Kane, checking the bag was zipped closed.

'Yeah, mate, and I got us a cut,' said Jerry. A self-satisfied smile tugged at his lips.

'Fuck, Jerry, you trying to get us killed? You know if the takings are down, Mr Joshua won't be impressed. He'll send the heavies after us,' said Kane with a startled look on his face.

'Fucking heavies? I am the fucking heavies,' said Jerry. His smug bragging drew a long, hard look from Kane. 'Nah, mate, don't shit yourself...all's good. I charged the mugs an extra hundred to cover us.' He roared with laughter and smacked Kane on the shoulder. As he lifted his arm, the notebook fell from his back pocket, unnoticed. I stopped walking and waited for him to realise his loss. The men walked on unaware. My heart sped up. Was I brave enough? I took a casual step forward and put my foot over the notebook, to hide it from view and watched the two men wander off together. I could hear the blood pounding in my ears and a small bead of sweat trickled down my temple.

Beside me Betty bounced from foot to foot eager to move on. 'Come on, Constance, it's too cold to stand around out here. I'll go get us some seats near the fire inside, you go get us a drink. Scotch for me.'

'Sure, Betty. I'll just be a minute. I need to re-tie my shoelace. You go on.'

As predicted, Betty didn't bother to wait for me. Casting my gaze around I made sure no one was paying any attention to me before sliding my foot out of my runner. I swooped on the notebook and quickly transferred it into my shoe. I shoved my foot back in and fiddled with the laces. As I pulled my jeans back over the top of my sock, fear and excitement sizzled through my gut. I was going to make Jerry sweat...serve the bastard right. Besides, I was curious about the notebook's contents. What did they say about curiosity and the cat?

***

We stopped at a pub in Carlton on the way home. Jerry had some business to take care of. We'd been to so many pubs over the months that I gave up trying to memorise their names. Kane and Betty sat at the table, sucking each other's face again. It was disgusting. I decided it was time to call a cab and disappear before I was left alone with Jerry. I gathered my gear and was just rising from my seat when Jerry pushed a small package in front of me.

'Hey, Princess, you see that guy over there?' he said, pointing to our left. 'Give him this, while I go to the bar and get us a drink.'

'Which one – the football beanie or the long-haired one?'

'Footy beanie,' he said. 'He'll give you some money. Make sure he gives you an even hundred. Count it, alright.'

'OK,' I said. I'd do this and then get out of here. Anything was better than watching Betty and Kane.

As I walked away, I heard Kane comment, 'What're you doing, Jerry?'

'Just getting a bit more control, mate. No biggie.'

What the hell did that mean?

I strolled over to the footy beanie guy. 'I have a package for you,' I said, putting it on the table. 'Jerry said it's an even hundred.'

The bloke's face went white. He grabbed the package and shoved it into his over-large jacket pocket. Throwing some money down on the table in front of me, he grumbled about the price rise. While I collected the notes together, he shoved past me and stormed out of the bar. Returning to our table, I dropped the money in front of Jerry and sat.

'He was complaining about the price. What the hell was in the package, Jerry?'

'Oh, just a little happy dust, Princess. How did you enjoy doing your first drug deal?' he asked, laughing.

Disgust swamped me. 'You bastard,' I said, and stood up, kicking the chair out of my way and grabbing my bag. 'I'm leaving.'

Jerry patted his pocket and began swearing to himself. As I stepped away he reached out, grabbed hold of my wrist, and threw me back into a chair. He went through the pocket patting process again.

'*Fuck.*'

Kane looked over at him in surprise

'What's up, mate?' he asked.

'My fucking notebook.' *Pat. Pat. Pat.* 'It's gone.'

'Shit, Jerry,' said Kane, removing his arms from around Betty and leaning towards his mate. 'When did you see it last?'

'At the dogs.' He glared at me. 'You were in a fucking big hurry to leave, why?'

I knew I was in serious trouble here if I said the wrong thing, so channelling my anger towards him I let rip. 'You, you bastard. Always using me. This time it's to do your dirty work.'

Jerry put out his hand and said, 'Give it to me, Princess.'

Be smart, Constance, I thought trying not to panic. Then I had an idea. I pointed to the table where I'd thrown his dirty drug money.

'It's there...your money's right in front of you.'

Jerry's hand lashed out.

The slap resounded around the room. My cheek began to burn and my eyes blurred with tears of pain.

'Not the fucking money, bitch...my notebook.'

I cradled my stinging cheek, and let a single tear run down my face.

'Notebook...what notebook? I've no idea what you're talking about.'

Before he could question me further, I stood up. I channelled my anger, not caring who in the bar heard, and yelled, 'And you can fuck off...I'm going home.'

Jerry grabbed my arm and started searching my jacket pockets. Not finding his precious book, he ran his hands over my body. As his hand passed over my breast he gave a hard squeeze. I struggled against his intrusive hands and brutish search by lashing out at his shins with my foot.

'Get your hands off me, you mongrel.'

He gave me a hard shove, snatched up my handbag and upended it onto the table. My purse, room key and feminine products spilled onto the table. People in the bar were staring but no one made a move to intervene. Kane stood and put a hand on Jerry's shoulder.

'She hasn't got it, mate. You must have lost it at the track. How about we head back now and take a look?'

Jerry nodded in agreement. I bent to the table, and with my arm scooped all my stuff back into my handbag. Glaring at Jerry, Kane and Betty, I yelled, 'Stay away from me, don't ever come near me again...any of you.'

With my left shoe weighing a lot more than my right, I stormed out of the pub and hailed a passing taxi. I was so angry, especially with Betty for pulling me into this horrible world. I was frightened by the violence I had just unleashed. I could never admit to having the notebook.

As the taxi pulled up, I saw David walking up the street from the Beaky pub. Not wanting to talk with anyone, I hurried to pay the driver and get inside. The gods were against me, I had the slowest change giver in Melbourne. By the time the taxi driver had done a slow and careful count of my coins, David was standing next to the door.

Climbing from the car I kept my head down. 'Hello, David, what's happening?' I said at the same moment David slung a friendly arm over my shoulder and said 'Hey, Mermaid, what's happening?'

He laughed and said, 'Jinx.'

I threw my head back and joined in his laughter, forgetting about the mark on my cheek. As the light from the hall lit my face, he stopped laughing and grabbed my chin.

'Constance, has someone hit you? How could you let that happen?' His hazel eyes flashing in anger.

Turning my face sideways, I pulled my chin free from his hand and my anger spilt over.

'*Let* someone hit me. No, you moron, I didn't *let* someone hit me,' I said. 'Men... why is it always the woman's fault?'

I didn't bother waiting for an answer. I turned on my heel and sprinted up the stairs, being careful not to slam the door to my room as it closed behind me.

Throwing myself onto my bed, tears of shame rolled down my cheeks. God, Constance, you stupid, stupid girl, you've really made a mess of your life.

My foot felt uncomfortable, so I sat up and removed Jerry's notebook. A quick glance at a page and real fear took over. Oh boy, now I'm really in deep shit. With shaky hands I hid the notebook with my other treasures under the floorboard.

In terror I lay staring at the grey wall wondering what to do.

10

Chapter Ten

The footsteps on the stairs paused. A soft husky laugh drifted down the hall, followed by a murmur of voices. I rose from my bed and eased the door open a crack and spotted Betty running her fingers along the contours of David's cheek and down his chest. A smug smile touched her lips when he whispered in her ear.

'Give me an hour,' she said, and turned towards our room.

The door closed with a soft click and I hurried over to sit on my bed, hairbrush in hand. The door burst open and Betty stormed in. She glared at me. I could see the fury bubbling just under the surface.

'What the hell was all that fuss at the pub about, Constance? Can't you take a joke?'

My blood began to boil at the unjust attack. Mindful of the other residence, I whisper yelled at her.

'That was no joke, Betty. Your friend Jerry's a psycho and his behaviour is getting out of control. I'm so pissed off with both you and Kane for not stepping in to help me. It's not the first time Jerry's lashed out and you two have just stood by and watched. What sort of people are you to allow something like that? In the future don't bother to include me in your so-called dates, I won't go.'

Betty took a step back in surprise, not only at the ferocity of my words but the fact that I'd stood up to her. Applying her version of a soothing balm, she crossed to me and placed a gentle hand on my shoulder.

'Come on Constance, don't be like that. It's not that bad...Jerry was just upset about losing his precious notebook. Look, I promise...I'll talk to Kane and get him to rein Jerry in.' she said. 'I'll admit he was out of line – there is no way you could have his notebook. How could you? You spent all night avoiding him.'

I made my first proactive decision since arriving in Melbourne.

'Don't bother with the snake oil, Betty. It's not going to work. Jerry is a brutal bastard. Nothing anybody does or says will change that. I want nothing to do with him ever again.'

Betty pouted her lips and threw herself on her bed in a sulk. I climbed into bed and closed my eyes, ignoring her, pretending to sleep. The bedside clock ticked away in the silence. As no snoring came from the other side of the room I knew she was still awake. Over an hour passed before I heard her bedcovers rustle and the floorboard creak. The door knob gave a small squeal as it was turned and the latch a soft click. Betty snuck from the room, I presume to meet David in his attic hideaway. At three in the morning she returned, in fumbling stealth and reeking of booze.

* * *

I found a bunch of sad-looking daisies lying on the front doorstep when I left for work the next morning. I picked them up and looked around. A blue Kingswood was parked up the street. A familiar ugly man sat in the driver's seat, watching me.

I made a deliberate and obvious movement and threw the flowers in the street rubbish bin. I turned away from the stationary car and hurried to catch the bus.

That night my favourite Sunday haunt, Café Italy, burnt down.

* * *

Jerry started haunting me. At the oddest time the hair on the back of my neck would stand up and when I looked around, there he was. He didn't approach me, he would just sit in the car, or stand across the street and stare.

Every day I would find daisies on the doorstep. I always made a point of tossing them in the bin. My hand started to shake in fear and worry. What happens if he decides to enter the boarding house? Even the formidable Mrs Simmonds wouldn't be a match for a determined Jerry. I couldn't even ask Paul for help, he was out of town. After our wonderful day at the races, I'd received an enormous bouquet of sweet-smelling yellow roses and a written apology. He'd been called away overseas on business and expected to be away at least a month. The month turned into two and there was still no word of his return.

I considered calling the police, though I didn't see it doing any good. Then Jerry stopped following me – and that was even scarier.

11

Chapter Eleven

Spring racing at Flemington had started. All week the socialites of Melbourne – cashed up and hunting for the perfect outfits to wear – had tried my patience and skills at work.

Exhausted, I was grateful to be on the bus heading back to my quiet room to enjoy the rest of the weekend off. I was thinking of going to visit Aunty Gladys and Uncle Richard and hiding for the weekend. A delicious home cooked meal wouldn't go astray either. Betty was a glitch in the ointment. I had seen little of her lately. On the rare occasion we were in the room together, she treated me with icy disdain. Her nocturnal visits upstairs continued on the nights she didn't spend with Kane. Late hours and drinking were taking their toll. She now had an unhealthy look about her. How would I explain her absence to her parents? I'm no good at lying, but I couldn't hurt them with the truth. Sighing, I climbed off the bus and dragged tired legs to the door.

A thick, crisp white envelope, addressed to *Miss Constance O'Hara* in a beautiful cursive hand, was pinned to the letter rack in the foyer. Running my finger along the seal, tearing it in my haste, I felt a flutter of excitement. I lifted the flap and drew out a white and gold embossed card. It was from Paul, an invitation to join him for dinner tonight. Seven o'clock at the Orion Club. Fantastic, he was back. Energy and excitement surged in my limbs. I raced up the stairs, fumbled to get my door key in the lock. In success, I burst into the room, threw my handbag and myself face-down on my bed and kicked my feet in excitement. I gave myself a full minute to act like a loon.

Finally composed, I sat up and reached down between my legs to slide my suitcase out from under the bed. Flipping the lid, I stared in awe at the Mon Cheri gown that lay within. It had taken me months to pay it off on lay-by. I'd hidden its acquisition from Betty's grasping clutches, waiting for the perfect occasion to show it off. The fine filigree of silver work on the dress shimmered, as I held up the white full-length evening gown in admiration. This was definitely the right occasion for such a beautiful dress.

I leapt up and rushed to snaffle the shower before any of the other residents could beat me to it. After scrubbing my body under the cascading hot water until it glowed, I applied a floral scented cream. It gave my body a subtle aroma of a blossoming garden. I did this in preference to the overpowering scent of heavy perfume that Betty favoured.

With my dressing gown on, I went back to my room, settled in front of the mirror and carefully applied a small amount of make-up. A thin layer of foundation and just a touch of mascara and eyeliner was enough to highlight my assets.

Dressing waist length hair is a lot of work, so I opted for an easy hairstyle. Coiling a braid into a bun, I pinned it into place on the crown of my head.

Stepping into the exquisite dress was a revelation. Reflected in the mirror stood an elegant and shapely young lady, who was about to be the envy of Melbourne society – or so I hoped.

In my excitement, I was ready and watching out of the window, fifteen minutes early. Not bad, I thought.

A shiny black limousine glided to a halt in front of the boarding house, affording some curious looks from the other residents. I hot-footed my way downstairs and out the door, before they could question me.

As the limo cruised to a halt at the club's main entrance, I saw the back of a man, with butterscotch hair, walking away. Curious.

Aidan, dressed in his doorman's version of a tuxedo, opened the car door and offered me a smile and his meaty left hand.

'Good evening Miss O'Hara. Welcome to the Orion Club.'

'Thank you, Aidan. It's nice to see you again,' I said as he escorted me along the red carpet. 'Who was that man?'

'What man?'

'The one in scruffy blue jeans and black tee-shirt who was just leaving as I arrived.'

Aiden's forehead and bald scalp wrinkled, he looked puzzled. Then they smoothed again. 'Oh, you probably mean the bloke looking for work. We get them all the time. Why?'

'I thought I recognised him, that's all. Doesn't matter, it's not important.' But I was curious, David already had a job, why was he looking for another, this time in Paul's club. Giving a mental shrug I asked, 'How's Robyn, the baby must be due soon?'

Aidan's smile could have lit up Melbourne. 'Bubs was born yesterday. A little girl. We named her Hope.'

Delighted, I squeezed his arm, 'How wonderful – congratulations. Please, give Robyn my best – Daddy.'

We took the three steps leading to the frosted, gold embossed glass doors. Glowing with pride and happiness, Aidan opened the door and walked with me to the dining room entrance, and handed me over to Marius the maître d'.

While Marius solicitously removed the wrap from my shoulders, I cast an eye over the room. Crisp white linen tablecloths adorned an array of tables, strategically placed in a half moon shape around a small central stage. The tables, illuminated by the soft glow of yellow tea lights, looked warm and inviting. Soft music played in the background.

'Mr Joshua sends his apologies, Miss O'Hara. A matter of some urgency has delayed him. He will join you as soon as he can,' said Marius. His English was tinged with a slight French accent.

'Thank you, Marius,' I said, hiding my disappointment with a polite smile.

'If you will follow me, Miss, I'll escort you to your seat.'

Wending our way between the outer tables, Marius paused at a central table, the best in the room. He adjusted a red velvet chair for me, making it easier for me to take my seat. A jeweller's box, tied with a pale-yellow silk bow, lay on the table in front of me. A gold embossed card attached. *Constance to match your beautiful emerald eyes, Paul*. Slowly untying the bow, I lifted the lid and gasped. Laying on a bed of rumpled white silk was a delicate emerald and diamond infinity bracelet. Breathlessly I ran my finger over the amazing stones and tears of delight stung my eyes, Oh Paul, so beautiful. Slipping the bracelet on, I held my wrist up to the light to see the diamonds sparkle.

The noise level around me rose as the well-dressed Saturday night crowd arrived and settled in. Across the room, I noticed Betty. I lifted my hand in recognition as the thought crossed my mind that standards seemed to be slipping. Marius flipped a white cloth covered wrist, and a waiter materialised at my elbow to pour out a glass of very expensive champagne. Tasty.

A commotion on the right had heads turning – Kane and Jerry, I observed in exasperation and despair, acting like they owned the club. Jerry, unsteady on his feet, was showing his true nature – shoving people and chairs out of his path. He was leading Kane. They made a beeline towards Betty. Protests froze on lips when they saw who the protagonist was. I watched Betty shimmy sexily to her feet and plant her painted red lips over Kane's, nearly sucking the tongue from his mouth. Kane reciprocated while running his hand intimately all over her body. As their lips parted, he grabbed her left breast and squeezed. Betty, preening with the attention, murmured something in his ear then resumed her seat.

Jerry stood swaying in place watching the couple, a smarmy smile plastered on his lips, before he threw himself with nonchalance into a nearby chair and lit a cigarette.

Betty glanced my way, smirked, and said something in Jerry's ear. Turning, he scanned all the tables in my direction before focusing on me. I sat back in fright as he staggered to his feet and bulled his way across the room yelling, 'Here she is...here's the princess whore.'

Before Jerry could reach my table, Marius deftly intercepted him.

'Get out of the fucking way, you jumped up little frog,' Jerry said, trying to shove Marius out of his path.

Aidan appeared behind Jerry and laid a beefy hand on his shoulder. 'Mr Martin, please rejoin your party or leave.' His high-pitched voice had deepened and carried a tone that brooked no argument. 'You know Mr Joshua won't be happy if you make a scene in his club. Remember our conversation last week. Your disgraceful behaviour towards her has come to Mr Joshua's ears and he has forbidden you to go anywhere near this young lady.'

Jerry gave a half-hearted grunt. 'Huh...fuck Mr Joshua, she's mine,' he said.

'No she is not, and you will stay away from her.'

Jerry flicked his cigarette butt at Marius, turned and blundered back to Kane and Betty. With violence he pulled his chair up, threw himself down, sculling a glass of beer from the table next to him. He sat there glaring in my direction. Well, that was fun – not. I might sound flippant but I was terrified. Jerry's behaviour was right out of control. I decided it was time to talk about it with Paul. I might even give him Jerry's notebook. I sat mulling over Aiden's words and a light bulb went on inside my head. Paul already knew and he'd stepped in. That explained why Jerry's stalking had stopped. But, I wondered, for how long.

Marius appeared in my field of vision. 'I do apologise, Miss O'Hara...with the dim lighting in the club, people are often mistaken about who they see.'

'Thank you Marius, you're very kind.'

'My pleasure, Miss. May I refresh your drink?' Lifting the bottle of champagne, he topped up my glass.

The floor show was well under way, a fabulous blues singer was keeping the crowd enthralled, but I was tired of the glares coming from Jerry's direction and sick of waiting for Paul. What the hell was keeping him. I had been waiting nearly two hours and he was still a no show. Maybe I should just go.

Marius materialised at my elbow. 'Mr Joshua, thanks you for your patience, Miss O'Hara. He'll be with you shortly. May I get you anything while you wait, more champagne perhaps?'

'No thanks, Marius, but I would like to use the bathroom. Can you tell me where that is?'

'Certainly, it's on the other side of the foyer, down the left-hand hallway. The blue door, on the right.'

I smiled my thanks, gathered up my silver beaded purse and slipped through the crowded room to the foyer. I headed down the empty hallway towards the blue door marked Ladies that stood facing a closed white door marked Store. As I neared the door, a hand slapped roughly across my mouth. I tried to scream as an arm reached around from behind, hooking tightly around my waist. I felt my feet lift off the ground. My purse flew from my hand.

With a crash the storeroom door shattered as it was kicked open. I felt myself sailing through the air. I came to a painful stop as my head and shoulders slammed into metal shelving. On impact, the air rushed from my lungs in a loud whoosh and I fell into a heap on the floor. Before I could regain my feet, my assailant grabbed what was left of my nicely coiled bun, and hauled me to my feet. A rough, calloused hand clutched tightly around my throat and squeezed. I could hear my heart pounding in my ears, as pulling air into my lungs became impossible. My back slammed back against the shelves as I was shoved and the pressure on my throat eased. I could hear my breath wheezing loudly as I pulled air into my oxygen-deprived lungs.

Hot breath, reeking of alcohol and tobacco, blasted me full in the face. Jerry shoved his face close to mine. 'Bitch! I'm not good enough for you, huh?'

His fingers tightened on my throat again, but I managed to gurgle, 'Let...me...go...you bastard.' I took an ineffective swat at his hand.

A hard, stinging slap to the face had my cheek burning and brought tears of pain to my eyes. Warmth trickled down my chin. I licked my lips and tasted blood. Before I could stop it, a sob escaped my mouth.

The squeeze on my throat eased. Jerry removed his hand long enough to replace it with his forearm. Pushing my chin up, he gave me a leering smile.

'Princess you always know how to turn a man on,' he said. Leaning forward, he put his horrible mouth over mine. I moved my head to the right, pulling away. I could feel a trail of hot spittle smear my cheek as his lips slid across it. Easing his weight back off my throat, Jerry rubbed his groin against me and pulled the shoulder of my dress down, tearing the material. He grabbed my exposed breast and squeezed. I could feel fear and adrenaline coursing through me. I sucked in a long, ragged breath, placed my hands on his chest, and shoved hard.

'Get off me you bloody mongrel,' I yelled.

Jerry fell back a couple of steps. Panting I tried to dash past him to freedom but Jerry lurched in my way. This time he grabbed my forearms and squeezed so tight my hands went numb. Dragging me towards his chest, he forcing my mouth to meet his. I clamped my lips shut, not allowing him to invade my mouth with his wet slobbering tongue. My back slammed against the shelving again. Jerry let go and began hiking my dress up. I lifted numb fingers to his face and raked his cheek with my long sharp fingernails, digging deep. To follow up I lifted my knee, fast and hard, aiming for his groin. My height was against me...I didn't make the contact I needed to put him down but it was enough to make him take a step backward.

The cords in Jerry's neck swelled and rage suffused his face with red. His open hand connected with my cheek. My head flew back and I saw stars as I collided with the shelf behind me. My air supply was cut as Jerry slammed his forearm across my throat. I gagged in an attempt to breath. He eased his weight a little and put some distance between my knee and his jewels.

Leaning forward, he glared and snarled, 'You're so gonna pay for that, you little bitch. I'm gonna root you...'

The space between us gave me enough room to lift my leg. I placed my right foot flat on his chest and shoved. Jerry flew backwards, tripping over some metal buckets. He landed in a noisy heap on the floor.

I gasped as I sucked oxygen into my starved lungs. My chest heaved. Seeing my chance, I leapt over Jerry's prone body and out the door. I ran across the hallway into the ladies' bathroom. Nearly wetting my knickers in fright, I pressed my back hard against the door, jamming it closed. I held in my sobs and listened for any sound of pursuit.

From the other side of the door came the sound of running footsteps and a man's voice said, 'What the fuck's going on.' It sounded like Kane but I couldn't be sure. A clatter of a metal bucket being thrown was followed by the slam of a door. There were more footsteps in the corridor and a muffled conversation. I heard Aiden's distinctive tone followed by a grunt and then silence.

I stood with my back against the door shaking. I looked for a lock – there wasn't one. Something to hold the door wedged closed...nothing. I could feel the panic rising in my throat. I wanted to run, hide, yell – anything but stand here with only a thin wooden door between me and a brutal man. The silence outside finally penetrated my frantic brain. I glued my ear to the door and listened. Nothing. I cracked the door and took a peek. The corridor was empty. I staggered over to the sink and ran the tap. Holding my scratched and bloody hands under the cold running water, I blinked away the unshed tears that blinded me. I stared at my face in the mirror, it was bruised and bloody. My hair was a mess and my dress torn.

I splashed water over my face. The rage inside me fought to escape. I gave vent to it and screamed at my image in the mirror. 'Bastard, bastard, bastard, bastard!'

The door crashed open. I leapt in fright. The scream died in my throat. Betty stood in the door way glaring at me. She flung the door closed and stormed over to where I stood, shivering at the sink. Betty grabbed my forearms and squeezed tight. The pain of the un-investigated bruising under her grip nearly floored me.

'Ahh,' I yelped. Twisting back and forth I tried to free myself from her painful grasp.

'What have you done?' she said. Her thin red lips were pulled back over her teeth, giving the impression of a rabid dog.

I glared at her in defiance.

'*Me...*,' I said, in a voice that shuddered and shook. 'I haven't done anything. Look at me.' I pointed to my torn dress and the cuts and bruises on my face and neck, 'It's your precious, psycho friend, Jerry...*He did this*.'

Betty shook me so hard my teeth rattled, 'Jerry's dead you fool.'

Her words stunned me.

'D-d-dead...what do you mean he's dead?'

'In the cupboard. Kane just found him.'

'He can't be dead. I only pushed him on his arse to get away. He was floundering around in a bucket when I last saw him.'

With a small shove, Betty let go. Whirling around she looked out into the corridor... it was clear. She grabbed my wrist. My bracelet cut the skin under her grasp, as she dragged me out into the hall towards the fire escape. Shoving the door open, she pushed me outside. I landed on my bum in a dark, empty alley.

'You have to go...leave...right now.'

My teeth began chattering. Wiping the tears from my face with the back of a shaking hand, I stammered 'L-l-leave...I can't leave. Jerry's dead...I have to talk to the police.'

'You can't be seen talking to the police, you stupid girl, it's too dangerous. Right now they can say Jerry was drunk and fell over. If anyone here gets even a whiff of you going near the cops, it's goodnight Constance.' Her voice and tone was full of bile and malice. 'Mr Joshua won't be happy you were in that room with Jerry. No matter what you say, he won't believe you weren't there by choice. Jerry told everyone you were an item. And if Kane finds you, you'll definitely be dead. You killed his best friend.'

'Then I'll go back to our digs and...'

'No. When I say you have to get out of here, I mean out of town. You're dead, Constance. You can never go home. Don't contact any of the family or your friends...ever. *Now get out of here.*'

She slammed the fire door, locking me out in the dark, shivering and scared.

* * *

The sun was just peaking over the horizon as I arrived at the boarding house. It had taken me all night to walk home from the club. By sticking to the shadows, I'd avoided being seen. I carefully checked the surrounding street for any movement. The streetlights were losing their energy to the coming dawn, and no longer cast circles of dull light. Beaconsfield Parade was grey and gloomy, the sea along the beachfront a pool of calm silence.

Sidling my way to the back door, I dug out Betty's hidden key. Removing my now ruined strappy heels, I crept up the stairs in my stockinged feet. My hands shook so badly I had difficulty getting the key in the lock. After three shaky attempts it finally slid into place. I paused before opening the door and pressed my ear to the wood panel to listen for any noise inside. Satisfied I was all alone, I turned the key and slipped inside.

Grabbing my old blue denim backpack, now faded and scruffy from use, I stuffed in a few changes of clothing. Nothing fancy, just plain underwear, jeans and tee-shirts. Everything else I would leave. I hoped Aunty Gladys would send it all home to Sarah, but I didn't care. I didn't want a reminder of this life anyway.

Prying up the loose floorboard, I scooped up my hoard of cash, my journal and the precious photo of Sarah and Dad and stowed them in my bag. The photo taken on our last night together with Sarah's new Polaroid camera, was the only memento from home I had. We were so happy then, the world at our feet.

Last item to go in the bag was Jerry's notebook. Who knows, the information about bribery, extortion and blackmail might save my life one day.

My beautiful Mon Cheri gown I abandoned on the bedroom floor. Betty can have it, I would never wear it again. Like everything of mine she'd touched, it was ruined. Stripped to my bare skin, I stood in front of the mirror and examined the damage Jerry's manhandling had done. My neck and shoulders were black, my arms dotted with a multitude of blue and purple finger marks. My face had a red hand-shaped mark across the cheek, which was starting to turn blue at the edges. Split and swollen lip, sore bum and a headache all added to my woes.

As tears streamed down my cheeks I pulled on faded jeans and my old tennis shoes. Searching through the mess that was Betty's wardrobe, I unearthed the long-sleeved, black turtle neck skivvy she'd never worn. It covered the marks on my arms and neck. Fair swap I thought, my torn dress for her new skivvy.

I smeared foundation on in a thick layer, concealing the marks on my face as best I could. The damage to my soul would never go away. To hide my auburn hair, I left it coiled in the now bedraggled bun and pulled a St Kilda football beanie over the top. A final glance around the room revealed nothing else I would need to start a new life.

Once again, I pressed my ear against the door to listen, and detecting no noise on the landing outside, I threw the backpack onto my very sore left shoulder and slipped silently down the stairs. Unlocking the front door I left Betty's precious key hanging in the lock. Let her get in late at night now. I stepped out just as the number 236 bus pulled up down the street. Running flat out, I jumped inside the bus doors, just as they hissed shut.

The driver gave me an amused look and said, 'That was close, lass.'

As I took my seat I saw David standing on the doorstep, watching.

* * *

I hopped on and off buses and trams, travelling all around Melbourne and some of the inner city suburbs. I was using the constant motion to cover my trail. When I was sure no one was following I got off and made my way into the botanical gardens. It was quiet so I found a bench under some trees, out of sight of any prying eyes and sat and thought about what I should do next. I figured I'd be safe hiding here for a few hours as I don't think Kane would consider it a likely place for anyone to hide, or if in fact he even knew the gardens existed.

What to do? I couldn't go to Aunt Gladys and Uncle Richard's, Betty would happily inform Kane where he could find me. I couldn't go home – Mother told me I was never to darken her doorstep again. Handing myself into the police would put everyone in the family in danger and I would be lucky to survive – Kane and Paul have a long reach.

The day passed slowly. I was a nervous wreck, jumping at shadows and flinching anytime someone came into view. The day cooled and evening closed in. I stole away from gardens just as they were closing, still with no clear plan in mind. I caught a city bus and scrunched down into a small ball on the back seat, frightened and lost. When the bus pulled into the main terminal it parked next to an orange and white interstate greyhound bus providing me with the solution to my problem. Interstate...*yes*...that's where I will go.

12

Chapter Twelve

I waited, impatient to be off. A long line of passengers, suitcases and luggage piled haphazardly around them, queued at the locked door of the greyhound coach. I'd secured first position at the door and clutched my one-way ticket to Adelaide like a life preserver. I tucked my backpack between my feet, the strap looped, ready in case I need to make a fast getaway. With rapid glances I kept vigilant watch. My bruised face I tilted away from the other passengers' inquisitive stares. I avoided making eye contact and stayed on the balls of my feet, ready to bolt if anyone recognised me.

The exposure of being out in the open was driving me nuts.

A bus driver wandered from the staff area and ambled in our direction. He walked with his weight on his heels and his rotund gut shoved forward. This forced the crowd to part before him. A beige, leather travel bag dangled from one hand and a set of keys hung from a looped chain on his belt. He eyed the long line of passengers and their bags, smirked and stopped to chat with another driver.

The phrase *hurry up* was on repeat in my head. But of course, he didn't.

After a bout of backslapping and laughter, the driver resumed his slow progress towards us.

He jangled the keys, taking his time to select the correct one to shove into the door's lock. Before opening the bus, he rocked back on his heels and gave an officious speech.

'G'day folks. Full bus today. You'll have ta put ya bags in the rear luggage compartment. Check ya labels. I won't take the blame if ya lose anything.'

The group grumbled. The driver smirked.

'Ya can only take stuff onboard that ya'll need for the trip. Everything else gets stowed...no exceptions.'

There was *no way* I was going to be separated from my backpack. The driver, eyebrow quirked in amusement, watched the passengers load their gear. I flashed my ticket under his nose and clambered onboard. Attention elsewhere, the driver didn't notice my bag.

Opting for a seat half-way down the aisle, I settled next to the window. I dropped my backpack on the seat next to me, to discourage anyone from sitting there, and pulled my knees up under my chin. I stared out the tinted glass, watching the passengers do the driver's job of loading their bags before they climbed aboard. I studied every face as it passed my field of vision. No one seemed to take an interest in me. At long last everyone was on board. The driver settled in his seat with a grunt and the door hissed shut, which gave me a small sense of safety.

The last person on board was a middle-aged man, dressed in a light blue, short-sleeved safari suit. His belt was notched so tight his fat gut hung over the top like a sagging veranda. Long beige socks and sandals further enhanced this good look. Lucky me...he stopped and stared at the seat occupied by my denim backpack.

Great.

I ignored him and hoped he'd change his mind and find another seat. No such luck. He stared at me. I lost the battle of will and moved my bag, shoving it on the floor in front of me. The seat next to me ballooned and sighed as the man plonked himself down. He wriggled and writhed, adjusted his overfull jacket pockets, then his bum. At long last, he stilled and was quiet.

Not for long.

He turned towards me and smiled, showing me a mouth full of crooked, gappy teeth.

'G'day, I'm Fred.'

Then I made a big mistake – I gave a small finger wave and said, 'Hi Fred.'

That was enough. Fred liked to talk and loved the sound of his own voice. He started a monologue that lasted the entire ten-and-a-half-hour trip to Adelaide. To start, I was blessed with a detailed run-down of the history of Greyhound Coaches.

To distract him from a subject I had absolutely no interest in, I waited for him to take a breath and asked, 'Where are you off to, Fred?'

He extracted a packet of cheese and tomato sandwiches from his pocket. 'I'm on my way to Perth. It's a trip of 2123.7 miles or in that new-fangled metric system they now use, 4417 kilometres. It's taking me the entire week to get there...from Sydney. Do you know, if I'd taken the Indian Pacific train, with the new switching system they've installed, I'd be there in 49 hours. Imagine that. Only 49 hours.'

My eyes glazed over.

Around a mouthful of food, Fred asked, 'You ever been to Kalgoorlie?'

I shook my head, hoping against hope he'd leave it at that. Nope, no such luck. Fred launched into a detailed history of the Goldfields and its surrounding districts. My ears hurt as he droned on and on. When he pulled a stack of Polaroid photos from his pocket, I hauled my backpack up from under my seat, propped it up as a pillow, and closed my eyes, pretending to sleep. As if I hadn't suffered enough, Fred had been sent my way. Boy, God must be really pissed off.

Tuning out the drone of Fred's voice wasn't easy as it continued to fade in and out of my consciousness while I tried to plan out the next steps of my escape. I couldn't afford to leave a trail for Kane to follow, or do anything to bring attention to myself. First thing I'd do is change my name. Nothing too radical, I was hopeless at that sort of stuff and I was a useless liar. A new name had to be something easy to remember. I tried a few on for size.

Lee.

Tansy.

Con.

Connie.

I'd hated Connie as a child and refused to answer if anyone used it. I sighed and resigned myself to the fact that the name would probably work for me.

Adelaide or Sydney seemed obvious destinations for anyone fleeing Victoria. I needed to cover my trail and travel farther afield. I had two choices from South Australia. I could go north to the Territory, but from what I gathered from Fred's waffle, there's a lot of nothing that way and few job options. My other choice was Western Australia. Job prospects were excellent. It was remote enough from the rest of the country that I wasn't likely to run into anyone who knew me.

Okay, west it is.

Now, I really needed to get off this bus. If I had to sit and listen to Fred all the way to WA, I'd be a basket case.

I could take another bus, but that would mean a delay. No – the train would be better, and quicker. The need to put some distance between Kane and me was paramount.

Where to go? Some of Fred's waffle had sunk in, because Kalgoorlie crystallised as a good place to start. With its many small towns and aboriginal settlements, I was sure to find work. I just had to remember to keep my head down and my mouth shut.

After a very long and weary night of Fred, I was relieved to reach Adelaide. The orange and white greyhound coach came to a gentle stop at the city terminal.

Fred was still talking. '...with a magnificent church or cathedral around every corner it's no wonder Adelaide is known as the city of churches.'

My relief that my Fred ordeal was nearly over gave impetuous to my movements. Before the door opened, I grabbed my bag and leapt over his legs. I grunted a 'See ya,' and took off.

I scurried off the bus, before my ears exploded, and headed into the city. Finding the right ticket office and organising my train travel took longer than expected and it didn't leave me much time to get to the shops to buy the few essentials I needed. I made it to the supermarket moments before the one o'clock lunchtime closure. The staff glared at me, willing me to hurry up. I snatched up some fruit, meals for the next couple of days. In the cosmetic section I found eyeliner, mascara and a pair of scissors and got out of the store before the workers went on strike for having their lunch break curtailed.

* * *

I sat under a droopy she-oak tree in the park and waited until the public toilet was empty before I went into Connie renovation mode. I stood at the sink and studied myself in the old cracked and dusty mirror. I pulled the beanie from my head and held my waist length braid out to the side and waited for courage. I sighed, picked up the scissors and in one fluid motion I cut it off level to my chin. My hair sprang into a curly auburn halo, my head was so light it almost floated from my shoulders. Who knew hair was that heavy! I fluffed my new bob, turning left then right as I checked out the results of my barber job.

Not bad.

Satisfied, I turned my attention to my face.

If I'd learnt anything from Betty in the last six months, it was how to apply make-up, in a way that changed your appearance. She was an expert at enhancing her qualities and hiding her faults, literally. I applied a thick layer of liner and mascara to my eyes, altering their shape. I studied the results in the mirror and barely recognised the girl reflected back at me.

I changed into clean jeans and pulled a long-sleeved check shirt over the black skivvy, shouldered my backpack and set off to catch the train with a new sense of purpose and freedom.

* * *

The train journey to Kalgoorlie would take 29 hours, so I propped myself up comfortably against the window in the air-conditioned carriage, intending to sleep most of the way. An elderly lady of indeterminable age sat next to me, her bejewelled fingers mesmerising to watch as she worked diligently at her knitting. She smelled of lavender and baby powder.

She smiled shyly at me. 'Hello dear, my name is Irene.'

I hesitated to try out my new name for the first time. 'Connie,' I said.

Irene's smile touched her eyes as she said, 'Now dear, you just settle back and don't feel you need to talk if you don't want to. I won't take offence. I know how tedious it is when you're travelling and you get some gasbag sitting next to you. The stories I could tell you would make your toes curl.'

My lip quirked in amusement and I nearly blabbed out my experience with Fred, but remembered just in time to hold my tongue. I didn't want anyone tracing me back to the bus. To be polite, I asked her about her trip.

'Well dear, I'm on my way home, to Kal. I've been in Adelaide visiting my sister. We had a lovely two weeks together. That was enough. I'm ready for my own bed again. How about you Connie, where are you off to?' she asked over the clack of her knitting needles.

'Kal?'

'Kalgoorlie dear. All the locals just call it Kal, it's too hot to waste time on full length words.'

I laughed and said, 'Ah, well like you, I'm getting off in Kalgoorlie.' Taking a risk, she wasn't another talker like Fred, I asked, 'Irene, where's a good place to stay in town? Nothing flash...I'm looking for clean and cheap.'

'Now, let me see.' She wrinkled her delicate powdered brow, sat in quiet thought, then she clicked her fingers. 'Why, of course! If you're looking for a place long term there's a boarding house on Egan Street. It's got an excellent reputation for being clean and reasonably priced. Or for short-term stays, there are plenty of motels along Hannan and Maritana Streets, more expensive of course. You don't want to stay at any of the hotels – not a pretty young thing like you. The pubs in Kal can be pretty rough and noisy, especially on the weekends when the miners are in town.'

'A boarding house sounds great, just what I'm looking for. How far is Egan Street from the train station?'

'Not far dear. The train pulls in at Forrest Street Station. Egan Street is a four-block walk.'

'Thanks, Irene. I don't want to be rude, but I'm going to get some sleep, I've had a long and tiring couple of days.'

'You go right ahead, dear.' Irene's eyes narrowed as she studied my face. 'I'll make sure no one comes near you and if you'd like to talk...'

I felt the corners of my mouth lift in gratitude at this kind and fierce old lady. Talk was tempting but I needed to keep my own counsel.

'Nothing to talk about, Irene.'

She frowned at my words but remained silent on the subject. I settled back into my seat and fell asleep to the rhythmic clicking of her knitting needles and the sway of the carriage.

I must have slept for a long time, because it was almost dawn when my growling stomach roused me. I opened my eyes and swivelled to look around in the dim lighting. I was the only person awake. Irene, sitting erect, her head propped against a small pillow gave a soft snore. I stuck my hand into my bag and eased out the banana I'd been saving for my breakfast. As I ate, I stared out the window, marvelling at the clear night sky ablaze with a million stars. It was an awesome sight to behold.

Jerry's ugly image reflected back at me from the glass. I jumped in fright and spun around. Everyone was still asleep, there was no movement anywhere. It was only a memory. I felt sick. Guilt and remorse churned around in my gut, threatening to give me back my banana. How could I have killed him? It made little sense to me. All I had done was shove him.

The memories of our encounter brought sweat to my brow and my bruises ached in response. Images rolled over in my mind, as if a film was stuck in a loop. Finally, I lost patience and forced the thoughts away, shoving them in into a drawer in my mind. I locked the draw and told myself, 'It's not your fault Constance, you were only protecting yourself from the bastard.'

Not ready to go back to sleep, I pulled out Jerry's notebook. It was split into sections. His notes were laid out in tidy, orderly columns of dates, names and currency. The names and payments seemed to relate to bribes. I flicked to another section. The later dates coincided with Jerry, Kane and Betty's trips to the country races. Looks like they'd been doing some race fixing. Some had been carried out with the knowledge and co-operation of the jockey and trainer. In other cases the horse had been nobbled. Page followed page listing the horse's name, method used and money won on each race. The winnings added up to a small fortune. One term I didn't understand but cropped up a few times – *Ring-in*.

The last section of the book had two pages of coded entries. The very last one caught my attention.

JW – knocked Fri19670–38 Special. Dumped Nightingale into PPB. Prints–PJ. In Fitzroy lockup.

Now here was a puzzle. I ran my finger under the code and tried to puzzle its meaning.

JW? Fri19670?

I knew what a 38 Special was. It was a Smith & Wesson revolver. Jerry had flourished it once, showing off.

Nightingale I also knew. It was Paul Joshua's fancy boat...PPB? Boat...PPB. Oh, of course...Port Phillip Bay. What the hell had Jerry dumped off a boat into Port Phillip Bay?

I shrugged – anything was possible with a psycho like that.

Fri19670. I scratched my head and mulled over the words, Fri...Fri? Oh, you're such a dope, Constance – of course Fri was short for Friday, which must make 19670 a date... 19th June, 1970, why was that familiar?

Images scrolled through my mind, a day at the races, Paul winning a lot of money, our dinner date cancelled because of unexpected business and the next day a radio news report came to mind, a body – according to David not drowned, but shot. Bloody hell, I'd cracked Jerry's code.

I didn't like what I read.

John Wilcox, knocked Friday 19th June 1970, 38 Special, dumped Nightingale Port Phillip Bay. Prints–PJ?

The only PJ I knew was Paul Joshua.

Did that mean that in Jerry's Fitzroy lockup – the storage unit where he kept a stash of gear relating to his criminal activities – he'd kept the gun used to kill John Wilcox? The way I read this he was either setting Paul up for the murder or Paul had actually pulled the trigger. Bloody hell! My stomach clenched, my hands went cold and numb as the blood drained from my face. Holy shit, I had nearly handed this over to Paul, thinking he was a nice man and would protect me. There was no way he would've let me walk away with the knowledge it contained.

In a cold sweat, I shoved the notebook away, deep, to the bottom of my bag. I stared out the window at the dark landscape, my mind frozen with fear.

* * *

'Connie. Connie dear, wake up.' A soft elderly voice buzzed in my ear, it pulled me from a deep slumber. 'Connie we're just about to pull into Kalgoorlie, dear.'

Connie? Who? Oh yeah, that's me.

'Kal, already,' I mumbled, rubbing my eyes and trying to clear my sleep fogged brain.

'Yes dear, and you're already sounding like a local. We'll be pulling into the station in about ten minutes. I thought you might like to use the bathroom, do a little make-up repair, before we arrive,' said Irene, waving a finger over her face to emphasise her statement.

'Thanks Irene, you're an angel,' I said. 'And thanks heaps for watching over me while I slept. It was a great comfort.'

I climbed over the smiling old lady and beat a hasty path to the toilet before the other passengers, stirring in their seats, could beat me to it. I used the facilities and then did some running repairs to my face. I studied myself in the mirror and noticed that the red hand mark had faded, now there was an ugly yellowy-green tinge to the skin. With a light smear of foundation, I hid the worst of it. As I left the restroom, the train slowed to a halt. I stepped off the *Indian Pacific* and received a hell of a shock. The mid-morning sun was shining gloriously in a clear blue sky but the lazy desert wind that traversed the platform cut through me like a hot knife in soft butter. It was cold, no freezing is a better word, and it bit me right down to my bones.

I shrugged into my jacket and zipped it up to keep the worst of the breeze out. I tagged along behind the flow of people heading for the Forrest Street exit. Before leaving through the gate, I took a final look back along the platform at the train. It was an awesome sight, two locomotives had pulled twelve passenger carriages plus as many freight carriages across the entire country without a murmur.

I hunched down into my jacket and followed Irene's directions. I looked with interest at the houses as I passed. They were so different from anything I'd ever seen before. Each structure was a collection of odd rooms with walls built from a mixture of cement sheeting, tin and canvas. It was like the builders had used anything that had been near to hand at the time. Every house had a tin sheeted roof, rusted red from time, dirt and weather.

A waist-high, chain-link fence delineated properties and surrounded gardens that would've broken Uncle Richard's heart. There was no greenery or flowers. The yards consisted of red dirt and tufts of straw-coloured dried out weeds. The occasional eucalyptus tree provided a modicum of shade. Green was not a colour of the Goldfields landscape – in fact, a rusty red glaze tinged the entire countryside as far as the eye could see.

I paused as I stepped onto the main thoroughfare, Hannan Street. Its width amazed me, designed and built in a bygone era for the fifteen-camel road trains used to cart pipes and other supplies to the mining and sheep industries around the district. The dray wagons needed a lot of room to turn around. A six-lane city freeway could be fitted comfortably here without disturbing any existing buildings.

The architecture of the main street was delightful – here was no boring symmetrical design but a collection of random sized structures thrown together from cement sheeting, tin and sandstone, built to suit the size of the owner's wallet. Single-storey narrow shops, had been squashed between double-storey commercial enterprises. Each block had been book ended by fabulous limestone and red brick buildings – the hotels and pubs of Kalgoorlie. At the peak of the gold rush, Hannan Street boasted fifty-two drinking houses up and down its 3km length – see, some of Fred's waffle had penetrated. A girl could get tired walking up and down here, when on a shopping spree.

A strong pull of curiosity drew me into the street. I decided to have a wander up and back down a few blocks. Strolling past each place of business was an experience – every building had a covered porch or veranda that had been built to its own design and abutted its neighbour's porch. This interesting concept provided the foot traffic protection from the elements, especially the fierce summer sun.

I walked as far as Maritana Street, crossed over, wondering if I needed a cut lunch to reach the other side. As I passed the side entrance of the Palace Hotel, a wave of men's voices and laughter rang out of the open windows. I hurried past, not wanting to attract attention, and spotted a lone signpost. Hanging by one screw a battered white street sign pointed to the ground. The faded dull grey lettering read, Egan Street. I looked left and right for some guidance, but it didn't help. Street numbers were non-existent. I took a punt, turned right and crossed the road on the diagonal. My hunch paid off, three blocks down, wired to a mesh gate, I came across a small paint-faded wooden sign on which I could just make out the words *Rooms – Egan Boarding*.

I lifted the latch and pushed at the gate. It screeched in protest but swung open easily. Hard packed red dirt marked out by a line of dusty white painted rocks formed the path that led to a wooden porch and the front door. Lifting my hand to the paint-flecked green door, I jumped in fright when it opened before I could knock.

A tall girl, black hair chopped as short as a man's and dressed in jeans and flannel checked shirt said, 'Oh sorry, I didn't know anyone was out here. I was just on my way out. Can I help you?'

'Yes please, I'm looking for a room, do you have anything available?'

I hitched my backpack more comfortably on my shoulder and studied her chiselled face. She was all angles and points, the harshness of which was softened by dewy brown eyes and long dark lashes.

'Oh, it's not me you want ducks, it's Norma, she runs the place. I just board here. My name's Sandra, by the way.' She held out a work-roughened hand with blunt fingers to shake mine.

'Hi, I'm Connie,' I said, quite pleased that I had remembered to use my new name so naturally.

'Hiya, Connie. Come on in, Norma's out back in the kitchen. That's where you'll always find her. I don't think she ever moves. It's not bad here, clean and comfortable. The rent's good. You could do a lot worse,' said Sandra. She strode down a long hallway, her scuffed Appaloosa riding boots clattering loudly on the wooden floorboards.

Trust me to notice the footwear.

A hall lined by closed and numbered doors, which finished at the number six, ran the length of the house. The wooden floorboards creaked and groaned as Sandra led me to the open door at the end. A kitchen. In the middle of the room stood a rectangular tubular steel frame table, it's green laminated top covered in an assortment of junk. Scattered around the table were six vinyl-padded chairs, of varying colours. Facing the doorway, so she had a clear view of the hall and front door, sat Norma, cigarette in hand and a cloud of grey smoke hovering over her head. Her fat body, encased in a giant yellow mumu that had sweat marks around the armpits, totally hid the chair she was sitting on.

Smiling in welcome, she revealed yellow-stained teeth.

Before I could speak, Sandra piped up. 'Hey Norma, I found a pixie on the front doorstep, looking for a room.' She turned to me and gave me a smile that was full of friendship. 'I'll leave you to it, Connie. We can catch up later, once you've settled in.'

She spun on her heel and clumped her way back down the hall. The front door slammed.

'Hi, Norma is it?' I said, getting straight down to business. 'My name is Connie Hara, I've just arrived in town. I'm looking for a place to stay long term, would you have a room available?'

Norma stared, her eyes running from the top of my head, pausing on my face for a moment then continued down over my travel worn jacket and jeans to my scruffy tennis shoes.

'I run a tight ship here. Rent is forty dollars a week. For that, you get your own room, shared bathroom and use of the laundry once a week. You keep your own room clean, including sheets and towels. You can use the kitchen to cook meals, but that will cost you extra *and* I expect you to clean up afterwards. There's no cooking or eating allowed in the rooms. And *NO MEN*! A deposit of fifty dollars on the key.' She paused, consulted her internal checklist, then held out a hand for the money.

'May I take a look at the room please, Norma, before I decide?'

Silently Norma scrabbled around in the mess on the table in front of her. The circular earrings dangling under grey, tight-permed curls, swayed with her body movement. She held out two fingers to me, a key dangling between them.

The key fitted door number 4. It was the middle one on my left, as I stepped from the kitchen. Brown-stained wood with a pewter number nailed in its centre, stood as a barrier to prying eyes. The room sighed as I unlocked and opened the door. I gave a silent thank you to Aunty Gladys for teaching me what to look for. Clean, dry, nice size, no bad smells. The dressing table glowed warmly from a coat of beeswax polish. Opening the matching two-door pine wardrobe, which stood like a silent sentinel behind the door, I ran my eye carefully around. No bugs, and oodles of hanging space – even Betty would struggle to fill that. The floral bedspread looked inviting, so I sat and bounce tested the mattress. Not only was it comfortable but the homely smell of clean linen wafted nicely into my nose. Sliding my fingers under the covers, I encountered crisp sheets. Well done Irene, you didn't lead me astray, this room will do me nicely.

I left my backpack and grabbed my purse. I paid my bond and two weeks rent. That should give me plenty of time to find a job. If I was unsuccessful, I still had enough money for a train ticket to the next town.

13

Chapter Thirteen

It was two in the afternoon. My feet were aching and swollen. I gave up my job hunting and entered the Victory Café, in search of a reviving cup of tea. I had walked all three kilometres of Hannan Street and then made the return journey on the other side of the street, making enquiries. I'd avoided the pubs after my first experience. Barmaid work in this town was a tough gig. You had to work long hours, late into the night, and every Thursday you were required to work topless! They had this thing called *Skimpy Night*. A topless barmaid serving beer to drunken, sex-starved men. Yeah, that wasn't demeaning or dangerous at all!

I slid into a seat at one of steel-framed laminated tables and lifted my hot sweaty face to the breeze being created by the slow motion of a creaky ceiling fan. I sighed, it was great to get off my feet. Today's job hunt had not been a success, though to be fair, some businesses took my name and address saying they'd let me know if anything came up. Most just shook their heads. Looking for work was the pits. Glum is the only word to describe how I felt and in desperate need of a cup of tea. I waited, but no waitress appeared to take my order. A clatter of plates drew my attention. I heaved myself up on tired limbs and approached a hatch that opened into the kitchen area. Maybe they hadn't heard me come in.

A loud crash, accompanied by a stream of Italian, blasted out of the servery. I stuck my head in and watched in amusement. A round, middle-aged, bald man, his head glowing from the heat of the room, threw a frypan across the room. It landed neatly in the sink, on a bed of frothy suds, with a resounding plop. White foamy bubbles launched themselves into the air and just missed landing on the nose of a woman who stood there with her hands folded neatly over each other at her waist.

The woman, dressed in a knee-length black dress covered by a stiff and starched, white apron, her dark hair tied back in a black scarf, reminded me of photos of European peasants in a magazine. Her sweet face was currently devoid of any expression, as she watched the pan sink to the bottom of the sudsy water.

'Maria, *abbiamo bisogno di aiuto*,' said the man. He switched to atrocious English, 'Help, we must hava the help, *il mio amore*.'

The woman, who I presumed was Maria, answered in a soft voice that bore the same accent as the man, though her grasp of English was better. 'I know Carlo, but finding the good help is no easy. Looka what the last girl she was like – useless.'

Now seemed like a good time to interrupt before Carlo threw anything else.

'Hi, I don't mean to bother you but, can I get a cup of tea.'

Both faces swung in my direction. Two sets of brown eyes stared at me blankly for a moment before Carlo flashed me a huge mouthy smile, all teeth.

'Of course Piccola, come, come,' he said, waving his hand in a motion to join them in the kitchen. 'The urn she is a stilla hot. We close at two, but for you no problemo.'

'Oh, I'm sorry, I didn't know you were closed,' I said as I stepped into the kitchen, 'The sign on the door still reads open.'

Maria took three dainty steps towards the urn and reached up to the shelf above her head for a clean cup and saucer. She measured a generous scoop of tea into a pot and filled it with boiling water from the urn.

'Come, you taka the seat in the dining room and I a bring it out, Piccola.'

I lifted my brow in puzzlement. 'Piccola? What does Piccola mean?' I asked.

A sweet smile touched her face and a small sparkle glinted in her eye, 'Piccola, she a means little one. Now come, come outta the hot kitchen.'

Collecting everything onto a tray, Maria led me out of the kitchen to a table under the noisy fan, then reached over and turned the sign on the door to closed.

I plucked up my courage.

'Excuse me, Maria, is it?'

She nodded.

I took a small steadying breath.

'I couldn't help overhearing...you need some help here in the café. I've just arrived in town and I'm looking for work. I don't suppose you'd consider me for the job. I'm honest and a very hard worker.'

The smile that bloomed across Maria's face lifted my depression and my lips. She turned her head towards the kitchen and raised her voice.

'Carlo, we hava the new waitress.'

And just like that I had a job.

* * *

The alarm awoke me at five-thirty. It took a moment to adjust my sleep confused brain before I remembered I was to start work at six.

Dressed in my black skirt and a white tee-shirt, I pulled a jacket on to ward off the morning chill and quietly slipped out of the house.

Carlo was heating the grills and Maria setting tables when I trotted in the back door. I pulled on an apron and pitched in to help by setting out the salt and pepper shakers, sugar bowls and bottles of tomato sauce in the dining room. A few hardy patrons were already standing on the street outside our window. As Maria quickly instructed me in my duties, she flung the door open and stood back. From nowhere a rush of people poured in. Pen and pad in hand, I started at the first table and took what turned out to be the order of the day…breakfast.

Maria pointed to the hatch, so I stuck my head in and said, 'Four Bonzas please, Carlo.'

Maria nodded and said, 'Faster Piccola, don't-a wait for the meal. Carlo, he will call when it'sa ready. We must hurry, soon ita be busy.'

Busy! The café was already full. I hurried along and took as many orders as I could and then Carlo started yelling, 'Grubatas up.'

I dashed to the servery, collected the biggest and best-looking meals I'd ever seen – Carlo's version of an Australian breakfast…a Bonza – bacon, fried eggs and sausages covered with an enormous pile of hot chips, all accompanied by a mountain of hot buttery toast.

Maria was running mugs of complimentary coffee and tea to all the patrons.

The café décor may have been basic - six steel framed tables with yellow laminated tops and matching chairs lined each wall, sat on rusty-brown coloured linoleum covered floorboards that creaked and groaned when you walked on it - but there was nothing basic about the food or its popularity.

Carlo, loud and voluble in the kitchen, happily crashed and talked his way through the workday, rapidly producing meal after magnificent meal.

Once I found my rhythm of seating customers, taking orders and payment, clearing, cleaning, setting up tables, delivering the food to hungry patrons and then doing it all over again, Maria retired to the kitchen and stoically manned the sink, quietly dealing with the huge volume of dirty dishes that came her way. I swear half of Kalgoorlie came to the Victory Café for breakfast before nine and the rest of the town came in after. Carlo's meals were in huge demand and I was run off my feet keeping up.

I loved it.

* * *

Saturday morning the café was busier than the weekday mornings. I'd expected it to be quieter, a day off for the workingmen. Boy, was I wrong! Miners living in camps on the outskirts of civilisation, working their gold claims, came into town in their droves. They spent their Friday night in a pub, guzzling enormous quantities of beer. Saturday morning they recovered from the excess of drink with a Carlo breakfast, then returned to their solitude. The beer fumes that reeked from them that morning had me propping the door open for ventilation, until I got used to the smell. The café opened its doors at six-thirty and hangover or not, the line of patrons ran down the street.

As I cleaned down the last table of the day, Carlo and Maria wandered in from the kitchen carrying a basket of freshly baked hot bread and a lasagne. The wonderful aroma started my stomach growling.

'Come, eat,' said Carlo, as he settled at a table.

'You havea done well this week, Piccola. Tomorrow she is Sunday...we rest,' said Maria. She handed me a plate of food and laughed. 'Next week we do it all again.'

'Other than Sundays, do you ever close, have a holiday?' I asked.

'The only time we-a close is Christmas Day. No, the miners, he woulda riot if we-a no open,' said Carlo with a bellowing laugh. His laughter was infectious and I chortled along with him.

I made a pig of myself on Carlo's delicious food, eating like it was a new hobby. I let out a delicate burp and said, 'That was an awesome meal...I'll just wash these plates.'

'No, Piccola, you-a go enjoy your weekend,' said Maria, removing the plate from my hand.

I leapt to my feet. 'Thanks, I'll see you both on Monday.'

I made a careful scrutiny of the street before leaving the safety of the doorway.

* * *

Sunlight hit my eye. I awoke with a groan. Sunlight, I sat bolt upright in bed. Shit I'd slept in. I checked the clock. Nine...oh blast, I was so bloody late. Why hadn't my stupid alarm gone off? With funds starting to run low the last thing I needed was to lose my job for sleeping in. I rolled out of bed and grabbed my work clothes...then woke up. I smacked myself in the forehead with the heel of my hand. You stupid idiot, it's Sunday.

Up now, with adrenaline still racing through my veins, I pulled on a pair of shorts and tee-shirt instead of work clothes and headed out for a stroll in the fresh morning air. As I was about to turn into Hay Street, a hand fell on my shoulder. My heart nearly flew out my mouth and I let out a small squeal.

I spun around and gasped. 'Crap, Sandra...you scared the bejesus out of me.'

'Sorry Connie, I didn't mean to startle you. I thought I had better stop you going down there,' she said, pointing down the street towards a row of bright tin huts with their dutch-doors painted in bold prime colours. 'That's the knock-shop district, and unless you want to get picked up by some sex starved miner, I'd stay away.'

'Knock shop?'

'Yeah, the knockers. Kalgoorlie's red-light district. You know prostitutes, brothel. Hay Street's quite famous and is known as the most legal illegal street in the country.' I felt my lips form a circle. 'Where are you off too anyway?'

'Just rubber-necking,' I said, 'Checking out the sights. You?'

'Avoiding my aunt and church. Do you mind if I join you? I can give you the lowdown on everyone and everything. I've lived in this town a long time.'

Sandra and I gasbagged as we made our way around the streets. She filled me in on the more disreputable history of the town and had me in a fit of laughter.

'Hey, how about some lunch? Being Sunday, most places are closed but the Towers Motel dining room will be open.'

I glanced over to where she pointed and felt the blood drain away from my cheeks and pool into my belly, like cold sludge. Parked outside a room in the motel's car park was a light-blue Kingswood sedan with Victorian number plates.

'Th-thanks Sandra, but I think I'll give it a miss.'

'You okay?'

'Yeah, I'm just tired. I think I'll head back now.'

Sandra gave me a puzzled look and then gave the parked car the same look. 'Okay, if you're sure. I should really go visit my aunt anyway, explain why I've neglected my soul this week and listen to a lecture on the moral delinquency of society – fun times. I'll catch ya later.'

As soon as she turned the corner, I ran.

* * *

Christmas came and went. I spent the day writing to Sarah and Dad, telling them about Maria and Carlo, my job and the life I was now leading. I hid the letters in the back of my journal, knowing it was too dangerous to send them. Maybe one day.

I had kept a careful eye out for the blue car, wondering if I needed to skip town, knowing I couldn't afford to just yet, but I didn't see it again. Must have been a coincidence, just someone passing through, but I never let my guard down. I remained constantly vigilant.

I awoke to the soft buzzing of my alarm and cursed. It was January 16th, my birthday. So now, I was twenty-two years old and a full twelve months had passed since I'd last seen my sister and father. I missed them both terribly. I can't tell you how much it hurt, the ache just settling over me like a fog. I dragged myself to work and quietly got on with business.

Maria noticed my distraction, 'Piccola, are you okay? Is something she wrong?'

'Nothing's wrong, Maria. I'm just feeling a little off colour,' I lied, giving her a small smile. 'I'll be alright again tomorrow.'

Maria, the sweetheart that she is, said, 'Go-a home Piccola, we-a cope.'

'No Maria, I'm okay, I'd rather work.'

I was much happier here than brooding in my room. To distract myself, I tuned into the customers and the gossip they'd picked up in the pub the previous night. Everyone was talking about the same thing. Setting a breakfast order in front of Scotty and Lanky Luke at table six, I blatantly listened to their conversation.

'I saw Ironstone and Dazza in the pub last night, they're back from working their Gwalia claim,' said Lanky, with a shaking hand lifting his coffee cup to his mouth. 'Lucky bastards...having two gold claims.'

'I heard Dazza's signed up for the footy season again this year,' replied Scotty, ignoring the obvious jealousy. He watched his mate slop coffee down the side of the cup. 'You wanna lay off that stuff, Luke...it's not good for you.'

'Yeah, you're probably right. You gonna play footy again this year?'

I delivered a meal to table nine and a similar conversation was under way.

'Ironstone Jack was telling me...'

And so it was, at every table. Boy, these blokes must be popular.

I reset table seven, gave the tabletop a final swipe with my cloth and stepped back. I fell into the arms of a tall, rangy and very handsome man, with an unlit rollie cigarette hanging from the corner of his mouth.

He removed a scruffy old hat from his head, revealing untidy dark blonde hair that was in desperate need of a cut but somehow suited him, and said, 'Sorry Miss, I hope I didn't hurt you.'

Drinking in piercing blue eyes, I felt my toes curl. A lone butterfly did a somersault around my stomach. Whoa! What was that all about?

Accompanying this sex on two legs was a short, stocky and very handsome dark-haired young man. He looked to be about 19 or 20 years of age. I recalled myself with a start, stepped out of his arms and blathered, 'Seven is vacant...if you gents like to take a seat, I'll be right back for your order.'

The young man let out a machine gun laugh.

'Hahaha, hear that Jack, we're gents, mate.'

He flashed me a killer smile, full of white dazzling teeth, I couldn't help myself, the corners of my mouth lifted.

The man named Jack murmured, 'Thanks Miss,' as he settled into the seat that gave him the best a view of the café.

His partner followed suit, sitting opposite and said to me, 'No need to take our order Miss, just tell Carlo we'll have the Ironstone and Dazza.'

Puzzled, here was a breakfast I hadn't heard of, I returned to the kitchen. Over the loud pop and sizzle of frying bacon and sausages, I yelled to the busy cook.

'Carlo, two Ironstones and Dazzas! Does that make sense to you?'

Carlo's lips parted in a big toothy smile. With his cheeks glowing from sweat and the heat of the kitchen, he looked like a cherub. 'Yes-a Piccola, now go make a two big cups of the black coffee, strong...ver-a strong and take them toast, lotsa toast. As Dazza would say, to tide them over.'

Tide them over...what the hell!

'Okay Carlo, two strong black coffees and toast coming up.'

I reached to the high shelf and grabbed two of the oversized enamel mugs we used for the miners. I added two heaped teaspoons of coffee into each, hoping that would be strong enough. Juggling the coffee and a plateful of liberally buttered toast, being careful not to dump the lot in anyone's lap, I made my way back to table seven. I scanned the dining room as a hush descended. The young man stood behind his chair, commanding attention.

'A bear walks into a bar and says, Give me a whiskey...*(pause)*...and coke. The barman asks, why the big pause and the bear said, don't know mate, I was born with 'em, I guess.'

Laughter erupted and someone sang out, 'You're a right one Dazza, how the hell do ya come up with 'em.'

Ironstone Jack, a smile tugging at the corner of his mouth, looked up as I approached. He removed the unlit cigarette that hung from his lip and carefully laid it in the ashtray.

'Your order's on its way,' I said as I slid the plate of toast onto the table.

The bell over the door tinkled, another group of chattering men entered. I busied myself seating them. Just as I finished taking their orders, Carlo's deep voice bellowed his Italian Australian version of *Grubs Up*. I rushed to the hatch to collect the food. The size of the feed amazed me. Carlo, famous for the generous portions of his meals, had outdone himself. Two platters – not plates – were loaded with T-bone steaks, lamb chops, sausages, a mound of crispy bacon, grilled tomato halves, baked beans and a mountain of chips. On top, four perfectly fried eggs with the golden yolks still runny. Staggering under the weight of the tray, I placed the platters in front of Ironstone Jack and Dazza without dropping them.

'Ahhh, bonza. I've missed this,' said Dazza, taking a seat and rubbing his hands together in delight.

He snatched up his knife and fork and tucked into his food with gusto.

'Thanks, Miss,' said Jack, lifting the salt shaker and liberally dousing his eggs.

'Please, call me Connie.'

He smiled, his blue eyes crinkling at the corners, 'Hi, I'm Jack. The cheeky young bugger is Dan or Dazza, whatever you prefer,' he said, pointing at his mate with his knife.

I nodded my head in greeting and said, 'Nice to meet you both.'

The bell tinkled again as men left. Others entered. I dashed over to clear and reset the tables. When I had a moment, I glanced over at table seven. Jack and Dan were just settling back in their chairs, making appreciative noises of contentment. In front of them lay two empty platters.

'I hope you enjoyed your breakfast gents,' I said. What the hell...life's too short to brood over a stupid birthday, besides here were a couple of handsome men, so I asked cheekily, 'Did you have enough to eat...can I get you anything else?'

Waving his cup in the air, Jack said, 'I could go another cup of your excellent coffee, thanks Connie. How about you, Dan?'

'Nah, mate, I'm good. That bonza feed should tide me over till lunch,' he said, rubbing a hand contentedly over his trim stomach. He pushed his chair back, 'I need to get down to the police station and then get that government letter into the mail. You got this?'

'Yeah, lad, go on with ya,' replied Jack, cocking his head towards the door, 'I'll catch you up, later.'

Dan leapt to his feet, flashed me a dazzling smile.

So that's how he'd earned his nickname.

'Thanks, Connie,' he said, waving a hand over his shoulder as he dashed from the cafe.

I collected the dirty dishes from the table, my mood lifted, and said, 'One strong black coffee coming up.'

Ironstone Jack stayed, savouring his second coffee for another half an hour. I was conscious of his eyes following me as I worked. When it became obvious his table was needed, he rose to his full six feet, replaced the unlit rollie into the corner of his mouth and doffed his scruffy hat. He gave me a two-fingered salute and sauntered with a casual lope from the café, chatting to people on his way out.

It was another week before I saw him again.

* * *

Every week we went through the same routine. The enormous platter of food, the second coffee, Jack watching me work, a two-fingered salute and then he was gone again. At the end of the second month, I wondered if Jack was ever going to say anything other than, thanks miss. Then Dazza opened his big mouth.

'Jack, you ever going to talk to her, or are ya just gonna sit there like a big goofball, watching, for the rest of your life?'

I didn't hear Jack's reply, but I heard the harsh scrape of his chair as he rose abruptly from his seat and left. To say I was disappointed was an understatement. The nicest and best-looking man I had met in a long time had probably walked out of my life for good.

Bugger.

14

Chapter Fourteen

My shift ended, I was hot, tired and my feet were on fire. They ached abominably. Depression formed a lead weight low in my belly. A blast of hot air stung my cheeks as I left the café. My step faltered. Ironstone Jack, clutching his battered Akubra in work-roughened hands, an unlit rollie hanging from the corner of his mouth, was leaning against a post.

He straightened when I emerged and said, 'Connie, may I walk you home?'

His shy and gentle manner bought a smile to my lips. All the negativity disappeared. My feet were no longer a problem. I decided to take a risk and see what the future held in store for me.

Slipping my arm through his I said, 'About bloody time...I thought you'd never ask.'

No one could accuse Jack of being talkative. He strolled along with me on his arm, a smile on his flushed face, but no words fell from his lips. It was frustrating. To fill the silence I blathered away, giving him the rundown on Carlo and Maria and the café.

Still nothing.

I racked my brain and recalled a funny incident that had happened during the week. I chattered away like babbling twit.

'I'm sorry Jack, here I've been talking your ears off,' I said, trying to encourage him into speech. 'I've not let you get a word in...how was your week?'

We arrived at the boarding house gate and Jack leant against it giving a soft laugh. He took my hands in his and gazed down, my whole body tingled but I had no intention of rushing things.

'I love hearing you talk, it's fresh, cheery and interesting. I have little to say – my life would bore you,' he said, lifting a stray piece of hair from my face and smoothing it back behind my ear.

'No Jack, it wouldn't...it's about you. How could that be boring?'

I caught a flash of white teeth, and a sexy little dimple formed in his left cheek. My heart gave an almighty thump, while the butterflies that had been casually fluttering around in my stomach leapt into action.

Jack removed his hat and twirled it around in his hand. A small flush stained his cheeks. 'Connie, there's a movie showing in the town hall on Friday night. Would you like to go?'

'I'd love to, Jack,' I said.

'Right...I'll pick you up at seven.' He straightened, removed the rollie from his mouth and leant down to place a soft kiss on my cheek. It tingled and my face warmed. Jack gave me a two-fingered salute and strolled away.

I stood with my hand on the kiss mark, staring, long after he'd turned the corner. A warm glow ran through my veins.

* * *

Friday seemed to take forever to arrive. Nerves and self-doubt interrupted my anticipation.

Should I be doing this?

The events of six months ago were still raw and painful. Guilt and remorse were my constant companions. Finally, I had a stern talk to myself.

Get a grip Connie. It is only a movie...what harm could it do?

A rapping on my bedroom door startled me.

'Come in.'

Sandra looked in and whistled.

'Very nice, Pixie.' She gave me a cheeky wink, pouted her lips and said, 'By the way, there's a handsome devil on the front porch...pixie hunting. You interested?'

I giggled – she always made me laugh.

'Thanks, Sandra. We're off to the movies, what about you?'

She shook her head. 'Nah, got other fish to fry.'

'Well have a nice time.'

I picked up my purse and hurried out to greet Jack. I'd made a tremendous sacrifice for our date and spent some of my precious funds on a pretty floral dress that didn't look too odd with my trusty, well-worn tennis shoes.

Jack kissed my cheek and said, 'You look beautiful, Connie.'

A smile of satisfaction tugged at my lips...good I'd not wasted my money.

'Thanks, Jack. You're looking very handsome. Like the hair.'

He ran a hand over his neatly trimmed crop, smirked and stuck his unlit rollie back into the corner of his mouth. He took my hand.

'Are you ready or do you need to grab a jacket, in case it gets cold?'

'I don't need a jacket...these autumn evenings are beautiful and warm, not like the eastern states.'

Oh bugger! You've gotta watch your mouth, Connie, be careful what you say.

'Yeah, I went east once. In fact, that's where I met young Dan. Big cities are not my cup of tea at all.' I don't know if my consternation showed on my face, but Jack didn't ask the obvious, like...where are you from? Instead, he told me a little of himself. 'I've been to the big smoke of Perth a couple of times, it was bearable...just. You ever been to Perth?'

Checking my internal meter, I thought it'd be a safe question to answer.

'No, not yet, I'm saving that adventure for the future. I'm quite happy living in Kal for now. I've got a good job and have met some great people.'

'So, you reckon you'll be sticking around for a while?'

'For the moment...but who knows what the future will bring.'

* * *

We strolled along, hand in hand. The warm evening air brushed my face like a pleasant balm. Jack and I were discussing the movie we'd just finished watching, *The Poseidon Adventure*. Suddenly Jack started laughing.

'Fess up, Jack, what's tickled your funny bone?' I asked, my curiosity, among other things, aroused.

He shook his head in amusement and said, 'It's just struck me...Poseidon. Poseidon is the mining company in Laverton – that's north-east from here. Bloody thing...oh, excuse the French...it's just gone belly up and here we've been watching another Poseidon do the same.'

Our laughter echoed down the empty street. Still chuckling, we strolled the footpath from Wilson Street into Hannan Street. A life-size statue of a man sitting on a rock came into view. My feet halted, pulling Jack to a stop.

'Oh, how stunning.' I ran my fingers along its contours, studying the exquisite curves the artist had captured. The bronze, still warm to the touch from a day in the sun, felt alive. 'Do you know anything about its history, Jack? Like who it is or how old it is?'

'It was commissioned in 1929, Connie...so I guess it's been sitting here a while. That's old Paddy Hannan...he was Irish you know...he discovered the first gold nugget that started a gold rush in these parts,' Jack explained.

I circled the figure. The play of the streetlight was fascinating.

'Did he really, I didn't know that. So, do you and Dazza have much luck in that department? You know, finding gold?' I asked, my curiosity nudging me into a delicate area.

You would think by now I'd have learnt not to ask too many questions.

'We do alright,' was his uninformative reply, 'We make a steady living.'

I glanced up at his face – it was blank except for a slight crinkle in the corner of his eyes.

'It's an unusual life, you know, Jack.'

'What is?'

'The way you live.' To ease his mind that I wasn't interested in discussing his money, I moved the subject on. 'Will you be doing it forever...or do you intend to retire in luxury on a beach somewhere?'

'No, I won't be doing it forever. We live this life because it's something Dan and I can make a living at. The life chose us, not the other way around. I'll tell you about it one day.' His eyes smiled and eased the tension that had been there. 'As for striking it rich, well who knows, maybe I already have.'

He reclaimed my hand, kissed my fingers and tucked them into the crook of his arm. I felt easier as we continued our slow wander down the deserted street. The sound of loud voices, raised to be heard over the laughter and talk of others spewed from the open pub windows. The noise flowed down the street in a steady stream. I moved closer to Jack, tense, as we skirted past the Kalgoorlie Hotel's service alley. As we did a noise made me stop. I swore I heard whimpering.

'Jack,' I whispered, as I took a squint into the gloom. The alley looked empty, except for trash. 'Did you hear that? There's someone down there. It sounds like they're hurt.'

'Stay here, Connie,' said Jack, and he took a step out of the light.

The whimpering came again. I couldn't just stand there doing nothing, so I tucked myself in behind Jack and followed. He turned and looked at me. I waited to be told off for not obeying instructions. Instead, he took my hand, not arguing. My heart fluttered with admiration for a man who would allow me to be myself. Together we crept towards the noise. It seemed to come from behind the bins and a pile of cardboard boxes left out for morning collection. The smell of discarded foodstuffs and stale beer was rank. I wanted to gag, instead I took to breathing through my mouth. I used my foot to push some dry refuse out of the way. A box near my shoe moved. I flinched and jumped back.

God, I hope it's not a rat, please don't let it be a rat.

I leant forward, pinched the edge of the box and held my breath ready to scream if something horrible jumped out at me. I lifted...and there he was.

Painfully thin, with huge soulful brown eyes and floppy soft ears, a golden-brown puppy. He stared up at me and whimpered again. I fell in love.

Ignoring the dirt, I fell to my knees and held out my hand. 'Oh, Jack...I've found a golden nugget.'

Jack reached around me and with gentle hands scooped the dog up.

'Is he alright?' I asked, following them back towards the street.

Holding the puppy cupped in his hand under the street light, Jack turned it left then right to check it over.

'He doesn't seem to be injured, Connie. He looks like he could do with a good feed though.'

I put a gentle hand on the top of the pup's head and stroked.

'We have to help him, Jack. We can't just leave him here.'

'We, Connie?'

'Well...you, Jack. I'm not allowed animals where I live, but you...you have all that bush. He won't be any trouble. Oh Jack...he's just a baby...please, please help him.'

Jack's lip twitched, he slipped the pup inside the front of his flannel shirt. The dog snuggled down, and with the tip of his nose and one eye showing, gave a contented sigh. His eyes closed.

'Come on, Nugget, let's go get you a feed,' said Jack.

I threw my arms around them both and squeezed tight.

'You wonderful, wonderful man,' I cried, a happy tear rolled down my cheek. Jack's arms tightened around me...he seemed to enjoy the moment.

I was lost...Nugget and Jack had just stolen my heart.

15

Chapter Fifteen

Jack sat in his usual seat, the front of his shirt bulging out in a round lump. It gave a little wriggle and Nugget popped his head out, announcing his appearance with a happy *yip*. I scratched the top of his head and he closed his eyes in ecstasy.

'Two breakfasts coming up and a bowl of milk,' I said with a smile. 'How's our little Nugget this morning, Jack?'

'He's bonza, Connie. Had a good feed of Carnation Milk and slept all night.'

'I blame you for my sleepless night, Connie. You've turned Jack soft on me. He let the little bugger snuggle up in bed with him. I had to put up with the pair of 'em, snoring all night,' said Dazza, with a soft rat-a-tat laugh. His gaze shot rapidly from my face to Jack's and back again, absorbing the change in our relationship.

'Don't worry, lad,' said Jack, a smug smile lifting the corner of his mouth, 'Nugget won't be sharing my bed again. From now on he'll be sleeping with you.'

'Be buggered...I won't be going soft over no stray mutt. Your dog, your problem, mate,' said Dan, leaning forward to give the pup an affectionate scratch between the eyes.

Leaving them to tease each other, I headed towards the kitchen, in a haze of happiness. The bell over the café door dinged. I glanced over. The smile of greeting froze on my lips. Two policemen stood in the doorway, staring in my direction. Judging by the stripes on the older officer's shirt, he was a seasoned sergeant. His companion, who didn't look old enough to be out of school, bore the markings of a constable. Moving fast, I quick-stepped into the kitchen and stood out of view of them, but in a place where I could watch their movements through the hatch. Greeting patrons along the way, the cops casually made their way to Jack and Dazza's table.

Carlo, pouring a large scoop of hot chips over a meal, paused and asked, 'Everything a-okay, Piccola?'

I looked over at him and plastered a false smile to my lips.

'Yep, Carlo, everything's hunky dory. I need an Ironstone and Dazza thanks.'

I mentally pulled myself together, ducked away from my spy hole and got on with making coffee and toast.

I loaded my tray, scanned the action in the dining room, to make sure the coast was clear, and dived back into the fray. The police officers were having an intense chat with Scotty and a very unhappy looking Lanky Luke at the far end of the room. The two miners had been in the act of rising from their seats, their empty plates stacked in a neat pile for me to collect. That would be Scotty, always considerate, unlike his short and creepy mate.

Before Carlo or Maria noticed I was neglecting my duties, I made a quick dash to Jack's table with my tray. Hastily arranging the coffee, milk and toast on the table, I rushed back to the kitchen. Fiddling around with unnecessary tasks, wasting time at the coffee counter, I prayed the cops would leave before I had to take out any more meals.

The door's bell rang, catching my attention. I watched the officers walk outside, talking with a group of men who were also leaving.

'Grubatas up, Connie,' whispered Carlo softly in my ear. He hung over my shoulder and looked quizzically into the dining room. 'You sure youa okay?'

Patting Carlo on the shoulder, I smiled.

'Yes, Carlo, I'm fine. Just keeping an eye on things. It's so busy today.'

Taking the loaded platters from his hands I hurried out.

'Was that the police I just saw in here?' I asked, as I slid the meals in front of Jack and Dan. I kept my voice as bland as possible.

'Sure was,' said Dazza. He uncapped the tomato sauce bottle and drowned his chips in sauce. 'They're looking for a couple of blokes who knocked over the hardware store and the bottle shop, yesterday arvo. Rumour has it, Coolgardie Lad and Lanky Luke were in the Shamrock Hotel last night, flashing a wad of cash around. Everyone knows Luke's always broke...he sticks all his money up his arm. He reckons it wasn't them and is claiming police harassment... 'cause they asked him where he was yesterday. Stupid bugger, he won't get away with it. The sarge is smarter than him.'

'I can't stand dishonesty. A man works hard for what's his. Anyway, Sergeant Henderson's a good copper, he'll sort it out,' said Jack. The tightness that was easing in my chest came back with vengeance at his words.

* * *

Jack was waiting for me as I stepped out the café door at the end of my shift. I hooked my arm through his, acting chipper, but I was worried. If he ever asked me about my life before we met, what would I say? I didn't want to lie, in fact I couldn't. I loved my new life in Kalgoorlie, but it might be better if I left before my predicament hurt Jack. If I left soon the only one hurt would be me. This man had stolen my heart and the thought of losing him from of my life was devastating.

My chirpiness didn't last beyond our first few steps. My mood sank and formed a hard rock inside my chest. I remained quiet all the way home. We stood at the gate and Jack lifted my chin with his knuckle and placed a gentle kiss on my lips. I tingled in all the right places and had a powerful urge to launch myself at him. I refrained. I was still gun-shy after Jerry's treatment of me.

'Connie, do you wanna come visit our camp...get a taste of gold mining, Jack style? You can also make sure I'm doing the right thing by our little friend here?' he said, pointing to his lumpy shirt.

I looked at Jack and Nugget, who were both giving me soulful eyes and smiled. One more week wouldn't hurt, would it? I'd just have to be careful, not get too attached.

'That sounds terrific, Jack, but I don't have a car. I can't drive anyway...I've never learnt, so getting there and back would be a problem.'

'No problem, Connie. I'll drive you, it only takes an hour. I'll pick you up after work and run you home early evening,' he said and then with a cheeky grin, tilted his head towards the house. 'You tell nosey, Ma Norma, I'll have you home by curfew. Okay?'

Grinning like a loon, I said, 'Will do, Jack. You have a safe week and I'll see you next Saturday.'

16

Chapter Sixteen

Leaning on the front fender of a gun-metal grey Land Rover, arms and legs crossed, staring at his shoes, was Jack. Sitting in the front between the driver and passenger seats was Nugget. I carefully checked the street before stepping out of the door and opening my arms. Jack drew me against his chest in a fierce hug. He released me with a gentle kiss on the cheek. Nugget gave me a happy dog smile. His pink and black spotty tongue hung out the side of his mouth and nearly reached his paws. A transformation had taken place in our new friend – his thin frame was beginning to plump and his golden coat shone with health.

'Good lord, Jack, what have you been feeding, Nugget? He looks like a different dog.'

Jack slid in behind the steering wheel, scruffed the top of Nugget's head with his knuckles and started the engine.

'Carnation Milk and roo meat.'

I ran my fingers through Nugget's soft fur. He crooned in delight when I rubbed his ears.

'Roo meat?'

'Yeah, kangaroo. The bloody things are all over the place. They come into camp all the time. Pinch the bread if we don't remember to lock it away. They're good eating...we shoot one occasionally for the spit. The wild pigs and goats are better though and there's plenty of them in the scrub.'

'Do they pinch the bread as well?' I asked, curious as to the habits of animals I'd only heard of as being farm creatures.

'Yeah...often. They charge through the camp and knock over the tents. We've gotta keep all the food locked away in metal boxes. The cold stuff's safe enough, that's kept in a kerosene fridge Dan's roped to a tree. The buggers haven't worked out how to get it open yet. Mind you, I've had to chase a goat or two off the top. Like monkeys they are...they'll climb anything if the urge takes 'em. I'm hoping to get the shack built before they work out how to open the bloody door.'

I laughed at the image of a goat standing on the top of the fridge, surveying the world.

'Did I hear right, you're building a shack?'

Changing into top gear, Jack pressed the accelerator hard and the Rover responded with a roar.

'Yep. The lad and I sleep in tents or out under the stars...depending how hot it is. That's great most of the time but it's not for everyone. The framework's up...a basic square. It'll be clad in cement sheets and roofed with tin. I'll line the inside walls with hessian, that'll help keep the dust down...it's also a good insulator.'

Drawing an image of the one-room shack in my mind, a thought struck me, 'But what about a bathroom, Jack?'

'Don't need one. We've got a great dunny already,' said Jack, 'Out by the main water tank is a useless old drill hole. It proved to be the perfect size for a cut off forty-four-gallon drum. Dan was very inventive – he glued an old wooden toilet seat to the top of the drum and named it the *Thunderbox*. It's a great place for sitting and thinking, or watching the sun rise and set, depending on the time of day.'

I couldn't help myself. I started to laugh so hard I nearly peed myself. The image of them sitting in the middle of the bush like that, really tickled my funny bone.

I brushed the laughter tears from my eyes and took a deep breath before asking, 'So how long have you and Dan been prospecting and mining.'

'I've been living in the bush since I was twelve.'

'Wow...didn't you have a family?'

There I go again...opening my big mouth and asking questions.

'I never knew my father, he died in 1944, fighting in northern New Guinea. Mum got pregnant with me on his last leave home. He died not long after that, never knowing he was going to be a dad.' Jack's voice was devoid of all emotion, it was like he was reading out a newspaper article. If possible, his voice became even blander. 'She remarried when I was about six and we moved to Beverley. My stepfather was a mongrel, always ready to use his fists on me or my mum. Anyway, one day he went too far. She died. The authorities put me in care of my step-aunt, his older sister. She was cut from the same cloth as him...I wasn't going down that track again. So I took off, hitched a ride to the Goldfields and have lived in the bush ever since.'

I could feel my eyes widen with each word he spoke.

'Oh my God, Jack. That's one hell of a story. I'm sorry about your mum...and you've been alone since you were twelve, that's tough. You don't have to tell me anymore, if you don't want to.'

Jack continued in his calm voice, 'No it's fine, Connie. I don't get caught up in the past. I've found you have to move on, leave your demons behind and work for something better. Anyway, I wouldn't have told you if I didn't want you to know.'

It honoured me that Jack would tell me something so personal, but I still wasn't ready to return the confidence. I changed the subject.

'So, tell me about Dan. How did you two meet?'

Jack gave a snort of laughter.

'Do you remember I said I'd been to the eastern states?'

'Yeah,' I said, sucking in a small breath and held it.

Please don't say Melbourne.

'In '63 I went to Sydney for the Ashes – the pommy cricket team was touring Australia. I'd had a good year prospecting. Being twenty years old and flush with money, I decided to treat myself and go and watch the Third Test at the SCG.'

'Wow, Jack...that must have been exciting.'

'Sure was, especially for a bush lad like me. First time on a plane. And the people. I didn't know so many existed.' I studied his face as he continued on with his tale. It took on a look of awe and excitement as he remembered the experience. 'The cricket was great...we beat the Poms by eight wickets, and drew the next two, so got to keep the Ashes.' Jack gave a happy sigh which amused me. I think cricket might be one of Jack's passions. 'Anyway, after close of play on the last day, I went for a wander around Sydney. You know, to have a gander at the Harbour Bridge, ride the ferry, and do all the things I may never get to do or see again. Anyway, while I was playing tourist, this young lad – so skinny and underfed the wind could have blown him away – tried to pinch me wallet. The lad was Dan. He was eleven years old and all alone in the world. His folks had died in a house fire, and as he'd no other family to take care of him, he'd been sent to a boy's home. It was brutal, he ran away and was living on the mean streets of Sydney. The lad was starving...even Blind Freddy could see that. I didn't bother with the cops. I took him out for a meal instead. He seemed like a decent enough kid, who just needed a helping hand, so I asked him if he wanted to come gold mining with me and here we are, eight years later. I'll never forget the date, it was the sixteenth of January.'

Before I could stop it old blather mouth took over and said, 'Huh, that's my birthday.'

'Well, there you go, it's also the date we met,' said Jack, giving me a wink, 'So, a great date all round.'

Flicking the indicator, Jack turned onto a faint, red-dirt track. He dropped the vehicle into a low gear, the Rover's tires skidded once before getting a grip on the loose surface. The engine groaned as the wheels ground over the rough terrain, brushing past a row of scrub, through a clutch of trees and into an open clearing. Here was the camp.

A large sandalwood tree shaded the main living and cooking areas. Tents formed a semi-circle off to one side. The men had scattered chunky wooden seats in a random group around the fire pit. Dan was relaxing on one, watching a juicy piece of meat rotate on a metal spit. As I climbed from the vehicle, the divine smell of the cooking hit me. My mouth filled with saliva and my stomach growled.

I walked towards him, smirking as I passed the kerosene fridge tied to the white gum. The afternoon sun caught my eye. I shaded my eyes and saw the windmill blades rotate slowly as they fed the steel water tank elevated on a large wooden stand. Sticking out the side of the tank was a pipe with a shower head attached. Beyond this very rustic bathroom was the famous toilet. Located under the hanging branch of a wattle tree, it faced towards the morning sunrise. At the base of Thunderbox was a small wooden box step, which served as storage for paper and access to the seat. The guys had thought of everything.

Jack lifted Nugget down from the cab and the dog did a happy puppy dance, which involved spinning and chasing his tail. He made me laugh. Nugget spotted Dan, gave a small 'woof,' and bounded towards the relaxing man. Dan's face broke into a brilliant and happy smile. He put his hand down and scooped the pup up. Cupping his hand he gave Nugget a vigorous knuckle rubdown along the spine.

Nugget groaned in delight and Dan cooed.

'Who's a good boy then?'

'Well, I'm glad to see you haven't gone all soft and gooey over the mutt, Dan,' I said, watching his antics with delight. The love of the pup was evident by his actions. 'Not playing footy today, is the season over?'

'G'day, Connie, welcome. No footy today, we have a bye,' he said.

Dan then surprised the hell out of me, he leapt up, rushed over and scooped me up in a big, warm, bear hug. He smelt of wood smoke and spice...nice.

'Meat'll be ready around four, Jack. You've got plenty of time to show Connie the sights,' he said over my head.

'Thanks lad, that's great mate. You can put Connie down now.'

Dan loosened his strong arms and released me. 'Connie, would you like a drink, or do you want to take a look around first?'

'Snoop first...then a cup of tea,' I answered. I found their easy affection warming.

Taking a gentle grasp of my hand, Jack led me around the campsite, pointing out its redeeming features. We left the clearing and strolled out into the bush a few metres, to view the shack that was under construction. The smell of roasting meat, eucalyptus and hot earth hung in the air. My stomach gave a loud rumble.

'Whoa there, Connie, I better get some tucker into you before you cause an earthquake,' said Jack, his eyes crinkling in amusement.

'Sorry, Jack,' I said. I felt the blood suffusing my cheeks in embarrassment. 'It's a long time since my apple this morning.'

I placed my hand on my stomach, trying to deaden the noise. It was determined to be heard – and growled again.

'Don't apologise. An apple's not enough for a busy girl like you. You should take better care of yourself.'

'I do take good care, Jack. Carlo and Maria are forever sharing their wonderful meals with me. Besides, I refuse to pay Norma's exorbitant price for use of the kitchen, when an apple will do me fine.'

'Well, I'm sure we can do better than a piece of fruit. The goat will be ready soon, you can eat as much as you like.'

We had wandered for nearly an hour. Jack, had done most of the talking. His love and respect for the bush shone through in his conversation and it gave me a real insight into this wonderful man. Everything I learned about him was good.

With contentment, I clutched the enamel mug of tea in one hand and a delicious piece of roasted goat's meat in the other. I sprawled my legs out in front of me and wiggled my foot. Nugget chased my laces. Looking up from our game I asked the question that had been bugging me all afternoon.

'So, where's your gold mine...or is it a secret?'

With a loud laugh, Dan lifted his finger and pointed to the right of the water tank.

'It's no secret, Connie. You've walked past it a couple of times already today. See over there?'

'What that small hole...the one with the wood box around it and that A-frame thingy on top?' I asked, shocked at how basic and unglamorous it all was.

'Yep, that's the one. The A-frame thingy's called a poppet head. We use it to hoist dirt, rocks and equipment up and down. The shaft underneath goes straight down, about ten metres, then a tunnel fans out to the left. You crawl on hands and knees for about twenty metres to a large cavern. The ore stopes spread out from there and follow the gold veins...wherever they lead. Next time you come to visit, you should go down. You're not really dressed for it at the moment,' said Dan.

I looked down at the black skirt and white tee-shirt I'd worn to work and agreed. He slid around in his seat and asked Jack, 'Is that alright with you, mate? Not breaking any rule or anything, am I?'

Jack raised his eyebrow at the question, his amusement plain to see.

'No lad, I don't have any problem with Connie going into the mine. I'm not superstitious...not like some of the old timers around here,' he said. He sat forward, stabbed a large chunk of meat with a fork and held it out to me, gesturing for me to take it and eat. 'Do you know, Connie, some of those silly old codgers think it's bad luck to have a woman underground...ridiculous. Would you be interested in crawling around in the dirt?'

'I'd love it. I've never been in a mine before,' I said, excitement bubbled in my chest at the prospect.

'Well then, how about next Sunday, would that suit you? I'll come collect you about ten. We can make a day of it. Dan'll cook, won't you lad...that way I'll know you're getting at least one good meal.'

So the following week, I was going to have my first experience in a gold mine.

17

Chapter Seventeen

As I stood at the head of the shaft, my hand shook. I was excited and fearful. Settling the hard hat more comfortably on my head, I pulled my gloves on tighter for a better fit. Jack was already on the ladder, just below me. I carefully placed my foot on the first rung and lowered myself slowly from one-step to the next. Jack kept a hand on my ankle, guiding my foot, so I didn't misstep and fall. I was enjoying his warm touch on my leg and took my time to climb down.

Stepping off the ladder, I stood very close to Jack's chest. I looked up at his lips and contemplated wrapping my arms around him and holding my lips up for a kiss.

Oblivious to the impure thoughts that were developing in my brain, Jack gave me a crooked smile and said, 'Cosy'. Then he leant forward and kissed the tip of my nose.

Damn, I should've been faster. A little tilt of the chin and I might've managed a lip lock.

'Now Connie, I'm going to crawl in here,' Jack said, pointing to a small tunnel at our feet. 'You just follow me, okay? It's not far, and then you'll be able to stand up. If at any time you want to leave, say so...we'll come straight out. Being underground's not for everyone. Some people can't take the enclosed feeling they get. Don't be ashamed to speak up.'

'Okay Jack, whatever you say. I trust you to keep me safe.'

'Good girl,' he said and then kneeling down, he crawled into the tunnel.

Taking a last look up at the sunlight, I saw two heads looking down past the poppet frame at me. Dan and Nugget...I gave a small wave, bobbed to my haunches, and looked into the tunnel. A metal rail for the ore cart ran in a parallel line along the floor. The ceiling was quite low. If I wanted to stay on my feet I'd need to bend nearly in half. Crawling was going to be more practical, so I dropped to my knees on the soft dirt. Dust kicked up, I coughed at a dryness in the back of my throat. I was wearing shorts, and it wasn't too uncomfortable, but next time I think I'll wear my cotton trousers.

I expected it to be cool, but the air flowing from the tunnel was quite mild. Crawling forward, the enclosing earth pressed down and the air felt heavy. I distracted myself by admiring Jack's butt as it wriggled along in front of me. I was very disappointed when he stood up. I looked around with interest before getting to my feet. We'd entered a spacious cavern, with enough room that four people could easily occupy the space and not touch. The air was quite fresh, although it had a dusty taste. The sounds we made seemed muffled, damped down by the surrounding earth. Dull light lit the area courtesy of the yellow globes hanging from an electrical cable looped through metal hooks in the ceiling. A faint beam of sunlight shone in, capturing my gaze. I looked up and saw a drill hole encased in a metal casing – it ran all the way to the surface.

Jack saw the direction of my gaze and said, 'It's a vent shaft...allows seepage of fresh air from the surface. The tunnel entrance is our other source of oxygen. On the surface a generator powers the lights and an exhaust fan. The fan draws out fumes and carbon dioxide that could otherwise build up and cause breathing problems.'

Crawl-size tunnels in the cavern wall ran off in all directions. I pointed to them asking a silent question.

'They're the ore stopes, they follow the gold seams. The waste goes into that ore cart,' said Jack pointing to a U-shaped metal bucket on rail wheels, which was sitting idle at the far end of the cavern. 'When the cart is full we push it along the rail to the shaft, hook the bucket to the poppet winch and hoist it to the surface.'

'How long are the stopes?' I asked, trying to picture the men at work and absorb all the new knowledge that went along with the image.

'A couple of them run a fair distance...a hundred metres or so. Others are only short...where the gold seam ran out, or the stope seeped water. You don't want to hit an underground stream...it would flood this place in no time.'

'Wow, this is a pretty good setup,' I said, admiring the cavern with its camp chairs and large wooden box, which was being utilised as a table for the coffee-stained enamel cups and crib boxes. 'Do you and Dan have a name for this area?'

'Yeah, this is the *War Room*. We meet here to eat, plan our work and discuss problems. We also have set check-in times, just to keep an eye on each other, though Dan talks so much, you can hear him no matter which stope you're in.'

Against the far wall, nestled behind one of the sagging chairs, was a large metal box, bolted with a heavy-duty padlock. Curious, I wandered over and gave it a discreet push with my foot. It didn't move.

Jack saw me, smiled and said, 'That's the gold safe.'

I made an O with my mouth but didn't ask if there was anything in it.

I stuck my head into the entrance of one of the stopes and looked around. It was chest height and very short in length. I could've sat upright very comfortably inside it.

'Would you like to see some gold?' asked Jack.

'Love too,' I replied, imagining a big chunk of bright glittering gold.

Before the words had finished coming from my mouth, Jack had lifted me by the waist and sat me on the edge of the short stope.

'Now Connie, I want you to lie back, facing the ceiling.'

I did as he asked, trying to push my helmet out of the way. It just tilted over my eyes, so I took it off and set it down beside me. Jack leaned in over me, smiling. My stomach knotted in excitement...but to my disappointment, he shone a torch onto a section of quartz just above my head. He wet his index finger in his mouth, ran it over a small section of the rock. There was no shine and glitter, like you see in the jeweller's shops, but a dull yellow horse shoe shaped line did appear. The gold vein was about a centimetre in length.

Jack scratched at the quartz around it with his fingernail and said, 'There you go, Connie...gold. We keep that one there in honour of our name...The Lucky Charm Mine.'

* * *

Climbing back up the ladder I had a slight headache, which I put down to the dull lighting. I sat on the shaft's framework to lift my legs from the void and back onto the surface. The sunshine nearly blinded me. I pulled my hard hat down over my eyes, to cut the glare, and sat waiting for them to become accustomed to the brightness. The bush insects, clicking and chirping, seemed so loud after the quiet of underground, it was almost deafening.

There was movement beside me as Jack climbed out.

'Are you okay, sweetheart?' he asked, his voice deeper than usual.

'Yeah, Jack, I'm fine. The sun's a little bright after the low light.'

'I suppose it is. Sorry...I should've warned you, but to tell the truth, after all these years I don't notice. Come on, give me your hand and I'll lead you back to camp.'

Holding Jack's hand was no hardship. With my heart doing little pitter-patters in my chest, I stepped carefully where he led, towards the smell of chops and potatoes cooking over the open fire.

The glare eased, and my eyes only watered a little. I spotted Nugget doing a bounce of excitement that turned into a tearing mad dash. He bounded towards us, yipping a greeting. Placing one knee on the ground, I put my hand out to pat him. Nugget had other ideas, he leapt over it and jumped into my lap, and proceeded to smother my face with doggy kisses. Laughing, I pushed him away and ran my long fingernails in the ridge between his eyes. Nugget closed his eyes and moaned in ecstasy.

'Grub will be ready in a couple of minutes. Lamb chops do ya Connie?' asked Dan.

'Yeah brilliant, Dan. They smell divine.'

I turned to Jack and waving my grubby mitts at him, I asked, 'Is there somewhere I can wash up before we eat?'

'Sure, come on over to the tank. There's a washstand and bowl set up. I'll run some water from the outlet for you.'

Taking hold of my hand again, Jack walked with me over to the tank stand. He paused, then wrapped his arms gently around me and drew me in close. As our lips met, I felt a tingle run all the way down my spine and warmth filled me to the very soul. A hot rush of passion exploded through my body. I tugged Jack in closer and more deeply. Our tongues met and swirled to their own choreographed dance, and I started moaning softly. Jack tightened his grip on me, then he slowly pulled away and cupping my cheeks with both his hands.

Looking deep into my eyes he said, 'Oh sweetheart, I'm very rapidly falling in love with you.'

I stroked his cheek softly and said sadly, 'Don't, Jack...that's not a good idea. I'm not the right girl for you.'

He took a step back, as if I had thrown a bucket of cold water over him. Without another word, he strode off into the bush. My heart broke.

Oh, Jack...I'm so sorry, I didn't want you to get hurt.

Tears filled my eyes and my throat closed over, but I refused to cry. Turning, I walked slowly back to the fire pit.

Dan looked up as I approached and said, 'I thought you went to wash up, Connie?'

'I'm sorry, Dan, I'm not feeling well. Would you drive me home. Jack had something else he needed to do.'

'Something more important than you...that's not like Jack!'

'Leave it be, Dan,' I said. My voice was having trouble moving past the lump in my throat and sounded high pitched and croaky. 'Would you drive me home, please?'

'Sure,' he said, placing a soft hand on my shoulder. 'If that's what you want.'

I nodded and made my way to the Rover and climbed up into the passenger's seat. I stayed quiet and stared out the window all the way back to town. I was barely holding back my tears. Dan didn't speak either, leaving me in peace until we had pulled up outside the boarding house.

As I slid from my seat and turned to close the door he said, 'Connie, Jack's a good man. I know from experience and trust me when I say he loves you. From what I can see, you two belong together. Please...whatever's happened, don't let it hurt you both.'

I took a long look at my young friend, saddened that he also was being hurt by my poor choices.

'Dan, you and Jack are both wonderful men and I think the world of you both. For reasons I can't go into, I can't let this relationship go any further. I'm sorry I have hurt you both, that was never my intention. Please, look after yourself and Jack for me. Goodbye Dan.'

With a gentle push, I closed the door and hurried inside to my room.

18

Chapter Eighteen

The tears streamed down my face in an unchecked flood. Blindly I reached for the backpack stored under my bed, then left it to hang loose from my fingers as I stared at the bedroom wall. My heart shattered, each shard inflicting indescribable pain. This wasn't fair, why couldn't I have love and happiness.

Well, Connie, you can thank your own stupidity for that. The first time you met Jerry should have been the last. Now you've hurt Jack.

Telling him the truth and still expecting him to love you, wasn't possible. Jack's already lost someone to violence. Confessing to a crime just like his stepfather's would only cause pain and ultimately hate. No, it's better he thinks I'm just not the right girl for him. It would be easier to live with that than have him hate me for what I really am – a *murderer.*

Time to leave Kalgoorlie, start a new life somewhere else.

Lethargy and a cold, heavy weight settled on me. The bag fell from my lax fingers. I left it where it lay and dragged myself over to the bed. Staring at the ceiling, silent tears leaking from the corners of my eyes, I grieved for what might have been. The tears I left to dry where they fell. Eventually, the well was empty but the pain in my heart went on. Sighing, I rolled to my side, faced the wall and curled up into a tight ball and watched the daylight on the wallpaper dim, eventually it disappeared. Night fell. I still lay not thinking or sleeping, waiting for my pain to ease.

With dawn's light, nothing had changed. I rose and dressed for work. I had to tell Carlo and Maria of my decision to leave. They'd been so good to me, welcoming me into their lives and giving me a chance when no one else would – I couldn't throw that back in their faces and just walk out. No, I would pretend a family emergency or something.

I set aside a change of clothes for travel and carefully packed the rest of my gear. I seemed to have acquired a lot more things since arriving here nine months ago, it was a struggle to close the bag's flap. Tidying the room, so I could pass Norma's eagle eye inspection and get my bond back, ensured I was leaving nothing of myself behind. Satisfied, I sat my backpack at the end of my bed, pulled on my jacket and quietly slipped out the front door for the two and a half block walk to the Victory Café.

The chilly morning air burned my face with its icy tendrils and I gave a small cough that hurt, deep in my chest. Ignoring my heavy, weary limbs, I forced one foot in front of the other and made my way across Egan Street onto Boulder Road. My regular route always took me past the Palace Hotel. The Palace was a great historical landmark in Kalgoorlie, and I would often stop and admire its 1897 architecture of ashlar stone and wrought-iron balconies. This morning it held no interest for me. I was on automatic pilot, head down, not paying attention to my surroundings. As I walked past the alley running behind the hotel, I heard a bottle clink in the gutter. The noise didn't penetrate my fogged brain until a hand clamped across my mouth and I was jerked backwards. The hand smelled stale and dirty, a finger slipped into my open lips and it tasted horrible.

A rancid breath blasted my face, hot and vile. A man's voice cooed, 'Mary, my Mary, I finally found you.'

Frantically I tried to wriggle from his grasp, but his grip on me tightened.

'Mary darling, where you been, girl? I've been looking and looking. Couldn't find you nowhere.'

This can't be happening – not again. Words screamed in my head, *you stupid, stupid girl, you should've been paying attention, not wallowing in self-pity*, as I sought a way to escape. I lifted my foot and slammed it backwards, connecting hard with his shin. Howling, the man retaliated with a one-handed shove, while maintaining his grip on my coat with the other. The coat pulled my arms backwards as I flew forward and slid from my arms. Unbalanced and not able to reef my hands back in front of me in time, I fell onto my knees and skidded along the rough bitumen surface. The skin on my knees and shins peeled back and burned. Alert now, I unsuccessfully tried to ignore the pain, but the sharp stinging changed to a throb. I cried out as I pulled my feet around under me, preparing to run.

'Ahhh...shit,' then slapped a hand over my mouth to hold back a wail of fear and pain as I looked up at my attacker, fearful of his next move. He stood swaying, his yellow bloodshot eyes staring up at the sky. I didn't know him, I'd never seen him before. He was filthy – his long hair and beard were matted from neglect. His skin was grey with ingrained dirt and his clothing ragged and unwashed. Thin wiry arms hung flaccid at his sides, my jacket pooled at his feet.

He seemed to be hallucinating. He talked to the sky, 'Mary, where'd you go, Mary.'

Taking advantage of his distraction, I leapt to my feet and took off running. Hot blood poured down my bare legs, and as my feet pounded the pavement small droplets flicked up dotting the front of my tee-shirt. My brain had shut down and gave me no idea where I was going, I just ran until I recognised the boarding house.

I nearly leapt the gate in my haste to make the front door. I couldn't seem to pull air into my lungs. I fumbled with the ribbon around my neck that held the key to my room. I finally managed to unlock my bedroom door, slipped inside and relocked it. Still not feeling safe, I tried to push the cupboard across in front of the door, but it was too heavy.

My body shook, my legs refused to hold me up any longer, I fell in a heap on the floor. I curled up in a little ball, hugging my head with my arms, trying to hide. Blood from my knees pooled around me and dried into a hard crust. The foul taste from his hand remained in my mouth. I couldn't move.

Why does this keep happening...? I tried to be careful and stay safe, just as Dad told me to, but things kept happening. Shit...my purse. I had put all my money in it. Where was my purse? A heaving sob escaped my lips, I quickly clamped my hand over my mouth, to hold back the storm. Once I started, I would never stop and then he would hear the noise and find me. My cheek froze to the floor, everything began to ache but I couldn't seem to get up. Then the shuddering started, it came in a violent, uncontrollable wave that went on and on. I clamped my jaw tight, so no noise could escape and waited for the shaking to ease. It lasted a long time.

I lay on the icy floor, exhausted and scared, not daring to move or draw attention to myself.

Tick, tick, tick, said my bedside clock in the silent house. It lulled me and I drifted into a twilight sleep.

Tap, tap, tap, I awoke with a fright.

'Connie,' it sounded like Sandra was talking to me, but how could I be sure? It might be a trick. 'Connie, are you in there?'

Not wanting to take the risk of being caught again, I waited.

Silence returned to my small haven. I let my mind drift back into the twilight world, where it was safe, as I stared ahead, watching the dust mites float in the air above the carpet, dancing their own private dance. The room greyed then darkened and hid them from my gaze, so I closed my eyes and let the black take me.

A beam of light touched my eyelid as the morning rays poured in my window. The light set off a chain reaction of exploding bubbles and zigzagging lines, my head pounded. It was excruciating. I began to burn...the fever came in waves of hot and cold. It washed through my body. I shivered and shook, my locked muscles cramped. Gritting my teeth against the pain in my head and muscles, I forced myself to hold perfectly still until the cramping eased.

Not game enough to move towards the bed, in case I set the cramps off again, I stayed curled up in a ball on the cold floor. My head throbbed, pushing shafts of hot pain down my neck and my mind felt like it was wading through thick mud.

The sun moved away from my tightly closed eyes. As the light left my face, the crushing pain eased a fraction. I drifted away towards a black hole, there I floated in a peaceful, warm darkness.

I was jerked back by a low moan. I wished it would stop. I just wanted to go back into the black, where it was warm, safe and quiet – there was no pain in the black.

A loud bone jarring *crash* reignited the pain in my head, something soft and cool stroked my brow, it was nice.

I dreamed about Maria, she was cooing Italian in my ear, '*Resisti Piccola, resisti.*'

The black moved closer.

'Connie my love, hang on. Please don't die.'

Jack, I had something I needed to tell him. Oh yes, I love him...no that's right – Jack doesn't love me...No that's not right...I'm sorry. That's it...I love you and I'm sorry, but the words evaded me. I began floating, it was like I was flying, and nothing made sense. I could hear the terrible moaning again and hated it.

I struggled with my eyes, trying to see the light, the pounding in my head was increasing. I could see the black inviting me towards it, so I gave up my struggle with the light and fell into the welcoming arms of the dark mist.

* * *

My eyes were gritty and sore as I opened them in a small slit, expecting a pain that never came – my headache was gone. My chest ached and I started to cough, hot needles peppered my lungs. I forced myself to stop by holding my breath and then allowed the air to leak from my dry parched lips.

Where was I? Without moving my head, I opened my eyes fully and looked around. I didn't recognise the white wall or green curtain hanging next to the bed. This wasn't my bedroom at the boarding house. Glancing down at the bed covers, I noticed the stiff white sheet and baby blue cotton blanket, neatly tucked around me on all sides. They didn't have a rumple in them.

I lifted my head off the plump pillow, to gaze further afield, but halted in fright when a deep male voice said, 'Lay still, Connie.'

'Where am I?' I croaked through a dry sore throat.

'You're in the hospital. You've been very sick – pneumonia. We only just got you here in time.'

'Jack?'

'Yeah sweetheart, it's me?'

'Jack, I'm sorry,' I said, and then started to cough.

The phlegm rattled around in my chest, sticking me with hot needles once again.

'Shhh, there is nothing to be sorry about. Here, sip this, then go back to sleep.'

A straw touched my lips, I sucked, and the cool fresh water eased the tickle in my throat. It tasted like heaven.

Jack brushed his work-hardened fingers over my brow. It must be safe, if Jack's here. He wouldn't let anyone hurt me. I let go and slipped once more towards the blackness. A swish and a squeak interrupted my descent. Rubber-soled shoes on polished tile floors, I'd know that sound anywhere.

'You shouldn't be in here, Ironstone. Miss Hara's in isolation,' said a stern, female voice that rose a pitch on the word *isolation*.

'I've had my shots, nurse. The doc's given me a big dose of antibiotics, so I could sit with her.'

'Hmm, well I suppose, as you've seen the doctor and Miss Hara is no longer contagious, it should be alright. But only for a minute okay, she's a very sick girl.'

I drifted into the dark, warm and safe.

Murmuring roused me back to the light. As I struggled to surface, I began to make sense of the soft speech going on around me.

'Have you been home yet, Ironstone, it's been days? No, I didn't think so.' It was the same voice as before. The nurse, still pitching the last word of her sentences on a higher note, continued to lecture Jack. 'She's on the mend, you know. The antibiotics are doing their job.'

'Yeah, I know, but I don't want Connie waking up alone. She'll be frightened. I'll just stay a little longer,' said Jack.

He sounded weary.

'Well don't let matron catch you, or my neck will be on the block.'

A cool hand touched my wrist.

I managed to croak some words from my dry mouth. 'Where am I?'

'Ahhh. Welcome back, young lady. You're in Kalgoorlie Hospital. You've been very sick.'

'Hospital?'

'Yes...Kalgoorlie Hospital. You can thank Ironstone and Maria Vittori. They got you here just in time.'

'I don't remember. What happened?'

'I'll leave Ironstone to tell you all about that. I need to get on with my rounds. Don't talk long, you need to rest. Ironstone also needs to go home and get some sleep. He's been haunting your bedside and this hospital for days.'

'Jack?' I croaked, as the nurse let go of my wrist. I heard her shoes squeaking their way out of the room. 'Jack, are you there?'

'I'm here, Connie. How are you feeling, love?'

'I feel so weak and tired. Why am I so tired?'

'It's the pneumonia. You've been very sick with it.'

'Jack what happened to me, why am I so sick?' I croaked before realising it was a pretty stupid question.

Jack was very patient with me. 'What do you remember?' he asked.

'I remember I was walking to work, I was really sad because I'd hurt you. I had my head down – it was stupid not to pay attention. Suddenly this man grabbed me...' My voice broke, and I hiccupped. A small sob escaped my throat, causing me to cough. I moaned in pain. Jack helped me sit up and drink some water – my chest eased its painful spasm.

'Shh, it's alright sweetheart, you're safe. I'm sorry you were accosted like that,' said Jack. 'It's all right now. The man who grabbed you was Digga Johnson. He owns a claim out at Kanowna. Him and his wife Mary lived and worked there for twenty years.'

'He kept calling me Mary,' I said. I was careful to manage my words by taking shallow breaths. I really didn't want another coughing fit.

'Yeah well, Mary was Digga's wife. She died last summer from a dugite bite. Digga was away prospecting a new claim, left her alone in camp for a few days. The snake got into her tent while she was asleep. Mary got out of bed and stood on the bugger in bare feet. Digga'd left her with no way of getting help,' said Jack, shaking his head, 'Stupid bloody thing to do, leaving her alone like that – you don't work alone and you don't leave people stranded like that.'

Forgetting myself, I drew in a lungful of air as I said, 'That poor woman.' After another spasm of painful coughing, I managed to ask, 'Jack, why was he acting so weird and why did he grab me, I didn't do anything to him?'

'Digga's been living in squalor out at that camp of his ever since his Mary died. He contaminated his water supply by not treating his septic waste and storing his drinking water next to it. He drank the tainted water and gave himself paratyphoid fever.'

'I thought typhoid had been eradicated in Australia.'

'You can still get it from unsanitised water.'

'I didn't know that,' I said, with a slow shake of my head.

'Anyway, Digga managed to get into his truck and drive into town...how is anyone's guess. He was pretty far gone. He crashed the car in the alley behind the pub. That's where he grabbed you. When the cops found him Monday, he was wandering the streets, hallucinating. It seems he was looking for Mary. They got him to the hospital but it was too late for the poor bugger...he died.'

'That's so sad. Poor man.'

Twining a lock of my hair around his finger, Jack gently lifted it off my face.

'When Sarge Henderson was getting the truck towed away, he found your handbag in the alley. He went around to the boarding house to return it to you. Sandra knocked on your door, but there was no answer. They didn't know you were in your room. Anyway, the sergeant went to see Maria and Carlo. They thought you were still out at the camp with me and Dan. It upset them you hadn't shown up for work, and not sent word that you weren't coming in. A comedy of errors really. I didn't come looking for you after you left us on Sunday because I was angry with myself.'

'Angry...Jack, why were you angry with yourself?'

'Scaring you like that, getting you behind the water tank, kissing you that way. It was clumsy. I'm so sorry.'

'Jack, don't be sorry, it's...' Another spasm of coughing hit me.

Jack put his finger over my lips and said, 'Don't speak, leave it for now, Connie. When you're better we'll talk, not now...not while you're so sick.' He paused and gave me a tentative smile, before continuing with the tale of my woes. 'Anyway, after giving it some thought, Maria and Carlo got worried. Your purse in the alley just didn't make any sense. Knowing the person you are, you would've sent word if you weren't going to be at work. It just wasn't like you to not show up. So, Tuesday morning, when you were still a no-show and couldn't be found, Maria kicked everyone out of the café and came out to camp to find me. I told them Dan had taken you home on Sunday and dropped you off at your front gate. When she told me about your purse showing up in the alley behind the pub I freaked. I went straight to the boarding house. We could hear you moaning through the door. So I kicked the door in and there you were on the floor.' Jack leant forward and placed a gentle kiss on my brow. 'No one knew Digga had attacked you or that you'd even had contact, until we bought you in to the hospital. The doc thought you had typhoid, but the blood test showed pneumonia. It must've been from lying on the cold floor all that time. I'm afraid your knees are also a bit of mess as well. What happened, do you remember?'

'I fell on the rough pavement.'

'I'm sorry I wasn't there to protect you, Connie.'

'It's not your fault, Jack. I wasn't well before that,' I said, remembering the dry cough and headache that had been plaguing me, along with no sleep. Not wanting to go down that path I changed the subject. 'I bet Norma's not too happy about you kicking open the door.'

'No, she's most *displeased* with me at the moment. I've got to do some major crawling to get back into her good books.' Jack gave a soft laugh and then said, 'The police want to return your things, Connie...and the sarge wants you to give a statement.'

'*No*...I can't talk to the police. Please, Jack, don't let them in here,' I said, my heart pounding in fright.

Jack pulled his eyebrow together in a puzzled look. He brushed his finger down my nose and said, 'Shhh, don't upset yourself. There's nothing to be afraid of. All that nonsense can wait. You don't have to talk to anyone, if you don't want too.'

'I know you think I'm being silly, but I don't want to go through it all again. The poor man is dead...can't we leave it at that?' I asked. A tear forged a lone path down my cheek.

Jack lifted it off my face with his finger tip. 'It's okay Connie. I'll tell the sarge you're not ready. He'll just have to put the statement on hold, for now. If you change your mind later, you can do it then.'

'No, I won't change my mind,' I said. There was no way I was going anywhere near the police, it was just too big a risk to take.

I heard the rapid squeaking of shoes on polished tiles. Nurse Gordon stuck her head in the room.

'Ironstone, skedaddle. It's matron, she's on the warpath. There'll be hell to pay if you're found in here.'

'Righto nurse,' said Jack. He stood and placed his lips gently on mine. 'Please get better sweetheart, my heart nearly stopped when I thought I was going to lose you.'

Lifting the window, he scissored his long legs over the sill and closed the glass behind him.

19

Chapter Nineteen

I spent ten days in that damn hospital, being poked and prodded by doctors. The nurses would pop in at odd times to wake me up, so I could take a sleeping pill. Matron would thunder through the wards, scowling at everyone, looking for wrongdoers.

The first day I could sit up by myself, without the world spinning around in a dizzy kaleidoscope of colours and nausea, the floodgates opened to a steady stream of visitors. Everyone was limited to five minutes.

Mid-afternoon Maria and Carlo blasted in. Maria enveloped me in a comforting motherly hug and a rapid stream of Italian. I couldn't get a word in, so I just hugged her back and enjoyed the experience. When she finally let go, Carlo cupped my cheeks with his big soft hands and gave me a huge toothy smile.

I returned it with a small one of my own and said, 'I'm sorry I've let you both down. I'll get back to work as soon as I can.'

'Piccola, I am very angry with you,' said Carlo, his gruff tone scared me. He flicked his forefinger over my nose, 'I'ma not a young man...you scare ten years from-a my growth. *Never do-a that again*!'

After a coughing giggle I said, 'Sorry.'

He glanced over his shoulder and when the nurse wasn't looking, slipped a container of warm lasagne under my hand. Carlo winked and said, 'You getta better, whena you're ready, you coma back...but getta well first, okay! We can'ta do without our, Piccola.'

'Thank you, Carlo. As soon as I can, I'll be back,' I said, my heart warm, touched by their genuine affection.

'You takea your time. Maria and me, we cope. Nexa time I visit, I bringa you some more good Italian food...you lika the ravioli? It build you up, putta the hairs on your chest.'

'They do feed me in here, you know Carlo,' I said, amused by his touching offer.

'Pwah...they no cooka the gooda food like Carlo,' he said, puffing out his chest.

'No, that's true,' I said and placed my cold hand over his warm one, 'but then, no one cooks like you Carlo. Thank you both, you're the best. I love you.'

With a surreptitious swipe, Carlo wiped a tear away from his eye. He cleared his throat. 'Okay...good. We hafta go now, that nurse she looka daggers at us. We coma visit again soon.' He leant forward and gave me a loud smacking kiss on the cheek.

Maria wrapped her arms around me in another enjoyable hug. '*Ti amo mia amica*,' she said.

My understanding of Italian was improving and I returned her words.

'I love you too, my friend.'

Their vitality and kindness dazed me and it took me a few minutes to recover from my Italian visit.

A clomp of booted feet on highly polished vinyl announced the arrival of Sandra. She clutched a small posy of flowers in her hand.

'God, Connie...I'm soooo sorry. I feel terrible that you were lying there all that time, alone and ill. Even Norma didn't know you were home, and she usually misses nothing.'

'It's nobody's fault, especially not yours, Sandra. I could've called out, but I didn't,' I said. 'Now, tell me all the gossip...how cross is Norma with Jack for kicking in the door? Do you think she'll let me come back?'

Sandra hitched her hip and sat on the edge of the bed and held my hand. Her fingers were strong and calloused. 'You'll have no problem on that score. Dazza and Jack have taken care of everything and installed a new door on your room. They've also taken the sag out of the front porch by relaying the floor boards. The house is now in the middle of a repaint. Norma's ecstatic, enjoying all the free labour and...having a coupla good looking fellas around the place to ogle.' She rolled her eyes heavenward, laughing. 'And you know Dazza, he's got this way about him. He's managed to charm the socks off, Norma, that's for sure. She even got up off her chair and made him a cup of coffee.'

I studied Sandra's face, had I detected a trace of wistfulness as she mentioned Dan?

She recalled me from my thoughts. 'Well, best be off...before Nurse Gordon hunts me out. They're being very strict about keeping visits short. I went to school with her you know.'

'Who... Nurse Gordon?'

My voice and eyebrows rose in surprise at the sudden change in the conversation.

'Yeah...she's a local girl...like me. Left and went to train in the city, in one of the big hospitals...Royal Perth, I think it was. As soon as she qualified, she hightailed it straight back here. Says it's because it's hard to get people to work in the country, but I think it's more to do with a certain police sergeant. A little old I would have thought...he must be a least thirty-five.' My heart jolted. I fought hard to keep any emotion from showing on my face. Sandra's conversation didn't falter, so I must have succeeded. 'It seems really weird to call her Nurse Gordon instead of Sue, but the matron's a real stickler about things like that. Anyway, I don't want to get her into trouble, so I better dash. You get well, okay.'

Sandra gave me a butterfly kiss on the cheek and with a cheeky smile said, 'See ya later, Pixie.' She bolted out the door. Her footsteps echoed in the hallway and faded.

Quiet descended, I closed my eyes and dozed.

Yip.

The sound tugged my lips into a smile. I opened my eyes and drank in the sight of Dan standing next to my bed, a sheepish look on his face. Nugget nestled inside his blue checked flannel shirt, his cute face hanging out over the top button. I held out my arms and pulled them both into a hug. His arms clamped tightly around me. I breathed in his wonderful smell of spice and the outdoors. Nugget's tongue slid across my cheek and then went to work on Dan's face. He roared with laughter and let me go.

I patted the bed, and he sat.

'How're you feeling, Connie?'

'I'm heaps better... not coughing up so much rubbish now that the antibiotics have kicked in. I'm just tired...all the time.'

Nugget nudged my hand with his warm, wet nose. I took the hint and scratched the ridge between his eyes. He closed his eyes and moaned in enjoyment.

'How'd you get past the nurses' station with him, Dan?'

'I have my ways,' he said. A dimple formed in his cheek as he gave me a mischievous grin.

'So I hear. I've had a visit from Sandra. She tells me you managed to get a cup of coffee out of Norma.'

'Yeah, and bloody awful it was too! You owe me big time for that one,' he said. 'When was Sandra here?' The casualness of the question didn't deceive me.

'Not that long ago...in fact you've only just missed her.'

The clatter of cups and saucers warned me that it was nearly time for one of matron's surprise visits. She was as predictable as the afternoon tea trolley.

'Dan, you better skedaddle, before matron rumbles you in here with Nugget. Besides, if you're quick, you might catch up with a certain young lady on her way to the boarding house.'

I smirked as Dan flashed me an angelic smile. He leaned over, kissed my forehead and said, 'I love you, Connie. Take care. We'll sneak back later for another visit, bye for now.' He shot out the door faster than lightning. A moment later, a frowning Nurse Gordon walked in, followed closely by the predictable matron.

Good call, Connie.

***

Gifts and messages of goodwill poured in and were left at the nursing station for me. The shelf in my room rapidly filled with flower posies, delicate handkerchiefs, homemade cards and even a new enamel mug. Get well gifts, from the men whom I saw daily in the cafe. I was touched.

Jack ignored visiting times totally. I'd close my eyes to sleep and he would materialise to hold my hand. If I awoke in the middle of the night, he would be at my bedside. He eluded the nursing staff with a stealth that would have done a ninja warrior proud. They never could catch him.

'Jack, you must have more important things to do than sit at my bedside all the time.'

Jack gave me a sweet smile, stroked his finger down my cheek and said, 'There is nothing more important in this world, than to be by your side.'

God how easy was it to love this wonderful, caring man. So once again I took the easy path and let things be, drifting along in a warm glow of love.

* * *

The day of my release from hospital finally arrived. Jack, Dan and Nugget arrived to collect me. Pushing open the glass doors, I stepped into the winter sunshine and held my face up to the sky. I sucked in a deep breath of fresh air laden with the scent of eucalyptus and sighed happily. It was wonderful to be alive and outside again.

Ignoring my doctor's parting words to take a month to rest and recover, I said, 'Jack, I think I'll go back to work on Monday.'

'Now, love, you heard the doctor. How about you come live at Lucky Charm...I can bodgie up the shack for you.'

'No Jack, I need to get back to my normal life and routine...otherwise I'll always be frightened.'

I could see he wasn't convinced, but didn't argue, instead he tried a new tactic. 'Let's swing by the café for a cuppa. Maybe Maria can talk some sense into you.'

As Dan opened the café door the bell jangled. Faces looked up to see who the new comers were. The room fell silent when I stepped in. Scotty leapt to his feet. He gave Luke a shove on the arm to get him to vacate his chair.

'Welcome back, Connie,' said Scotty, his face wreathed in a smile. 'Here take this table, we're finished.'

Luke scowled. Dan opened the door for him, waited for Luke to make the street and said, 'Choof off ya bloody flog.'

I had a quiet chuckle, but not wanting to encourage him I said, 'Shush, Dan.'

Maria burst into the room, arms spread wide her dainty feet moving at a fast clip. She covered the distance between us in an instant and enveloped me in a warm hug. I was beginning to understand the supportive love a real mother gives...how it soothes the places inside our heart that are scared and lonely.

'Youa home. Come sit...tea?'

At my nod she dashed back to the kitchen. A stream of Italian announced the arrival of Carlo. He ran a hand towel over his sweaty face and bellowed across the room, 'Piccola, should you be outa the bed. You musta come home with us. You so skinny, you needa the feeding up.'

Maria stepped around his bulk and placed a delicate china tea cup in front of me. She poured in the perfect amount of milk from a pretty little jug. Jack started a soft conversation with her and I caught the words, 'talk some sense...'

Dan sat in front of me, a big grin on his face.

I held up my hand and said, 'Stop fussing, all of you. I'm fine. I'm not going to stay with anyone...I'm going back to the boarding house. Jack you're to go back to your camp. Come and see me on the weekends, like before. As for you Dan...you and Nugget have been popping in and out of the hospital every five minutes and not getting any work done. Maria, Carlo...' I paused for breath, gave a small cough that only hurt a tiny bit and went on, 'next week I'll come back to work. While I recover my strength, I'll sit on a chair at the sink and wash dishes, while Maria serves the customers.'

You could hear a pin drop in the silence. Everyone looked at me in awe, I hadn't been this decisive or firm with any of them before. I hadn't been myself in a very long time.

I made one concession.

'Carlo, will you pick me up and drive me to work each day?' I asked. When I felt stronger and wasn't jumping at shadows, I'll learn to walk by myself in the mornings again...but I wasn't ready for that yet.

The tension in the room broke. Everyone started talking at once. I picked up my tea, took a sip and ignored them.

* * *

Carlo was waiting out front in a powder blue Morris Minor. I'd often seen the car parked behind the café but I'd never really twigged who owned it. It was a great car, surprisingly roomy. The original interior was cared for and shone like new. I remember seeing cars like this in the old war movies I'd watched as a kid.

'I love the car, Carlo,' I said, enjoying the scent of lemon polish that filled my nostrils.

'Yesa, after Maria, she is the love of my life. I waited many, many years to buya this beautiful baby. Maria she say she feel likea the queen riding around town,' he said with a beaming smile of pride. 'Now Piccola, Maria and me wanted to tell you, we-a making changes in the café. We-a have taken on the new waitress.'

My heart dropped to the pit of my stomach.

'Are you sacking me, Carlo?'

I felt sick...my small amount of savings had been seriously depleted over the last few weeks. I needed this job to get back on my feet.

'No...no, Piccola. You're one ofa the family...no. We're just soa busy. Maria, she no as young as she was, so we hafta have more help. So the new girl, Tegan, she starta the work today. We all train her, maybe one day she be good like you.'

Relief swept through me at his words.

'You said a few changes, Carlo?'

'Yesa, we buya the cappuccino machine, you know it makea the coffee.'

'Yes, I know what a cappuccino is. They make a lot of fancy coffees like that, in the Greek and Italian districts of Melbourne...very nice they are too.'

'Maria and me, we missa our espresso and cappuccino after work. You know the Capuchin friars in Italy, they introduce-a the cappuccino in my country, many years ago. These Kalgoorlie miners, they ina for the big treat,' said Carlo. He drove at a sedate pace down Egan Street. 'Maria, she fulla big plans. She wanna the carpenter to build a new counter, so she cana make the Australian meat and salad sandwich, and sella the hot pie so the men can buy lunch from us.'

'That's a marvellous idea, Carlo. Boy you're going to be busy.'

'Yes-a, that's why we getta the new waitress. You teacha her to be good, then we getta another and another, then Carlo can retire the rich man.'

I gave a bark of laughter and said, 'Carlo, if we have all that extra work, then we will have more dirty dishes. I think you should buy an electric dishwasher. Maria can't keep doing dishes and make the sandwiches.'

'You'sa as bad as my Maria, Piccola. How canna I retire a rich man, if you keepa spending my money?' he said, pouting and laughing as he parked the car into its space behind the shop.

'Sometimes you have to spend money to make money, Carlo,' I said, trying to keep a straight face.

Climbing out of the car, I looked around scanning the back lane before hurrying to the kitchen door. Carlo said nothing – he opened the door and gave me a gentle pat on the shoulder as I rushed past.

* * *

Tegan stood with hands clasped in front of her apron pocket, watching Maria set the tables. Young, with a lot of fly-away blonde hair hanging around her face – she didn't offer to help – the girl had a lot to learn. Some would come with experience, the rest Maria and I would take care of – she'd soon be whipped into shape.

Maria started the first lesson by addressing Tegan's footwear. She gave the girl tasks that were hampered by the high heels she was wearing. Mid-morning Tegan disappeared for a few minutes and returned wearing canvas lace-ups, similar to the ones I wore. I smiled at Maria across the room when I saw the shoe change and thought to myself, well that's lesson one successfully completed.

It was nice being back at the café. As I sat at the sink, my hands immersed in the hot sudsy water washing dishes, a few of the regulars popped their heads through the kitchen hatch and sang out a welcome back. My heart filled with happiness.

As the weeks passed, my strength returned. I came to the realisation that this was the place I belonged. At least until I had the courage to tell Jack and my friends the truth.

20

Chapter Twenty

A month after my return to work, I started a new job.

Jack and Dan settled in at their usual table. I wandered out of the kitchen, carrying their coffee. I'd made it just the way Jack liked. I didn't trust Tegan with my boy's beverage of choice, just yet...besides, I'm entitled to say good morning.

'Hello my handsome men, how are the three of you today?'

Sitting beneath Dan's chair, his tail moving in a slow, sweeping arc, Nugget was watching the comings and goings of the room with unabashed interest. As I set the coffee down, he *yipped* hello and went back to his people watching. Jack rose to his feet and, to the hoots and whistles of the other patrons, pulled me close and sank his lips into mine. Warmth rose from the tips of my toes to all the right places. The world disappeared for a moment as I merged into the kiss. Our lips parted.

Wow!

Not an unenjoyable experience, it just left me yearning for more.

With a self-satisfied smirk, Jack returned to his seat. He ignored the ruckus that had started in the cafe and said, 'Good Morning sweetheart, I missed you this week.'

'I missed you too,' I whispered, running my finger down his cheek. Then clearing my throat, I pulled myself back into reality.

'So what's the plan for the day?'

'Well, Old Girl, how'd you like to go to the footy? Dan's playing rover today...the regular guy's out.'

'Yeah, that sounds great. What time does the game start?'

'Seniors bounce down is at two-thirty. Digger Daws Oval's a ten minute drive from here.'

'Terrific, that'll fit in nicely with my knock-off time. I'll pack us a picnic lunch. We can kick back and enjoy the food, while Dan here does all the running around.'

'You're all heart, Connie,' said Dan, his machine gun laugh rattling away. 'I hope I can kick a couple of goals for you today.'

'Sounds like a plan. Alright boys, I have to get back to my sink, before the dishes flow out the door. You enjoy your breakfast and I'll see you this arvo,' I said, blowing them both a kiss.

Tegan rushed to their table, pulling her notebook from her apron pocket. I smiled to myself at her puzzled expression, when Dan said to ask Carlo for the Ironstone and Dazza.

In the kitchen, I found Maria up to her elbows in sudsy water, scrubbing dishes.

Seeing my raised eyebrow, she said, 'That new girl, she's doing okay. We'll leave her cope on her own, hey. You're to help Carlo, as assistant cook and I...I go back to my sink,' she said, running her hand lovingly over its surface.

With each passing day, I'd become stronger and was now nearly back to my normal healthy self. As my energy level increased, I'd not only been doing the dishes but had also helped Carlo, in small ways, around the kitchen. Much to his delight, I'd taken over the smaller cooking tasks, peeling and preparing vegetables, and streamlining the way we did things, so we didn't fall over each other.

Carlo was pleased with my help, happy the work was running smoother than ever before.

As a reward, he'd been giving me cooking lessons, teaching me to make the most divine pasta dishes. When I suggested we should serve the pasta as part of the menu, he muttered something about sending a man broke, but added it to the menu. The meals were an instant hit.

'Piccola,' Carlo said, 'youa to make today's lasagne. Starting Monday morning, asa my new assistant cook, I teacha you other delicious meals, which we'll testa on that rabble outa there, okay?'

I was stunned at the new opportunity opening up before me. The look on my face must have been amusing. Maria started to giggle, she set Carlo off. He barked out a deep belly laugh that filled the kitchen. I tried to act nonchalant, but bubbles of excitement were fizzing in my stomach and I found myself bouncing up and down on my toes.

'Are you sure Carlo...about me cooking lunch? I don't want to mess it up.'

'You, you a terrific cook. You hava the flair for the *presentozione* and the taste. So, nowa you become Victory Café's *maestra* cook, under my brilliant guidance of course.'

'Yes, chef.' I nipped around the grill and gave him a kiss on the cheek. 'Thank you, Carlo.'

'Humph...'

I flicked his cheek with my finger, 'Are you blushing, chef? You are, you're blushing!'

'Pwah...go away, you little imp, and starta the pasta sauce,' Carlo said, ducking his head, trying to hide his red face.

* * *

Jack was waiting in his usual spot in front of the café, when I bounced out the door after work.

'Wow, you look happy,' he said, taking the food basket from my hand.

I wrapped my arms around his neck and said, 'I got a promotion today. You're looking at Victory Cafe's newest *maestra* cook, specialising in Italian meals. Carlo is going to train me, and then we'll make some changes to the menu.'

'Wow, Connie, that's great. Congratulations.' He swooped me up in a delicious hug.

A worry wrinkle formed on his brow. I ran my finger over the crease.

'What's wrong?'

'Carlo's not going to change my breakfast is he?'

I burst into laughter, 'No, Jack, heaven forbid.'

* * *

Amusement was bubbling like a happy cauldron in my chest. For the entire drive, Jack's nose had been twitching as he sniffed the air and dropped blatant hints.

'Hmm...something smells good.'

I kept a smug silence, knowing hidden in the depths of my basket was a generous serving of the delicious lasagne I'd made that morning, along with fresh crusty bread. The first Italian meal I'd ever cooked for my man.

To distract him, I didn't want to blab and spoil the surprise, I said, 'Okay, Jack, you've got to tell me who's who, in today's match. Who are the Panthers?'

'The Panthers are Kalgoorlie Railways Football Club. They wear red and black and are our biggest rivals. They were last year's grand finalist. We *don't* barrack for them.'

Right, check, we don't barrack for the Panthers.

'And the Mine Rovers?'

'The Rovers, also known as the Diorites, are the Mines Rovers Football Club. They wear royal blue and white, *and* were last year premiers. They're Dan's team. We *do* barrack for them.'

'Woof,' confirmed Nugget.

Well, I guess I know where my allegiance lies.

'What about, Nugget. Will he be alright at the footy?'

'Connie, my love, you haven't experienced Aussie rules, until you've watched a game with Nugget. It is the damnedest thing. That dog just loves his football. I won't say anymore except you're in for a real treat.'

Jack parked in the shade of a salmon gum tree. Nugget began doggie talking and nudging Jack with his nose, his excitement apparent. Jack opened the driver's door and Nugget leapt clean over his lap and raced away. He positioned himself halfway down the field on the boundary line. He ignored everyone and everything around him. As the teams ran onto the field, he gave a bark and locked his gaze on the ball.

Worried he might run out onto the field, I said, 'He won't get in the way will he, shouldn't we called him back?'

'No, Connie...just watch. He won't move from that spot, until the game's over.'

The siren sounded for the start of play, the umpire bounced the ball. Nugget's gaze followed the play of the ball intensely. Dan flitted past and suddenly he had the ball, he wove and kicked, Nugget gave a woof of approval.

Short, skinny, his rat-like gaze focussed on a group of bikies parked further down the field, Lanky Luke made a beeline along the boundary line towards them. His route took him past Nugget. As he came level, his foot lashed out at the dog. In a deft manoeuvre, Nugget avoided the boot and showed Luke the full set of his sharp white teeth. Luke sidestepped and scuttled away. Dan scored a goal and Nugget leapt to his feet and did a small dance.

I followed Luke's progress down the field, my temper simmering as thoughts of payback flinted through my mind. Dan had rightly called him a flog...a wanker. I cast a glance towards the group he was heading for and saw a familiar face.

'Jack, is that Tegan sitting on the Harley motorbike?' I pointed to the leather clad Twisted Heads bikies, who were laughing and throwing beer cans at each other. Jack took a quick look and then re-focussed his attention back on the game. 'Yeah, Scotty's playing half back today.'

What's Scotty playing football got to do with Tegan sitting on a motorbike? Before I could ask, his opponent threw Dan to the ground. Jack started yelling, tooting the horn and accusing the umpire of blindness.

I settled back in my seat and propped my feet up on the dashboard. I listened to the murmurs of appreciation as Jack wolfed down his plate of lasagne. I bit into a piece of fresh bread, closed my eyes and savoured the thick layer of butter, as it filled my mouth. My pleasure was interrupted by tooting car horns and Jack cheering – Rovers had just scored a goal and Dan was being thumped on the back by his teammates. Damn missed it. Nugget hadn't, he was dancing in a circle and barking.

As Jack was distracted, I leant over and swiped a forkful of food from his plate, and laughed at the look of consternation that crossed his face.

The Panthers scored, Jack leapt into action, tooted the horn and booed. Nugget lay on the ground and covered his face with his paws. It was the funniest and most entertaining game of football I'd ever been too.

The final siren blasted, the Rovers won by a point.

Jack pointed to Nugget and said, 'Watch.'

The dog jumped to his feet and tore off across the field, towards his hero, Dazza. Casually, Dan turned from his congratulatory teammates to the oncoming dog, held out his arms. Nugget shot through the air like a torpedo and landed neatly in them. He smothered Dan's face in wet doggy kisses.

I laughed and asked, 'What happens if the Rovers lose?'

Jack smiled and said, 'Nugget howls and then races out to congratulate Dan on a good game.'

I couldn't help it. I got a fit of the giggles. My side ached by the time I finally managed to catch my breath.

I hiccupped, 'How did you guys teach him that?' I asked, trying to steady my breathing, without much success.

'We didn't, he's always done it. Dan tried to leave him in the car once, but Nugget just howled. I tried keeping him at camp but he snuck off. When I found him he was halfway to Kal. How the hell he knew Dan was playing baffles me. Eventually, one of the players' wives said she'd keep an eye on him, now he's a permanent fixture on the sideline.'

So the rest of the season passed. Dazza's team made it to the grand final, and I had to say goodbye to my three boys.

* * *

Grand final day. I dressed for work in a royal blue and white spectator's jumper and beanie and did a mental review of the last twelve months. This time last year, I'd arrived by train, a naive and scared girl, with no job prospects and only a small amount of cash. I'd nowhere to live and no friends. Now I was still a scared girl, but scared for a different reason. I'd so much more to lose, a fulfilling new life, full of love, friends and prospects.

I'd spent the previous Sunday at Lucky Charm with Jack and Dan. Jack had proudly shown me around his almost completed shack. The walls were up and the roof on.

'The truck from Perth is due in next week. It should have the windows on board. Then I just need to make some furniture and it is ready to be lived in.'

'It looks great, Jack. You guys should be real comfortable.'

'Only one of us will be living here.'

Before I could ask what he meant, he took hold of my hands and locked his blue eyes to mine.

'Connie, there's something important I need to talk to you about.'

My heart gave a jolt, I felt the blood drain from my cheeks. Yes, it probably is time to sit down and talk about my life. My eyes burned and my throat tightened.

I have to tell him...but I'm scared...don't want to lose him.

Jack leant forward and cupped my cheek with his hand.

'Don't look so frightened. You can trust me with anything.'

He studied my face for a moment.

'I can see you're still not ready to tell me what haunts you...Connie, I need to talk to you...tell you...I'm leaving.'

My heart squeezed tight and hurt.

Oh god, I'm losing him.

My hands shook as I grabbed both of his with mine.

'Leaving...why?'

Jack pulled me into his arms and held my cheek against his chest. I could hear his heart beating away strongly.

'We hold title on a gold lease, just up the road from here, in the old mining town of Gwalia.' Then drawing me away from his chest, he looked down at me and asked, 'Do you know where that is?'

I shook my head. 'No.' My voice sounded rusty and cracked.

'Its north of here...just out of Leonora. It was once the country's biggest gold mine...closed in '63, the year Dan joined me.' I studied a trail of ants as they crossed the dirt floor in a busy scurrying line, not wanting him to see the pain in my eyes. Jack continued, 'Anyway, the lad and I were looking for a couple of good prospects...we picked up this lease dirt cheap because of the mine closure. Only there's a catch, we have to work the lease continuously for a least a month, every year, or we lose the mineral rights. It's a rich prospect...too rich to lose.'

He placed a finger under my chin and tilted my face up.

'Do you understand? Every year, after the footy season, we go to Gwalia for a couple of months, and work the claim.'

'Is that why I didn't meet you and Dan, until January?'

'Yeah, that's right, love. We'd found a sweet gold vein and mining that seam kept us busy, for four months.'

'So, what's at Gwalia?' I asked, 'Is it a big place, with lots of people like Kalgoorlie?'

Jack gave a snort of laughter.

'Not anymore. When the mine was running 1200 people lived there. When it closed, they just packed their bags and abandoned everything they couldn't carry. Gwalia's a ghost town. The buildings still stand, curtains blow in the breeze through broken windows. Gardens are overgrown with weeds, and the kids' swings screech from rusted links. It is quite eerie actually. I'll take you there one day, so you can see for yourself. It's really an experience you shouldn't miss.'

I studied his face, memorising each line, and decided not to make this too hard on either of us.

'You think of the most romantic ways to show a girl a good time, Jack. When do you guys leave?'

'Well, the shack's windows are due this week, the grand final's next week, so probably the following Monday. Are you okay with this, Connie, I'll stay if you want me to?'

'I'm going to miss you, desperately, but this is important. I'd hate to be responsible for you losing the lease. I'll be fine, don't worry. Carlo still won't let me walk to work...and I have so much still to learn. The time'll just fly by.'

'If we hit another good seam and it looks like we'll be gone for an extended period, I'll drive back and visit on Sundays. It takes three hours to reach Kal in the old Rover. I could be here and back in a day.'

Taking the bull by the horns I said, 'Jack, when you get back, we need to talk...there are some important things about me you need to know.'

Pulling me into his arms our lips met, a hot fire began to lick its way through my body. The temptation to throw caution to the wind, gave me a mighty nudge and I deepened my kiss. Jack walked me backwards to lean against the wall and he pressed himself in, as close as possible. I could feel his excitement, hard against my stomach. I felt an overwhelming desire.

'Jack, Connie – grubs up,' yelled Dan, accompanied by Nugget's commanding bark.

The mood was shattered.

Panting, I hung on to Jack for a moment longer, and then stepped away, feeling the blood rush to my face as shyness at my actions took hold. What must Jack think of my bold behaviour?

That question was answered a moment later as he gave the front of his jeans a wiggle, and shook his leg in a funny jig.

'Coming, Dan,' he yelled, before adding a soft, 'or not.'

I couldn't help myself, I started to giggle and had to lean against the wall again, until I could stop. Flicking the tip of my nose with his finger, Jack smiled, took hold of my hand and together we made our way at a slow walk towards the fire pit. It gave us time to regain our composure.

So here we were, grand final morning, my lust still unfulfilled, and the last day I would see my men.

Breakfast devoured, Jack and Dan left for the oval to help set up the barbeques. Nugget, wearing his own personal Rovers scarf, had gone to watch the Juniors and the Colts play their final.

Sprinkling cheese over the top of the lasagne, I slipped the four large trays into the oven to slow cook for the lunch crowd. As I closed the oven door there came a loud *Crash* from the dining room and Tegan, cried out in distress.

I raced to the hatch to see what was going on. Scotty with a fist full of shirt and his face up close and personal, was pushing a scrawny looking bloke against the wall.

Dashing in to the café, I said, 'What...the...hell...is...going...on? *Scotty,* put him down at once.'

The floor was littered with broken crockery and the remains of an unserved breakfast. I stepped over the mess and placed my hand on Scotty's shoulder.

'Let go Scotty and back off...I've got this.'

Scotty pushed the man into a chair and let go. He eyeballed him. The rage was coming off him in palpable waves. He stepped back, as I had asked, and turned to a sobbing Tegan.

I heard him take a shuddering deep breath before he spoke, 'You okay, T?'

The scrawny young man smirked. He crossed his sleeveless tattooed arms across his chest and slouched back in his chair.

'I guess you owe me a free breakfast,' he said.

Her hair hanging over her face, Tegan sobbed. 'He put his hand up my skirt as I walked past.'

Scotty's face went red, beads of sweat sprang to life on his face and he clenched his fists.

I held my hand up to him and said, 'I've got this Scotty...you go sit.'

I took Tegan by the hand and said, 'Go into the kitchen, tell Maria what's happened.'

Tegan nodded and pointed at the mess.

'Don't worry about it, love. I'll fix it.'

I turned to the smirking man and slammed my fists on my hips, and let rip.

'How dare you accost a young lady like that.' He sat back in shock and the colour left his face. 'Get your arse off that chair, and get out. *NOW*. Any man who could treat a girl in such a manner, is lower than pond scum. *Get out and don't come back*.'

You could have heard a pin drop in the silence that followed. The young upstart, his face mottled red and white in fear, stood up, knocking his chair over in his haste. He looked at the faces around him and bolted out the door. The room erupted in applause. I turned and faced the room, my heart thudding hard in my chest, and took a bow. As I straightened I saw Carlo, cheeks glowing and smile beaming. He was standing at the kitchen door with a huge carving knife in his hand.

Ten minutes later Jack came dashing into the kitchen and stopped dead when he saw that all was calm and as usual.

'Jack, what are you doing here?' I asked, 'It's not closing time yet.'

Jack said, 'I heard there was trouble and I came straight away.'

Good god, it didn't take long for the bush telegraph to get word around town. Carlo gave an amused chuckle as he cracked six eggs onto the grill.

'The trouble isa all for thata man, who was rude to our Tegan. Connie, she ripa the skin from him. He no be disrespectful to women again, not ever. She a fierce tigress this one,' he said, patting my shoulder.

'Are you alright?' asked Jack, coming over to me and placing his hands on my cheeks.

'I'm fine, Jack. I don't like men treating women that way...so I told him.'

Tegan, eyes red and cheeks blotchy from crying, came in from the back alley. She had tidied her hair and straightened her clothes and seemed more composed. She came over to me and wrapped her arms around me.

'Thank you, Connie. I wish I'd stood up to him, like you did... it was awesome. I feel better now he's gone.'

I returned her hug, gave her back a pat and said, 'We've got a café full of hungry men all waiting to go to the footy, you okay to get your apron back on?'

Tegan nodded, took a deep breath and marched into the dining room.

I kissed Jack's cheek, 'Rack off you, I've got work to do. I'll see you at the footy,' and shooed him out of the kitchen.

* * *

Poor Nugget didn't get to celebrate a grand final win that year. The Rovers were runners up in 1971, beaten by their nemesis the Panthers.

21

Chapter Twenty-One

The late afternoon sunshine was nice and warm, seeping right down into my bones. It was a relief after the biting cold of winter. I was enjoying the glorious weather while it lasted, knowing that summer and its forty-degree days were just around the corner.

As I made my way along Egan Street, I thought about the last two months. October and November had passed slowly without Jack, Dan and Nugget. Changes had been underway in the café. The Carlo and Maria Sandwich and Pie Bar, was being well patronised – the cappuccino machine a real hit. Carlo had even begun talking about new furniture. With Christmas only two weeks away, Tegan suggested we spend this coming Saturday afternoon jazzing up the café with festive decorations. Carlo cracked me up, moaning that we were sending him broke and he would never retire a rich man...while agreeing with the idea. Scotty volunteered to climb ladders and hang lights. I watch him and T – as he called her – make eyes at each other and felt the sharp barb of Jack's absence in my life.

I took the step up to Norma's nicely renovated and painted front porch and was nearly bowled over by Sandra as she flung open the door.

'Connie, we've got letters,' she said, waving two envelopes in my face. 'From Dazza and Jack.'

I smiled at her as she bounced from foot to foot in excitement. The ice-cold lump in my heart thawed and warmed to match the heat of the day.

'Lovely, Sandra...what do they say?'

'I haven't read mine yet, I was waiting for you.' she replied.

'That was very restrained of you...I don't know that I could have waited.'

Sandra blushed.

'Well to be honest, I've only just got in from work. I haven't had a chance to open mine yet,' she confessed. 'God, I hope they get back soon, I really do miss the rascal.'

'Who Jack?' I said feigning ignorance.

'*No*. Dazza of course. Just as things were getting interesting, he buggers off to go mining. Sheesh...men.'

'They had to go...you know that, don't you?' I said, concerned she didn't understand the importance of what they were doing.

'Yeah, I know...I'm just being selfish.' A self-deprecating smile touched her lips. Handing me a thick envelope, she said, 'Here, go lock yourself away in your room and have a good old cry over this – I know I will. We can compare notes later.'

I held the envelope to my nose and took a deep breath. I could smell fine dust, eucalyptus and sandalwood, all the smells that made up Jack. His smiling image rose before my eyes. Cradling the envelope to my heart, I made my way to my room and with a soft click closed the door. My eyes stung with unshed tears, and I hadn't even opened the letter yet. I went to my dressing-table, stuck my hand inside a drawer and took out a handkerchief. I sat on my bed and opened the letter, being careful not to tear the flap. I slipped out two sheets of paper. The first was from Dan and on one side of the page he had written,

Dear Connie, the mining's going well. We're all safe. Miss you badly and hope to see you soon. Say hi to Sandra, love Dan.

On the other side of the page was Nugget's muddy paw print and Dan had written, *love Nugget*. I laughed at this beautiful gesture. Putting the letter down beside me on the bed, I took up Jack's missive. For a man who had never finished school and spent his days working with his hands, his writing was quite elegant.

My darling Connie, Dan, Nugget and I are all fine. The lease is proving to be very rich and we've found another large gold seam. It runs through good stable rock so the mining is quite safe. There's enough gold to keep us busy for a very long time, but life is not the same without you by my side. I sit at my campfire, watching the stars in the night sky and imagine your beautiful green eyes and cheerful laugh. I've a hole in my chest where my heart once was and I know that place can only be filled by you. Because Dan and I are both pining for our beautiful girls, we've decided to come home before Christmas. So expect us any day soon. Stay safe my love, Jack.

A sob caught in my throat and I felt my heart swell with love. Hugging the letter to my heart, butterflies of excitement swirled around in my stomach. Jack was coming home. I blew my runny nose and dried my eyes...yeah, I know elegant, but it happens when you cry over a man.

Well, Connie, the moment of truth is rapidly approaching. You need to stop hiding...from yourself. Its time to take responsibility for your actions and talk to Jack about your life in Melbourne.

The resolution solidified in my mind and I locked it into place.

* * *

After giving the griddle and hot plates a scrape down and scour, I rubbed hard to buff the stainless-steel surface to a shine. My shoulders ached and a river of sweat poured down my face. I used my hand towel to wipe my sweaty brow and sighed. The heat in the kitchen had not diminished even with everything off.

'Carlo, the extraction fans, hotplates and oven are all done,' I said as I took a clean cloth and plunged it into the bucket of hot sudsy water. 'I've just got the condiments shelf to do and the kitchen will be spick and span – ready for a new week.'

'*Grande*, Piccola, youva done well. When the shelf, he is done, come join me in the dining room, fora bowl of the pasta and espresso.'

'It's too hot for coffee, Carlo,'

'It'sa never too hot for espresso,' he said, flashing me a toothy smile. 'But ifa you like, we can just watcha Maria, Tegan and that young man Scotty hang the Christmas decorations and givea our gooda advice.'

I smirked at Carlo's mischievous ways and said, 'You're a brave man, Carlo.'

'Or a stupid one...maybe they one and the same,' he said. His loud laughter echoed around the room as he strutted out into the dining room. Uproar eschewed as he offered some sage advice.

Smiling, I emptied my bucket in the sink and ran the tap to rinse my cloth. There was a faint rustle of cloth behind me, and a warm breath tickled the back of my neck. A chill of fear ran down my spine and with a clenched fist I spun around, ready to ward off my attacker. I halted my fist mid-air, my heart pounding so hard and fast it nearly flew out of my chest. Jack softly cupped my cheeks with his hands.

'Hello, my love.'

'Oh, Jack.'

I launched myself into his arms, held on tight to his muscular frame, as I captured his mouth with mine. Jack's arms closed around me. My feet left the ground. Warmth ran from the tips of my toes, fizzling its way up my body to the ends of my hair. The kiss was hot, it was passionate, and it tasted of Jack...and home.

'Now there's a greeting a man likes to come home too,' he said as I leant my forehead against his and looked deep into his smiling blue eyes.

'You can put me down now, you big lug,' I said, in amusement.

'Never,' he murmured and began to nuzzle my neck.

'I'm so happy...I've missed you so much. It feels like you have been away forever.'

'I've missed you too, my love. *Marry Me.*'

My breath caught in my throat, hiccupped and then came out in a rush. Jack opened his mouth to speak, but I placed my finger on his lips.

'Jack, before I can answer that, I need to tell you some things. I can't do it here...we should go somewhere quiet and talk. After that, if you still feel the same way...ask me again.'

22

Chapter Twenty-Two

Shocked into action by Jack's proposal, I grabbed his hand and dragged him to the local park, seeking the privacy of the trees. Somehow, I found the courage I'd been seeking all this time. I couldn't cope with the repulsion I was sure to see on his face, so I fixed my gaze on my white, clenched fingers. I held tight to my emotions, even though they hurt and I told Jack the story of my childhood, my mother's bullying ways and the ultimatum that pushed me to leave home. Then came the hardest part, I described the life I'd led in Melbourne and the poor decisions I'd made. When I got to Jerry and his sexual attacks, brutish ways and finally the confrontation that resulted in his death, I felt Jack tense beside me.

I stopped speaking. The shame of what I had been filled me.

There was silence.

I lifted my eyes to meet his, the welling tears blurring his face but I didn't let them fall.

'Jack, my name's not Connie Hara. It's Constance O'Hara. Connie is the name I gave myself after I murdered that brutal man and ran away. I can't go to the authorities...I don't know who to trust. Paul Joshua has a long reach, and Kane is still out there somewhere, hunting me. I'll always be in danger from them and so will anyone I'm close too.'

His lips parted. I lifted my finger and placed it on them to stop him speaking.

'Jack, that's not a risk I want you to take on a whim. Go back to Lucky Charm, and think over all I've told you. If you reckon I'm still worth knowing and loving, then come and see me next Saturday, we'll talk again. *Please,* do this for me, so that I know your decision isn't rash or spur of the moment. But whatever you decide, *please don't despise me.*'

I placed a soft kiss on his cheek and got to my feet. My heart weighed me down as I dragged myself away and walked home. I didn't look back at the man I loved more than life itself.

* * *

Crash!

A chunk of ice smashed through the windscreen of a vehicle parked in the street. Another frozen lump followed. It bounced and sizzled on the hot bitumen. Pedestrians dashed for cover, as a devastating wave of hail poured from the sky. Ice, larger than golf balls, danced and ricocheted in all directions. Hailstones punched holes in the thin, tin pedestrian roof which protected the footpath, as if it was paper, creating a colander effect.

The noise in the café was deafening, the loud drumming on the roof made conversation impossible. I raced from the kitchen to the dining-room window, eager to watch the show. Carlo, who was dogging my steps, hooked his arm around my waist and pulled me under the nearest table. A chunk of ice bounced off the glass, right where my face had been, cracking the glass.

'Everyone, getta down,' he yelled.

Patrons dived for cover. Scotty put his arms protectively around T and huddled in next to us. I watched Luke take advantage of Scotty's abandoned money on the opposite table, with a superior sneer on his pointy, rat-like face – he filched it and shoved it deep into his own pocket. He glanced around, checking out the other tables but a loud thump on the window, as more ice smashed against it, helped change his mind. He scuttled under a table. The noise eased to an occasional *clink*, *clink,* as single pieces of ice fell.

Bang.

A clap of thunder rattled the café. A picture on the wall tottered and fell from its hook and landed face down in a plate of congealed eggs and chips. The rattle faded away, only to be replaced by a whistling and roaring, as wind tore down the street and ripped the sheeting from buildings in a grinding, groaning clatter.

Silence.

I breathed a sigh of relief and crawled out from under the table to stare out the window. The rain came. It hurled from the sky, pounding on the roof in a loud thrumming downpour. There was so much water, it overflowed gutters, cascaded from roofs and streamed down the window in a thick viscous sheet. The hard packed ground, unable to absorb so much water, became the bed of a fast-flowing river, which surged down the main street.

Then it was gone and so was the river.

Iron sheets lay bent and twisted, like crumpled pieces of paper. Shop windows had been reduced to small cube size pieces of shattered glass. The Palace Hotel's ashlar roof facade was pitted and chipped, while the outer wall of the shop next door was a mess of fist sized holes and its porch had been ripped away. Glancing down the street I could see the same story everywhere.

'Bloody summer,' Carlo growled.

Muttering further words under his breath in Italian, he stomped into the kitchen to check for damage.

'That was a ripper storm...is everyone okay?' I asked, glancing around the room to ensure none of the walls or ceiling had been pierced by the deadly hail.

'Got nothin' on '69...that one blew us off the map,' some wit said.

Men's laughter filled the room. Voices increased in volume as everyone tried to outdo his quip with something better.

I took a detour that afternoon, to walk the long way home...and check out the destruction. While some buildings had sustained extensive damage, walls and windows smashed, roof sheeting torn away, others were totally untouched. The Victory Café was lucky...we only had one cracked window.

The town's clean-up crew were busy. As I pushed my way through the watching crowd, I caught a flash of a black jacket with a Twisted Heads insignia on the back. I focussed on a hand and watched it reach into an unguarded pocket.

I stepped up behind the sneak thief and said, 'Hello Luke, anything interesting happening?'

He leapt about a foot in the air.

'Not much,' he replied, spun on his heel and took off at a fast pace.

I smirked after his retreating figure, satisfied I'd done my bit for community policing, but the smugness didn't last. The horrible nausea and funk returned. I'd been like that ever since Jack's surprise return from Gwalia. I hadn't slept and it showed...black bags under my eyes and a dark depressive mood had taken hold of me – not good. Since making my confession, I hadn't slept...I was so sure I'd ruined everything that I had started to pack my bag – again. Deep in my gut I knew I'd finally done the right thing and I prayed Jack could forgive me my past. If not...I'd move, and leave the great life I'd made for myself. Staying would be too painful. Guess I would find out on Saturday.

* * *

D-day arrived. I was as jumpy as hell. The morning ticked by at a slow pace – there was no sign of Jack. No Dan either and that worried me. I was sure he'd come in for breakfast before his usual visit with Sandra.

A voice in my head nagged at me. *Something's wrong*.

I glanced into the dining-room, for about the hundredth time and growled, 'This is ridiculous.'

Waiting and not knowing finally got too much for me… I had to know.

'Carlo, at the end of my shift today, can I borrow your car? I need to check on something.'

'Sure thing, Piccola. You tella that Ironstone, my business, she goa bankrupt, if he no come in for his weekly breakfast.'

'Carlo, I didn't say I was going to see Jack?'

'Please, Piccola, you'va been moping around my kitchen all week. You no sleeping,' he said, running his finger under my eyes, 'It's obvious, howa mucha you two love each other. You needa to marry that man soon, put him, anda me, out of our misery.'

'That's not going to happen, Carlo. I've ruined everything,' I said, wrapping my arms around my waist. 'I need to go see Jack, so he can tell me it's over.'

'*Sciocchezze*, how you say…eh…rubbish. That man, he adores you. Nothing you could do would change that,' said Carlo, handing me his car keys and making shooing motions towards the door. 'Go.'

'Carlo, I haven't finished my shift yet,' I protested as he leant forward and untied my apron strings. 'The lasagne still needs to go in the oven.'

'You think I donna know how to cook in my own kitchen, little *maestra*. Go, I getta Maria to cover.'

I whipped my apron off and kissed him on the cheek. 'Thanks Carlo, you're the best,' I said. 'I promise I'll be very careful with your baby.'

I've only driven a couple of times in my life, so as I pushed gently on the accelerator and released the clutch the car kangaroo hopped forward…and stalled.

I restarted it and tried again.

The Morris slowly moved forward in a jerking motion. Pleased, I guided the car into the traffic on Maritana Street, positive the other drivers didn't notice my poor driving skills. As my head rocked backwards and forwards with the motion of the vehicle, I changed gear. The gearbox crunched. After a colourful word from me the gear engaged. I pressed harder on the accelerator. The car picked up speed and the jerking eased. Very carefully, my hands almost welded to the steering wheel in a death grip that so reminded me of Uncle Richard when he drove in Melbourne traffic, I drove along the narrow bitumen highway. An hour later I came to Lucky Charm's turn off. Not wanting to dirty Carlo's beautiful car, I changed down gears and let the car crawl along the faint dirt track.

A tension headache crept its nasty way up the back of my neck.

Throughout the long slow drive, my mind had been on overdrive. I'd imagined so many scenarios of my meeting with Jack but I was totally unprepared for what reality was about to throw my way.

* * *

The car jerked and stopped. I gazed around in horror. The campsite was destroyed. Dan's sleeping tent was shredded. Torn pieces of canvas gave a lazy flap in the slight breeze. Jack's tent and the store tent lay on the ground, acting as a dam to a pool of water and mud.

Screech.

I cupped a hand over my eyes and looked into the mid-morning sun at the steel tank and windmill. The mill's blades, bent and twisted, cried out in protest as they tried to turn. The water tank was pitted and full of small holes, its precious contents slowly leaking out onto the hot, red earth.

Oh god...what the hell's happened here?

The gnarled gum had been uprooted and was lying on the ground, its roots sticking out like a bad hair day. The fridge, still attached, lay with its door flung open, contents strewn everywhere. Blowflies were feasting in their thousands.

The Rover was here, parked in its usual spot, untouched. So the men must be around somewhere.

I climbed out of the car and looked around – nothing.

Where was everyone?

A movement in the sky caught my glance. A wedge tail eagle slowly circled the camp.

Cupping my hands around my mouth I yelled, 'Jack,' pausing to listen before yelling again, 'Dan...Nugget.'

A mournful howl rent the air. I leapt into action and sprinted towards the noise.

'Nugget...Jack... Dan.'

The howling stopped and the dog barked. Emerging from a clump of white gum, I spotted Nugget, digging at what was left of the mine's entrance. He paused, peered down the shaft and went back to digging. Falling to my knees beside him, I peered down into the gloom. Halfway down the shaft, there was a litter of broken timbers, rocks and clumps of red mud. The remains of the poppet head. Only a small corner of the shaft was free of rubble. The collapsing timbers had created a barrier which held back the worst of the loose dirt and rock that filled the rest of the shaft.

Shit, a cave-in.

Leaning as far down into the void as I dared, I filled my lung with air and screamed.

'*Jack.*'

Nugget joined in, barking.

A slight movement caught my attention.

I placed a gentle hand on Nugget's muzzle, 'Shush, mate.'

I squinted down into the gloom, trying to get a better look.

The sound of small stones rolling caught my attention and as I stared, a clump of red dirt moved right where the tunnel's opening had once been. I opened my mouth to yell again, a hand popped out of the dirt. The fingers wriggled, then disappeared. A muffled voice floated up to me.

'I'm through, Dan mate. Hang in there.'

'*Jack...Dan*,' I screamed.

'*Connie? That you love?*'

Jack...he was alive.

Crying out in joy, 'Yeah, Jack, it's me and Nugget. Are you guys okay? What can I do to help?'

'I'm okay. Dan's taken a knock to the head. He's unconscious. I need to dig us out, but there's nowhere to put the rubble. You'll have to haul it up top, Connie. Will you be able to do that, love?'

'Sure Jack, just tell me what to do and I'll make it happen.'

'In the back of the Rover there's a coil of rope. In the stores tent you'll find a tin bucket and a shovel. Oh...and some water, Connie, it's thirsty work down here.'

'Right, I'm on it – don't you go away,' I quipped.

I turned to Nugget and pulled him into a tight hug.

'They're alive, Nugget...*alive*.'

Nugget's tail spun in a mad circle, his wet tongue ran up my face, leaving a trail of doggy slobber from my chin to my temple. I didn't care. I released him and leapt to my feet.

'Stand guard, Nugget. I won't be long.'

I raced back to the camp and haphazardly searched through the mess looking for the equipment I'd need. At long last I located the shovel, by kneeling on it, buried under a piece of wet tent. I hauled away at a corner of the heavy canvas, my shoes filling with mud and water, while my arms protested at the effort it took.

It took me ages to find the bucket, it was wedged under the Rover's muffler, bent and battered but it would do the job. I wriggled it free and carried the gear back to where Nugget was sitting, staring down the shaft.

Now for the rope.

I flung open the back of Jack's vehicle and found a large coil of slender rope. Oh boy, I had to carry that! I fed my arms through the centre of the coil and pulled the rope onto my shoulders and back. Staggering under the weight, I stiff-legged my way back to the shaft head.

Panting, I fell to my knees and let the coil slide to the ground in relief. Taking a moment to catch my breath, I wriggled a few kinks out of my shoulders.

'I've got the rope, Jack,' I yelled, 'I'm attaching the bucket now and sending down the water.'

He stuck his hand out the tiny hole and gave me a thumbs up.

* * *

My hands were burning in fiery tendrils. The rope slipped, irritating them further, as I clutched at it tightly and pulled another bucket load of rubble to the surface. My neck and shoulder muscles screamed in protest but I couldn't concede defeat. For hours I'd stood in the hot sun, lowering the bucket to Jack's waiting hand and when it was full of dirt and rocks, I'd haul it back up.

The bucket made the lip of the shaft, I grabbed it and lugged it over to the flat area called the waste. I dumped its contents into the growing heap and wiped my sweaty face on my shirt sleeve.

Slowly the tunnel hole was widening, and as the sun set and the day cooled, I lowered a lamp in the bucket to dispel the gathering gloom and give Jack more light to see by. I began to see more and more of his arm as he fed rock and dirt into the bucket.

I sent the bucket down again and wondered how many more loads I could handle before I'd need to take a break.

Jack's head popped into view. He turned a grubby dirt encrusted face upwards and his teeth flashed white as he smiled.

'Won't be long now, love,' he said.

The task sped up after that, Jack was able to use the shovel to clear the tunnel debris and load the bucket. With renewed vigour I hauled up rubble. Within the hour, Jack was able to slide through the new tunnel, and squeeze into the clear area at the bottom of the shaft.

After I hauled up the last load, Jack said, 'Right, get ready to brace the rope for me. First, I'm going to shift Dan into place and then tie the rope around him. I'll climb up to you and together we can pull him to the surface.'

'Hang five, Jack. I don't think I can hold your weight that long all by myself. How about I fetch the Rover and secure the rope to it?'

'That's a bonza idea, Connie. The keys are under the visor.'

Nugget heard the word Rover and raced ahead of me to the vehicle, winning the race with ease. When I opened the driver's door he leapt into the cab, taking possession of his prized seat. Making effective use of the roo bar, I planted my foot on the accelerator and with the engine screaming in first gear, bashed through the bush to the patiently waiting Jack. I wrapped the rope three times around the roo bar and braced my feet on it to be ready if the rope slipped.

'Righto Jack, go for it.'

The rope in my hand tightened, I felt the strain on my sore tired body and cursed. I heard scrambling and cursing behind me...I wasn't the only one messing with the language. The strain eased and a dirty, calloused hand was placed on my shoulder.

I looked up to the most wonderful sight in the world, Jack's smiling face.

Coated with dust and smeared mud, he resembled a dried salt lake, all cracked and grey. Pulling me to my feet, his bright blue eyes, the whites slightly red from dust, shone with intent. Drawing me close, he lowered his head and our lips met. My mouth exploded in a hot swirl of lust and passion. I wrapped my arms around his neck, my toes curled, and I lost the ability to stand on my own. Jack's arms tightened, drawing me even closer. A wave consumed me, spreading its tendrils of hot, sweet desire. My nipples hardened and an ache of need clutched me deep inside. Jack ended the kiss, pressed my cheek gently against his chest and kissed my brow. Panting, I clung to him and listened to his rapid heartbeat. We stood there just holding each other. Nugget ran circles around us in excitement, and barked like a mad thing.

'Right, let's get Dan to the surface,' said Jack stepping back.

'Oh shit, *Dan*. How bad is he hurt, Jack?'

'I don't know, Connie.'

Hand over hand, I inched the rope between my sore hands, as Jack and I pulled the unconscious man to the surface. When the top of Dan's head was level with the surface Jack tied the rope off and leant over the edge of the shaft. He hooked his arms under Dan's armpits and lifted him up and out. I continued to hold on in case the knot slipped, but I should have had more faith – Jack knew how to secure a rope. I ran to the back of the vehicle, threw open the rear door and grabbed the blanket from the seat. I wrapped it around Dan's unconscious form and rubbed his cold limbs vigorously to get the blood circulating. With soft probing fingers I checked his head and face for injuries. Behind his left ear there was a large egg-sized lump, surrounded by a purple bruise and a little dried blood. I looked but couldn't find any other injuries.

I placed a gentle hand on his cheek and said, 'Dazza...Dan...wake up, mate.'

His eyelids fluttered for a moment, then stopped.

'This isn't good, Jack. We need to get Dan to the hospital, fast. He's been unconscious a long time and may have cracked his skull and be bleeding inside.'

Always a man of action, Jack said, 'Righto...Nugget, in the car.'

Nugget made a mad dash for his seat. With infinite care, Jack lifted Dan's still form and carried him to the vehicle. I clambered in the opposite door, while Jack slid him into place on to the rear seat. I placed Dan's head in my lap and stroked his face with soft fingers. With more care and respect than I'd shown his car, Jack set off back down the track I'd ploughed with the roo bar, and we headed out to the main road. Once we made the bitumen, Jack planted his foot. The engine screamed in protest but he didn't ease back.

Dan mumbled incoherent words. My hand on his brow seemed to soothe him, so I gently stroked his forehead and said, 'It's okay, Dan, you're safe...Jack's safe. Shush, my boy.' While I tended to Dan, I asked, 'What happened, Jack?'

'Dan and I decided to go down the mine early yesterday morning. We thought we'd get in a full day's work, then come into town and see our girls. Yeah, I know, you *said* Saturday but I couldn't wait any longer. There must have been a summer storm.'

'Yeah, there was and it was a doozie. Half of Kal was wrecked.'

Jack nodded his head at my words, no surprise showing on his face.

'Of course, being underground we didn't know what was happening up top, until water started rushing down the air vent. Dan was standing at the entrance of my stope, yelling for me to evacuate, when there was an almighty crash, dust and rocks started flying everywhere. A small chunk of rock ricocheted upwards and caught him under his helmet, knocking him out. The war room had a few rocks and dirt come down, but the main cave-in seems to have come from the tunnel and shaft.'

'Yeah, your poppet head collapsed. Lucky it didn't completely block the tunnel entrance.'

'Lucky alright. We could have been trapped down there permanently,' he said. 'How did you know we were in trouble, love?'

'It was Saturday and you didn't show up for your breakfast.'

Jack chuckled, then said, 'Hang on tight, love, we're here.'

With a squeal of tires, we zoomed around a corner into the emergency department driveway. Jack slammed on the brakes, causing the tires to screech as he brought the fast moving vehicle to a standstill.

Our arrival at the hospital created a flurry of activity. I sat in the back seat cradling Dan's head and stroking his brow. Jack raced into the emergency area and yelled for help for his mate. Two white clad orderlies, carrying a stretcher, dog-trotted over to the vehicle. I slid out of the way, while they manoeuvred Dan out. Bearing his weight between them, they dog-trotted back inside. The silence left behind was broken by a single cricket chirping in the night. I leant forward and pushed Jack towards the door.

'Go, Jack, go be with Dan,' I said. 'I'll park the car.'

Jack kissed the tip of my nose and took off.

Much to Nugget's disgust, I kangaroo hopped and stalled the Rover at least half a dozen times while trying to park it. In the end

I gave up, left it at an angle that took up two parking bays. As the dog and I climbed down from the vehicle to make our way in the dull street light to the emergency door, a police vehicle came tearing into the car park. Sergeant Henderson leapt from the driver's seat and came rushing up to me. I was just preparing to run when he began rapidly speaking in a surprisingly deep baritone voice.

'I just heard there was a cave-in at the Lucky Charm. How's Ironstone and Dazza? Are they badly hurt?'

I stepped back from his intensity and answered, 'Dan's just been taken into emergency, he's unconscious. Jack's fine, a bit shaken and dirty, but not injured. He's just gone in to check on Dan.'

'And you, Connie, are you alright?' he asked.

His concern surprised me, as I'd always done my best to stay out of his focus.

'I'm fine, I wasn't down the mine when it collapsed. Nugget and I are just a bit tired from digging, aren't we boy?' I said, giving Nugget's head a gentle rub.

'Woof,' said Nugget.

'It didn't take you long to hear about the cave-in, sarge. You've really got your finger on the pulse of things.'

Sergeant Henderson studied my face and said, 'I have spies everywhere, young lady. You should know that by now. I need to get inside, on another matter. I'll check in with Ironstone on my way through casualty. Are you coming in?'

'No, not yet. Nugget and I have to park the Rover.' I said, pointing to the crooked car.

What was really going through my mind was, *I don't want you getting a good look at my face and making some connection with a wanted poster.*

The sergeant flipped me a wave, as he disappeared through the doors.

I heaved a sigh of relief.

'Well, mate, that was close. As soon as he leaves the hospital, we'll sneak in and find out what is happening with Dan, okay?'

The door opened and Jack stuck his head out.

'Are you coming in, love?' he asked.

'I can't, Jack, what about Nugget. I don't think they allow dogs in the hospital. I don't want to leave him sitting out here by himself.'

'He can come in, I've asked, everyone's voted to ignore his presence. He's a legend in these parts you know.'

Walking towards me, he drew me into a warm, dusty hug.

'What about me Jack and the police, we haven't talked about that yet. I'm scared...scared I've lost your love...scared I'll be recognised by Sergeant Henderson...get sent to Melbourne to be tried for murder... scared of losing you. I can't lose you now because I love you.'

His arms tightened around me.

'Shh...everything's okay, my love. The sarge's gone to sort out some trouble inside. He won't be a problem. As for all the other stuff you told me, well didn't I once say to you I don't live for the past? From what you told me, you were only protecting yourself. That's good enough for me. I love you and together we can face anything.'

Jack smiled down at me and added, 'If you'd hung around for a few minutes longer last week, when we talked, I would've said the same thing and we'd be married now.'

'Oh, would we just. I haven't said *yes* to you yet.'

Jack pulled me even closer, melded his lips to mine. My legs went to rubber and I held on tight.

Pulling away slightly, he smiled down at me and said, 'Now say *no*.'

I cupped his cheek with my palm.

'I'm not stupid, you know. I was never going to say *no*.'

Taking my hand in his, a smile of pure happiness on his face, Jack led me into the waiting area with Nugget at our heels.

Pointing to a corner chair, he said, 'Hide, Nugget.'

Nugget slipped under the chair and curled into a small ball. He lay perfectly still, only the movement of his eyes, as he watched the comings and goings in the room, showed that he was still alert.

'How'd Sergeant Henderson know about the cave-in?' I asked.

'Bush telegraph at work...nursing staff told him, when they rang to report that Lanky Luke's been admitted...overdosed on some sort of drug. The sarge's worried...he's got kids knocking over shops, houses and people for money, all to buy these new drugs in town.'

'Scotty's mate...that Luke?'

Jack nodded.

'Well, I hope the sergeant can put the dealers out of business, quick smart. I hate that stuff, it destroys lives,' I said.

I glanced around the room and spotted a pay phone.

'Jack, I'll be back in a minute. I've got to ring Sandra, let her know that Dan's here in casualty.'

An hour later, Sandra came charging in the door, looking dishevelled and upset, just as the doctor came into the waiting area.

'Dan's regained consciousness. He's fairly woozy and has a hell of a headache. We've X-rayed his head, no fractures or internal bleeding. We'll keep him in overnight, for observation. If he's okay in the morning, you can take him home. He'll probably be concussed for a couple of days, so he'll need to rest.'

'That's great news, doc, thanks. When can we see him?' asked Jack.

'Just give us a little while to get him settled into a bed, then you can have five minutes. In the meantime, Ironstone, I want to give you a quick check over. Sucking in all that dust can't have been good for your lungs.'

'I'm fine, doc,' said Jack. 'No need to trouble yourself.'

'Indulge me, Ironstone,' said the doctor with a smile, and then looking at me he added, 'And you young lady, need to get those hands seen too before they get infected.'

Jack whipped around and grabbed my hands gently in his. He turned them over and examined my raw and blistered palms.

Looking at me with pain in his eyes, he said, 'You didn't say anything, Connie – we could've had these seen too while we waited.'

'It's fine, Jack, a couple of rope burns and a blister or two is not going to kill me. Dan was our first priority,' I said. 'I'll make you a deal. I'll get my hands looked at now, *if you promise* to let the doc listen to your chest. I can't have you conking out on me before the wedding.'

23

Chapter Twenty-Three

We married at the courthouse, 11am Christmas Eve. I signed my real name Constance O'Hara – I wasn't going into this marriage on a lie – and nobody seemed to notice the discrepancy.

Once we were sure Dan would fully recover from his accident, Sandra and I, giggling like school girls bugging out on a day of classes, went shopping.

'Connie, a girl has to have a wedding outfit – and a sexy negligee,' said Sandra, leering ludicrously and winking.

My eyebrows rose as I fought to keep a straight face.

'What good's a negligee...I *don't* intend to keep it on?'

Sandra's eyes widened in surprise and I burst into laughter. She grabbed me by the hand and pulled me into *Golden Treasures Boutique*. I held my breath and looked around in delight. Treasures certainly lived up to its name – racks of glamorous gowns, rows of sexy shoes and a wall of amazing accessories, all offering a world of promise for our mission. I turned in a circle, taking in the sight and not knowing where to start.

'Hey Mavis, you've got a couple of customers,' yelled Sandra, sticking her head between the curtains that hung in front of the office area.

Mavis, middle-aged, tall and willowy, stepped into the room bringing with her a discrete floral scent and a strong image of style.

She gave us an even-toothed smile and said, 'Hello Sandra...not like you to put a dress on.'

'Connie's getting married, she needs an outfit...and as women's lib only goes so far I'd better have one too.'

A warm smile touched Mavis's lips. 'Do you have anything in mind, Connie.'

I shook my head, 'Something simple.'

She touched a finger to her lips, ran her eyes over my proportions and clicked her fingers.

'I've got just the thing.'

Disappearing back behind the curtain, the quiet she'd left behind was interspersed with the sound of box lids being lifted and closed and a mutter of, 'Now where is it?'

She re-emerged holding a long white box and a shoe box. With a flourish she slid the dress box in front of me and said, 'Try this.'

With tentative fingers I lifted the lid and gasped. Buried in a layer of tissue paper was a pale-cream, silk dress. The bodice and three-quarter sleeves was decorated with net appliqué. It was gorgeous.

Mavis set a pair of matching high heels next to the box and said 'Try it on...see what you think.'

The fit was...perfect.

'Oh, Connie,' breathed Sandra, when I modelled the outfit, 'you look stunning. Ironstone's not gonna know what's hit him.'

I stood in front of the mirror and loved what I saw.

Ignoring the price tag, I said, 'It's perfect, Mavis, I'll take it.'

I arrived at the courthouse in a taxi – extravagant I know, but there was no way I was going to get red dust on my outfit. Jack stood waiting on the courthouse steps. He looked drop dead gorgeous in tailored black trousers and a silk shirt, the exact colour of my dress. Nugget, tail swishing in excitement, a black bow tie neatly adorning his neck, sat at Jack's feet. Bless Sandra, she'd thought of everything.

Jack came forward and helped me from the cab. He took my hand, looked deep into my eyes and smiled. My heart gave a flutter, I reached up and ran my shaking hand over his hair, tamed and neatly combed in place. The unlit durry was nowhere to be seen.

'I love you, my beautiful Connie. Will you marry me?'

My heart swelled and nearly burst from my chest.

'I love you too...and *yes*, I'll marry you.'

Sandra appeared at my side and handed me a small posy of flowers she'd *borrowed* from her aunt's garden.

'Carlo, Maria, Scotty and Tegan are waiting inside,' she said.

Dan, dressed to match Sandra's outfit, tugged on Jack's arm, pulling him towards the door. 'Come on, Romeo...'

I tucked my hand into the crook of Jack's arm and together we strolled up the steps and into the registrar's office. The celebrant, amused he was assisting one of his brethren in taking the plunge, conducted a simple but quirky ceremony. I'm sure Dan had a hand in writing the vows, they smacked of his humour.

'Jack Evan Downy do you promise to ensure there is always tea in the larder, limit your cricket stories and put the toilet seat down?'

With a loud chortle Jack said, 'I do.'

'Connie, will you let Jack rescue you from spiders and creepy crawlies on a regular basis and laugh at his poor jokes?'

'I will.'

'Good, I pronounce you chained and shackled. Now go...enjoy your life together.'

Looking at my new husband and friends as we trooped up the street in a happy laughing group, I felt a warm rush of love and satisfaction for my new life.

The café, closed today because of the wedding, was to be the venue for our wedding lunch.

I settled into my seat and looked with interest at the tomato and herb bruschetta on my plate. Sniffing delicately I detected a hint of garlic.

Carlo beamed in delight at my look of approval, 'I mighta add this to the menu, Piccola, what you say?'

'Something for the ladies of Kal,' I said, nodding my head in approval.

Giving Maria an affectionate look, Carlo lifted his bruschetta to her, then to us.

'I wish to bestow upon Piccola and Ironstone an old Italian blessing. My *noona*, she blessa Maria and me when we marry...now itsa time to passa that gooda fortune on. Thisa bread, is so you may never knowa the hunger,' then sprinkling salt over the top, he continued, 'Salt she isa so your marriage will always hava the flavour. Wine...so you will always hava something to celebrate.'

Pop!

The cork flew off a bottle of champagne to a rousing cheer.

Taking a small sip, I swirled my tongue in the bubbles as they danced and exploded in my mouth, tickling the back of my nose.

The men chowed down, like it was the first meal they'd eaten in years.

Maria rose and disappeared into the kitchen. She returned and set a bowl of soup, full of delicious vegetables and parmesan cheese meatballs, in front of me.

She spoke quietly in my ear, 'Italian Wedding Soup – *minestra maritata*, married soup we call it, Piccola...to givea you the energy for tonight.' I felt my stomach do a flip of nervousness – my wedding night.

After a main course of roasted peppers and chicken pasta, Dan rose to his feet. His face flushed pink as everyone stopped talking and stared at him.

'Time for the Best Man's speech,' he said, running a finger around the inside of his collar and pulling a face of make-believe embarrassment. Dan played the crowd like a maestro, and held us in the palm of his hand.

'There comes a time in a person's life, when they meet their one true love, their soul mate, their destiny. The one person that will know and understand them...for the rest of their life. That moment came for Jack, *nine years ago,* when he met *me*, his best man.'

He waited patiently for the uproar and laughter to subside, before continuing: 'I do have to point out, Jack, just how lucky you are. You'll leave here today with a beautiful wife, who is warm, loving and caring. Connie, you'll get to leave here today with a wonderful dress.'

Jack threw his napkin at Dan, who easily dodged the missile. The laughter took a long time to down. When it did, Dan raised his glass.

'But seriously...I love you both dearly, and wish you the very best in life. To the bride and groom...Connie and Jack Downy.'

'The bride and groom, Connie and Jack,' chorused everyone.

Carlo stood, rubbing his hands together, 'Now I hava made the traditional wedding dessert.'

My mouth watered, as my spoon broke into rich crumbling pastry. When the hot sweet berries touched my tongue I moaned in delight. The tart was divine.

Where Carlo managed to get the berries from, I've no idea. I suspect he'd had them freighted in from Perth on last week's truck...just after Jack and Dan got back from Gwalia. Carlo saw a lot from his kitchen.

Jack lifted my fingers to his lips, a gleam in his eyes.

'Thank you everyone, for a memorable day...but I'm now going to take my beautiful wife home.'

Before I could protest, he rose from his chair, scooped me up and carried me out to the door. I could hear hoots and laughter coming from the café, but I chose to ignore them. I snuggled into his neck, breathing in his wonderful and unique scent of sandalwood and red earth.

***

Jack kicked the motel door shut and stood holding me cradled in his arms. He'd carried me from the Rover to our motel room, without taking his eyes from mine. Slowly he lowered my feet to the ground, our lips met. Cupping my face with his hands, he slowly almost lazily savoured the taste of my mouth, lighting a fire deep within me. My skin began to tingle, as flickering tendrils of heat and desire coursed my veins. Our tongues danced, our passion rose and then I learnt the true meaning of making love.

Early the next morning, snuggled together in bed, Jack said, 'Good morning my darling wife, Merry Christmas.' He slipped a small gift into my hand.

'Merry Christmas...husband.'

I tore the wrapping paper, in my rush to open my present. Inside was a small blue velvet box and inside that lay a shiny gold nugget hanging from a delicate gold chain. My eyes widened in awe, as I lifted the beautiful necklace up to admire it.

'Oh Jack...it's gorgeous,' I said, leaning over and kissing his cheek. 'I don't want to spoil the moment, but can we afford this? I know you lost everything when the shaft collapsed.'

Jack just smiled.

'We haven't lost anything, Connie. The safe's still in the war room, right where we left it. It might be buried under a bit of dirt and rock but it's easily dug out, and there's always Gwalia. Excuse the pun, but, that little lease is a real gold mine.'

Relieved by his reassuring words, I kissed the nugget and put the chain around my neck, running my fingers over it, enjoying the texture. I reached down beside the bed and picked up my gift to Jack.

'For you, my darling,' I said, handing him a plaited, leather trimmed Akubra, to replace his old battered hat, lost in the cave-in.

'Brilliant, Connie. My heads been feeling a bit cold without my lid,' he said, putting the hat on, a look of pleasure on his face.

Much later, after appreciation for presents had been shown, I gave myself a mental slap.

'Oh dammit, Jack...I didn't wear the beautiful negligee I bought.'

'Well, you could always put it on now,' he said, with a wicked grin and a wiggle of his manhood below the covers.

'You greedy dog,' I said, giving his arm a small shove, secretly amused by his antics, 'I don't think I could. I'll be lucky if I can walk, as it is.'

Jack laughed.

'Well to tell the truth, I think I need a feed and a little shut eye myself, before we go again...but if you insist.'

I gave a squeal of delight as he pulled me down under the covers and began nibbling at my neck. The phone on the bedside table rang, interrupting our enjoyable play. Jack reached across grumbling but I just laughed and climbed out of the bed, heading for the shower.

'Hello, what time of day do you call this?' he grouched into the receiver.

I heard a tinny voice, jabbering away.

Jack said, 'Okay we'll be down in half an hour.'

My footsteps faltered, 'What's wrong?'

Jack didn't answer, instead he lay back and ran his gaze over my naked body.

'Jack?'

He smiled wickedly and said, 'What? Oh...yeah, that was the motel manager. We're supposed to check out at ten, evidently it's after twelve. I don't know where the time's gone...must have slept in or something.' He leapt to his feet and chased me to the shower.

We checked out at three and headed over to Egan Boarding House, to collect Dan and Nugget.

* * *

Ever since Dan's hospitalisation, Norma had been in a funk. She'd fussed about his care, and worried that if he went back to camp, he wouldn't rest properly. She insisted he stay with her, at the boarding house. Dan laughed and accepted, that way he didn't have too far to travel to visit Sandra. The house was quiet when we let ourselves in. I gave a soft tap on Sandra's door. She opened it, looking rumpled and dewy eyed.

I smiled and asked in a quiet voice, so Norma wouldn't hear, 'Is Dan with you Sandra?'

'Yeah,' she whispered, a small secret smile touching her lips, 'give him a moment, to slip out the window and back to his own room.'

'Okay, tell him we'll be in my room, collecting my gear,' I said. 'And Sandra...Merry Christmas.'

'Merry Christmas to you and Jack,' she said, laughing and throwing her arms around me, squeezing tightly before disappearing back into her room and quietly closing the door.

I nodded my head towards my room, 'Come on Jack, we'll give my room a final check and stow my gear...while Dan sorts himself out. We better get him out of here before Norma rumbles them and Sandra finds herself out on the street.'

'Righto love, you're the boss...just show me what needs loading.'

Dan's door burst open and he bounced into the hallway. His mere presence seemed to add life to the room.

'Merry Christmas, Mr and Mrs Downy. How was the honeymoon?'

Jack smirked at him and said, 'Probably as good as yours, you cheeky bugger. Now go get your gear lad...we're off in ten minutes. There's still a camp to sort out and a mine to salvage. Oh yeah...you've also got a Christmas spit to organise, so don't waste time 'cause I'm starvin.'

Dan's laugh echoed around the hallway, it bounced off the ceiling and filled the crevasses in the walls.

'Righto,' he said at full volume, but as he headed back to his room he lowered his voice and spoke quietly over his shoulder at us. 'I'll just slip Nugget out the window...Ma Norma doesn't know he's here. Open the Rover door will ya, Jack?'

'Yeah, no problems, I'll just grab Connie's gear...meet you out front in a minute.'

Dan wouldn't be Dan without some witticism.

'You sure you should be doing that. You're an old married man now, you might hurt yourself carrying heavy loads.'

Before Jack could put him into a head lock, Dan dashed away, leaving only his machine gun laugh echoing around us.

My overstuffed backpack and Dan's knapsack joined a large pile of gear, already loaded into the back of the vehicle. Jack had spent the week stocking up, in preparation for our return to Lucky Charm. I spotted a new tent in the mix.

I took both sets of keys and strode confidentially down the creaky hallway, to make my farewell to Norma. A bit different to the day of my arrival, when I had been quite hesitant and unsure of what lay before me.

Norma was sitting at the table in a cloud of smoke, dressed once again in her yellow mumu. It was déjà vu all over again.

'Thanks Norma,' I said, handing over the room keys, 'for a safe and comfortable home.'

She smiled, tossed the keys onto the messy table and said, 'You tell that young scoundrel Dazza, if he was staying any longer, I'd be putting a padlock on Sandra's window.'

Amused, I crossed my arms and waited for the punch line.

'Oh, and the dog snores too!' she added.

Norma really had a handle on everything.

* * *

I expected our arrival back at Lucky Charm would entail a lot of clean-up work, but I should have known better. During the week, Jack and Dan had accomplished miracles. The wrecked tents had been dismantled and disposed of, while the surviving ones had been dried out, cleaned and pitched on the opposite side of the fire pit.

The rotting food was gone and the entire camp had been raked clean of debris. The old gum still lay where she'd fallen, but most of the branches had been removed, split and stacked to dry as firewood. The kerosene fridge, scratched and dented, still functioned and was tied to the sandalwood.

I laughed when I saw the steel water tank. It was covered in a multitude of cream patches and looked like it had a bad case of chicken pox.

Shouldering my pack, Jack took my hand and together we walked to the shack. As we reached the door, he scooped me up into his arms and carried me over the threshold.

'Welcome home, my love,' he said, and lowered my feet to the floor.

My head swivelled around as I tried to take in all the changes since my last visit. Dominating the room was a gigantic four-poster bed. The frame, handmade from twisted tree branches, had been varnished to a high gloss. The thick, comfortable looking mattress, dressed with white sheets, fluffy pillows and a handmade crocheted rug looked homely and inviting. Jack dropped my backpack next to a large wooden tallboy and hung his jacket on the wooden hat rack.

'When did you get time to do all this?' I asked running my fingers over the beautiful bed frame. 'Surely you didn't do this in a week?'

'Nah...Dan and I've been working on the bed for months. In fact, we started the day after I met you.'

'The day after, Jack. Surely not?' I said, wrinkling my nose in disbelief.

'Connie, one look at you was all it took, my love. When you fell into my arms, that first day, I knew you belonged there.'

Looking up at this wonderful man, my eyes filled with tears.

'Now don't you start blubbering, you know I hate to see you cry.'

He walked over to the right-hand wall and opened a door, one that hadn't been there last time I was in this space.

'I have a surprise for you.'

I stuck my head in the doorway, curious and a squeal of delight burst from my lips.

'Oh you wonderful, wonderful man. My own indoor shower and toilet! You've thought of everything,'

I flung my arms around his neck and kissed him soundly.

'I so love you, right now.'

Another long passionate kiss had Jack readjusting his jeans.

'As much as I want to test out the bed with you right now, I can't. I need to go give Dan a hand. I'll leave you to unpack and get settled.'

Laughing I smacked his butt and said, 'Get going, I'll be out soon to give you guys a hand. I don't have much to unpack. Oh, and Jack...tell Dan to get some food on, I could eat a horse.'

Laughing, my husband left the shack and went off to do the man stuff with Dan while I explored my new home.

***

That evening we shared the best Christmas dinner I'd ever eaten. While Dan started the fire, Jack unloaded the Rover and went to work pitching the new tent. Dan fussed around with the food and suddenly the most delicious aromas filled the air. A leg of pork, popping and hissing as it rotated over the hot coals attracted me to the fireside.

'What's for dinner, chef?' I asked Dan, as he wrapped potatoes and carrots in aluminium foil.

Dan smiled and said, 'Roast Pork, veg and hot damper dripping in butter.'

My stomach gave a loud growl.

'That sounds awesome, Dan. Can I help?'

'Yeah mate, but not with the cooking. I've got that covered. Could you load the stuff from the esky into the fridge, and stack the groceries into the food lockers? Then dig out the coffee...or in your case, tea. I think we could all do with a strong hot cuppa while we wait for the dinner to cook.'

I was starting to feel at home and useful as I loaded up the fridge. Glancing up from his work, Jack smiled before going back to banging pegs into the hard ground.

In the cool of the evening, under a glorious night sky, I settled back with a gentle burp and said, 'Dan, that has to be the most wonderful meal I've ever eaten. Thank you. Now I have something for you.' I handed him a brightly wrapped gift, 'Merry Christmas.'

Dan rubbed his hands together in excitement and ripped it open. His face lit up as he lifted the personalised Rovers Football Club jacket, to reveal his number and Dazza emblazoned on the back.

'Bonza, Connie, this is fantastic. I've always wanted one of these...just never gotten around to ordering one,' he said. His eyes narrowed and he looked at me speculatively. 'You have to order these, they take months to arrive. When'd you do that?'

'Oh, I have my ways. Jack and I do talk you know,' I said laughing and sticking my hand under my seat. I picked up a blue and white dog collar, 'For Nugget.'

Dan leapt from his seat and racing over, he lifted me up out of my seat and engulfed me in his arms. My laughter muffled against his shirt. I could hear Jack in the background, his amused voice saying, 'Put my wife down you scoundrel.'

Letting me go, Dan danced away calling, 'Nugget come here mate, look what Connie and Jack got for you.'

I watched him fasten the collar on Nugget, before the pair of them went racing off into the dark yahooing and barking at the night.

'Well, that was a hit, Jack. We had a real winner with those gifts.'

Jack gave me a lazy smile and said, 'I have one more gift for you, my love.'

'No Jack, you've already given me so much. You, Dan, Nugget...a new golden life. It's all so wonderful, I don't want anything else.'

Jack leant forward and kissed me on the tip of my nose, 'This is a gift for me as well, Connie. I know you want to keep working at the café and it has been worrying you, the amount of time it would take out of our day to drive you into work and pick you up each day. Dan and I bought you something to help with that.'

Rising to his feet, he held out his hand to me, drawing me to my feet.

Jack looked into the dark and called out, 'Now, Dan.'

I heard a motor start, lights lit the darkness, suddenly next to me stood a little yellow Mini.

Dan leapt from the driver's seat, 'Ta da...Merry Christmas, Connie.'

I wrapped my arms around both my men, and did a jig of delight.

Then reality struck.

'I suppose this means I'll have to get a driver's license.'

Dan let out a long laugh and said, 'If Connie gets her licence, Jack, should we get ours as well?'

Jack just smiled, 'All in good time, Dan, all in good time. You can't rush these things.'

Life can be so wonderful and then it kicks you in the guts.

24

Chapter Twenty-Four

Dan regaled us with one of his more humorous exploits. Jack threw a load of wood on the campfire. Taking a sip from my morning tea, I watched the horizon crack open, tinting the black with a bright orange pre-dawn light. The days were passing fast. It was already January, my birthday and Dan's *found day* were rapidly approaching...this year I intended to make it a celebration – for all of us. Nugget snuggled in close to my right leg to keep warm. He was staring blankly down the access road, day dreaming his idea of dog heaven.

Jack chuckled softly and said, 'Dan, you're such a bullshit artist, how do you come up with these things.'

'Nah...fair dinkum, mate, it really happened like that.'

'Yeah right,' Jack drawled. He slid his arm across my shoulders, gave a gentle squeeze and settled back to sip his morning coffee. 'Connie my love, Dan and I'll be coming in for lunch today...we've got some business to take care of at the bank. I want to sell some gold. The market's up and it's a good time to cash in. Dan, how much do we still owe on the vineyard?'

'Two more payments, Jack...then we're done.'

'Hmm...what do you reckon...cash in enough and pay it off today?'

'Ripper idea Jack, we should take advantage while we can. The finance boffins reckon the nickel market's about to boom, you know what that means...' Dan leant forward and filled his enamel mug with more coffee, 'If nickel goes up...gold will go down.'

My jaw slackened as I listened to the conversation. I looked from one man to the other in confusion.

'What's up, love?' asked Jack, as I gave him an extra long stare.

'A vineyard, Jack?' I stuttered, scrubbing a hand in my hair to check if I was awake. 'You're buying a vineyard?'

Dan started to laugh. Startled, a pink and grey galah took flight from its perch high in the sandalwood tree and shrieked its protest at being disturbed.

'Yeah, Connie...a vineyard. Well, it's not really a vineyard yet...will be once we've finished planting the vines. Fifty sweet acres of Swan Valley real estate. Nice flat ground, a few gentle slopes and good supply of underground water. It's the life we've been working towards. Didn't Jack tell you?'

Jack smiled and said, 'Not yet...I was actually going to discuss it with you both tonight. Our family's growing, Dan, I need to make a will and sort the finances out. It didn't really matter before if anything happened to me, you'd have been okay. You know where the gold is and how to cash it in, when you need funds. You also understand the value of keeping a small bank account and staying under everyone's radar, but now I need to make sure Connie's taken care of.'

'I'd take care of Connie, Jack...you know that right?' said Dan, his brow scrunched in a frown of concern.

'Yeah I do, mate. I've complete faith in you,' said Jack, nodding his head in acknowledgement of Dan's commitment. 'But we're worth a great deal of money. The safe downstairs is full and there's also our hidden stash. The world's full of crooks who'd love to get their greedy hands on what we have. From today, we're going to teach Connie the finances, lad. Show her how the leases and markets work. I also want to make sure she's got access to the gold. You can't be too careful.'

'Yeah righto, Jack. What's the problem, Connie, you look a bit stunned?' asked Dan.

'I'm sorry if I seem a little slow this morning... actually I'm rather gobsmacked. I knew you'd had some mining success...I just didn't realise how much.'

'That's why we keep a low profile...safer not to come to anyone's attention,' said Jack. 'We've worked hard and lived rough so we could set ourselves up for the future...the vineyard is that future. Dan's been studying wine making, in his spare time. I wrote to a bloke, a neighbour, asking if he'd teach us the trade...got his reply yesterday. He's happy to help us with advice. In return we'll lend a hand on his property when he needs it. Would you be happy with that kind of life, my love? Living amid fruiting vines and sipping wine in the shade of blossoming fruit trees, all in the quiet of the Swan Valley?'

I heard the yearning in his voice, a new sense of purpose flickered to life inside me.

'Sounds wonderful...tell me, are there this many flies on our vineyard?' I asked, swatting at the buggers as they tried to dive bomb my cup of tea. Both men gave a chuckle of laughter.

Nugget shifted restlessly against my leg, stood and stared down the track, his tail stiff and still. A soft growl rumbled from his chest. He cranked it up a notch, as the sound of a vehicle changing gears echoed down the track. Jack leant his head back, cocked his ear and listened.

'It's okay, mate,' he murmured, placing a hand on Nugget's head, 'It sounds like the paddy wagon.'

Dan, his stocky brown legs sticking out of tan shorts, stood up in his work socks and stretched, then casually leant his left elbow on the branch of the sandalwood, as he too stared down the track.

Taking a sip coffee, Dan said, 'Wonder what's up, the cops don't come this far off the beaten track very often...and early in the morning too.'

I gave a small jerk of fright. Jack stuck the unlit rollie in the corner of his mouth and replied to this query in his usual philosophical way.

'I'm sure we'll find out in a moment.'

He gave me a thoughtful glance.

'Connie my love, would you do a job for me?'

I nodded.

'Go and fuel the water pump at the tank. Dan and I'll deal with these blokes.'

Dan gave us a puzzled look.

'Sure Jack, can do,' I said and kissed him.

In the background I heard Dan muttering, 'Get a room you two.'

I just smiled as I leapt to my feet, eager to be away from police eyes.

'Come on, Nugget...let's go.'

Nugget turned his head to stare at me, looked intently at Jack for a moment and then glared back down the track. He growled at the approaching vehicle.

'Go on, mate, go with Connie. *Guard.*'

Nugget takes the verb *guard* seriously, he gave a soft *wruff*. I kicked off my canvas tennis shoes, pulled on a pair of thick socks and slid my feet into my work boots. Dan crossed his feet at the ankles, and taking on a more relaxed stance against the tree said, 'Don't worry mate, we won't let anyone take her.'

I stopped and stared at Dan.

'I don't need to know what's going on, Connie. Jack loves you, I love you. You're my family. I'll protect you to the bitter end.'

My heart lifted, I flashed him a happy smile and blew a kiss. Dan's face turned pink and he blinked rapidly a few times, like he had something in his eye.

I grabbed the heavy jerry can with two hands and headed off, with it banging against my leg. Nugget dogged my heels guarding me against hidden dangers.

The campfire was still within sight and sound of where I was working, so I kept one eye and ear on the action there. As I removed the cap from the fuel tank I heard Jack say, 'Dan, grab a clean mug, will ya mate. I'm sure the sarge would appreciate a strong hot cuppa.'

'I better make it two...he's not alone.'

A white Land Cruiser, with dark blue letters reading Police emblazoned down the side, halted next to our parked cars. A young constable, one I'd never seen before, sat behind the wheel. In the passenger's seat I could see the familiar large frame of Sergeant Henderson. Well, that's a turn-up for the books...he usually does all the driving. Something big must be up.

I watched, from the corner of my eye as they climbed from the cab and stretched. With a firm tug Sergeant Henderson settled his police hat in place before rounding the front of the vehicle and shaking hands with Dan and Jack. He accepted a steaming mug of coffee and settled himself on the seat I'd just vacated. The constable fidgeted and moved restlessly in his seat but kept quiet.

Nugget watched the group, gave a small growl and then nudged me on the leg. I placed a hand on his head in comfort.

The conversation around the fire looked amiable...Dan's laughter was soon joined by the others. I began to relax. As there was no effort being made by anyone at the campfire to move, I primed the pump and started the bloody thing... it kicked in and began topping up the water tank.

Still no indication they were moving on.

Good god, how long does it take to drink a coffee? Say your piece and go.

I'd run out of excuses to stay away. I gathered up my gear and was about to head back when Sergeant Henderson rose to his feet. The atmosphere in the group changed. Jack and Dan tensed. The young policeman, fitted his cap securely on his head, stiffened his backbone and with a mournful look on his face did something unusual, he handed Dan an envelope.

Since when did the police begin delivering mail?

God, I hope Dan hasn't done something wrong, gotten himself summoned to court or anything silly like that.

Sergeant Henderson patted Dan's shoulder, walked towards his vehicle and glanced over at me. He gave me a sad shake of his head and a small wave. Doors slammed, the vehicle did a three-point turn and slowly drove off down the track.

Jack's head dropped and he started to weep. Dan's face showed no emotion at all. He put the hand that was clutching the envelope on Jack's shoulder but didn't speak. My stomach churned and a large hard lump formed in my throat. Fear sizzled through me.

Jack's crying.

I dropped the fuel can and funnel, left them where they lay. I pumped my arms and legs and pelted up the dusty track. Nugget dogged my heels and kept pace easily.

I skidded to a halt and cried out, 'What the hell's going on? Dan...why's Jack crying?'

Jack wiped his eyes with the back of his hand and pulled Dan into a fierce hug. It seemed to go on forever.

'*Dan...Jack,* please,' I pleaded, 'what's wrong?' Tears began forming in my eyes, my throat tightened and I found it hard to breath. 'Please tell me...'

In unison they turned to look at me...two sad men.

Speaking softly, Dan said, 'I've been conscripted, Connie. I've got a month before I have to report for a medical and training...looks like I'm going to the war in Vietnam.'

My world crashed down around me.

'No, Dan, no,' I croaked. I launched myself to his chest, locked my arms tightly around him and hung on.

'*No*...I won't let them take you.'

I felt two sets of arms go around me and tighten. As a family unit we stood locked together...I wanted to stay like that forever.

'You have to let me go, Connie. It's the right thing to do.'

My tight throat gave a sob as my chest heaved. 'Jack, *please*,' I pleaded, 'don't let them take Dan from us.'

Jack stroked my hair and with a catch in his own voice, answered the only way he could. 'If I could change things, I would, my love.'

'Connie, I love you...and Jack...but you have to let me go. I want to do this,' said Dan.

Nugget circled us and whined, not understanding we'd lost Dan, and nothing would ever be the same again.

* * *

Dan's departure day arrived far too quickly. Jack booked us rooms at the Tower Motel and we drove into Kal, the night before he was due to leave. Farewell drinks were organised at the Exchange Hotel. A few of the boys from the footy club wanted to have a beer with their Dazza – word soon went around and half of Kalgoorlie rocked up. The pub was packed to the rafters by the time we arrived, more people milled around out in the street, laughing and drinking without a care in the world.

It was loud, raucous and hot inside. I had one beer and said, 'I'm going back to the motel, Jack. You stay with Dan as long and as late as you need to.'

'You sure, Connie?'

'Yeah, I'm sure. This farewell's too public for me. I can't say goodbye to Dan like this,' I said. My heart weighed a ton and ached.

'Well, let me see you safely to the motel and then I'll come back.'

'No, Jack, stay. Keep an eye on Dan. The way they're pouring the beer into him, he'll be legless in no time. Just ask the publican, Rory, to telephone me a taxi will you. I'll just let Dan and Sandra know I'm going.'

I shoved hard and pushed my way through the crush, to where Dan stood, chugging down another beer. My heart bled for Sandra. She stood by his side, looking forlorn and tired.

I placed a comforting hand on her arm and yelled, 'I'm going...this is not for me. I'm at the Tower Motel, if you want to talk.'

Sandra lowered her mouth to my ear and yelled over the roar of the crowd, 'Thanks Connie, but I'll stay. If this is all I can have, then I'll take it.'

I nodded, I understood. I waved a hand in front of Dan's face to get his attention and raised my voice again. 'Enjoy yourself, lad. I'm off. I'll see you for breakfast. An Ironstone and Dazza at the Victory Café before you go.'

Dan rocked forward and kissed my cheek.

With a puff of beery breath on my face, I heard him slur, 'Love you, Connie, see ya in the morning.'

* * *

We literally had to pour Dan onto the train. Lucky for him the train trip would take four hours. I hoped it would be enough time for Dan to sober up. The army was probably used to conscripts showing up a little seedy but I didn't want Dan making any life changing decisions in that poor state. We had no idea where he was going, other than he was scheduled for a medical in Merredin tonight and had a ticket for the midnight bus to Irwin Army Barracks in Karrakatta. I suppose the military didn't want to give the conscripts an opportunity to take off. These were to be our last moments together.

We met for breakfast and Carlo produced a magnificent feast. With a belly full of beer and I suspect a headache to rival his concussion, Dan still managed to put away the giant plate of food. I could see Jack was hurting bad, he hardly touched his food, but he maintained a calm exterior. Men! Me, I kept tearing up and sniffling.

'I'll write when I can,' slurred Dan, emptying a bottle of tomato sauce over his chips. 'I'll send the letters care of the sarge...he'll always know where to find you.'

Pushing a gift box towards Dan with his forefinger, Jack's voice broke as he said, 'For you lad. So you can always find your way home to us.'

Dan lay down his knife and fork and took up the gift. He opened it and stared at the contents. Sitting on a bed of white satin was a beautiful gold watch, water and shockproof. In its face the jeweller had cleverly included a small compass. He lifted it from the box, scrunched his eyes and read the inscription on the back out loud.

'The sand may brush off, the salt may wash away but our love will remain forever. Jack and Connie, 1972'

A single tear ran down Dan's cheek.

He put the watch on and in a cracked voice said, 'Thank you both.'

Pushing a second cup of coffee in front of him, I asked, 'Where's Sandra this morning. I thought she'd be here?'

Dan looked at me cross-eyed and said, 'I told her not to come. It's too hard. Connie, promise me you'll look after her? I know I'm young, but I'd like to marry her one day.'

I patted his hand, took a deep breath and promised.

'Sure Dan, I'll take care of her.'

The food and coffee seemed to be helping. Dan was steadier by the time we made it to the train station. The train stood, doors open, ready to suck our lad into an unwanted future. As Dan grasped Jack's hand in farewell, a reporter from the *Kalgoorlie Miner* tried to butt in.

'Sir, how does it feel to be sent away to become a baby killer?'

My stomach churned, shocked at his cruel words. As a group we turned and stared, horror written on all our faces. Suddenly the bulky frame of Sergeant Henderson, blocked the reporter from my sight.

'Move along please, sir.'

The reporter started to argue.

'Obstructing a police officer in the course of his duty might get you a night in a police cell, sir.'

The reporter stopped arguing, held up a camera and madly started clicking. The sarge put his hand over the lens and snarled, 'Move it.'

The reporter stomped away but kept glaring back over his shoulder at us.

'Bastard,' said Jack. 'Thanks, sarge.'

The tall policeman stepped towards Dan, patted his shoulder and said, 'Keep your head down, Dazza. Come back to us safe.'

He nodded at me, touched the brim of his cap, 'Connie,' and walked away.

'All aboard,' yelled the conductor.

I flung my arms around Dan. He held tight for a moment, then stepped back, gave Jack a chin lift and climbed onto the train. A final flap of the hand and he was gone.

25

Chapter Twenty-Five

'Connie, Sergeant Henderson's in the dining room...says he needs to speak with you,' said Tegan, hands fidgeting with her apron, a worried look on her face. 'I hope everything's alright...nothing's happened to Scotty or Jack.'

My head shot up and my heart nearly stopped at her words. After his drug overdose, Luke had become even more unreliable and was keeping bad company. Scotty had terminated their partnership saying it was too dangerous to have him around. He now worked at Lucky Charm as a paid employee – not filling the hole Dan had left in our lives.

Jack and Scotty had spent the last month rebuilding the poppet head. Today they were due to start clearing the rubble from the shaft. Everything had been fine when I left for work this morning.

'Tegan, tell the sarge I'll be there in a sec,' I said, giving the oven a final swipe with my cloth and slamming the door closed.

Please don't let there be a problem...I don't need any new worries in my life.

Wiping my greasy hands on my sweat towel, I hurried around the work bench and headed for the dining room.

Sergeant Henderson's deep baritone stopped me in my tracks.

'No need to come out, Connie,' he said, leaning in through the kitchen hatch. He held out an envelope. 'And don't look so frightened, young lady. There's nothing to worry about, I've a letter for you...from Dazza.'

Unbidden, a smile of pure happiness lifted my lips.

'Fantastic. Jack will be thrilled. We really miss him.'

'The whole town does, Connie,' he said, handing me the envelope. 'Give my best to Ironstone.' He doffed his hat and disappeared from view.

I looked down at the envelope cradled in my hand, and then clutched it to my breast. I took a deep uneven breath and slipped it into my pocket, for later. I went back to my cleaning, with a lighter heart.

Relaxing beside the campfire, cup of tea in hand, I said, 'Jack, we got a letter today...from Dan.'

The lines that had formed at the corners of Jack's eyes in recent weeks lifted. He smiled in pure happiness.

'What did the lad have to say for himself?'

'I don't know...I haven't opened it yet. I wanted to save it, so we could read it together.'

I slipped the envelope from my pocket and showed him.

'You read it to me, love. I like to listen to the sound of your voice.'

With a warm heart, I opened Dan's letter.

Dear Jack and Connie,

Well, I passed the medical. It was never in doubt really, had a thumper of a headache that day, must've had a touch of flu or something! Anyway, it wasn't something to make me fail the test. After passing the army doctor's scrutiny, the military was real quick to bundle us off to the Recruitment Training Centre at Kapooka. The base, just outside Wagga Wagga, is far enough out of town to keep us from getting into trouble with the locals and I suppose so nobody can bugger off. We're here for twelve weeks for our initial training, then it's off to Queensland, for some intensive jungle warfare stuff. The QLD grounds are in Canungra, so I'll be getting around, seeing the world. So here I am, a NASHO – that's what they call us lucky bastards who lost the national service lottery. Recruit Daniel Babcock at your service, (says he with a salute and a jaunty smile). The blokes here are mixed bunch, some are really pissed off at being called up. I stay out of their way, not worth getting in a fight over something I've got no control over. I'm bunking in next to Don Donaldson, everyone calls him Bluey, on account of his red hair. Nothing like your gorgeous curls, Connie. His is carrot red and he has the freckles to match. Poor bugger burns to a crisp out in the sun, his face is always peeling. The sarge here reckons he'll be a great target in Vietnam, glowing the way he does. Bastard, imagine telling a bloke that! Bob Hawkins, you remember him Jack? He played district footy out in the Wheatbelt. Well, he got called up as well and is bunking on the other side of me. Being an inventive lot, the team's dubbed him, Hawk. I am still Dazza. Hawk saw to that the first day, by yelling it across the bus to say G'day. He said to say hi to you and hopes you're doing good.

Training's been pretty full on, the army needs to turn us into soldiers, real fast. Not just doing physical stuff, but weapons and hand fighting as well. Lucky I'm fit, I can tell you. Some of these guys can't even run the ten kilometres before chow in the mornings. They're finding the training really hard, I can tell you. Well, its lights out, so I'm off to bed. Say hi to Sandra for me. Tell her I'll write later, it's too hard at the moment. Give Nugget a big scratch. My love to you both, Dan

I sighed, the relief at having Dan touch our lives again was a little melancholy. 'It's great to hear from Dan, but he really should write to Sandra. I saw her yesterday...she's so sad.'

She'd looked ill and had black marks under her eyes. When I asked if I could help she said everything was fine.

'I do miss the lad,' said Jack, in the understatement of the year.

'Did you see that horrible article in the local rag, the one that reporter wrote about Dan, and all the other recruits. It was just plain nasty, saying all those awful things about our poor young men at war. Someone should send him over there...let him get a taste of reality,' I growled, getting up a head of steam, 'If he comes into the café I'm going to lace his meal with a laxative.'

Jack's chest rumbled with laughter. He leant forward and kissed the tip of my nose.

'Remind me not to upset you,' he said with a smile. 'Come on, let's go test the strength of the bed frame...I'm worried something's coming loose.'

* * *

The months dragged by until finally we got another letter from Dan. I guess with training and the travelling, his new life was busy and he didn't have much time for writing home. The letter was only short and looked like it'd been written in a hurry. After reading it, a solid lump formed in my belly.

Dear Jack, Connie and Nugget, well training's complete and my knapsacks packed. You wouldn't believe it, Jack, the buggers have issued me a L1A1 self-loading rifle.7.62mm, gas operated with an internal piston, and has a 20 round staggered box magazine. Talk about WOW! A bit different from the old .22 we keep in the back of the Rover. I'm now Private Daniel

Babcock and things are starting to get real. We got our marching orders today and we're off in the morning, going to Vietnam. Being shipped out on the HMAS Sydney, more commonly known to us boffins of the 1st Australian Task Force, as the Vung Tau ferry. By the time you get this, I'll be in someplace called, Nui Dat, Phuoc Tuy Province. I'm not supposed to tell you, but one of the blokes here is sick and not coming with us. He said he'd mail this letter to you when he gets home. They censor all our mail, so in future I won't be able to tell you where I am, but I wanted to let you know where I was going... just in case. Miss you, love Dan.

* * *

The Mini merrily chugged around the corner and glided neatly to a stop outside Egan Boarding. A small smug smile pulled at my lips – I was rather proud of my improved driving skills.

I knocked on Sandra's door, Dan's letter clutched in my hand. She didn't answer.

I headed into the kitchen. Norma raised an eyebrow.

'She's gone to live in Perth.'

I stared at Norma, speechless. Sandra hadn't said a word.

'Did she leave me a note, with her new address or phone number?'

'Nope.'

'What's going on, Norma? Is she ill or something?'

Norma just shrugged her chubby shoulders, setting her earrings twirling, her face blank.

Strange...there's more going on here than was being said.

* * *

Football season was under way. I'd expected Nugget to take off to the playing fields while Jack ate breakfast. He didn't. He lay under Jack's chair, head on paws, eyes closed and tail still, until I finished work.

I threw my bag into the Rover's cab and climbed into my seat. Jack drove us to the oval, to watch the first game of the season. We parked in the shade of a tree and Jack opened his door. Nugget turned, climbed into the back seat, curled up and went to sleep. Jack's eyebrows rose into his hairline. My heart started to ache.

Poor Nugget, he was taking Dan's absence hard. I placed my hand on his head.

With a break in his voice, Jack said, 'What do ya say, my love... let's just go home. It's not the same without Dan.'

* * *

I parked the Mini at the back of the café next to the Morris Minor and huddled into my jacket. The early morning temperature left a lot to be desired. I let myself in the back door. The kitchen was empty, the grills as cold as the outside temperature. Hurrying into the empty dining room, I glanced out into the street, looking for Maria and Carlo.

Where the hell was everyone?

Carlo stood with his arm around his wife, under the shelter of the pedestrian veranda, watching a large crowd mill around Hannan Street.

Stepping out of the door I asked, 'What's going on? There seems to be a lot of people in the street.'

Carlo turned his head, worry lines creased his eyes.

'The Oriental Hotel, shea gone. The brewery knocka her down'

'*What*! You're kidding. They knocked down the whole damn pub?'

Carlo's head bobbed up and down frantically.

'Yesa, ina the night .'

Maria clutched her hands to her breasts, and said, 'There's a gonna be hell to pay. The blokes around here won'ta like it. Remember whata happen, Carlo, when they demolish the Shamrock in Boulder.'

'Yeah, bigga trouble that day.'

'Is that why there are so many people on the street?' I asked.

Carlo nodded. 'Yesa, the peoples they were coming in to protest the demolition today, but when they arrived it'd already happened. The mood is a very bad, I think we no open today. Go home, Piccola, before the trouble starts. Maria and I will lock up.'

As the words left his mouth, two police vehicles, tyres screeching, hurtled around the corner of Cassidy Street. Breaking glass and yelling reverberated up the street. The windows of the hardware store, only a block down from us, shattered. We scurried back into the café. Locking the front door, Maria rapidly pulled down the blinds. I flicked off the lights.

'Go...out the back door, now,' she said, 'Go home to your husband...be safe.'

With a pounding heart, I kissed Maria's cheek and said, 'You and Carlo take care too.'

I raced out the kitchen door and leapt into my Mini.

There was no kangaroo hopping today, only speed. I planted my foot hard on the accelerator. With a chirp of the tyres, the little yellow car shot out of the alley, onto a thankfully quiet Maritana Street. She had never been driven so fast but stood up to the challenge well and took me safely home. I sedately pulled to a stop next to Jack's vehicle and turned off the key. Nugget, his legs going like the clappers, came tearing over from the poppet frame, barking his greeting. Jack looked up from his task, dropped his tools and ran towards me, worry lines creased his face.

'It's okay, I'm okay, Jack. There's a bit of trouble brewing in Kal. Carlo and Maria have decided not to open today.'

'Must be bad if they're not opening. What's going on?'

I told him of the brewery's underhanded tactics to avoid trouble. 'Carlo's worried there's going to be a riot.'

'Well, I'm glad you're home, where I can protect you. I'll go let Scotty know what's going on. He might want to go and get Tegan,' said Jack, kissing my brow. 'You my love, can go get into your work clobber, I've got a job for you.'

I looked at him with suspicion. 'Work, what kind of work? I was going to kick back and enjoy a day of leisure. You know, sit in the lovely warm sunshine, soak up a few rays, work on my tan and watch you show off your muscles, *while you worked.*'

Holding out my arms for him to admire, I suddenly realised, I no longer had milky white skin. My body glowed with a golden tan.

'Well, you can work on your tan, while you help me sift the waste pile. I'll even get you a chair. How's that sound?'

Happy I could be of use and spend time with him, I said, 'Slave driver. Give me five minutes to get out of my skirt and put on my shorts and boots.'

'And a hat, Connie. The sun's a real killer, no matter the time of year. In fact, maybe I should give you a hand to get changed.'

'*No, Jack*. You go tell Scotty what's going on. If I let you help, we'll never get any work done. I'll be there in a minute...with my hat on.'

I watched in amusement as Jack strolled back to the work site, muttering that I was a spoil sport.

Sitting in the shade of an umbrella, sifting waste, I said, 'Explain to me why we're doing this Jack.'

'Two reasons, love. One – the poppet head is finished and the shaft's rubble almost cleared. A couple more bucket loads and I can access the war room. The mines good to go, but I don't want Scotty or anyone other than you, me or Dan to get a look at what's down there. Don't forget, the safe's full, and a large portion of our wealth is hidden here as well. As much as I trust Scotty, it only takes a couple of beers in the pub, a wrong word and we'll be the target of every crook in the district. I'm going to install a lockable gate at the top of the shaft and we'll hide the key. Whenever we're not here...keep it locked.'

I nodded my head, not seeing any holes in his plan so far.

'Secondly – the waste is ore bearing, and it'll keep Scotty busy till the end of the month.'

'Why the end of the month? I know you don't like to work alone, and Scotty has his own lease to get back to? What are we going to do in the long term, without Dan around? You know his national service is for two years?'

Jack gave me a long, considered stare.

'I have a huge favour to ask of you. Would you take some time off from work, come with me to Gwalia? With Dan away and Nugget not interested in the football, we can go while the weather's still cool.'

'Well that's a no brainer, Jack,' I replied, my spirits lifting in excitement, 'Of course I'll take the time off. I'll talk with Maria and Carlo tomorrow, let them know I need a couple of months. If they want to give my job to someone else, so be it. I can't see me being much use to you though...I don't know anything about mining.'

'Not much to it, just hard work,' he said, his eyes crinkling with a smile. 'This'll be the last time, anyway.'

'Last time, why's that Jack?' I asked, tilting my head in concern. 'You're not going to let the lease lapse are you?'

'No. I may be a country hick, my love but not a foolish one,' he said, with a booming laugh. '*No*, I've had some serious inquiries the last twelve months, from a mining company. They want to re-open the Sons of Gwalia mine. They're very interested in buying our lease. Dan and I know how rich it is, so we've been hanging out for a percentage deal, rather than a straight out purchase. They've just come back with a 2 per cent life of the mine deal. That means that for every million dollars profit they make, we'll get a twenty thousand dollar payout. If the mine proves to be as profitable as I suspect, then our children and grandchildren will be set for life.'

My heart nearly stopped, and I had to clamp my jaw tight to stop it dropping into my lap. No, Jack was no country hick...in fact I think he and Dan are extremely smart when it comes to the financial stuff.

'Will that mean I can run a café at our winery?'

Jack laughed and nodded.

'Alright then, Jack you'd better start teaching me how to become a miner.'

Jack whispered as he leant over to kiss me, 'Thank you.'

* * *

Tomorrow we're off to Gwalia. The camp was beginning to have a deserted feel with the tents and equipment we needed for our venture all packed into the Rover.

Carlo and Maria, sad I was going away for a while, had agreed they could cope without Piccola for the time being, but not permanently. I wandered out from the kitchen, carrying a large plate of lasagne and warm crusty bread for Jack. The day was quiet, by our standards. Carlo had left me in charge of the kitchen, while he sat in the dining room enjoying an espresso with his mate, Ironstone. They were having a high old time laughing and telling tall tales.

The bell on the door tinkled. Sergeant Henderson stepped into the café and I held my breath.

'Ah good, I'm glad I caught you, Ironstone,' his voice boomed in time with his heavy tread as he strode up to the table. 'I've got a letter for you from Dazza. One for Sandra too. Norma says she left town. You don't have her address do you, Connie?'

'No sergeant, I don't. I haven't heard from her at all. All I know is she went to Perth to live.'

'Well can I leave this letter with you? Either forward it or give it back to Dazza.'

The sergeant wasn't his usual calm self. As he handed me the letter, his hand shook slightly. There were frown lines on his brow and dark smudges under his eyes.

I said, 'Sure, I'll take it. Are you okay sarge...you look tired and frazzled?'

'Yeah, I'm alright, just weary. We've been conducting a few late-night raids around town. I'm still trying to get on top of this drug stuff...not having much luck I'm afraid.'

'Why'sa that, sergeant? We've all a heara rumours...they deala outa of the Mineral Rights Hotel and the Twisted Heads clubhouse,' said Carlo.

'Yeah, I've heard the same rumours. Trouble is the buggers always seem to know when we're coming. We raid – they have already shut up shop. The person we're looking for has just left town. I'm chasing my tail and it's frustrating.'

'Well, can't help you there sarge...not our scene at all,' said Jack, taking a sip of his coffee.

'No, I know. I'll get it sorted, just takes a little perseverance. Anyway, you and Connie take care in Gwalia. When do you expect to get back?'

'The end of the year, all being well. If we decide to stay longer I'll drop you a line.'

'Appreciate it, Jack. Like to know you're safe. I'll get the lads to call in with any mail when they do the North East Goldfields patrol.'

'Thanks sarge,' said Jack, 'and you take care of yourself. This town would be a real mess without your strong hand.'

A slight pink tinge came to his cheeks. He lifted his hand in farewell and strode to the door and out into the street. My eyes followed the burly copper as he stopped a young lad, who had just thrown some rubbish on the ground, and gave him a stern lecture.

'Good man,' said Carlo, drawing my attention back to the room. Jack was nodding his head in agreement and staring at the letter in his hand.

Carlo rose to his feet, collected his empty coffee cup and said, 'You sita with you husband and reada the letter from Dazza. I go takea care of the kitchen.'

'Thank you, Carlo.'

Much to his delight and embarrassment, I kissed his cheek.

As I sat down Jack handed me the letter saying, 'Fire away, Connie. Let's see what the lad has to say for himself.'

Dear Jack, Connie and Nugget

It's been a while, I know, but I'm still alive. I've been posted as a Nasho recruit to an experienced team here and have been in constant training with them. They're not particularly welcoming as they've lost quite a few mates. I've learnt to keep my mouth shut, listen and do what I'm told. I am not allowed to say where we are, or give details of our missions so I'll tell you about a typical day. First light here starts at 5:30 every morning, the sky cracks with pre-dawn light. Full dawn arrives bang on 6am. We head out on patrol with the light. In the dry season the heat stays at a constant 36 degree Celsius. In the wet it's 30 degrees Celsius and humid as hell. We sweat like pigs and our clothes are always wet. I keep a dry set in a waterproof bag, to wear at night, so I don't get chilled. I re-bag them every morning and I pull the old damp and sweaty one's back on, to patrol in. It rains all the bloody time. It's not like home at all, everything here is wet and smells of rot and mould. The mozzies are atrocious, buzzing around your ears and face at night. It's enough to drive a man crazy or to drink! Our patrols usually last four days before we head back to camp for a shower, a hot meal and try to catch up on some sleep.

They've a nickname for the Viet Cong here, he's called 'Charlie' or 'Gook'. They're fierce opponents. On the rare occasion we get to the boozer in camp, we pick the brains of the other soldiers, trying to suck up as much knowledge as possible. Who knows what little piece of information will be useful. I sleep lightly these days, with my ears open, not like the old days when nothing would rouse me. Out on patrol, we maintain a constant vigilance, always expecting trouble. When we rest, we sleep on the ground and post a sentry. We always sleep head to bum to stay safe. That means whoever is the sentry puts their bum between our three heads and you pray like mad they don't fart. If the sentry nods off, he'll fall on a sleeping man, waking him up. Hey...we're human and things like that happen after a day of tense and tiring patrol. We look after one another and are regimented in our actions and constantly train for each patrol. I reckon, Jack, that I'll be able to sneak up on those bastard pigs and tickle them behind the ear and they won't even know I'm there! Something to look forward to hey.

I've had another first since being here. I can now add helicopters to the list of things I've done. The Hueys are our main form of transport, other than our feet of course. We often hitch a lift into some remote area and patrol back by foot. There's a lot of green here, it's nothing like the rust red country we're used to. The jungle is thick with trees and shrubs and the bird and animal noises are totally different from the constant buzz of cicadas of the Aussie bush.

I'll write again when I can, but it may be a while. Is Sandra alright? I've sent her a couple of letters now, but I haven't heard from her. Connie, tell her I love her and miss her. Can you guys send me some socks, the nice thick wool ones I used to wear to work. They seem to be the best for our feet, and yes I am looking after my feet. The care package you sent to HQ arrived last month and was greatly appreciated. The guys really loved the vegemite, it was gone in a flash, send more if you can. love Dan.

So, with a letter from Dan and a new mining career to look forward to, Jack, Nugget and I headed off to Gwalia with a light heart. I promised myself when I returned I was going to make a concerted effort to find Sandra.

26

Chapter Twenty-Six

I quietly opened the Victory Café kitchen door and stuck my head inside. Maria was standing at the sink, up to her elbows in hot sudsy water. She looked up, startled by the opening of the door. I did a finger wave at her.

'Hi,' I said.

'Piccola, you're home. Carlo, come see whata the wind shesa blown in. Whena you and Ironstone get back?'

'We've just driven in,' I said, as I kissed her cheek. 'I'm on my way to the shops...we need to stock up on supplies. Just thought I'd stop in and see how everything's going. Busy?'

'No,' she replied, shaking her head. 'The mining company, he a buy all the leases, our peoples all selling out, leavinga town.'

Carlo's voice boomed across the kitchen, 'Piccola, my little maestro, hello. You'va been away too long.'

Arms spread wide, Carlo rounded the grill and swooped on me. I enjoyed being enveloped by my big friend's arms and hugged him back.

'Oh, it is so nice to see you both. Sorry to have been away so long, but we've had a busy six months. We ended up selling the lease, negotiations took longer than expected.'

'Youa leaving too?' asked Carlo, his concern apparent by the frown around his eyes.

'No. Gwalia was just too hard without Dan.'

Shaking his head at the mention of Dan, Carlo asked, 'Youa coming back to work? Business, she's a not good, Piccola. There a new peoples in town, not nice like our regulars. These a people all here for other business, not the mining.'

'Why, what's going on?'

A look passed between Maria and Carlo, 'Nothing. Things are just changing – I'sa must be getting old – I no like change. Anyway, how a you and the Ironstone doing? What you hear from that young rascal, Dazza? Isa he a coming home soon?'

Deftly the conversation was changed, with Carlo and Maria asking lots of questions about our time away.

* * *

Dawn cracked the horizon in a riot of orange and purple as I drove to Kal for my first shift at the Victory Café in six months. The soft breeze coming in the open window carried a scent of eucalyptus and cleared the sleep from my brain.

The café was quiet. I pulled on my apron and looked out into the dining room, only six tables were occupied. The current customers didn't resemble the hard working and rough miners I was used to. The table nearest the door was occupied by two lads, in their early twenties, dressed in blue singlets and unbuttoned flannel shirts. They slouched with their dirty work boots up on the adjoining chairs and were amusing themselves by throwing rude comments at the other customers.

'Carlo, you see what I see?'

He shrugged, 'Whata can you do, Piccola, the peoples they are like that now.'

Tegan hesitantly came into the kitchen, her mouth pulled into a frown.

'Carlo, table nine. They want a full breakfast but are refusing to pay. They told me to put it on their tab. Since when do we run a tab?'

Carlo's shoulders sagged, 'Give them what they want. Theya pay me later...maybe.'

I narrowed my eyes and leant forward, giving him a gentle shove on the arm.

'What do you mean they'll pay later? Carlo, what the hell's going on?'

'Leave it, Piccola. It's no something you can fix.'

He sighed in defeat.

'No, bugger it, Carlo. You can't let them use bully-boy tactics on you,' I said.

Determined to fix this, I picked up my large wooden rolling pin.

'I'm giving them a piece of my mind.'

Carlo reached out and laid a gentle hand on my arm.

'No, Piccola, theya only come back and makea the more trouble.'

'Carlo, if you don't stand up to them now, then it'll only get worse. Eventually they'll bleed you dry. When you can't pay anymore, they'll beat you up or burn you out. I've seen these tactics before. You can't let them boss you around.'

Carlo stared at me. Unblinking. He looked at his wife and chewed his lips. Maria lifted her eyebrows, their eyes met and an unspoken message passed between them.

'Piccola, thisa the type of thing the Mafia they do. They bad criminals, back ina my old country. Yousa expected to pay to be protected...from who – from them. Ifa you no pay, bad things theya happen to you and your family.'

'Yes I know, Carlo, but by standing up to them now, you're showing you're not a pushover. Bullies are cowards. Please...let me go teach them some manners. Then we'll let Sergeant Henderson know he's got another problem brewing in his town.'

Before my darling friends could object, I walked out into the dining room, rolling pin in hand. I casually strolled to table nine and slammed it down hard on the table.

Both men sat up startled, I said, 'Get your feet off the furniture. What do you think this is, a school yard? Now, if you want a full breakfast it'll be five dollars each...cash...payment upfront. A full breakfast is inclusive of unlimited toast, tea and coffee. We don't offer credit in this establishment. Pay up or leave, we've got other customers who are waiting for a table.'

The dark-haired lad's lip curled. I kept tapping the rolling pin gently on the table, in beat with the clicking of the overhead ceiling fan. The *tap...tap...tap* on the table top unnerved him. He reached into his pocket and threw a ten dollar note on the table.

'Thanks. Your breakfast will be out in five minutes. In future, remember to keep your feet off the furniture. Have a nice day.'

I turned and made eye contact with Scotty, he gave me a half smile and a wink.

On my way back to the kitchen, I greeted some familiar faces. As I stepped inside I sang out, 'Two full breakfasts, table nine.'

Tegan was handing Maria her apron. 'I'm sorry Maria, I can't do this anymore. Can you find another waitress?'

Maria neatly folded the apron and patted Tegan's cheek. 'It'sa difficult for you, Bambina. It'sa hard to be of two worlds.'

Puzzled by her comment, I took a glance into the dining room, then studied the worry lines on my friends' faces.

'Maria, I'll waitress until trade picks up,' I said, hoping that I could lighten the load for them.

'Thank you, Piccola.'

* * *

The weather got hotter, unrelenting as summer progressed, and I began to regret waitressing. Underground mining was so much cooler and a more comfortable prospect than running around in a hot café in forty-degree heat.

In late February we got a letter from Dan. It was six months since the last one. Worry had been churning away in the back of my mind all that time, so I was looking forward to reading his letter and have some of my worries about him eased.

Dear Jack and Connie, I can't remember when I last wrote, sorry. Most of the guys have been pulled out of Vietnam now and the military boffins hope to have all of the 1st Australian Task Force out soon. Not me though, looks like I've been seconded to a training team and will remain here in Vietnam for a while yet. I don't know when I'm coming home but being a trainer has got to be better than what I've been doing. Hopefully no more patrols, I'm glad. I can't picture your faces anymore. I can't picture anyone's face. We've lost so many. Bluey copped it early in the piece and Hawk, I don't know what happened to Hawk, do you? My mates here look after me and I look after them but shit still happens and blokes die. I told you about my mate Arctic, didn't I? He's our medic, a great bloke. He's so tall he towers over everyone and is so strong he can carry two wounded blokes at the same time. He's got a cool head on him, especially under fire, and is a good man to have beside you in a fight. He hails from West Aussie, grew up pretty close to our fifty acres. He'd like to meet you guys when we get home...if we get home. They still call me Dazza, me mates reckon a smile from me can dazzle Charlie from his tunnels.

I overheard some Yank slagging off the other day, about the Aussie soldiers. He reckoned the Aussies had it easy and didn't face Charlie as much as they did (which is bullshit by the way), but I fixed him good and proper. I told him Charlie was scared of us and that's why he stayed away. Mouthy bastard! We're all doing our bit in this damn war. It's hard to know who to trust, these days. You think the locals are helping you, then they turn around and betray you. They're working both sides. You can't trust anyone other than your mate.

Someone said the other day it's 1973, is that true, how long have I been gone? I must be 21 now, I feel so much older. Jack, did I ever thank you for saving me all those years ago, when I was a snot nose kid? Trying to steal your wallet was the best move I ever made and being with you and Connie the best time of my life. I've lost track of time. Give Sandra my love and tell her I'm going to marry her, as soon as I get home. Ask her to write, I still haven't heard anything from her. I love you both. Scratch Nugget's belly for me Dan

My eyes burned with unshed tears.

Jack said, 'Dan's sounding a bit off, don't you think, love?'

'Yeah Jack, I do. He sounds lost, there's desperation in his writing like he's only just holding on. I hope he's okay. I can't even write and give him news of Sandra, I've failed him there. I've no idea why she left, or where she's gone.'

My eyes met Jack's – I could see worry lines carving new rivets along his face.

'I'm going to see Norma tomorrow, give her the third degree. I bet she knows exactly where Sandra is.'

I glanced down at the date stamp on the letter.

'Jack, this letter was posted months ago.'

'No surprise there. I heard postal workers were refusing to deliver mail from our soldiers...reckon they shouldn't be in Vietnam.'

'Bastards,' I murmured, as I wiped away a tear that trickled down my cheek.

Jack pulled me tight into his chest. I rubbed my face against the soft flannel of his shirt and the hard muscles underneath. I breathed in his scent, accepting the peace and comfort he gave me. We sat like that for a long time before he gave a deep sigh and suggested bed.

* * *

Finishing work the next day, I pointed the Mini in the direction of Egan Street Boarding. I'd procrastinated too long over Sandra, shame on me for that.

Norma sat in her usual seat in the kitchen, cigarette dangling from her fingers and the newspaper spread over the mess on the table before her. She looked up warily at my entrance. I marched over, pulled out a chair and sat, not waiting to be asked.

'Hello, Connie, come in, make yourself at home. What can I do for you?'

Sarcasm dripped from her words.

Smiling sweetly, I dug deep for my courage. I wasn't going away without an answer this time.

'Hello Norma, how are you? How's business, keeping busy are you, lots of new tenants?'

'Business is reasonable,' she said, cocking her head to the side, waiting for the punch-line. 'Why, do you need a room? Has Ironstone finally lost interest?'

'Ha ha, Norma, good one. *No*.'

Looking directly into her brown eyes, I squinted my own, trying to look tough, and asked, 'Norma, how much do you care about Dazza?'

Norma took a long slow breath in and released it, just as slowly.

'I wondered how long – took longer than I expected. I suppose being away in Gwalia slowed you down some. Before I tell you anything, I want to ask *you* a question.'

'Fire away?'

'How much does Dazza care for Sandra?'

'Heaps – the last thing he said before he left was, he wanted to marry her. In every letter, he sends her love and asks her to write. She never has...it's breaking him. The wars hard, messing with him, I can't add to that by telling him I don't know where Sandra is. We love her, Norma, miss her and want to help, nothing's going to change that...so *please*...what's going on?'

Norma gave a firm nod of her head, accepting what I said as the plain truth.

'So, she hasn't written, huh. I've forwarded a stack of Dazza's letters...she's being a silly goose...reckons she won't force a marriage.'

'Why'd she think he'd be forced...'

Suddenly understanding dawned. Thick, Connie, thick.

'Oh...boy or girl.'

Norma smiled smugly, 'A little boy. He was born in October – she named him DJ, short for Daniel Jack. She's living with a cousin and is very unhappy.'

'Why didn't she tell us, we'd have given her a home.'

'Oh, you know the old biddies of this town and their attitude about having a baby out of wedlock – shame. Her aunty, the religious nut, did a real number on her. Sandra's worried they'll force Dan to marry her and he'll end up hating her. She doesn't want him on those terms.'

'But there's no shame in having a baby, married or not. Dan will want to be a father to DJ,' I said. 'I'm so angry with myself for not coming and seeing you sooner. We could have been helping her all this time. Please, give me her address and phone number, I need to fix this now.'

Norma gave me the first genuine smile since I had stormed into the room and said, 'I knew you could be relied upon, Connie. When you first arrived here in Kal, I could see you were only just holding your life together. I've always admired the guts you showed, getting your life on track. Sandra's going to need your support, her family hasn't been kind. Her cousin's under a great deal of pressure to turf her out. He's resisting, but his wife has sided with the family. If you can offer her something, give her some breathing space, I'm sure Sandra can sort out a life for herself and DJ.'

Norma handed me a piece of paper and pointed to the telephone.

'My shout.'

Will wonders never cease, Norma had just put her hand in her pocket!

* * *

I was daydreaming, my life already so full, had been blessed again. Jack and I now had welcomed two new members into our small clan. After speaking to a tearful Sandra, on the telephone and reading out the letters from Dan, she'd agreed to let us help. Jack and I wired her the money needed to set up a home for her and DJ.

I rubbed the heel of my hand over the warm feeling in my heart and looked across the dining room at Jack. He quirked a lip at me and I gave him a wink. He was tucking into his breakfast while chatting with Scotty. Nugget played invisible dog under his chair. I bustled over to table one, my order book in hand, and smiled at the old-timer sitting there.

'Hi ya, Toothless, how's it going?'

Bruce had a mouth full of gums, no teeth. He grinned and ran his fingers down his grizzled grey beard.

'Not bad. Some geezer from the mining company came round...wants to buy my lease. Looks like I can finally retire.'

'Hey that's great Toothless...what'll you do with yourself in retirement?'

'Oh, probably buy me a metal detector thingy, hook up the caravan, an' go prospecting, I reckon.'

'So not a real retirement then, huh?'

Toothless Bruce chortled and stroked his beard again.

'No, I suppose not...though working on the surface instead of underground would be a change. What do they say – a change is as good as a holiday.'

'Well before you head off on retirement, what can I get you for breakfast?' I asked pencil poised, 'The usual, scrambled eggs, no toast?'

'Got it in one, Connie – can't chew nothing else without me teeth.'

He lifted his lips wide and gave me a full display of his gums.

I shook my head, amused. 'Righto...one double order of scrambled eggs, coming up,' I said, as I slipped my pad back into my apron pocket, and patted his shoulder in affection.

I headed for the kitchen. The doorbell tinkled. I glanced around. My feet stopped and refused to move, frozen in place. I watched the new customers stroll in and the blood drained from my cheeks. A ball of fear erupted in my stomach. Reaching out blindly, I grabbed the back of a chair and gripped it tightly. My peripheral vision darkened, as a black cloud moved in. I forced myself to concentrate on the light, as I watched a man I'd hoped never to see again in my life, walk towards me.

'Well, well, well, look who we have here. Hello Constance,' he said.

I didn't speak, couldn't. I stared up in horror at the smiling handsome face of Kane Hansen! Smirking, Kane casually stepped to the right, and revealed his companion.

'You remember my good friend, don't you Constance – I seem to remember, you and he used to be quite chummy.'

My glance flitted to his companion's face and the world spun. There stood the man I feared and hated even more than Kane. A man whom I thought was dead.

Jerry Martin!

He sneered, eyes dancing in amusement, at my obvious fear. My legs started to tremble. My skin crawled as he reached out a hand, now missing three of its fingers, towards my cheek.

'Hello Princess, did ya miss me?' he asked.

Before his mutilated hand could touch me, a deep blood-curdling growl started next to my right knee. Nugget, hackles standing stiff and upright, his top lip pulled back to expose a full mouth of very sharp teeth. He locked his eyes on Jerry and stood guard. A stream of saliva dripped from his canines and pooled at his feet. Nugget stepped forward. Jerry's hand dropped quickly to his side and he took a hasty step back. Confusion and wariness showed on his face.

The clatter of cutlery ceased, voices around the room hushed, only two sounds remained, the slow methodical clunk of the ceiling fan and the dog's growl.

A strong sense of warmth and safety invaded my being along with the smell of sandalwood, eucalyptus and dust.

'Is there a problem, Connie?' asked Jack, his voice as hard as steel.

'Connie. Hey, I like that...better name than Constance. Seems you've made a few changes since I last saw you, Princess. Must say, I like the hair. It'll be nice to run my fingers through – what's left of them anyway – when we visit the cupboard again.'

I refused to verbally react to Jerry's nasty comments and laughter. I gave him a look that reflected the utter contempt and loathing that was churning in my gut. I shifted my gaze to Kane for a moment, trying to gauge his intent. He was watching Jack, his eyes crinkled in wariness.

Jerry opened his mouth to deliver another wisecrack but was interrupted. The door bell jangled. Kane glanced over his shoulder, slapped the back of his right hand onto Jerry's chest, and indicated behind him with his head. Entering the café were Constable Rawlings and Sergeant Henderson.

Jerry half turned, inspected the policemen, and cocked his eyebrow at his friend.

'Not now,' was Kane's enigmatic reply to the silent query.

Jerry slid his eyes up and down my body. I wanted desperately to take a shower and wash away the smear his grubby leer left behind. The feeling disappeared when Jack placed a warm comforting hand on the small of my back.

'I'll be seeing you, real soon, Princess...we can take up right where I left off,' said Jerry. He bulled his way past the policemen and out the door. Kane dogged his heels.

I turned towards Jack and the world went black.

* * *

Something cool and moist pressed against my forehead, two strong arms cradling my limp body. Jack was holding me in his lap. It seemed very quiet. I opened my eyes and realised the café was empty of customers – Carlo was just locking the door and Maria pulling down the blinds. I let my glance roam to the man seated across the table from us.

Sergeant Henderson removed his hat, frowned in Jack's direction, and said, 'Are you sure we don't need an ambulance, Ironstone? Connie's looking awfully pale.'

'Nah sarge, she just fainted. Give her a moment, and then we'll find out what the hell's going on.'

Maria, her gaze locked on my face, rushed over.

'Ah Piccola, yous awake. Good...good...you no move, I makea the cup of the tea, lotsa sugar.'

She patted my cheek softly, before bustling away. Nugget put his cold wet nose in my hand and nudged my fingers, whining.

I moved my fingers, stroked his silky ears and murmured, 'Thank you Nugget. I couldn't have bared for him to touch me.'

I struggled to sit up. Jack's arms around me tightened.

'I'm okay, Jack. Can I sit up please?'

Removing the cloth, he kissed my brow, and gathered me close to his chest for a moment longer, before helping me into the chair beside him. Maria came hustling back, cup in hand.

'Thanks, Maria,' I said taking a reviving sip of the hot sweet liquid, 'I'm sorry to have blanked out like that...I had a rather big shock.'

'Alright Mrs Ironstone, I think it's time you told me what's going on,' Sergeant Henderson said.

I studied the policeman's face, reviewed in my mind all that I knew about him and decided on trust.

'I'll tell you, sarge – but only you – send the constable away. I don't know whether I can trust him or not.'

I was blunt and to the point. The young constable narrowed his eyes, offended. I didn't care, Paul Joshua had a long reach. Jerry and Kane were experts at blackmail.

'Has this anything to do with those two men?' asked the sarge.

I nodded and waited.

'Rawlings, go back to the station, see what you can dig up. I want to know who and what I'm dealing with. Also, find out what Lanky Luke's up to, he was acting very strange when we saw him out in the street just now. I'd like to know what he's gotten himself mixed up in this time.'

At a nod from his superior the fresh-faced young man pulled on his cap, rose to his feet and left.

I locked my gaze with the sarge's, not blinking.

'Now Connie, drink your tea and tell me what's going on,' he said.

I gripped Jack's hand tightly and drew in a deep breath.

'Their names are Kane Hansen and Jerry Martin. They're from Victoria and work for a man called Paul Joshua. They are extremely dangerous men.'

I stared at the water-stained ceiling as I recounted the full story of my life. My possession of the notebook, I left out for the moment, as that was my insurance policy.

I lowered my gaze to the faces of my friends and told them, in full detail, Jerry's attack on me at the Orion Club. The lie Betty had told me, which had sent me fleeing for my life, left a bitter taste in my mouth.

I'd expected to see condemnation and disgust for the person I had been. Instead, Maria sat hand over her mouth, eyes full of tears, and Carlo reached over to take my hand, his eyes shining with love.

'So, you thought you'd killed this man, and the Melbourne mob and corrupt police were chasing you,' Sergeant Henderson said. 'No wonder you were twitchy whenever I was around. Connie, I wish you'd have come to me...I could have made discreet inquiries.'

I shook my head.

'No, Paul Joshua has a long reach and some very high-ranking friends. Any inquiries made by you would've set off the alarm bells. Even now, what you've got Constable Rawlings doing scares me.'

'The recent increase in crime now makes sense,' said the sarge, 'Not so much the drugs, they've always been a problem in a small way. It's the scale. If I can get a bead on who these blokes have been dealing with locally, I may be able to shut them down. As for the other stuff you told me...well, that happened in Melbourne...I can't do anything about it, not without something concrete.'

'I have proof, sarge,' I said, steepling my fingers in front of my lips, '*But* we've got to be careful how we use it. There's a lot of influential people involved, very high-profile. If we just hand the evidence over, it'll probably disappear, us too!'

'Er...sarge,' said Jack, tapping his fingernail slowly on the table for emphasis, 'I reckon you might've been making more headway into this drug ring than you realise. Why else would this Joshua character send his two main men to Kalgoorlie?'

Seargent Henderson studied our faces for a while, then gave voice to his concern. 'I wonder if this Kane bloke's here on a recruitment drive – looking to put people in place. He'd need to get some dirt. That's how they work...isn't it?'

'Sure is, they'll show someone a good time, get photos of them in a compromising situation. Then it's *you scratch my back and I don't tell the wife you've been down in Hay Street.* Gambling is another hook in their arsenal,' I said, then added with some concern, 'You need to be careful sarge. Remember how many unsuccessful drug raids you've had? Check out your officers, see who they've been hanging out with. Anyone young and inexperienced, like Rawlings, is a prime target for Kane. Out for a beer – what's your vice – into a back room. Can you help us out, a nod on a raid maybe. Here's a little cash, just to sweeten the deal and take the sting out of any threat.

It's not long before an officer rises in the ranks and is in a position to make charges go away.'

'Itsa scary world, this one of the criminals,' said Carlo, shaking his head in disbelief. 'Ima glad you got away, Piccola. Now we musta hide you from the bad mens, so they can no hurt you.'

Jack leaned towards me, capturing my gaze with his. His lips brushed my cheek as he spoke quietly in my ear.

'Connie, do you trust the sarge?'

I nodded.

'Tell him everything.'

I nodded again.

'Sarge...there's something else. I have in my possession a notebook. In it, Jerry Martin has documented every transaction they made on behalf of Paul Joshua until June 1970. In it, he names corrupt officials and the bribes they were paid. There's also details of race fixing, a financial sheet of all the money extracted by extortion, and the punishment meted out for non-payment.' Nausea swirled in my stomach but there was one more important piece of information. 'In the back of the book, there's a section that's truly horrifying...murder victims and where to find the bodies.'

As a collective, everyone drew in a deep breath, faces blank, eyes unblinking.

Silence.

I gave a small cough and broke the tension.

'Connie, have you been sitting on this powder keg all this time. *Bloody hell girl*, no wonder you were frightened,' said the sarge. He dragged his fingers over his thinning hair and sighed. 'I'm honoured you're trusting me with this information. I'll do what I can...make sure it goes to the right people.'

'If you can arrest Jerry, search him. He'll have another notebook, either on him or somewhere close. He's obsessive, and enjoys writing it all down.' A thought struck me, 'Maybe that explains why, even though Mr Joshua disliked Jerry, he kept him around. In their world, blackmail is power.'

'Sarge, we're leaving the police work to you...good luck with it. Come out to Lucky Charm tonight and collect the evidence. Tomorrow'll be too late,' said Jack, placing his hands on the table in front of him and rising to his feet. 'I'm taking my wife and getting the hell out of Dodge. Maria, Carlo, we'll say goodbye for now – later, when it's safe, we'll be in touch. Thanks for all the fabulous meals over the years and your great friendship.'

As our friends opened their mouths, Jack said, 'No I'm not saying where we're going.'

Jack slung his arm over my shoulder and looked deep into my eyes.

'It's time, old girl.'

'It sure is,' I said, adding cryptically, 'The lad will know where we are?'

Jack smiled, nodded, and without looking back, we walked into the kitchen and slipped out the door. Nugget as always, on our heels.

27

Chapter Twenty-Seven

Striding to the blossoming sandalwood tree, I rubbed my shirt sleeve across my top lip, wiping away the beads of sweat. Thick socks and work boots heated my toes and they felt like sausages ready to burst on the barbecue. A cool breeze wafted past, I dropped the box I was carrying and held my face up, enjoying its touch on my cheeks. I looked around the half-packed camp, melancholy had kicked in. I was going to miss Lucky Charm.

We planned to leave before dawn, there was still a full night's work ahead of us. Jack was currently in the bowels of the mine collecting tools and the contents of the ore safe. While he did that I emptied the shack, stored our clothes and bedding in the Mini and then laid out the winch gear ready for him. When it was dark we'd salvage our gold cache from the water tank.

The next job on my list, retrieve the notebook hidden in the lockbox under the Land Rover's chassis. Sergeant Henderson was welcome to it. The evening breeze lifted my hair slightly. I breathed the scent of the Aussie bush on the breeze deep into my lungs and admired the blood-red sun as it began to set, so beautiful. Turning I gathered together our skinning knives.

Nugget, not understanding my rush, paced the perimeter of the tents. He halted, stared down the road, sniffed the air and cocked his head. His scrunched muzzle gave him a puzzled expression. I walked over to him and stroked his ears.

'Good boy, Nugget.'

He panted, his tongue lolled from the side of his mouth and he leant against my leg. Suddenly his head whipped around, he looked down the track and growled. I stopped scratching his ear and listened. In the distance, a vehicle changed down a gear.

'It's probably the sergeant,' I said, and placed the razor-sharp boning knife I was holding flat on the branch of the sandalwood tree.

I dusted my hands clean. Head down, I walked over to the Rover. Nugget's growling increased in volume. I glanced at him in surprise. His top lip was giving a good display of his fierce looking teeth. I recognised the look...he'd shown it to me this morning in the café.

My head snapped around and I stared into the dusk that sat lightly on the track. A dark-blue four-wheel-drive, raced along it at high speed. The vehicle bounced and skidded chased by a trail of red dust.

'*Run,* Nugget. Go get Jack,' I screamed.

I pumped my arms and legs and ran towards the shaft leaping over the tufted weeds that got in my way. As I neared the poppet head a cloud of dust enveloped me, stinging my eyes.

Crack

The dirt at my feet kicked up.

'Now where do you think you're going, Princess? We still have a little unfinished business, you and I.'

I halted, half raised my hands. Panting from fear and effort, I turned to face the voice. Jerry, his bare arm hung out of the passenger's window, waved a pistol at me. He had a mean crooked smile on his face.

Nugget launched himself and latched on to Jerry's forearm, sinking his teeth deep and tearing a chunk of flesh away. Jerry screamed, the gun fell from his grasp and Nugget dashed away.

I raced forward and swooped on the weapon. Just as my fingers gripped the warm muzzle of the gun my hair was grabbed from behind. My eyes began to water and my scalp burned with pain as I was yanked backward. In the act of falling, I hurled the pistol as far as I could.

Score. It disappeared down the mine shaft.

Still clutching my hair, Kane dragged me to my feet and held me above the ground. I reached up, grabbed his arm and dug my nails into flesh. Kane snarled and threw me against the car. My back hit hard and the air rushed from my lungs in a loud whoosh. Warmth ran down my chin, I brushed my hand under my nose and it came away covered in blood.

Jerry flung open his door and staggered from the vehicle. His left arm was clutched against his chest, staining his white tee-shirt with blood. He came towards me and swung an open right hand at my face. The slap connected hard against my cheek. My head snapped back and my face began to burn. He bunched his fist into my shirt front, pulled me forward pushing his face in close to mine.

'You fucking bitch,' he screamed. Spittle sprayed from his lips, showering my face.

I narrowed my eyes and glared at him, not giving him the satisfaction of cowering me. Jerry flung me away in disgust and stood clutching his injured arm. He peered around and began to laugh.

'All alone Princess – no one to hear you scream. This is gonna be fun.'

The hairs on the back of my neck stiffened with his maniacal laughter. This was not a road I ever wanted to travel again. Kane stood beside Jerry with a thoughtful expression on his face.

'I don't reckon she's alone out here, mate. The boyfriend's here somewhere...two cars.' Jerry's laughter ceased abruptly.

'Well, why don't you go *find* the fucking boyfriend,' he snarled, not appreciating having his fun interrupted. 'Me, I have other fish to fry. Oh, and Kane, kill that fucking mutt.'

Jerry leant forward and grabbed my wrist. He pulled hard, dragging me towards the camp. My shorts offered no protection against the hard-packed dirt and gravel. My skin peeled from my thighs and knees as my bare legs scraped over their sharp teeth.

My face on fire, my head pounding and my eyes stinging with unshed tears, I was determined not to go down without a fight. I spun my feet forward and dug my heels into the hard surface. I wrenched my wrist sideways from his tight grasp and fell on my arse. Jerry lashed out with his foot and kicked me in my stomach. The air exploded from my mouth and I dry retched. I curled into a small ball and clutched my stomach in protection. Fury burned deep inside, ready to explode.

Nugget's blood-curdling growl caught my attention. I looked over and saw him leap at Kane, aiming for his windpipe. Kane managed to knock the dog sideways and scuttled into his vehicle. He slammed the car door. The vehicle started and raced towards us. Rolling to my feet, I took off running... making for the water tank. Stupid me, I took my eye off the ball, didn't I. I should've headed for the trees where the vehicle couldn't follow. Kane sped past my running form, spun the vehicle in a half circle and skidded to a halt in front of me. He hung out the driver's window and levelled a gun at me. Of course, Kane would have a gun too!

Stupid girl, was my last thought before the bullet struck me and I face planted in the dirt.

Still some distance away Jerry began to stomp in our direction, screaming, 'Fuck, Kane don't kill her, I haven't finished playing.'

'Just a flesh wound Jerry, it won't interfere with your fun. She needed reminding of who's in charge.'

My stomach quaked, from where I lay I watched Kane climb from the vehicle with a self-satisfied smirk on his face. The muzzle of the gun was still warm when he used it to push my chin up further. Eyeballing me he said, 'Call the fucking dog, Constance.'

'*No.*' I spat at his face.

Casually Kane lifted his foot, placed it on my right arm and pressed down hard. Blood from the bullet wound squirted and a searing pain shot up and down my arm, burning through my muscles, even my toes hurt.

I screamed. The breath left my lungs in a long, loud, '*Nooooo.*'

Nugget appeared from beyond the water tank. Kane raised his gun. As he squeezed the trigger I lashed out and kicked his knee as hard as I could with my steel capped boot. Kane staggered back a step. The gun exploded. Nugget yelp.

Silence.

'Mate, did I get the bastard?' Kane asked as Jerry charged towards us.

'Yeah, looks like it,' rasped Jerry. Almost as an afterthought he booted me in the stomach again. 'Come on, let's get the bitch tied up and find the boyfriend. I want no more interruptions.'

Kane smiled, 'Sure mate. There's also the small matter of the gold. According to that mug you did over earlier, there's a large stash out here somewhere. That'll put us back in Mr Joshua's good books.'

'Oh fuck him…any gold I'm keeping.'

'Haven't you learnt your lesson? He'll have Aidan take more than your fingers next time. Fuck Jerry, you know Mr Joshua doesn't like you helping yourself…not to his money or his women,' said Kane.

He glanced down at me laying on the rough ground and then back at Jerry. 'I'm surprised he didn't kill you.'

'Fucking Aidan...he enjoyed giving me the chop, the bastard. He was soft on this bitch you know. Blabbed when he found out I dragged her into the storeroom. I told Mr Joshua she was the federal police spy, Wilcox gloated about before he was shot. I did it to protect his interests...he took my fingers anyway.'

'Mate, you need to be careful, your blackmailing notebooks won't keep you safe forever. One of these day's he'll find the lock-up...'

'Well, what he doesn't know,' said Jerry. He reached down, hooked his arm around my waist and picked me up. He smelt of stale sweat and blood. 'Come on Princess, you can tell us where all the lovely loot is. Then I think I might retire to a tropical island somewhere. Before that though I think I'll put the bed to good use.'

My arms were jammed in tight against my body as Jerry lugged me, under his arm, towards the sandalwood tree. The only weapon available to me was my teeth and feet. I shoved my face against his stomach and tried to bite him. All I got was a mouthful of tee-shirt. I screamed a profanity I didn't even know was in my vocabulary and lashed my booted feet wildly hoping to kick him in the back of the head or anywhere that would make him let go. All I struck was air.

Jerry laughed at my antics, 'Princess you always did know how to turn me on.'

We arrived at the fire pit, he opened his arm and let me fall to the ground... his mistake. In fury at his callousness and the threat he posed for the future I bounced to my feet and kicked him as hard as I could in the nuts. As he doubled over, I reached up into the sandalwood tree, grabbed the skinning knife, and bought it straight down, aiming for the side of his neck. He moved at the last moment and the knife plunged deep into his shoulder. Blood rushed out in a hot, pulsating fountain over my hand. Twisting the knife, I pulled it free and revelled in his scream. The lust to inflict more pain overrode my normally gentle nature.

'*Fuck,*' Jerry screamed falling to his knees.

I backed away, holding the knife out in front of me in protection. Kane dashed towards us. I slashed the knife at him making him back away. He started to raise the gun clenched in his hand. From behind one of the tents, Jack appeared and leapt at Kane, tackling him to the ground. The gun flew from Kane's hand but it went the wrong way for me. It skidded across the ground and came to rest under the Mini. Kane and Jack kicked up a cloud of red dust, as they rolled over grappling with each other in the dirt, both trying to get the upper hand.

The rolling stopped with Jack on top and Kane on his back facing the sky. Kane clenched his right fist and took a swipe at Jack's jaw. Pulling his head back at the last moment, the punch sailed under Jack's chin to land on his right shoulder.

Jack retaliated with three rapid, hard left jabs to Kane's ribs, landing them strategically under his right arm. Air exploded from Kane's mouth in a loud *whoosh*, followed by a whistling wheeze as he tried to pull air back into his lungs. The jabs were quickly followed up...a right-hand punch that had all the muscle of years of mining behind it. It landed on the side of Kane's face.

Crunch.

Teeth and blood exploded from Kane's mouth and decorated the ground around his head. He gurgled as blood frothed from his nose. His eyes rolled back and no one was home. *Lights out sucker,* I thought in satisfaction.

My attention snapped back to Jerry. He'd managed to regain his feet and was hunched forward, one hand clutching his groin, the other the bloody wound. He snarled, his eyes dilated, became black as midnight and burned with hate.

'You fucking bitch. I'm going to enjoy killing you,' he ground out, taking a step forward.

Holding the knife ready, I bounced from foot to foot waiting for his move. From the corner of my eye I caught a glimpse of Jack as he leapt to his feet. Something whizzed past my ear.

Thunk.

Not comprehending what my eyes were seeing, I watched stunned. In slow motion Jerry slumped into a boneless heap on the ground in front of me. A large stone rolled off his forehead and nestled next to his face.

Jack raced forward and scooped me into his arms.

Pain seared through my whole body. Startled I cried, '*Shit*, Jack, watch the arm.'

His grip loosened. I reached up and brushed gentle fingers down his cheek, before turning in the safety of his arms. I stared speechless at the figure standing before me.

Our lad, the soldier, home from the war.

'Dan,' I cried, my heart leaping in joy. 'Oh Dan, is it really you?'

Dan, his face covered in fine lines, eyes hard and alert, mouth grim, less joyful, said, 'What the hell's going on? I go away for five minutes and the bloody place turns into a war zone.'

'I'll tell you everything in a moment lad, but first we need to get this scum tied up...before they wake up and cause more problems,' said Jack.

'On it,' he said, and carefully removing the knife from my lax fingers, cut two pieces of rope from the nearest tent and hog-tied Jerry.

Moving to do the same to Kane, Jack quickly outlined all that had happened and why.

Dan took me gently in his arms, being more careful of all my cuts and bruises than my husband had been. I hugged him fiercely and asked the question that was burning in my brain.

'How is it you're home? We got your letter and you said that you had to stay in Vietnam.'

'You gotta love the military, they don't explain anything. One minute I was told I was needed to be a trainer, next minute I get orders to be on the transport back to Australia. I didn't argue. I arrived in Perth yesterday and was given a 48-hour pass. I hope by the time I get back my discharge papers will be ready.'

I stepped back and cupped his face with my battered hands. Tears of happiness coursed down my face. The world around me looked so much brighter, our family was whole again. I couldn't resist, I hugged him tight.

'Do you trust me, Connie?' asked Dan.

'With my life...and so much more,' I replied, lifting my face to stare at him. 'Why?'

Dan peered over my head at Jack. I watched him lift his eyebrow in an unspoken question. From the corner of my eye I saw Jack nod.

'If we do this, we have to make sure it's far enough away that no one will find them for a very long time...if ever. I'll give you a hand,' said Jack.

'No, Jack, there's no 'we'. You need to be here when the cops show up. No one knows I'm home, so I won't be a suspect.'

Puzzled, I shifted my gazed back and forth between them.

The tension got too much. 'What're you talking about?' I asked.

Dan cupped my face with soft hands.

'Connie, these two will never stop hunting you and Jack. I'm going to fix it, so they go away, forever. Word won't get back to Mr Joshua...he doesn't know you're here.' Muttering to himself, Dan said, 'Who the hell gives themselves such a ridiculous name anyway. Mr Joshua for God's sake!'

I couldn't help myself. I put it down to shock, I lay my head on his chest and started to laugh.

Jack came over, held us both tight. 'Let it out, my love. You've been through a lot today and handled yourself magnificently. I especially liked the kick in the nuts.'

I laughed even harder.

'Nugget's the real hero...looking after Connie the way he did,' said Jack.

I stopped laughing.

Nugget our wonderful dog...shot.

I started to sob.

'Kane killed Nugget, our beautiful, faithful boy,' I said. My words were muffled against Dan's chest.

Dan let out a piercing whistle, held me at arm's length and pointed. 'Look.'

Nugget came limping along the track.

'Nugget's fine. He has a graze along his shoulder and lost some blood but otherwise he's okay. He was waiting for me at the main road when I arrived on the motorbike. I could see straight away something was up, so I walked in.'

I embraced my hero. Nugget tolerated my highly emotional hugs and scratches with closed eyes and a soft deep rumble of happiness.

28

Chapter Twenty-Eight

Jack and Dan loaded the trussed-up men into their vehicle. Jack propped Kane into a sitting position in the front passenger's seat and filled the thug's top pocket with a large handful of gold.

Dan clicked the seatbelt around Kane's unconscious form, and asked, 'What time are you expecting Sergeant Henderson?'

'We didn't set a specific time. I told him we'd be packing the camp up and would be outta here by first light. I don't reckon he'll make it too late, you know what the roos are like on the road at night.'

Jack shrugged the unconscious Jerry from his shoulder onto the back seat.

'Okay, here's the plan,' said Dan. He glanced into the vehicle and smiled at the sight of Jerry trussed like a chicken ready for the oven. 'We'll load the motorbike into the back. I'll park behind that large stand of white gums near the highway. When I see the paddy wagon, I'll skid the four-wheel-drive out in front of it and race down the highway. That way the sarge can swear blind he saw these mugs leaving. He's gonna come check on you and Connie and find you locked down in the mine. As a bonus, you got a police sergeant as a witness...you've got nothing to do with what happens next.'

'Dan,' I said, taking his hand, drawing his gaze to mine. 'What are you going to do?'

Dan's mouth twitched with the slightest of smiles. 'Let's just say, there's some deep and isolated abandoned mine shafts around here, that will happily swallow a vehicle.'

'*Dan*!'

I squeezed his fingers.

Dan gave me a bland look. I thought about all that had gone before, and the future to come. Rough justice tugged a grin to my lips.

'Be careful...we've only just got you home,' I whispered.

Dan's face lit up and there it was, the smile I'd missed so much in our life.

'See you at the vineyard, Connie,' he said.

Blowing me a kiss, he jogged away to retrieve the motorbike. Turning to my husband, my eyes watering, I said, 'I love you, Jack Downy. Thank you for giving me a great family.'

He cupped my face and ran his work-roughened thumbs under my eyes, mopping up my tears.

His face was grim. 'They hurt you my love...that's unforgivable.' With a nod at my arm, he said, 'Come on, my sweet let's go have a look at that gunshot wound of yours.'

'No, not right now. We'll do it in the shaft later. There's a lot of cleaning up to do around here before the sarge arrives.'

'Alright, you're the boss, but at least let me tie a clean cloth around your arm, to stop the bleeding.'

* * *

Collecting the guns, I cleaned our fingerprints from the weapons. I opened the back of the vehicle to throw them in and stepped back in shock.

Wearing a Twisted Heads leather jacket, was Scotty. He been tied and beaten.

I slapped my hands over my eyes and screamed. Jack dropped the jerry can he was carrying and raced over.

'Connie my love, what's wrong?'

'No,' I sobbed, my stomach churned, I backed away from the vehicle, 'No...oh Jack.' I put my hand on my stomach and heaved.

He grabbed my arms, once again forgetting about my wound. I yelped at the pain.

'Sorry...you're scaring me. What's wrong?'

I couldn't make the words leave my mouth, I just pointed.

Jack carefully put me aside and went to look. His face went white. He leant forward and checked for a pulse. There wasn't one.

'He's dead. Took quite a beating. I bet that's how the bastards found us – by torturing Scotty.'

'Why's he wearing a Twisted Heads jacket?' I asked.

A look of surprise crossed Jack's face. 'Didn't you know, Connie – Teagan's the gang leader's daughter. Scotty joined to become a more acceptable son-in-law.'

Dan, followed by a trail of dust, came tearing down the track with Nugget riding shotgun on the bike, their faces wreathed in a happy smile. The smile dropped from Dan's face when he caught a glimpse of Jack's pallor.

'Change of plans, lad.'

Dan looked into the back of the vehicle.

'Shit, yeah you're right, Jack we can't dump a good friend...too cruel on the family, not knowing what happened to him.'

'What say we get the Twisted Heads to take care of the problem?' murmured Jack.

Dan laughed and slapped Jack on the shoulder. 'I like your thinking.'

While the men loaded the motorbike into Kane and Jerry's vehicle, I cut a leafy branch from the sandalwood tree and used it to brush away its tire tracks. That done I threw the branch into the fire...another piece of evidence gone.

Dan hung his arms over Jack and my shoulders and walked us to the mine shaft. 'I'll wait for the sarge as long as I can,' he said, 'but I've only got eighteen hours left on my pass and I need six hours to get back to Perth. I'll have to change the plan if he's late. You stick to your story no matter what you hear.' Dan gave me a quick hug and pushed me gently towards the shaft ladder. I scissored my legs over the frame and took my time to climb down. Jack stayed perched on a step half-way and watched Dan lock the grate above us and wipe away his fingerprints.

Dan peered down at him and said, 'Jack, I'll leave the key a couple of metres away, for the sarge to find. Nugget will let him know where you are.' He pointed to the grate and issued an order to the dog, 'Good boy, Nugget...guard Connie and Jack.'

Dan gave us a two-fingered salute and was gone.

Nugget settled on the grate.

I slumped in the corner of the shaft and stretched my sore dirty legs. Resting my hand on my belly, I groaned.

Jack, took one look and said, 'Hang on, my love. I'll go fetch the first-aid kit from the war room. You look like you could do with some TLC.' He scurried down the tunnel and within moments was back.

'A good strong cup of tea more like...no Jack, leave my legs. They'll need a soak to get them clean, besides the worse I look, the better the report the sergeant can file. Just see to this blasted arm will you, it hurts like buggery and it's bleeding again.'

To keep my mind off my aches and pains as Jack cleaned and dressed my wounds, I asked him how he'd managed to get out of the shaft, without being seen.

'They weren't very smart, those two,' said Jack, wrapping some gauze around my arm. 'I heard the gunshot and was just heading for the ladder when a pistol landed at my feet.'

'Yeah, I threw it into the shaft. I couldn't have that mongrel Jerry running around with a gun,' I said, holding the bandage in place while Jack fiddled with a safety pin to secure it. 'I'd hoped you'd see it...know I needed help.'

'Smart thinking...it worked. I knew we didn't own a pistol. I climbed up and while the big blond bloke had his back turned, to shoot at Nugget, I rolled out and hid behind the poppet frame. You know the rest, I saw you watching. Nice distraction, by the way, all that kicking and swearing. It nicely covered the noise I made following you.'

'So, what do we tell the police?'

'The truth...up to a point. Those bastards came to the site, looking for gold. Found you alone, they attacked and you fought back...escaped, but Kane shot you. They put a gun to your head and as I came up from the shaft, forced me to give them the gold. That handful I put in Kane's pocket is worth a small fortune. Not by our standards...but no one will know that. Anyway, we had a tussle and managed to get away and hide in the mine. They locked the grate and left,' he said, packing up the first aid kit. 'It's close enough to the truth to explain the scuff marks and blood around camp. Dan will made sure their fingerprints are on the keys and lock. One thing...we can't mention Dan.'

'Duh, that's a no-brainer, Jack. He's still in Vietnam,' I said, flicking the tip of his nose with my fingertip.

Jack smiled and settled in beside me. He reached over and drew me close, 'Oh god, Connie, I've never been so frightened in my life. I thought I'd lost you when that bastard pulled the trigger.'

I snuggled in close to my husband. My body ached, but nothing important was damaged. With a heart that was full of love, fatigue swamped me and I closed my eyes.

* * *

I awoke with a start. Nugget had barked. With bleary eyes I looked up the shaft, a faint light illuminated the dog as he sat guard.

Rubbing the sleep from my eyes, I carefully stretched, cranked the stiffness from my neck and asked, 'Have I been asleep long?'

'Most of the night, my love...it's first light,' answered Jack, as he watched Nugget above us.

'Where's the sarge... shouldn't he be here by now?'

My husband shrugged, his face blank.

'I'm scared, Jack. Dan's plans not going to work...he'll be seen...recognised.'

Jack squeezed my shoulder.

'Shhh...it's okay, Dan will adapt. We'll just stick to our story...'

Nugget gave a loud mournful howl, paused, and howled again.

'Showtime,' said Jack rubbing his hands together. 'Stay here and rest my love.'

He kissed my cheek, clambered to his feet, and climbed the ladder. Lights brushed over the howling dog and the sound of a vehicle's engine reached me. The light steadied and illuminated the poppet head. Nugget stopped howling and barked. He stopped at Jack's command.

Footsteps crunched on loose gravel, close to the shaft entrance and a deep baritone voice, sounding flustered, yelled, 'Ironstone...Connie. Can you hear me?'

Nugget gave a yip and Jack called out. 'Sergeant Henderson...that you?'

'Yeah, Ironstone. What the hell's going on? Are you okay...Connie?'

'We're locked down the shaft. Connie's alive...she's been shot,' yelled Jack. 'Watch yourself, sarge, there's a couple of bastard gold thieves out there and they've got guns.'

The crunching footsteps stopped. Sergeant Henderson started issuing orders, 'You men...draw your weapons...fan out and search. Rawlings, get on the radio...shooting and a robbery at Lucky Charm.'

Silence. The morning light lit the shaft. We waited.

'Ironstone.'

The sarge's head appeared at the top of the shaft. 'I've got the key...I'll have this lock off in a jiffy. How bad's Connie? Do we need the flying doctor?'

Clang.

The sergeant heaved the grate open. He reached a hand out to Jack and helped him to the surface.

Jack's words floated down to me. 'We won't need the flying quack...Kal Hospital can cope. Connie's got a flesh wound to her arm that needs stitching, she's covered in cuts and bruises...the bastards hit and kicked her.'

Jack glanced down at me, the worry lines evident even at this distance.

'Can you hang on another minute, love? I'll come down and get you. Don't try climbing the ladder...we don't want you bleeding again.'

Aching lethargy coursed through me, I was happy to rest.

'Alright, Jack...but can you make sure they're gone.'

'It's alright Connie, I've got my officers combing the site,' said Sergeant Henderson.

He turned to Jack and asked, 'Do you know who attacked you...did you get a good look at them?'

'Yeah I did, sarge. It was those bastards from the café yesterday. They got here just on sunset...waved a coupla guns around, demanding our gold.'

'Are you willing to make a statement to that effect? I can't make any charges stick if you won't testify.'

Dodging the question for the moment, Jack asked, 'What happened to you, sarge, I thought you were going to be here, early last night?'

Sergeant Henderson delivered the blow we'd been expecting later.

'I was, but I got held up. I finally got free about midnight and was heading this way, when I got a radio call...I'm sorry, Ironstone. It's Scotty Pearson, mate, he's been murdered.'

The sarge placed his large beefy hand on Jack's shoulder, a comforting gesture. 'I need your statement. I know it's a big ask, especially for Connie. The blokes who attacked you both were seen dragging Scotty into a vehicle yesterday. I need something to hold them on until we get evidence of their involvement in his death.'

Jack lifted his leg onto the ladder, stared directly at the sergeant and said 'We'll make a statement, sarge.' Jack's tone was fierce, his words clipped. 'You just make sure you get the evidence to make the murder charges stick. Those bastards have got to be stopped.'

Jack climbed down the ladder and lifted me up. I wrapped my arms around his neck, my legs around his waist, and snuggled in while he simply climbed back up as if I weighed nothing at all.

A police constable was talking to Sergeant Henderson when we got to the surface.

'All clear sergeant. There's no one here except for us. I did find some shell casings, over near the water tank and a small patch of blood further on. It looks like the spot where Mrs Downy was hit. Closer to the tank, there's a bloody bullet, must be the one that wounded the dog. I didn't touch anything, just made a note in my book. Was that correct?'

'Well done, Walker. Go and get Mrs Downy a blanket, she's suffering from shock and blood loss. We need to get her warm.'

Sergeant Henderson looked at my sad dishevelled state and shook his head. 'Connie lass, I'm sorry this happened to you, on my watch. Unfortunately, because of the murder...I'll have to call in the Criminal Investigation Branch. The CIB investigate all major crimes....standard procedure. They'll probably be here late morning. Because Scotty worked out here, they'll need to speak to you both. Any plans you had, put them on hold.'

Jack opened his mouth, I could see the protest forming on his lips.

The sarge shook his head, 'Don't argue, Ironstone. If you up and disappeared now, CIB will think you've something to hide. They'll put out a state-wide hunt for you both. Not what you need when you're trying to keep a low profile. Just answer their questions...leave the rest to me.'

The radio in the police vehicle squawked. Constable Rawlings stuck his head out the door.

'Sarge, we've got a car crash...east on Norseman Road...multiple fatalities.'

'*Shit*, it never just rains, it always pours. Alright, Rawlings, you and Simons get loaded up. Leave Walker here with a radio, he can guard the site for the CIB. Ironstone...I need that statement.'

'Sure sarge, but first I want a doctor to look at Connie's arm and the vet to check Nugget. That dog's a hero...it could have been so much worse for Connie without him to protect her.'

Sergeant Henderson nodded his head in agreement. 'Rawlings, you go with Ironstone and Mrs Downy...stay with them and watch yourself. There's a couple of killers on the loose. When the doc's finished, bring them straight to the station.'

'Will do, sarge,' said the constable, tucking his notebook away in his shirt pocket and buttoning it closed.

He followed us to the Rover and perched on the edge of the back seat keeping a vigilant watch as we followed the police Land Cruiser into Kalgoorlie.

* * *

It was late afternoon. I was exhausted and my arm throbbed like a bitch. Fatigue and nausea still plagued me. So much for the flesh wound – the doctor had put thirty neat little stitches in my arm, cleaned and patched my legs, jabbed me with tetanus and antibiotic needles, and confirmed the good news.

'Everything's fine Connie. Just take it easy...no more adventures, okay.'

I smiled, until the needle went in. 'Ouch doc, haven't I had enough pain for one day.'

He smiled and patted my hand.

'Just a precaution, you're very lucky, the damage from that bullet could have been a lot worse.'

'Tell me about it. Thanks for the patch-up,' I replied, giving him a tired smile.

Poor Nugget went through a similar experience with the vet, except they shaved his beautiful golden coat to expose the bullet wound, before stitching it. He wasn't a happy dog.

Jack found a parking space right outside the police station's front door. I climbed out on legs that felt like rubber and wobbled.

Constable Rawlings placed his hand under my elbow as support, and asked, 'Are you alright, Mrs. Downy?'

'Yes, thanks, constable, but I think I've just about had enough,' I answered.

'Well, let's get you inside and I'll make you a nice cup of tea.'

'Hmm...tea...that'd be lovely.'

Jack rounded the front of the vehicle, concern etched all over his face.

'I'm fine Jack...don't fuss. Let's get this over with, find a hole to hide in, and sleep.'

'Righto,' said Jack, and then he made me laugh. He turned to our dog and growled, 'Come on Nugget, stop sulking. It's only a bit of fur, mate, it'll grow back.'

Nugget stiffly climbed down from the Rover, stuck his nose in the air, offended, and stalked inside.

* * *

Being invited into the interview room to make a statement was not an experience I wanted to repeat again in my lifetime. Constable Rawlings led us down a long hallway that was in serious need of a coat of paint. We passed a series of closed doors that offered no hint as to what they were guarding but, along with the hallway walls, created a claustrophobic effect. It was a relief when Rawlings unlocked a dirty paint-chipped door at the end of the corridor.

He pointed into the small room at a metal table and four chairs, all bolted to the floor, and said, 'Take a seat. I'll go rustle you up that cuppa.'

He left, the lock clicked softly behind him. I wrinkled my nose and surveyed our small prison.

'It's hot in here, Jack. Smells bad too...like stale sweat and dirty old socks.'

Jack lay a gentle arm across my shoulders and guided me to a chair.

'There's no ventilation, the air just sits and stews. Sit down, my love...we'll get out of here as quickly as possible and then go get Carlo to cook us some breakfast.'

My stomach churned at the thought of food, but I held my peace. I sat on the hard seat. Nugget settled himself under my chair with a deep sigh. I looked down, he was weary too. I dropped my hand under the chair and stroked his head. Nugget closed his eyes and began to snore.

I nestled back against Jack's shoulder and laid my head on his chest, staring at the off-white dirt-stained wall. We sat for a long time. The sound of approaching footsteps drew my gaze from the study of the walls' scuffmarks to the back of the chipped door. It opened abruptly and I squeaked in fright.

'Shhh...it's okay love, you're safe,' Jack breathed softly in my ear.

Two men, arms loaded with paperwork and files, bustled into the room. Sergeant Henderson followed at a sedate pace behind. He was carrying a tray loaded with steaming mugs and a plate of biscuits.

He placed a red mug in front of me, and said, 'Here you go, Mrs Downy, you look like you could use this.'

He placed a matching cup on the table in front of Jack.

'Coffee, strong and black, Mr Downy.'

Hmm, very formal. Interesting.

The sarge took a stance behind the two seated men, legs spread wide and hands clasped behind his back.

'Thank you, sergeant,' I said and picked up the cup from the table.

As I blew on the hot tea, I studied the two men over the cup's rim. Dressed alike in long-sleeved white shirts, black ties and dark trousers, they looked out of place in a town full of scruffy, dirt-encrusted miners. I guessed the younger of the two was aged in his mid-thirties. He had chubby cheeks and dark hair that was neatly combed back, exposing the beginnings of a receding hairline.

His companion was older, maybe late forties or early fifties. He wore his sandy coloured hair close-cropped and carried his thin frame with a weariness that was belied by a shrewd gaze. He noticed my scrutiny and smiled thinly.

'This is Detective Sergeant Albert Nielsen. I'm Chief Inspector Peter Lawrence. We're from the Criminal Investigation Branch. DS Nielsen has a series of questions for you both. Please answer them truthfully and with as much detail as you can.'

With a nod of his head, he handed the reins over to his subordinate.

The detective sergeant pointed to a cassette deck.

'For the purpose of this interview everything we say here today will be recorded. That recording will be transcribed into a statement for you both to sign,' he explained.

He scrabbled his fingers around in the pile in front of him and pulled out a cellophane-wrapped cassette tape. He opened it and inserting it into the tape deck. With a flourish, he pressed the record button and commenced the interview by identifying the police contingent present in the room.

The detective sergeant levelled his gaze at Jack and said, 'Will you please identify yourself, sir.'

'Jack Evan Downy.'

Nielsen looked at me.

I said, 'Connie Lee Downy.'

'Thank you.'

DS Nielsen selected one of the files in front of him and opened it. His eyebrows rose and fell while he contemplated the words before him.

'Now Mr Downy...if that's your *real* name...'

My head shot up and I looked at Jack, flutters of fear started swirling around inside my chest. Jack stayed relaxed in his chair, his left arm casually draped over my shoulder, but his eyes had gone an intense blue.

'We don't seem to have very much information about you on record sir. What we do have, makes for an interesting read.' Nielsen placed his finger on a point in his notes and raised his gaze to Jack's face. 'You've no fixed street address, no driver's license, there's no record of you attending school in this state and, your father Robert Moresque is currently a guest of Her Majesty's prison system, serving a life sentence for murder. Now, what do you have to say about that *Mr Moresque*!'

'Stepfather.'

'I beg your pardon, sir?'

'Robert Moresque's my stepfather,' replied Jack. 'My father, Captain Evan Christopher Downy, was killed in Northern New Guinea in 1944 during the Aitape-Wewak campaign. My mother remarried, when I was six, sent me to school as Jack Moresque. If you check your records a bit closer, you'll see I was never adopted, so my real name is Jack Downy.'

DS Nielsen's eyebrows twitched up and down again, giving his face a startled appearance. 'Why the name change, sir?'

'Detective sergeant, if some bastard killed your mother, would you want to bear his name for the rest of your life?'

Nielsen glanced at the chief inspector, who gave him a slight nod.

Nielsen asked, 'Why's there no record of you attending school under either name, after the age of twelve?'

'Because I didn't go back to school after my mother died,' replied Jack, studying the fingernails on his right hand.

'Where do you and Mrs Downy currently reside, sir?'

'At the Lucky Charm mine site. If you check your records, a bit closer, you'll see that I'm the current lease-holder...all properly registered and paid up!'

Closing the file in front of him, DS Nielsen selected another from his stack.

'In 1963 you lured a ten-year-old boy from Sydney, crossed state borders, and bought the lad to Western Australia. What is the nature of your relationship, sir?'

'Once again detective sergeant,' said Jack, his tone calm, level and firm, 'check your records. Dan was an orphan, living on the streets of Sydney. He was homeless and starving when I met him. The NSW welfare and court system awarded me guardianship over him...and gave permission for him to come to WA. Three years later, after meeting all their stringent requirements, the courts approved my adoption of Dan. To all intents and purposes, he is my son.'

Jack peered over at Sergeant Henderson.

'Sergeant Henderson has a copy of all the relevant documents, he's carried out regular welfare checks over the years, until Dan was eighteen. *Isn't that right sarge!*'

Chief Inspector Peter Lawrence leant forward, clasped his hand together in front of him on the table and in a soft voice asked, 'Where is he?'

'Where's who, chief inspector?'

'Daniel Babcock...he seems to be missing. He's not at your lease, he's not in town.'

I couldn't stand it any longer, these people were out to crucify Jack and I couldn't work out why.

'*What do you mean, where is he*?' I growled.

The chief inspector's gaze flicked to my face and his top lip twitched in surprise. I glared at him, switched my disapproving look to Nielsen before returning it back to Lawrence. 'Dan's in Vietnam...risking his life to serve his country.' I put everything into my growled words, all my fears, anger and pain. The men in the room sucked in their breath...even Jack. 'Now, what the hell's going on? We're quietly going about our business, some bastards attack us, and we get the third degree.'

'Connie,' said Jack, his arm tightening slightly around my shoulder. 'The police are just trying to establish the validity of our identities, gauge our honesty, isn't that right chief inspector?'

The DCI gave Jack an amused smile. I exploded in rage.

'I don't care,' I yelled at them. 'Jack's a good person. What you're doing is wrong.'

And before I knew it red-hot tears were welling and overflowing.

'Connie love, don't cry. You know I hate it when you do,' said Jack, pulling me close.

'I got shot...for God's sake...I'm entitled to a good cry,' I wailed.

Through wet eyes I watched embarrassment tinge the cheeks of the three policemen in the room.

DS Nielson turned to Sergeant Henderson and said, 'Another cup of tea perhaps, and maybe something to eat.'

Nugget crawled out from under his chair, placed his head in my lap, and whined. I sucked in a long, ragged breath, stopped my tears, and patted his head. Chief Inspector Lawrence, passed me a crisp white handkerchief, folded neatly into a small square. With a loud honk I blew my nose and scrunched it into a ball.

'We're sorry this is so upsetting for you, but there have been some very serious criminal acts carried out in the last forty-eight hours. We're just trying to get to the heart of it all. We'll take a break and then just a few more questions and you can go home,' said the DCI.

In unison, they stood and left the room.

Jack leant forward, kissed my temple and whispered with a grin, 'Well played, my love.'

'Hmm...not play, Jack. I'm fed up. Both Nugget and I are in pain, we need to rest. You do too,' I said, running my hand over his cheek. He drew his breath in, to protest. I wagged my index finger at him. 'No, don't pull any of that macho rubbish with me. I know you too well...there's lines of fatigue around your eyes, Jack.' I ran my fingers over the invaders on his handsome face. 'Here and here.'

Kissing the tip of my nose, Jack placed his forehead against mine. He cupped my cheeks and murmured, 'Alright love. I'll call the sarge back, get our statements done and then we'll go. Okay?'

At my relieved nod, Jack rose to his feet, banged on the locked door, and hollered, 'Sarge, can we get this done. Connie's had the bomb and needs to rest.'

Bloody cheek, what about him!

The same trio returned to the interview room. This time Detective Sergeant Nielsen only carried two files. Detective Chief Inspector Lawrence took charge of the interview, by asking the DS to start the tape. After stating the time, date and those present in the room, he then asked us to describe the events of the previous evening. Jack and I recited our agreed story. Sergeant Henderson confirmed finding us locked in the shaft and that the evidence his officers had found on site agreed with everything we said.

'Now Mrs Downy, yesterday morning, in the Victory Café, you were seen talking with the two men, who you say later attacked you. What did you talk about?'

'Chief inspector, I didn't speak to those men. I was taking Toothless Bruce's breakfast order when they came in. They did all the talking, especially the short ugly one. He made some vile suggestions about playing kissy in a cupboard and wanted to run his horrible hands through my hair,' I answered truthfully, I didn't suppress the shudder that ran through me.

'Hmm yes, that seems to match what Toothless said,' then blowing out a frustrated sigh, he added, 'Why don't people in this town have proper names?'

Detective Sergeant Nielson leant forward and said to Jack, 'Sir, did you recognise either of these men?'

'Nope, I'd never laid eyes on them before,' answered Jack, truthfully.

The chief inspector placed the necklace that Jack had given me our first Christmas together on the table.

'Do either of you recognise this?'

Surprised, I lifted my hand to my neck where the piece of gold always hung and said, 'Oh, my necklace!'

'Mrs Downy, why was your necklace found at a crime scene?' asked the chief inspector.

Chills ran up my back and the blood drained from my face.

'C...c...crime scene,' I stuttered, 'wh...wh...what crime scene?'

'This necklace was found on the floor next to the dead body of one Scott Pearson.'

So the twisted heads hadn't quite done us a favour then. Was this their subtle way of diverting attention back away from themselves?

'Explain! How can I explain, what I don't know? It must've come off yesterday in the struggle when I was being dragged around. I didn't notice. The men who attacked us said they were after gold. I can't see them leaving a nugget like that behind. Can you?' I said, while I frantically tried to come up with an explanation that covered Dan's involvement in the moving of Kane and Jerry's car. 'The men must have dropped it when they killed Scotty.'

'No, he was killed before you were attacked and not where he was found.'

'Well I don't know, why don't you ask them?'

'This morning, a vehicle travelling at high speed on Norseman Road, failed to take a turn, left the bitumen and crashed into a tree. It exploded on impact. The badly burned bodies of three men have been recovered from the crash site. Two of the men had been shot in the head. So I need an explanation for your necklace.'

Jack's grip on my shoulder tightened slightly, I reached up and grabbed his hand.

'Well maybe they dropped it when they dumped his body - I don't know. I can't give you an explanation for something I have no knowledge about.' Even to me the stress of the situation was apparent in the quavering of my voice. To divert the chief inspector I asked, 'Is that who was in the car...those men? Who was the third man?'

'We're hoping you could tell us. From your description, the man in the front passenger seat matches a man called Kane Hansen. He had a handful of gold in his top pocket...confirms what you told us. The one on the back seat matched the description of Jerry Martin, a well-known standover man from Victoria.'

'And the third?' I asked, my gut churning in fear. 'There were only two when they attacked us yesterday.'

The DCI didn't answer my query. Instead, he slid from his seat and said, 'That's all for now. DS Nielsen will get your statements transcribed and written up. I want you to come in tomorrow morning, check them over and sign them.'

Nielsen switched off the cassette recorder, collected the files and together the CIB officers strode from the room.

I broke the silence they left in their wake.

'Sarge, what do you think of these CIB johnnies?' I asked, running a hand over my tired face. 'Honest opinion now...do you think they can be trusted?'

'How do you mean trusted, Connie?' asked the sergeant, giving his ear lobe a gentle tug as he looked at me warily.

'With the notebook? If you, or one of your officers, found the notebook in the car wreck, gave it to CIB, do you think they'd act upon it? Use the information to bring down Paul Joshua?' I asked, watching the wrinkles furrow deeper in his brow with each word I spoke. 'That would keep us safe...away from any fallout wouldn't it?'

He began to chuckle, his brow clearing. 'You, young lady are quite devious,' he said, amusement lines appeared around his eyes. 'I think something can be arranged. I've made some discreet inquiries, since we last spoke on this subject. The Beach Inquiry is currently under way in Victoria. The federal inquiry team report directly to the Attorney-General. Their focus is corruption within the police force. I think the contents of the notebook could greatly assist them to clean house. The Western Australian CIB has a great reputation, for honesty and integrity and people like Chief Inspector Lawrence would use your information to dismantle the Joshua organisation.'

I felt a surge of relief at his words. I reached down and pulled off my shoe and removed the notebook. A heavy weight seemed to pass from me to the sergeant as I handed the book over. A dangerous burden had just been passed on. I prayed that I had finally made the right decision.

My control started to slip and I made a dash for the bathroom. I locked myself in the small room, took some gulping breaths. It didn't help...I threw up. Turning on the white plastic tap marked cold, I splashed my face with the tepid water. Drying off on the paper towels, I took some more deep breaths. My nausea abated, my control returned. I went back out to join the men.

Jack and Sergeant Henderson were standing near the entrance, chatting. As I approached, Constable Simons walked in from the street, escorting a well-dressed man, with neatly trimmed butterscotch hair. He looked vaguely familiar.

Jack took my hand and said, 'If we're finished, sarge, I'll take the old girl home, she's all tuckered out.'

Sergeant Henderson nodded and said, 'Yeah, you two get off. I've got another interview booked – the new manager of the Mineral Rights Hotel. It's frustrating, someone must have some information about Scotty's murder.'

29

Chapter Twenty-Nine

Sleep eluded me. I lay curled in Jack's embrace, listening to his soft snore. How could he sleep while I had butterflies of fear fluttering around in my chest? There were three bodies in that burnt-out wreck...was one of them Dan? I didn't care about Kane and Jerry, as far as I was concerned, they got what they deserved.

Who was the third man?

I pushed down on my fear and locked it away in a small box.

Another rose in its place.

I'd finally recognised the well-dressed man with butterscotch hair. My blood ran cold at the memory of a good-looking young man, surfboard tucked under his arm, bright happy eyes joyously watching the surf and asking probing questions.

David!

He didn't resemble a happy-go-lucky surfer now, neatly groomed with quality clothing and, apparently, managing a hotel here in Kalgoorlie known for its criminal connections. What the hell was going on? Does he and has he always worked for Paul Joshua?

Did he recognise me today?

None of this made any sense.

I sighed and slipped quietly out of bed. I pulled on the shorts and Tee-shirt that lay where they'd fallen, in my rush for bed. I picked up my boots and slipped from the shack. I stared up at the moonless night in awe – ablaze with a million stars that shone crystal clear in a peaceful sky. I turned my boots upside down, banged them together, to dislodge any creepy crawlies that may have taken up residence, and pulled them on. The last thing I needed was to share a space with a scorpion or wolf spider, that would really make my week – *not*.

The night-time insects didn't pause in their noisy chatter, undisturbed by my movements. The coals in the fire pit glowed faintly. I picked up the metal poker and gave them a stir. Sparks rose on a current of warm eucalyptus scented air and danced away into the dark. I grabbed a large log from the woodpile and threw it on the embers, pushed the billy closer with my foot, and settled back on a cushioned seat. Staring up at the stars, I waited patiently for the water to heat. Nugget stuck his head out of the tent flap and glared at me.

'Go back to sleep, boy. I'm just making a cup of tea.'

Being a faithful companion, Nugget lay down where he could keep an eye on me. He takes my safety very seriously.

'You okay, love?' asked Jack, emerging from the gloom, naked except for his boots. Amusement tugged at my lip.

'You really should wear your hat, Jack. You're going to scare the wildlife.'

He chuckled and wandered over, slipped his arms around me and scooped me up.

'Hey,' I protested, 'I was sitting there, watching the sky.'

Jack settled on my seat and cradled me in his lap. We lay back together and gazed up.

'What's wrong, love. I could hear your thoughts ticking over in bed.'

'Oh...so they were only pretend snores were they?' I quipped.

Laughing softly in my ear, my husband said, 'Come on, Connie love give. What's eating you?'

'I'm worried about the car accident...the third body. Is it Dan?'

Jack stroked my hair.

'I don't reckon...the sarge said nothing about a motorbike in the wreck. We had a good old chinwag while you were in the toilet. He described the driver as a really short bloke...had to use an old swag to see over the steering wheel. There was a needle and some heroin rolled up in it.' Jack stared off into space, his blue eyes glazed. I turned my head and watched his face. He blinked and said, 'The sarge reckons there was a box of files in the back of the vehicle, unfortunately mostly burnt. It wasn't there when it left here. Also Scotty wasn't in the car when it crashed – he was found earlier.'

'Where?'

'In his digs, laid out neatly on the bed, with respect. Cops received an anonymous phone call.'

'That was kind of Tegan's father...' I said.

'Yeah...it's also a good indicator that Dan got to the clubhouse...what happened then is anybody's guess.'

Jack sucked in a deep breath and let out a long sigh.

'Thinking about it...I wouldn't be surprised if the driver was Lanky Luke. He's been trying to get in with the gang for a long time. As an initiation they may have told him to get rid of Kane and Jerry and all their stuff...if he was doped up, his driving would've been shot to hell.'

'So, what happened to Dan?' I asked, turning my head to watch his face as he gazed up at the heavens. Jack gave a sad smile.

'I don't know love...the missing motorbike's a good sign. I pray he's safe...but knowing that cheeky bugger, he's parked the car at the twisted head clubhouse, rung the doorbell, and skedaddled before they even realised he was there.'

'I suppose – it certainly sounds like Dan,' I said, giving a small chuckle of relief. Jack had a way of putting me at ease. 'There's something else I need to tell you.'

'Hmm,' said Jack, as he started to nuzzle at my neck.

'Oh, stop that, Jack,' I said, pulling away exasperated.

Jack did a perfect imitation of a boy whose treat had been taken from him. With soulful eyes, he dropped his bottom lip. I raised my eyebrows at his antics and snorted.

'You're such a boy,' I said. 'No, don't take that as encouragement, this is important, Jack. Do you remember when we left the police station today, Constable Simons came in with a man.'

Jack nodded. 'Yeah, the new manager of the Mineral Rights.'

'Well, I thought he looked familiar...I've just remembered from where.'

Gazing off at the stars, I stopped talking. A sense of betrayal from one who I'd considered a friend hurt in my chest.

'Connie, who was he?' asked Jack, giving me a small nudge with his shoulder.

Sighing deeply, I replied. 'A man I thought was a friend. His name is David. He lived at the same boarding house as me in Melbourne. We used to sit and talk about things, especially what was going on in my life. Now it seems he may have been one of Paul Joshua's crew...otherwise why is he here, running one of his businesses?'

'We need to warn the sarge. I'll have a quiet word with him tomorrow, when we go in to sign our statements. Then, we're definitely packing up and getting out of here. It's getting far too crowded for my liking.'

'I'm sorry for bringing all this trouble to our life...'

Jack cut me off by placing his lips over mine. He scooped his arm under my knees and rose to his feet.

'Finished looking at the night sky, my love...I've some different stars to show you.'

* * *

I awoke with a start. Nugget was standing with his nose pressed against the door growling. Jack, already dressed in boots and jeans, carried the .22 rifle. In a quiet motion he turned the handle and cracked open the door. I threw off the sheet, swung my legs out of bed and pulled on my clothes, for the second time that night.

'Shhh, Nugget,' ordered Jack, as he paused to listen. He whispered, 'Connie, we've got a visitor. Stay here...until we know who it is and what they want.'

Not bothering to argue, I pulled on my boots and went to stand behind him. I hooked my hand into the back of his jeans. He looked over his shoulder at me, eyebrows raised.

I mouthed, 'My place is with you, Jack.'

He nodded with a half-smile on his lips.

'To be expected...stick close, my love.'

We stole out the door. David was standing at the still glowing fire pit, hands empty and held up at shoulder height.

'I'm alone and mean you no harm,' he said, looking into the dark towards us.

Nugget circled, halted in front of David, growling softly.

Jack motioned me to stay, shouldered his rifle, and stepped into the firelight.

'A good way to get yourself shot, mate, sneaking into a gold miner's camp in the dead of night. Who are you...what do you want?'

David slowly turned his head, gave a benign smile and said, 'Didn't Constance tell you about me? We're old friends from Melbourne.'

Jack stared at David and cradled the rifle in his arms, his face held no expression.

David tried his goofy look and said, 'Look mate, I'm not here to cause any trouble. I just want a quick word with Constance, then I'll leave.'

Jack stared at David with the rifle cradled in his arms, his face held no expression.

David lowered his hands slightly and began to fidget, rocking from one foot to the other. Nugget gave a soft growl. David halted his restless activity and stood still. A bead of sweat trickled slowly down his cheek.

Jack stared at David with the rifle cradled in his arms, his face still held no expression.

Amusement and a touch of sympathy for our visitor lifted my mood.

I walked over to stand next to Jack and said, 'Hello David. What do you want?'

A look of relief flashed across his face.

'Hello Mermaid, it's nice to see you again.'

'Connie.'

'What?' David asked, his bemusement evident in the puzzled look he gave me.

'My name is Connie. You didn't answer my question. What do you want?'

A tentative smile touched his lips, it didn't reach his hazel eyes.

'I wanted to see you...make sure you're okay. I've been concerned.'

'Cut the bullshit, David. It's three in the morning, we're standing in a mining camp in the middle of the West Aussie scrub. I haven't seen you in three years and you suddenly show up saying you're concerned about me! *Come on.*' I crinkled my nose up in disgust at the glib lies that fell so easily from his lips. 'You used to be a much better liar than that. You're not here to check up on me, you're here to make sure I don't blow your cover. Now I've had a tough twenty-four hours...which has included being used as a punching bag, being shot, doctored and interrogated...so I *will not* ask you again. What...do...you...want?'

David flashed me a smile, full of boyish charm, then his face turned serious.

'Would you... *please*...call off your attack dogs. Can we sit and talk?'

I looked up at Jack who continued to stare at David, with the rifle cradled in his arms, his face still held no expression. I returned my eyes to David's face.

'No, I don't think so...you've given us no reason to trust you,' I said. I crossed my arms across my chest. 'Now answer the question, what do you want?'

David sighed deeply and scrubbed his hands through his neatly trimmed hair.

He opened his mouth, but the words were halted on his lips when Jack said, 'Sarge, it's been a long and busy day. You want to come take a seat. I'll put the billy on. A cup of tea, Connie?'

A hearty chuckle from the dark, followed by footsteps and a deep baritone voice, came from our left.

'I warned you, sir, that this was entirely the wrong approach. You need to be upfront and honest with these people if you want to get the answers you need.'

Jack smiled.

Taking my cue from my husband I said, 'Love a cuppa thanks, Jack.'

Sergeant Henderson wandered into view, he took a seat at the fire pit and sighed as he propped his feet up on a spare seat.

'Close your mouth, David, before you trip over your tongue. Do you think we're a bunch of hicks, just because we live out in the bush?'

I waved him towards a seat, took the rifle from Jack's hand, and returned it to the gun safe at the foot of our bed.

* * *

Settled back, blowing steam from my tea, I studied our visitor.

'Okay David, none of your surfer boy, dude stuff, what are you doing here?'

'Before I explain, Connie, I just want to say – one of the happiest moments of my life was today, seeing you walk out of the police station. I thought that bastard Paul Joshua had killed you.'

'Now why would he have done that, David? I was no threat to him. In fact, he was always attentive and nice...'

David shook his head.

'That's just one of his many personas...anyway I'm getting ahead of myself.'

David looked each of us in the eye, frowned, and said, 'What I'm about to tell you, is not only highly confidential but can also cost me everything. The sergeant here knows most of what I'm about to say. My handlers gave me the green light to speak to him, but you two...I'm trusting with my life.'

Jack leant forward and said, 'Mate we've no intention of getting you or anyone else killed, or of messing up your investigation. Just tell us what you can, ask what you need to know, leave the rest.'

A look of surprise crossed David's face.

Sergeant Henderson smiled into his cup and in a soft murmur said, 'Told you – smart and trustworthy.'

David took a deep breath, settled back in his seat and spilled the beans.

'My name's not David Wellard, for the safety of my wife and children and future investigations, I can't tell you who I really am, but I can tell you I'm a federal police officer. I've been working under cover for a number of years, in organised crime. The original plan was for me to get close to Kane and Jerry, get a job in the Joshua organisation and work my way up into a position of trust. We thought the best way to get an introduction would be through Betty...so I was to move into her neighbourhood and start a friendship. Instead, I came across you Connie, a beautiful pixie standing amongst the flowers enjoying the sun. You told me you girls were moving to St Kilda, so I had to make a quick change to my plans.'

'So, David, our friendship was just part of a plan?' I asked, as disappointment washed over me.

'No, Connie. I could see immediately you'd nothing to do with that life, but I could also see you being slowly sucked in and trapped. When you told me about meeting Paul Joshua and his interest in you, I was scared. I'd heard stories. Then a jealous Jerry became abusive, I tried to guide you away but there wasn't a great deal I could do, without compromising the investigation.

My handlers leaned hard on the Beaconsfield Pub manager, John Willcox. Got him to turn informer and give me a job, in return AFP would protect him. Willcox was a fool, he thought being an informer meant he could short change Joshua. In the end it got him killed. After that, I took over the pub as manager and got a foothold into the Joshua organisation. Since then I've been moving up the ranks. His organisation is growing fast. Paul Joshua's started to branch out from Victoria. Jerry and Kane were sent to WA about six months ago to collect dossiers on people and open new avenues for his drug trade. The Twisted Heads offered them a local base for their operations in exchange for a cut of the proceeds. Paul Joshua doesn't share. He sent me here last week to take over the Mineral Rights pub and weed out the gang. Someone was gaining too much attention in the wrong circles.'

David glanced at the sergeant with a half-smile. 'That would be Lanky Luke. He had no idea how to keep his head down and mouth shut,' said the policeman.

'Or how good a copper he was dealing with. It was just bad luck Kane and Jerry found you, Connie. They were due to return to Melbourne next week.' David rubbed his chin, sucked in his bottom lip then asked, 'What happened to you? According to Betty one minute you were sitting in the club and the next you'd disappeared.'

'And of course you'd trust anything that comes out of that skank's mouth,' I said. Harsh and unforgiving were my feelings towards Betty and her lies. It would be a long time before I forgave the anguish she'd caused me. 'David, you were listening with the wrong part of your anatomy. I know you and Betty were having an affair. She used to sneak up to your room in the middle of the night.'

'Yes, Betty and I used to meet late at night...but I never slept with her. We'd meet on the landing outside my room, she'd drink my scotch and tell me all about the wonderful Kane. A good source of information was Betty. Unfortunately, she got herself deep in debt...gambling. She's currently working at one of Mr Joshua's brothels to pay it off.' Leaning forward, elbows on his knees and wrists hanging loosely in front of him David asked, 'Why shouldn't I trust what she says? Why did you disappear like that, Connie? Tell me everything...right from the beginning.'

So, for the second time in as many days, I recounted my story, starting the day I moved into the boarding house. It hurt me to talk of the events I'd witnessed, the attacks and my escape, and my throat tightened on my words. Jack took my hand and the burden eased. I pushed on with my story but didn't mention the current existence of the notebook.

'I thought you saw me leave David, you watched as the bus pulled away.'

David snapped his finger.

'The boy running for the bus!' he exclaimed. He sat back, eyes shining bright in the firelight. 'Connie, I didn't recognise you. Wish I had, I could've saved you a lot of grief, by telling you the truth about that night. Then I'd have helped you go somewhere safe.'

'Then I'd never have met Jack,' I said with a smile at my husband. '*No,* this is better. So, why've you come to see me now?'

'Paul Joshua's a slippery bugger, I'm having trouble getting any hard evidence on him. He runs extortion rackets, race fixing, illegal gambling clubs, brothels, drugs. John Willcox and others have been murdered, on his say so, but I can't quite get the proof I need to bring him down. I'm tired, Connie. I want to go home to my family, but I can't. I'm stuck on this undercover job, until this thing's finished. I was hoping that you may have noticed something or heard something that could help me.'

'How about the murder of John Willcox?' I asked.

'Jerry Martin shot him.'

'Nope, he didn't actually – set him up...*yes*...killed him... *no*. Paul Joshua pulled the trigger, his fingerprints on the gun prove it.'

Silence.

Wood crackled in the fire and the faint scent of sandalwood wafted past.

Everyone stared at me.

David's eyes narrowed, as he carefully asked, 'How do you know that, Connie?'

I held my hand out to Sergeant Henderson. He placed the notebook in it.

Turning to the page I'd read on the train, I said, 'Jerry was supposed to dispose of the weapon. He kept it for his own purposes.

He stored it along with evidence relating to other crimes in a private lockup he owns. The details are in this notebook. Take it David...shut down the Joshua organisation and go home to your family.'

David leapt to his feet, picked me up by my arms and kissed my cheek hard.

I yelled at him, '*Shit* David...watch the stitches.'

* * *

Sergeant Henderson wasn't around when we went in to sign our statements. He and his officers were out of town, clearing up the mess from the previous day. The CIB detectives were also absent.

Constable Rawlings manned the enquiry counter and carefully walked us through the process. As we turned to leave, he gave Jack an envelope.

'Sarge thought you might be needing these.'

Jack took a peak in the envelope and started to laugh.

We walked out into the sunshine and climbed into the Rover.

'Come on, Jack... give,' I said. 'What's the sarge left for us?'

Jack dropped the contents of the envelope in my lap, started the vehicle. Looking down, I started to laugh.

In my lap lay three drivers licenses, in the names of – Jack Evan Downy, Daniel Samuel Babcock and Connie Lee Downy.

* * *

Lucky Charm was beginning to resemble the ghost town of Gwalia. Our bed, the fully loaded Mini, our fridge, tents, pumps and generators were all loaded and secured on the trailer. As I helped Jack pull down the hoist we'd used for gold fishing in the water tank, I swiped sweat from my brow with the hem of my tee-shirt and took a final look around. A lone tumbleweed rolled past, propelled by a cool breeze that wove its lazy way through the bush.

Jack, his bare chest wet from his dive in the tank and glowing with a honey tan, came and stood beside me. I studied his face, looking for signs of regret.

'Will you miss it?' I asked.

Shaking his head, my husband smiled whimsically.

'Nope. I'm looking forward to the next phase in our life. Besides, it'll always be here. I'm hanging onto the lease, who knows what value it may have in the future.'

'What about our lovely shack? I'd hate to think, after all the hard work you and Dan put in building it, that it'll just sit here and rot.'

'Not gonna happen. I'll come back with the lad, soon. We'll pull it down and move it to the vineyard. I'm not letting all that great building material go to waste.'

Quirking an eyebrow at my frugal husband, I laughed.

'Skinflint.'

Jack smiled, whistled, and said, 'Nugget, Rover mate...we're off.'

* * *

The Rover creaked and groaned under its heavy load. Taking the last turn in the road, Jack swiftly changed into the lowest gear. The old girl growled as she ground her slow way up a steep incline.

Jack pointed to a turn-off at the top of the hill.

'Ups and Downs,' he said. 'Dan's name for it.'

My bum was numb, the vibrations of the vehicle had dulled my hearing, and I was busting for a pee...again. Our early morning start from Lucky Charm had gone without incident. The only thing that had gone to plan this week and it made me suspicious. I kept waiting for another problem to jump out at us. Jack drove all day and well into the night. I'd insisted on numerous pee and fuel stops just to make sure he took a break.

Nugget, alert, stared out the windscreen, a godsend for spotting wildlife on the road.

Yip, meant kangaroo.

Yip, Yip, a mob of kangaroos.

Stupid buggers blindly bounced onto the road oblivious to the dangers of a moving vehicle.

Jack flicked on the indicator to turn off the main road.

Woof.

'Yep Nugget, we're here,' he said, heaving a large sigh of relief.

Turning the steering wheel to guide the vehicle onto a graded road, Jack said, 'There's a dam just over the rise...we'll park up there for the rest of the night, unload in the morning.'

I squinted my eyes, looking out into the gloom and caught a glimpse of a row of grapevines strung along wire trellises.

'Jack, do you already have the vines in?'

'Only some, love. Don't forget we've had a manager working the property the last few years. We've planted five acres of vines, here on the valley flat, but there's still a lot more work to be done. You'll see better in the morning light.'

'White or red?' I asked, curious to what I was now a part of.

'Hmm...oh, white. Chenin blanc and muscadelle,' he said.

The meaning of that went straight over my head. I opened my mouth to ask for more information, but Jack got in first.

'There's a campfire up ahead!'

Looking past his pointed finger, I could see the glow of hot coals. The Rover's headlights illuminated a pitched tent.

'Dan?' I breathed.

As the words left my mouth a figure stepped from the tent. Not Dan.

Jack gently applied his foot to the brake, the Rover creaked and squeaked, ticked and groaned as it settled to a halt. I studied the giant man who stood in the beam of our headlights. Six feet eight and a muscular frame that looked fit and toned. His blonde hair was shorn short and his square shaped face was lightly scarred down the left side. He stood next to the fire, his very large arms and hands folded across his chest and a .22 rifle.

I knew it, things had been going too well.

'Don't suppose you'd consider staying in the vehicle while I deal with this would you, love?'

'No Jack, where you go, I go. You're the love of my life, I need to protect you!' I tried to sound tough and confident.

Jack's lip quirked, and taking a deep breath he popped his unlit rollie into the corner of his mouth and slid from the driver's seat to saunter to the front of the Rover.

'G'day mate, saw the camp fire, thought we'd stop and have a chat. Name's Jack,' and as I came around to the front of the vehicle, he added, 'This little firecracker's my wife, Connie.'

Before the stranger could reply, Nugget shot from his seat and raced towards the stranger. To my surprise, he sat down at his feet, gave his happy dog smile and wagged his tail.

A soft, deep, gravelly voice, said, 'Aaron Trace.'

Silence as everyone stood staring at each other.

Taking the bull by the horns, I said, 'That's Nugget...he seems to like and trust you. As he's a good judge of character, I'm going to go with his instincts. Jack, let's get the billy on. I need my cup of tea.'

Aaron, the wariness in his face receding slightly, said, 'Dazza did say you're a gutsy one.' He turned and put the rifle back into his tent.

'Dan...I've been so worried, have you seen him?' I asked.

Aaron paused and looked at our concerned faces. In the firelight the scars stood out like silver, along his left cheek.

'Three days ago he got a forty-eight hour pass, borrowed my motorbike to go see you guys in Kalgoorlie. He hasn't returned it yet. If he was running late he'd have gone straight back to base and returned the bike later. It wouldn't be smart, going AWOL, just as you're expecting your discharge papers. Why?'

'Let's get the billy on for Connie...if she doesn't get her cup of tea there'll be hell to pay. Then we'll talk,' said Jack. He strolled to the back of the Rover. 'I take it, you know Dan well?'

The wary look returned to Aaron's face.

'Yeah, we served together in Vietnam.'

Recalling Dan's last letter describing his tall and calm mate, I said, 'Arctic right?'

Reaching down to give Nugget a good belly scratch, Aaron smiled.

'Perceptive too.'

***

Giving a deep sigh of contentment, I took another sip of my much longed for cup of tea. Jack gave me an amused look.

'What?' I said, settling more comfortably on my camp chair. 'You've got your rollie, I've got my tea.'

Aaron was watching us, a bemused look on his face and offered Jack a smouldering stick for his rollie.

'Thanks, mate,' said Jack, 'but I don't smoke.'

'He's quirky, Aaron. He's a man who wears his hat at night and always has a cigarette in his mouth, that he never smokes, but a bigger heart you'll never find on anyone else. That's why I love him.'

Smirking I watched as the blush rose on Jack's face and a small smile came to Aaron's. Good, he was relaxing.

'Okay Aaron, I think we'd better tell you what's going on...just in case we need to send out a search party for Dan.'

I told Aaron the story of the attack at Lucky Charm, but included an edited version of Dan's role.

'Dan was going to run the baddies off, then come back here. That's the last time we saw him.'

'The Dan I know, is more likely to find a deep abandoned mine shaft and drop them in. He loves you guys, talks about you and your life all the time. I can't see him letting them get away with hurting you.'

Feeling a warm glow at his words, I said, 'Well, he didn't do that. They were found dead in a car wreck, the other side of Kalgoorlie and no motorbike. Jack, we should go back and search for him,' I said as the worry started to churn in my stomach again.

The last thing I needed – I was sick of throwing up.

'I'll see what I can find out in the morning. I'll ring the base at Karrakatta. See if Dan's returned. If not, then we'll go looking for him,' said Jack. 'Now, my love if you've finished pouring that poison down your throat, we have a tent to put up.'

Rising to his feet, he put out his hand to pull me up, so I handed him my empty cup and smiled.

Aaron watching the exchange leapt up and said, 'I'll give you a hand.'

So instead of waiting for the morning light we unloaded the trailer and set up our tents and camp.

Aaron and Jack got quite chatty while they worked. It turned out Aaron was camping at the vineyard because on his return from Vietnam and discharge from the services he'd returned to no home or job. His wife – using the time he was away to find a new partner – had left taking all with her. Dan had invited Aaron to join forces with us, in setting up the winery. Jack just smiled at Aaron's tale and nodded his head in agreement. It crossed my mind that we had now collected another lost soul into our family.

The sky began to awaken in a beautiful red blaze.

Jack placed the meat esky and skillets near the fire and grumbled, 'A man could starve before the days out. Connie my love, would you cook us some breakfast, while Aaron and I finish up here.'

'Sure Jack, an Ironstone and Dazza I suppose?' I said.

Sarcasm is always wasted on Jack. Kissing my forehead he said, 'Ah, love that'd be tops.' He patted Aaron on the arm and added, 'Mate you're in for a royal treat.'

Tents erect, swags set out, the fridge fired up and emitting its kerosene hiss, I got to work on my version of Jack's favourite breakfast.

Kicking back with a contented sigh, both men were letting out discreet belches and savouring their coffee when Nugget rose to his feet and stared off down the track. I paused in the act of pouring my tea, placed a hand on my belly, feeling the life growing there and followed his gaze with mine. A tingle started at the base of my neck and ran down my spine. Very faintly I could hear the noise of a vehicle.

Looking at Nugget's body language, I picked up the skillet and said to Jack, 'We're going to need another breakfast.'

His head whipped up and I indicated the dog with my head. Nugget had started doing his happy dance, and as we watched, a man yelling in delight came belting over the rise on a motorbike.

Dan was home!

Today was a good day to share my news.

About The Author

K.A. Hudson was born in New South Wales. As a child her family moved around Australia, living and working in a variety of mining towns. She met her husband and they continued to follow the family tradition for many years. This has given her a wealth of experiences and characters to draw upon when crafting her novels.

Now retired and living in Perth, Western Australia, she is an avid reader and passionate about the written word.

For more information about K.A. Hudson please visit :
Arrowsmith Publishing: www.arrowsmithpublishing.com.au
or https://kerriehudsonauthor.wixsite.com/website-1